Other works by D. Brumbley

The Eleusis Project*
The Initiative
The Rebels
The Fugitives
The New World

The Ironborn Cycle
The Ironborn Claim
The Heartborn Mate
The Lightborn Queen

The Broken Isles
Rise with the Tide
Run with the Wind*
Down with the Fallen*

Pact
Life for a Life
Love for a Memory
Live for Today**

*forthcoming in 2024
**forthcoming in 2025

D. Brumbley

Rise
with the
Tide

The Broken Isles, Book One

D. Brumbley

ISBN: 978-1-968827-08-3

Copyright © 2024 D. Brumbley

Published by Two in One Publishing.

Cover art by thecovercollection.com.

To our children,
for whom, like Adriana and Destin,
we hope to leave a better world..

.

CONTENTS

PROLOGUE

"Alright, everyone, that's enough, our break is over. Gather up, now. Vensa, if you'd fix the classroom floor for us, please?" Leander moved to the instructor's stool at the edge of the cliff, the seaside wind fluttering his robes. The deep violet matched the glint of his eyes in the afternoon sunlight, just as the softness of the fabric matched that of his expression. Rambunctious as they were, it was clear he enjoyed his post tutoring the children.

Vensa, a small girl with bright blonde hair and dark brown eyes, looked at their teacher and pouted a little. "It looks better this way, Teacher." She glanced down at the ground and sideways at her peers before a mischievous smirk appeared.

Ripples in the ground went outward from the small girl wrapped in petite brown robes, and one particular ripple went higher than another to knock a boy on his rear. Vensa giggled uncontrollably as she sat down on the now-smooth spot of earth that her fledgling power had flattened. Behind those brown Earthborn eyes, she was nothing but trouble.

The rest of the class filled in, laughing as the boy righted himself in his space. Leander just shook his head. "When he thinks you look better with vines growing through your hair later, I don't want to hear about it." The boy's green

Forestborn eyes sparkled with the thought of eventual revenge, but he kept his place as the class settled. The low grasses around him swayed idly to lie against his legs as he came to rest.

"Now, let's see if you've all been paying attention." Leander raised a single, dramatic finger, pointing it up at the afternoon clouds at first. "I'm going to point this finger at a spot on the horizon, and the first pup to tell me correctly what's *beyond* that horizon gets to run a lap and make one change to the class circle before they take their seat."

He lowered his arm dramatically and moved it along the horizon to make sure he had the children's attention before he allowed it to come to rest, pointing almost due east, past the palace rising in the distance.

The Forestborn boy's arm shot up. "That way's the Banished Isle! It's tiny, but it's there!"

"Very good, Danas. And remember, that's where they send you if you're very, very naughty. Try to keep that in mind while you're plotting your revenge on little Vensa here, will you? I can hear you getting carried away in there." Leander tapped the side of his head with a knowing smile.

The Forestborn boy went a little pale, viscerally reminded that their Heartborn teacher could read his thoughts. Still, he got up and took his lap around, beckoning thorns up from the ground around Vensa's space with a gesture, without pushing any of them actually close enough to sting her.

"Who is next?" Leander's arm rose and fell again, this time pointing due south.

More tiny arms shot up, and Marella, Leander's Earthborn mate, chuckled from her spot off to the side. She was there mostly to help corral any rowdy children. She nodded toward a small girl with dappled blonde hair, brown streaks through it, and slate grey Stoneborn eyes.

When Leander called on the little girl, Calla, she blushed a little, shy but eager. "The Reef. My mama says her family is from there."

"More properly known as The Burning Reef, while you're at your lessons, thank you very much. But very good, Calla, that is right." Leander looked over the children and put up a hand to his eyes, to warn them to prepare themselves.

As the children closed their eyes, he reached out to each of their minds, images of barren landscapes and bare stone moving from his memories to theirs. There were visions of lava flows cascading down hillsides to pillow out into the ocean. "It's a beautiful place, in its own way. Just different from here."

"Very different." Another little girl spoke up, Millie, her eyes screwed tight, but there was a breeze that whipped around her easily. With her excitement, the wind picked up around her, answering her emotions. "I heard Skyborn can fly from their cliffs! They're so high. Higher than here."

"They are, and they can!" Leander whispered back, as if there was some private conspiracy to the conversation in front of the other dozen students. "But only the strongest and bravest are strong and brave enough to try. It's no small thing to fly. If you try, you'd best know how to land."

An Earthborn boy in the back still had his hand raised insistently, and he made squeaking noises of urgency to be called on. "The Genvin is that way too, right, Teacher?"

"The Genovin Kingdom," Leander corrected gently, "is farther than the Reef, yes, but it's more . . ." he pointed south toward the Reef again, but moved his indication a bit more southwest, pointing into the clouds as if he could launch a thought and hit the distant kingdom. "Full of Earthborn and Forestborn . . . it's supposed to be a huge place, bigger than the Isles or the Reef all together. I've never been there, myself. One of you will have to go there someday and tell me if it's true or not."

Vensa looked excited by the idea. She looked over at Marella, since she felt a kinship with the Earthborn grownup that was mated with her teacher. Marella smirked at Vensa. "It's not an easy ride to get there. You'd have to cross through the waters of the Reef, and Lady Asira does not take kindly to strangers passing through. Maybe the fearless Captain Destin could get you there, but it's an adventure for only the truly brave."

"I'm brave!" Several of the children piped up at the same time, shouting their confidence. A little boy with black hair and dark blue Oceanborn eyes said he could swim there, and a little girl with dark skin and stark red Fireborn eyes said that Lady Asira would let her through because Lady Asira had a Fireborn brother and would be nice to a Fireborn.

All the children were attempting to one-up each other until Marella quaked the ground a little beneath them to get their attention. "Listen to your teacher. This is a lesson, not a game. Games will come later."

"She's right, you know." Leander looked over the children with a hand out to settle them, their emotions responding to his influence as easily as the earth did to his mate, or the breeze to Millie's whims. "Games are for later. Now is the time for you all to learn as much as you can about this wide world of ours. That way, when you grow up, and you are no longer pups, but full-grown wolves, you'll know your way around. Then you can find your place in it, to make it your own."

Leander got up from his seat and grabbed a stick to draw in the loose earth between his students, a loose collection of blobs above, a long strand of individual threads in the middle, and a large mass far below.

"The Seven Isles. The Burning Reef. The Genovin Kingdom." He repeated as he stabbed each of the three major regions, then tossed the branch to his Fireborn student to burn. "Don't forget them. They are the only world we have. It is a broad and empty ocean otherwise."

He looked up at the approach of a plainly-dressed woman hiking up the hillside toward them. Leander straightened up to step down toward her, while the children made their own doodles in the ground behind him. "Is their dinner ready?"

The woman smiled, even though she was a little dirty, and clearly dressed for hard labor. Her brown hair was braided down her back, and the few children who looked up dismissed the sight of her easily. She held up a basket for Leander to see.

Adriana, a human slave, was of no importance to most wolfkind. Even to the wolf children.

"I brought yours and Marella's. Snacks for the little ones, if they want it. The meal isn't quite ready for all of them yet."

"I'll have them run themselves tired for a while first, then. Thank you." He took the basket from her with a nod, even as another of the guards nearby gave him a confused look. What was he doing exchanging pleasantries with a human? Thanking her? Leander didn't seem interested in explaining himself, and ignored the look as he handed off the basket to Marella.

"Alright, little ones, enough geography for the day. The first one of you to make it three times around the pond will be the first to get treats with dinner. Ready . . . off with you!"

Before he was even finished speaking, the children were leaping out of their robes and landing on four legs instead of two, rushing and tumbling over each other on their way downhill to the pond that stood between the hilltop and the palace in the distance. They were faster as wolves than they were in their humanlike form, after all.

He walked beside Marella and handed off some of the food with a grin. "There, now we can eat in peace."

Marella grabbed some dried meat from the basket and gave some to Leander before she popped some into her mouth. She smiled over at Adriana, who hadn't left yet. "They're so cute. Someday I'll convince this mate of mine to make some of our own." She looked over at her Heartborn mate as lewd thoughts easily slipped from her mind into Leander's.

"Someday." Leander agreed, sending a few thoughts of his own back in answer to hers. Neither of them blushed easily, but they did their best to keep each other on their toes regardless. "In a . . . more peaceful time, maybe." Leander nodded out to sea, where they could all see ships coming into harbor, sleek hulls and broad sails of ships from the Reef, not commonly seen in port on the Queen's Isle. "I doubt they're bringing good news."

Adriana looked out at the ships, but she kept her voice low as she responded, since guards still stood nearby. "Does a more peaceful time exist?" She glanced down at her calloused hands, a new gash on the back of one of them from her day's work. Although most wolves thought of her as nothing but a disposable tool, not all of wolfkind hated humans. "Especially after what happened with the rebellion?"

Leander waited until they were far enough away from the other guards set to watch for the safekeeping of the children, his violet eyes still on the ships. "You're assuming the rebellion is over."

His eyes shifted to the palace, where some of his oldest friends had died a mere year ago for their plots against the king and queen of the Seven Isles who lived there. Their monarchs thought that by killing the leaders of the rebellion, they had squashed it for good and intimidated the population into quiet servitude again.

The thoughts that Leander heard constantly as he moved through the Isles said otherwise.

"I can assure you, it is only beginning."

ONE

Stone slabs rained down from the ceiling on all sides as Destin tried to pull himself to safety. The lavish tables and benches of the hall shattered in the fight raging through the chamber, food and wine thrown everywhere. Blood mingled with the stone and fire scorching the air.

He rolled to one side, narrowly avoiding a piece of the wall behind him that was ripped outward to try and crush him. Pieces of his world crashing down all around. He caught a glimpse of his brother, chained in the center of the room. Defiant to the end.

Destin had seen it all before. Seen the same scene over and over again so many times that he knew he could do nothing to stop it. Nothing to change it.

He pushed himself over a pile of rubble, scratching across the floor as he reached out to help, to do something, anything to stop what he knew was coming next. Nothing he could do could stop the flames from engulfing his father. Nothing could stop the Queen's power from overcoming Devon's and consuming him in turn. The damage was done. Their lives were lost. There was nothing else Destin could do but scream.

Adriana slept tucked into Destin's chest, but as soon as he started thrashing and screaming, she woke immediately and shook his shoulder to wake him. "Destin." She spoke softly into his ear, though if she was a smarter human, she'd move away from the clearly distressed wolf. "Destin, wake up. It's a nightmare. Wake up."

He came awake with a final shudder, and his hand shook as it gripped the blankets covering them. A few quivering breaths helped steady him as he opened his eyes, and he made sure the world around him was not the one he'd just left behind in the memories that haunted his dreams.

He kissed her forehead and laid a still-sweaty hand on her arm to thank her for waking him, then looked around past the beautiful blackness of her hair. Gone was the shredded banquet hall of their king and queen where his brother and parents had been murdered. The nightmare would be back. It never stayed away for long.

Destin and Adriana were entangled in a lounging alcove just above the sea, a veranda belonging to his family's estate stretching away from them along the curve of the low cliffs. The sound of the ocean lapping against the rocks immediately calmed his racing heart and stilled his shaking hands.

"I'm sorry." He pressed another kiss against her cheek as he laid his head down on the curve of his arm. "You put up with enough from me without having to put up with nightmares as well."

"Don't talk like that." She pulled the blanket up a little higher and curled into him again. Adriana kissed along his jaw, then tucked her head under his chin and ran her fingers along his chest. "I wish there was some way I could help you."

"All you do is help me." He wrapped both arms around her back to hold her tightly against him even as he stretched away both sleep and the nightmare he'd passed through hundreds of times. The sun was barely visible at the edge of the stone awning covering their hiding place, marking the time as mid-morning. Neither of them was likely to be missed on a day of rest, but he knew they would have to go their separate ways sooner than he wanted. "Did you sleep well enough?"

"Always, when I'm with you." Adriana loved the way he held onto her as though she was precious and special, even though she knew that she was just lucky. He could choose any human he wanted, but she was glad he had chosen her. "You're much warmer than the hay they give us in Chainhome."

"I try to be." He attempted a smile, but the reminder of the home she had to go back to was enough to put a note of melancholy into his voice. There were mixed emotions in his eyes as he leaned back to look her over. He was glad he had the time with her he managed to steal, but there was also anger over the limits on the time they had.

"We could go back to sleep and forget that we saw the sun in the sky for a while." He pulled the blanket up over their heads and kissed down to her neck playfully. "It's still night in here, as far as I'm concerned."

Adriana laughed softly and was glad to play along. "So we just pretend we never fell asleep?" She ran her hand down his side, still amazed, as usual, how defined his entire body was. "I'm convinced there is no such thing as too much time together."

"I'm convinced of a lot of things where you're concerned. Mostly I'm convinced that you're the tiniest bit insane." He laid back on the cushions and let the blanket fall away just a little, so he could get a good look at her in the morning light as she moved to sit on top of him.

She was the most beautiful creature he had ever seen, at least in his own estimation. He'd heard others criticize her for being obviously favored by him, since she had none of the malnourished skeletal quality of most slaves, but she was by no means plump. She was strong, and Destin knew exactly how strong she could be when the need arose. Her dark hair flowed down over both her shoulders like dark ripples of the ocean he loved, her green eyes made all the more beautiful against the shadows of her hair and her deeply tanned skin.

She was perfect in his eyes, and she was his, and there were many moments in which he had to remind himself that those were the only things that mattered in the world. "Tell me what you dreamed about. I'll borrow your dreams until my own decide to behave themselves."

"That sounds like a good idea." Adriana smiled and gave him a quick kiss before she sat up straighter on top of his stomach again. "The last thing I remember before I fell asleep was the feel of your hand rubbing my back, so that's how my dream started out. We were in a place that didn't look anything like this island, or anything I have ever seen." She tucked some of her hair behind her ear and she smirked as his eyes wandered along her body while she spoke. "We had a house of our own, right by the water. We didn't have to hide, we didn't have to rush anywhere, it was just our house and our life. No secrets. Just smiles and time. Lots and lots of time."

He ran a hand up along her side to her neck, before he pulled her down slowly into a heated kiss. "I like your dreams much better than mine." He rested his forehead against hers afterward and sighed as he sat up, since the day wouldn't wait for them, as much as he would like it to.

He sat against the side of the alcove with her still mostly in his lap, and tried to reconcile himself to get up and join the day. It was always hard to move away from Adriana. He ran a hand over his hair and beard, both of them peppered black and grey, though he was nowhere even close to old age for his kind.

After rubbing the sleep from his eyes, he leaned his head back and finally opened them again, turning them on Adriana with all the inherent ferocity in his nature. "Tell me more about this home. Were my idiot brother and sister there? I can't imagine I would have invited Daiva, but I wouldn't be able to leave Taimon and Kaia alone very long. I'm convinced they'd end up getting themselves killed if they were unsupervised for more than a few hours."

"I didn't really see them there, but I'm sure they were nearby. We wouldn't go without them, you know that." She moved her hand so she could slide her fingers along his beard, and she ran her thumb underneath one of his perfectly depthless blue eyes. His eyes were as seducing as the underwater current they were born of.

"Anyway, your sister makes the food. Of course she has to come along." Adriana's smile brightened as she locked her knees at his hips. "We can run away from here, right? Just tell them all to come with us and find an island of our own."

He smiled at the idea, since it wasn't the first time it had crossed his mind. "If it were that simple, I would have found one for us already." He hated facing reality, but he knew the longer he went without being realistic about their situation, the more it would end up hurting them both when they had to return to the world they actually inhabited.

"I've sailed to the ends of the world my mother ever knew. If I thought there was a single scrap of land somewhere we could live and never be found, we would leave right now." He looked out at the ocean longingly as he held her against him, his eyes reflecting the sparkles of the sun on the water without any of the warmth that always came with such a sight. "Maybe there is, someplace beyond the lengths she ever sailed. But to find it, I'd have to leave you for months and years just to find out. Somewhere you'd never have to hear the sound of another chain as long as you lived."

Her smile of hope faded, and she sighed along his skin as he held her. "Did you think about it some more? You know, the Turning?"

He kissed her shoulder and answered without looking up into her eyes. "I always think about it." His lips moved to her neck in a calm caress that was as fearful as it was hopeful. "I don't want to lose you."

"I don't want to lose you either." She sighed contentedly as he nibbled along her skin, the act distracting her from the severity of her request. "But they're bringing in new people. They're going to put me with someone new this season, I know it, and I don't . . ."

"I don't either." He gripped her body tighter against his, jealousy evident in his grip before he kissed her. "If I keep you here for good, they will kill you. I can't take that chance either. I'll think of a way. I don't know how yet, but I will."

It was the same thing he promised her for so many months, ever since they started sneaking away from the world to have a few stolen moments of peace to themselves. He never felt as though he was any closer to keeping his promise than he had been the first night he'd made it to her. The world kept pushing them farther and farther apart with every passing crisis.

"Would they really kill me?" She didn't know why anyone would waste their time killing a slave. She wasn't the strongest or the most skilled, but she wasn't useless either. "There are a lot of wolves that take humans for lovers. Pets. I could handle that, I don't care what anyone would say. I just want to stay with you." She liked his possessiveness, and she especially enjoyed being regarded as precious by him. "I don't want to go back and meet whoever I'm supposed to create another baby with. I don't want to lose another baby, Destin."

The thought of her going back and being with anyone else was something that made his vision swim in a red haze for a moment, but he pushed down his anger and reminded himself that it wasn't something Adriana was choosing for herself. It would be chosen for her, like everything else among the humans.

"If you'd been foolish enough to fall in love with any other wolf, they might have been able to keep you as a pet and keep you safe. But the moment anyone whispers in the princess' ear that I'm keeping you here as a lover while still turning her down?" He shook his head and looked back up at her, the mingled black and grey hairs in his beard appearing like mixed shadows on his face in the bright morning light. "She'd have one of her brothers end you. Slowly."

Adriana kissed him several times as though each kiss was an attempt to convince him to change his mind, even though she knew nothing would change. She would go back to Chainhome, and she would go about her breeding season, this time without the fear of being paired with Miris. She kissed Destin once more, without any vigor at all before she pulled away. "I should get back, then."

He returned the last kiss a little more forcefully than she had given it, but got up with her, sighing at the constant leave-taking between them. "Come on and take a swim first. And you can at least make sure you eat before you go back there." He knew the wolves that monitored the humans in their prison always rode the line of mistreatment when it came to Adriana. They hated her for being favored by him, but they feared Destin more than they hated Adriana. Destin made sure to keep it that way.

She looked toward the water, and she wanted to stay, but she was hesitant. Saying goodbye was the worst part, and now that she had started thinking about it, she didn't want to make it worse by putting it off. "I don't know. I'm sure I'll eat when I get back."

Destin moved to the edge of the veranda that overlooked the water below, then turned around and leaned back against the stone railing to look at the image of her in the morning light.

Behind him, a single column of water slid up like a well-beloved pet along his shoulder, the sunlight refracting through it in dancing rainbows of color that flashed along the grey stone, giving it life. It bent and twisted through the air as Destin smiled at her, trying to bring the world back to being theirs and theirs alone for just a little longer as the water coiled closer to her under his control. His eyes were the deep blue of the ocean's own heart, as if it had claimed him for its own at his birth and had never let go in all the days since. "I could always bring the swim to you, you

21

know."

Adriana couldn't help but smile, but she shook her head slowly as she stared at him with his true pet sliding effortlessly along his bare arms and shoulders. He made the water look like a living beast, which was always fascinating. "Do I need to bathe that badly?"

"That's not what I'm saying." He chuckled as the water closed the distance between them and moved up in a single thin tendril to brush up against her cheek. "But the ocean misses you when you're away. You haven't gone in to say hello for several days. It's a lonely creature, you know."

That got a small chuckle, and she moved a little bit closer to Destin. All of the furs and bedding behind them would probably get soaked, but she knew he could dry it out just as easily. "Oh, so it wants to show me how much it loves me, then?"

"Let's not go so far as to say love." He smiled as she got closer, the water circling around her as she walked. It ran over her bare back to encourage her with small, cold splashes against her skin. "If it were to love you, then the ocean and I would be fighting over the same woman, and I would rather not have to fight that war."

She squealed and squeaked every time the water splashed against her skin, even though she was used to this kind of taunting from Destin. When Adriana was close enough, she reached out and touched him. "So you still love me that much?"

"I will always love you that much." He pulled her in roughly and kissed her as the water moved up her spine to send shivers all over her body.

The kiss was broken a moment later when Destin looked off toward the stairs leading down from the veranda on the land side of the stone. He held her tightly as the muscles in his body tensed, but after the kiss broke, she could hear footsteps coming up along the stone walkway that had stolen his attention.

"Who is that?" He demanded loudly, in the commanding

tone she had heard him use on so many others before, but never on her.

Adriana shivered as both his demeanor changed and the thrill of the water against her skin completely vanished. She looked behind her as he looked past her before she rushed to find something to cover herself with. She was the one who shouldn't be there, after all.

"It's just me." A woman's voice carried easily, and her steps slowed as she moved closer to the top of the steps. Dola was wrapped in a dress dyed bright blue to match the icy sky color in her eyes, tight against her curves. The way she carried herself, however, had the manner of a commander behind it. Not some lady of the court who cared for nothing but pretty dresses. She fixed Destin with a look that was only mildly apologetic for whatever she clearly interrupted. "Your sister is coming. The Queen wants to meet with all of her captains. Immediately."

Once Adriana was covered, the tendril of water that remained on the veranda moved past her into their alcove to lift a rectangle of dark blue patterned fabric. The water dampened the top edge before the tendril tossed it to Destin and receded back into the ocean from whence it had come.

He wrapped the fabric around his hips and tied it into place deftly before he leaned against the railing again, visibly relaxing. "Meet with us about what?" He asked to let her know it was safe to come the rest of the way. Dola was one of only a few wolves he trusted with the knowledge of his relationship with Adriana. Even though she wasn't an Oceanborn like him, he was closer to her than most other wolves he knew, even among his own kind.

When Dola moved up the rest of the way, she barely glanced over at Adriana before she looked at her captain. "She wants to move against the Genovin, but I do not know the extent of it. Maybe she wants to send us all out to gather information. All I know is that she's impatient, as usual, and now means now." She looked over at Adriana briefly before continuing. "Miris is watching closely today, and the new arrivals should be starting to come in. Chiara will be lurking about too."

"You're just full of good news this morning, aren't you?" Destin sighed and looked back at Adriana as he prepared to walk away with her and his friend. Adriana looked the same as she'd looked the day he met her, in a plain rough spun dress that had been worn smooth by constant washing over its years of use. It was so simple and drab that most wolves never gave her or any other human a second look, but to Destin, she still looked amazing without even knowing it.

"I'll send Taimon with you to make sure you get back to Chainhome alright. And I'll come find you later tonight after the meeting to let you know what's going on." They both knew it probably meant he would have to leave, and there was always a chance of him not returning, especially if they were going up against the Genovin.

"If you can." She responded softly as she walked slightly behind Destin down the stairs, with Dola just ahead of him.

"Do you want me to send a message to your brother now?" The Skyborn woman offered. "He's never been quick to come whenever you're looking for him."

"Please do. And be as threatening as you like. The boy needs to learn to jump a little faster when asked." He looked at Dola's light blue eyes as they walked, smiling in spite of himself even though the news she'd brought hadn't exactly lifted his spirits. After spending a full day with Adriana, he felt as though there was nothing in the world he couldn't face.

Dola was distracted for a moment as she sent the message across the winds, and Adriana took the opportunity to touch the back of Destin's hand. She knew once they reached the bottom of the stairs she was just a slave again, and the world could be watching. "I can go back by myself, I can sneak in . . ."

"I know." He stopped on the bottom step, aware just as she was of the limitations of their shared world. He turned around to face her, almost the same height as she was once he was a step down, and looked up in her eyes as he held her hand. "I just prefer to know you're safe."

"I wish I could have that same comfort where you're concerned." She stared into his dark blue eyes for a moment before she looked away. Adriana took a deep breath as she reminded herself that as much as she wanted to dream, as much as she wanted to be with Destin, and as many times as he promised her anything, she knew the truth. They didn't belong together. "I'll get started in that direction. Taimon will find me."

He obviously didn't like it, but he didn't want to argue with her either, so he didn't press the issue. He pulled her in for a last kiss and squeezed her hand. "I love you. I'll see you soon."

"I love you." She echoed softly, but she didn't know if she would see him soon, so she didn't repeat the phrase as she pulled away. Adriana felt heavier as she walked away, but she forced herself not to look back. There was no reason to torture herself.

Dola looked over at Destin, and though it was hard to read her expression, she did feel pity for her captain. He was in love with a fragile human, a woman whose life wasn't likely to last very long. "Taimon will be with her soon."

"Good." He forced himself to look away from Adriana when she slipped into the trees lining the edges of his estate. It was still hard to look around the grounds and think of it as his own, since his parents had been killed only a year before, but he forced himself to get more accustomed to it every day. He walked briskly beside Dola, his hands clenched into fists at his sides as he chafed against being ordered around by the queen who had murdered half his family. "Is Gale at home with your pups or has he been called out by Her Majesty's nagging as well?"

"She's keeping the Earthborn here, so he's at home with them. We'll see if any of them are still alive when you and I return." Dola shook her head as she watched Adriana disappear. "Do you mean to turn her?"

It wasn't the first time someone asked him that question, but every time felt just as heavy as the first, and incited the same panic, hidden as it was beneath the surface of his expression. "I have no immediate plans. It's not a chance I'm willing to take right now." He'd lost too many of his loved ones too recently to take the chance of losing Adriana too.

"It doesn't make much sense to be with a human." She remarked simply, even though she knew he had feelings for Adriana. "How do you know one of a thousand other things won't kill her anyway? Miris being one of them. He hates her."

"Miris won't touch her. He knows better." There was deep confidence in his voice and a hint of a smile on his face, but it faded quickly. "I've never claimed to make sense, Dola. To you or to anyone else."

"Of course, Sir." She looked back at him again with sarcastic indictment in her eyes. "Just making an observation."

"Your observation is noted." They got back to the steps of the house just in time to see a blond wolf rushing out of the open stone doors toward them.

Destin had to sidestep on the path to keep from being hit, but the wolf dodged a moment later and fell into a roll along the grass. Mid-roll, the wolf changed form in the blink of an eye and became a mass of flailing human limbs, until Taimon managed to untangle himself and move into a crouch.

"You said to follow Adriana, right?" He was panting for breath as he looked up at Dola and his older brother. Taimon's eyes were the same iridescent sky blue as Dola's, and the breeze around them picked up at his presence. He was incredibly young by wolf standards, and barely capable of controlling himself, much less the element to which he'd been born. As a human, he was a grown man, but by wolf standards he was still quite young.

Dola looked at the young wolf and shook her head as

she stared at him. "What did you eat? Or drink?" She looked him over before meeting his eyes. "You're running like a forest is on fire. Anyone around you is going to think that they need to panic. Calm down, follow your nose, and you'll find her."

Taimon lowered his chin as if she'd just beaten him instead of correcting him, though he knew Dola was right. He looked up at Destin as if his brother was going to rescue him somehow, though they both knew that wasn't likely.

"Go on. Just make sure she arrives safely, and try not to destroy anything on your way. That includes yourself." Destin didn't move from where he stood, and his face didn't soften. His younger brother and sister had been through just as much in the past year as he had, but they needed to learn restraint if their family was going to survive.

"Sure. There safe. No problem." Taimon nodded again dutifully, then shifted back into his wolf and set off running, first at a more sedate pace, then at the breakneck speed to which he was more accustomed.

Destin shook his head and turned to go back into the house. "Was I ever that awkward? Daiva insists I was, but I trust your opinion of our childhood more than I trust hers." Dola was only a few years younger than he was, and they'd known each other almost all their lives. She was one of the few friends he still had who went back with him quite so far.

"Your version of trying to get a female's attention always started with, 'Let's go for a swim.' If that answers your question." She laughed and kept an eye on his brother for a moment before he was gone. "I'll try to help guide him more often. That pup needs some training."

"You've been a lot of help to him already." Destin assured her. He retrieved a formal set of blue robes from his house, which he pulled over his shoulders and tied in place as he spoke. If he was being summoned to a meeting with the queen, he was not going to look like some feral wolf she thought his family was suited to be. "What he needs, you and I can't give him." Once dressed, he waited with her near the entrance of the lavish home, looking out the windows at the walkway. "Where is Daiva? You said she was on her way?"

"She's nearly . . ."

"I'm here." Daiva replied as she entered Destin's wing of their family home, though she had been outside for most of the day and night. "I heard about the summons and knew you would be coming back." She wore steely grey robes that matched the color of her eyes, meticulously clean and perfectly fitted. "We should get going."

He looked her over without saying anything and waited to see if she was going to elaborate on her abrupt arrival. His lone surviving littermate, Daiva was an impressive woman, and Destin knew that he was one of the few wolves on all the Isles who wasn't immediately intimidated by her as soon as she walked into a room. Even he had moments when that was no longer the case.

Daiva was slightly taller than he was, with the dark hair of their father's side and none of the silver that he'd inherited from their mother. Her features were sharp and generally unreadable, even to Destin, but he knew where the roots of her ferocity were planted, and he was more grateful for it than scared. "I went looking for you last night when I arrived home and couldn't find you. Kaia wasn't sure where you'd gone."

Daiva kept quiet as she thought about how she should respond to her brother. She didn't think she truly owed him an explanation, even though she knew he was only concerned about her safety. "I spent some time with some of the queen's guards. Most of the Stoneborn are quite fond of me." Fond to Daiva meant something else than it did to most people, but she spent a lot of time with her own kind. "I fight with them, for practice, and they tell me things their majesties would not want me to know. It's a beneficial relationship."

"Have they told you anything lately that I should know?" He started walking with her, Dola falling into step near him but at a respectful distance. The three of them together made for an impressive sight as they headed out of the estate grounds, past the pair of guards trusted to watch over his property, out into the main road toward the palace. A few Stoneborn and an Earthborn, wolves attached to Destin's family as guards, fell into step unobtrusively behind them. All of them kept an eye on the streets as they passed. Nothing and no one could be trusted. Not anymore.

Daiva sighed. "Just that war is coming sooner than we think. And according to some of them, who swear that they are favored by Chiara, she's still very much under orders to claim you after this breeding season, whether you like it or not."

Destin winced in spite of himself at that declaration, but it was nothing he hadn't expected. He knew better than to imagine Daiva delivering any news gently, no matter how devastating, but it wouldn't have changed what she said even if she had. "I'm amazed she's waited this long to try. She's been back from the Barren Isle for months and hasn't so much as visited the estate."

"They took her toy away from her." Daiva's tone was filled with bitterness after everything that had happened between the Heartborn princess and their dead littermate. "I don't think she's so keen on rushing into your arms when she wanted to be with Devon." She still felt the pain inside her chest as though wounds had been ripped open again when she said their lost brother's name, but the expression on her face never changed. Calm, collected, and untouched. Or so she appeared. "But she's still a Heartborn. She can't survive without someone thinking about her or talking about her or ravishing her in some way or another."

He shook his head as they walked, keeping his voice low as he glanced around them. There were Skyborn ears everywhere that could hear every word he said, but he found himself not caring what they did or didn't hear. "We won't be ready by the end of the breeding season. We need the winter."

"Then you're going to be a father before you are ready." She looked over at her brother, looked him up and down, and kept walking. "I'm beginning to think even that would not be enough. The queen wants to go to war against the Genovin. Half our people will be dead, if not more. You and I could be dead, and the queen would probably love it."

"Only one kind of wolf falls in love with a Fireborn, sister." Destin said without looking away from the path ahead of them. He had loved their brother, but the nature of a Fireborn was anything but restrained. Devon had been no exception, and their queen was the rule personified. "The kind who loves the scent of the world burning down around them. I don't claim to know Chiara well, but she never seemed to care about anyone in the world, herself included. Our deaths would bother the queen more than anyone else, though I still don't really understand why."

Daiva could see the torches in the distance, which meant they were closer to the gathering, though she certainly wasn't looking forward to it. "I know you are an Oceanborn, but you should not let your mind be limited by your tastes. Devon may have been over-zealous and thoughtless at times, but he knew that the world would mean nothing if it was all burning down around him. There would be nothing to burn later if you burn it all at once."

"That's fair enough." He certainly wasn't going to get into an argument with his sister about the virtues of their brother's worldview. It was a view that had gotten him killed, and Destin didn't intend to make the same mistakes a second time when dealing with the royal family. The queen and the king had set their sights on him years ago as a match for their daughter, for reasons Destin still couldn't comprehend. He had never returned that interest, or Chiara's numerous attempts to kindle something genuine between them. All he wanted was Adriana, and that, to him, was enough.

"We need a new plan." Daiva said softly as she moved a little bit closer to her brother while they meandered. As strong as she was, as emotionless as she pretended to be, she still found herself wanting to be close to her brother. "And we don't have much time to figure it out."

"War first." He said reluctantly as they approached the bridge that led onto the grounds of the royal fortress. The high walls of the palace towered over the landscape and the rest of the island all around them. He could hear the assembled crowd through the open gates, signaling that they were some of the last to arrive. He didn't mind, or care. Many of them reported to him, and they could wait. "Then plans."

TWO

Cadmos stood just behind his mate, surveying the captains who attended at their call. He silently noted the different conversations happening, each in their own corners. None of them were foolish enough to speak an ill word against him or Melyssa while in the same room with him, but still, his ears took in every scrap of conversation, while his clear blue eyes scanned the hall.

"He'll be the last to arrive." He said to Melyssa, his words traveling on their own tightly controlled current of air directly to her ear so that she would be the only one capable of hearing him. The words whispered through the pure white tendrils of her hair as it fell around her shoulders, but another breeze tucked it back for her just as quickly. "I have to wonder if little offenses like this give him any kind of satisfaction."

"I am sure they do." She wished at the moment she could hear everything her mate could hear. Her skills with flame were very different from his with the air. "Even if he is the last to arrive, he will still be here. That's all that matters to me."

He pretended to look over the maps laid out in the center of the room on the floor, a huge depiction of the vast territories around which their lives were built. In the north were the Seven Isles upon which they lived. The long archipelago of the Burning Reef stretched roughly east to west in a kind of belt just to the south of the Seven. Finally, the sprawling land mass of the Genovin Kingdom sat still farther to the southwest beyond the edges of the Reef. It was all the world they knew, and all the world they needed.

He walked along the part of the map where they were about to send their fleet, but still spoke to Melyssa and listened to the conversations going on around them. "Most of them are eager to volunteer." He smirked, a private expression only for Melyssa to understand. "If I had known killing Naisa and Kensin would make the rest of our subjects this eager to please, I might have suggested doing so years ago."

"We will never know the difference it could have made." She followed after him slowly before she stopped on the depiction of the Burning Reef. She looked up and across the entire room once more. There was a small group of wolves that weren't familiar or socializing with anyone else, but she expected that. "Even Hassir wasn't the last to arrive." Melyssa hadn't called the meeting until after the ship from the Reef had arrived, since she wanted all of those under her reign to be in attendance. They would need the feral wolves of the Reef to destroy the Genovin, after all.

Cadmos raised his eyes from the map and took a good look at the wolves she mentioned through strands of light blond hair that fell in his eyes. Rather than adopt the formal robes suited to their element as subjects of the Isles, the wolves of the Reef wore clothing made from tanned leather, supposedly from their own kills, according to Reef tradition. Two of them were even in attendance in their wolf form, sitting near their master on the floor and keeping an eye on the room.

Hassir, lord of the Reef and grandson of the wolf that Cadmos and Melyssa had killed in order to bring the Reef under their rule, stood at the center of the delegation from his homeland. He was clothed in dark leather just as the rest of them. Nothing set him apart from his companions as their lord except the brilliant red hair for which his line was known. It was cut short against his scalp and trimmed close against his face, leaving the harsh lines and hard set of his jaw well defined beneath his beard.

"The fact that he came at all says that he still knows what's best for his people." Melyssa heard a faint growl behind her mate's voice. He hated the Reef just as much as she did, for reasons she had never quite understood. "He'll do as he's bid."

"That's what dogs do." She indulged in a self-satisfied chuckle as she glanced over at her mate. "We just need to make sure they don't make a mess of the furniture in the process."

As Daiva, Destin, and Dola climbed the stairs toward the meeting, Daiva took notice that Cadmos made sure they were well in his element by being in a part of the castle that was high and lined with windows. As high as they were, though, she could see some of the ships in the distance whenever they passed a window, and one in particular caught her eye. She hadn't grown up with Oceanborn as parents without learning a thing or two about the ships that belonged to the Isles. "Isn't that ship from the Reef?"

Destin was distracted by his thoughts and hadn't been paying attention to the call of the sea far below and beyond, but he followed his sister's glance and quickly picked out the vessel she indicated.

Unlike the broad, stately ships of the Isles that Destin knew, the design and construction Destin himself had overseen for years, the ship from the Reef was long and narrow, with runners out to either side that allowed it to sit high in the water. They were faster than the ships of the Isles, most of the time, but they were also much less sturdy. "It is. I wonder what Melyssa called them in for."

Daiva looked up the remaining stairs, and as she looked at each step of stone, her thoughts flooded with memories. When she was younger and playful, she remembered knocking Devon and Destin down similar stone stairs by shifting the marble. She also remembered the trek up granite stairs only to see her parents and her brother die in front of her eyes.

Now she thought about what might wait for them above, and who, if the Reef was now also in attendance. Other than the Queen and her youngest son, Daiva hadn't seen many Fireborn around the Isles. She also didn't know much about the Reef, except for their reputation of ruthlessness and as a Fireborn haven.

How the Reef could maintain that and still be controlled by a truly insane wolf like Melyssa was beyond Daiva's logic. Their reputation led her to believe *the Reef* should be ruling the Isles, not the other way around. "She must be quite serious about taking over the Genovin." Daiva mused, as she wondered if she could find a way to talk to the representatives from the Reef. She and Destin could benefit from that kind of firepower. "Maybe we can . . ."

"Not here." Destin cut her off quickly as he felt a breeze from Dola whip around them, further obscuring what his sister started to say. He gave her a quick glance, though, to let her know that he'd thought the same thing. "Her Majesty is very serious about many things. I'm sure the violence of the Reef's fighters will be a welcome addition to any kind of attack she's planning. That is all Melyssa knows how to do, after all. Live on the offensive."

Daiva kept her gaze on the stairs as they neared the entrance. "That is if the actual fighting ability of the wolves living on the Reef is more than just a tall tale." She wasn't completely convinced of anything, especially since she didn't know any wolves personally from the Reef. "They sound more like crazed beasts than anything else, we know what happened with . . ."

"They may be crazed, and they are certainly beasts, but their reputation is not just hearsay." He felt much more comfortable talking about the Reef than about anything else, under the circumstances, so he glanced out a window at the ship again, noting several wolves moving around on deck waiting for their lord's return. "I saw one of their Skyborn decapitate a man once with a solid column of air. The rest of the body was left spinning like water down a drain, while the wolf who'd done it couldn't stop laughing. They are not to be trifled with."

"I am not afraid of them." She stepped up behind her brother near the doorway. "Other than watching you, Taimon, or Kaia die, there's nothing left in this world that can scare me."

"Well then when I die, I'll try and make sure I'm out of sight." He gave Daiva a final glance, then stepped into the meeting chamber as every eye in the room turned toward them.

Cadmos was already looking toward the door, having smelled the three of them before they got anywhere near the chamber. "You were summoned hours ago, Admiral."

"And I am here now, Majesty." Destin quipped without backing down as he strode to the center of the room, leaving Daiva and Dola behind as he approached. "My queen." He said coldly to Melyssa as he bowed near the edge of the broad map, then rose to wait for whatever instructions she'd called the captains together to give.

Melyssa looked down and watched him as he rose and backed away, though she was quick to begin addressing all of her captains. "I have called you together so that we can discuss the strategy that has been devised for an attack on the Genovin. I know we cannot enter battle with them lightly or quickly, but I also know that we will not be successful if we try to hold a war entirely on their homeland. We have to find a way to draw them out, to weaken them, and then attack them in waves." She looked down at the map underneath her feet carefully.

"It has been decided that we will commit less than half of our forces to mass patrol north of the Genovin's nearest shores. It may prematurely draw some of them out, believing the gathered force to be all we can muster. If it is, then we will destroy those who are drawn out and take whatever ships they have that are functional. It may help us to gain access to their homeland if we can get in close with their own ships."

The Queen continued on with her initial plans of attack with all of her captains listening carefully, but Daiva remained back along the wall, her dark grey eyes scanning the room. She looked over at the small group from the Reef several times as her fingers ran against the smooth stone behind her. The stone rippled and shivered underneath her touch, and several times it cracked and shook some pebbles down onto her before she sealed it up again, making it look as though nothing had happened.

How was she going to talk to the impatient-looking Fireborn wolves if Melyssa was just going to send them off on a ship? What good would Fireborn do out on the water anyway?

The one who stuck out most to her was a man with shocking red hair and black fur lining the edges of his clothing around his shoulders, who looked increasingly bored as Melyssa continued to talk about her plans. Several of the other captains rushed to chime in and make themselves seem useful in the conversation, but the Reef captain remained silent. There were several small arguments about which direction to sail first and who should be sent, but Destin only watched the flow of the arguments and listened to all positions.

Eventually an unexpected sound entered the chamber, and Daiva could see, as those talking over each other subsided one by one, that it was coming from the red-haired wolf from the Reef. He was leaning back against the same wall that Daiva was touching, with his arms folded over his chest, bouncing with the low chuckle that escaped him, and which had silenced the room.

"Is something funny, Lord Hassir?" Cadmos' voice came irritably from the center of the chamber, standing over the map's depiction of the wolf's homeland.

"Oh yes." The wolf responded in a deep, hissing voice as he raised his eyes to look at the rest of the gathered captains. His red eyes seemed to glow with a fire of their own, and he stepped up through the others to approach the king and queen, impeded by no one.

"Something is very funny. Because just before I came to answer your summons, your majesty," he came as close to spitting out the title at Melyssa as he dared in a formal setting, but no one missed the acid in his tone, "my sister received a report of several ships that stopped on their way north. They claimed to be merchant vessels headed for the Shield Isle delivering Genovin wine, but Asira thought they were too well armed for merchants.

"When her Oceanborn fleet followed them south, she found a fleet of thirty more ships, all crewed with soldiers, moving westward along the Reef. Appears they were looking for a place to cross our borders and come north to pay you a visit." He shoved one of the other captains out of the way to free up a spot on the map, and spat on the floor at Cadmos' feet, pointing at the spot afterwards. "There is where she found them, and if you want a fight, that is where you'll find it."

"And you decided," Melyssa said slowly, as if she was speaking to a wolf with no intelligence whatsoever, "that you wanted to withhold this information until you thought you could pass it off as entertainment?"

"You did not ask for a report upon my arrival." He shrugged, as if he was speaking to a wolf who didn't rule over him and his kingdom. "I am tasked with the safekeeping of my people and protecting the borders of your territory. I have done both."

Melyssa's own fiery eyes locked with Hassir's, and no one missed the shimmer of heat that rippled off her skin as she thought about ways that she would love to incinerate the wolf in front of her with her own flames. "Reports of such events should be offered willingly, not upon command. You should . . ." She felt a slight breeze across her skin from

Cadmos to remind her to not push for a battle right there in the middle of their meeting, so she averted her gaze back down toward the map. "We should break momentarily so that we can all consider this new information. We will reconvene shortly."

Hassir inclined his head in the most condescending way imaginable but didn't move from where he stood. Clearly, though Melyssa might have a mate to keep her under control, Hassir had no such restraint. "As you command, Majesty, of course."

Several of the captains left the room to go to another where food and wine were prepared and waiting for such a break, but Daiva didn't even look for her brother as she remained against the wall. Against whatever her brother thought about the situation, she decided to approach the Fireborn as they eventually made their way across the room.

"I do not think we have met." She stepped in front of Hassir and blocked his path.

He looked her up and down once, his red eyes burning into her own as he took in the various details of her face and hair. It was an uncomfortable moment of silence as he studied her, but he let it go on for a long while before he spoke. "You entered with the admiral, Destin. You sail with him?"

"I intend to this time, but usually, no. He is my littermate." Daiva studied him as well, though she wasn't sure what she thought she would find. He didn't seem crazy, but he didn't seem altogether sane either. It was difficult for her to pin down, even if Destin said they were ruthless and a bit unhinged.

"Daiva." He dug the name out of his memory, since he briefly became acquainted with her Fireborn brother when he visited. He watched her closely without attempting to walk away or brush past her. "Do you have some personal vendetta against the Genovin, then, or do you simply not trust your brother to do his duty as he's been commanded?"

Daiva stared for a moment in silence before she looked

past him at Cadmos and Melyssa. The king and queen seemed to be in a heated conversation, but she knew the Skyborn was still capable of hearing things she didn't want him to hear. "You could say that I have a personal vendetta." She left the reply hanging, since she didn't care about the Genovin at all, and her vendetta was certainly not against an island of Earthborn wolves.

Hassir turned slowly to see where her glance fell, then turned back around before grinning broadly, in an expression that would have made most wolves look at least marginally friendly. For Hassir, though, it only made him look more vicious. "Don't we all?" He asked without expecting a reply, then cocked his head to one side toward the room where food had been laid out. "Walk with me, Stoneborn."

She walked beside him in silence but exited ahead of him, though she wasn't sure exactly where he was headed. What she didn't do, however, was look around for her brother, since she didn't want him to stop whatever conversation she was about to have with the Reef. They needed the Reef. Or at least some help.

"I understand that your brother is a capable leader." He looked over the wine and passed it without even considering it. He instead grabbed a hunk of bread and dipped it into a sauce, shaking his head at the food the entire time. "If the Genovin have thirty ships and there are a paltry ten in the fleet of the Isles that are anywhere near those of the Genovin in size, do you still think he can win?"

"If anyone can, he can." She looked over the table as well, but she didn't pick up any of the food. It was more satisfying to hunt when she felt anxious. "Which is why I am sure she will send him out in the front, hoping for a truly miraculous victory. Or, in the very least, for his ship to sink to the bottom of the ocean in his efforts." She looked away from the food and at the Fireborn again. "You don't seem to care in the slightest if he can win or if he cannot."

"I don't." He took another bite of the bread, moving

along down the table and picking up various pieces of the offerings as he went, without actually eating very much of it. "Melyssa will never conquer the Genovin, as she believes. It doesn't matter whether she loses her ships now or loses every fighter loyal to her later on their soil. Which makes the outcome of this fight pointless, unless her ambition is to anger the Genovin enough to attack us here in your home. Besides," he finally looked back at her, "though I may have respected your parents, I do not know Destin. I have no reason to wish him alive or dead."

"I can understand that logic." She looked away from the table, but this time when she looked for her brother, he was nowhere to be seen. "You are a wolf with nothing to lose, it seems. Why are you here if you clearly support no part of this?"

"Why are you?" He shot right back at her, and when she looked back at him, he was only a few inches from her face, holding the remains of a slice of fruit on one hand near his chin as he looked back at her. He was almost exactly her height, and the haughty manner in which he bore himself made her easily forget their similarity in stature. She could feel the heat rippling off the man wherever he walked, feel the power that seemed to resonate from him along with the heat. He was filled with untapped potential, barely restrained in polite company.

Daiva didn't back away, and she didn't look away again when he challenged her and shot the question back at her. "Because no one is going to feel the weight of their crimes unless they are made to pay for them." She knew it was vague, but she also knew that too many people could be listening. While she didn't care if someone came after her for the anger she felt toward the king and queen, she did not want Destin to have to lose another sibling.

Hassir chewed a bite of the food in his mouth slowly, but his lips turned up in the same slow grin that she'd seen a few moments before. If her own lost brother hadn't been a Fireborn, it might have been unsettling to be on the receiving end of such a vicious smirk. Instead, it was almost comforting, as if some kind of barrier had been erased between them, and they could speak a little more freely.

"I too, intend to sail south with whatever force Melyssa intends to command after your brother. My sister's waters are the ones that have been violated, after all. It is only correct that I should defend her rights. We'll have more opportunity on the way to discuss exactly how steep a price is fitting for such heinous crimes."

"I am sure we will." She wanted to smirk herself, but she didn't want to seem too confident before having a frank and open conversation with the Fireborn. He could be talking about anything, or anyone, really. "Are there any supplies that you need for your ship or your crew?"

"We're quite well equipped, actually, but if there is anything I require, we'll be sure to let your brother know before we depart." He didn't sound concerned at all that they were most likely going into a fight in which they were terribly outnumbered. They might as well have been talking about the weather or planning a hunting excursion farther inland for the afternoon.

He glanced past her for a moment as someone called for his attention, and took a final bite of the table's offerings before he started to move away. "This has been a very informative conversation, Stoneborn. I look forward to continuing it, but there is business to be done here first."

"My name is Daiva." She reminded him as he walked away, since she didn't want him to think that she was just any wolf that would be dismissed so easily. He knew her name already, and he would use it. "I am sure you have not forgotten." Daiva watched him for a moment longer as he moved away, business or not.

He stopped when she snapped at him, and turned to look over his shoulder at her, the grin on his face showed approval of her tone, rather than being insulted. "I forget nothing." He growled over his shoulder at her, then continued away from her to rejoin his companions without saying anything else.

THREE

Daiva didn't move again until Hassir started to converse with his fellow wolves, and after a look around the room, she still didn't see her brother. She left quickly and started down the stairs only to find him halfway down the flight, speaking with Dola. They both looked up when they heard someone approach, but Dola gave Destin a nod and continued down the stairs alone. "I looked for you several times."

"It appears this time you found me." He started back up the steps with her to the hallway, but he obviously wasn't in a hurry to get back. "How did you find the Lord of the Reef?" He didn't seem happy that she'd gone and spoken to Hassir against his advice, but he wasn't exactly chastising her. He sounded more tired than anything else, and she knew him well enough to see his mind spinning with anxiety behind his deep blue eyes.

Daiva didn't know what she thought of the Lord of the Reef, since their brief conversation hadn't been exactly enlightening. "He said he and I would discuss certain topics at a later time. I don't know exactly how it will end up, but at least it will be a discussion." She stepped closer to her brother and put out a hand onto his arm to stop his ascent. "I think we should convince the queen not to go to battle yet. This is not something that our fleet is prepared for right now. We need more time."

"I agree." He turned to look out the windows at the sprawling harbor with the ships of the fleet at anchor, and shook his head. It had been a busy few years for him, overseeing the rebuilding of the fleet after many of the ships of the Isles had been destroyed in a storm that had decimated much of the islands themselves.

There was a single great warship, which Destin commanded, but there were only about a dozen ships completed that were prepared to be sent south. The Genovin hadn't suffered through the same storm or incurred the same losses. The subjugation of the Reef was the only thing that kept the Genovin at bay so long. "But I think Melyssa knows that too. If I suggest a delay, she'll make it seem like a sign of my weakness in front of the other captains. She would love that."

"We don't have a choice, then?" She worried she already knew the answer. "Should we send Taimon and Kaia away? If we die, she might have a terrible fate in mind for them."

"If we die, Gale will make sure they're sent away." He said quietly, though he knew that was no guarantee of privacy between them. "That's part of what Dola is on her way to tell him. I'll make sure Leander knows his instructions as well, before we leave." He hadn't looked away from the ships outside the window, and sighed heavily as he considered the weight of the world crashing in around them at the moment. "The queen will have her way. Until she doesn't."

Daiva looked up the rest of the stairs. "Let's go hear what she has to say. Better to hear it now and plan than to wait and worry. Isn't that what Father always said?"

"Father said a lot of things." Destin finally turned away from the window, reaching up to brush a tear away from his beard. He was Oceanborn, and tended to show his emotions just as easily as the rest of his kind. It wasn't something he would ever apologize for. Thoughts of their parents would always draw tears from his eyes.

He started walking up the stairs with her, heading past other captains who were watching him expectantly, waiting to take their cues on the situation from him. He knew them all, respected many of them, and trusted a precious few of them to have his back in whatever conflict would come. "If I thought ordering you to stay home would do any good, I would attempt to do so."

"It won't." She almost growled as they returned to the main room. "If you die, I'm going with you."

"Good thing I have no intention of doing that any time soon, then." He grabbed a glass of wine on his way back into the room and sipped as he waited for Melyssa and Cadmos to reconvene. As he surveyed the room he caught sight of Hassir and his companions, standing on the other side of the floor map from him and Daiva.

Hassir looked back and forth from Daiva to her brother a few times, then glanced sideways at Melyssa and Cadmos, having a heated but private argument with one of the more foolish captains of the fleet. Seeing them occupied, he turned his attention back to Destin and Daiva, and lifted the glass in his hand toward them with a smile.

Destin wasn't quite sure what to make of the gesture at first, but he returned it subtly after a moment's consideration, though he didn't return the smile as both of them drank. He wasn't certain of exactly what they were toasting to, but the Fireborn was not a wolf Destin wanted as an enemy on any terms. He had enough of those.

Once the meeting adjourned and it was decided that their small fleet would go after the Genovin fleet by a route that would keep the element of surprise on their side, Daiva and Destin left the meeting as quickly as they could. They had a day to prepare, to figure out their own plan, and to come to terms with the idea that they could be dead very soon.

"I'm going to go meet with the Fireborn on their ship." Daiva moved quickly, even though she knew that Hassir and his comrades were still behind them. "Should I even make a guess about where you're going?"

"Dola's first, then to the harbor to set the fleet in order, then after that," he shook his head without looking over at her, since he could already see in his mind her disapproving glare, "no, you probably shouldn't guess."

"I suppose I shouldn't judge a wolf on his goodbyes." She watched her brother for a moment before she continued down the stairs. "Make sure you stop by and see Taimon and Kaia too. They always loved you more."

"Talking about me in the past tense already? Give me just a little more faith than that." There was a trace of his usual humor in his tone, but only the faintest trace, given their situation. "There's nothing the two of them would not do for you. And they'd do whatever you asked happily if you were to occasionally give them the impression you didn't want to pulverize them."

"I am strict with them because I want them to be careful. Neither of them are *ever* careful." She shook her head and continued down in silence before she stopped at the bottom and reached out for her brother when he stepped down. "I'll see you on the ship."

He took her arm and pulled her into a brief hug, even if he knew it wasn't really in her nature to be affectionate. He kissed her cheek and looked her in the eye before he let go of her arm. "Be careful." He said with more intensity behind the warning than he normally gave her. "We don't know them. Make no assumptions."

"I will be careful. I am always aware of the situation around me." She liked to think that she was, anyway. "Go on."

Hassir and his companions moved past them as they spoke, and Daiva watched them walk down the long stone paths toward the harbor at the bottom of the steep hill of the palace grounds. They moved without speaking to each other or looking to either side, with a direct purpose and no curiosity whatsoever.

As she followed, she noticed the footprint one of the

Stoneborn wolves left behind on each flagstone he passed over. It was a silent and innocuous act of rebellion against the imposed order of the wolves that had built the place. The haughtiness and condescension of Hassir and his companions almost dripped from their shoulders as they walked, appearing like lords of everything they saw rather than subjects called upon by their mistress.

Daiva followed after them casually until she knew they were close to their ship and she called out to the Lord of the Reef. She knew they all must be aware she was following, but they showed no signs of caring.

"Is now a good time to talk?" She said loud enough for him to hear, though she did wonder if he would stop or even look back.

All three of them stopped when she called, and she finally got a good look to see that one of them was indeed Stoneborn, the other a Skyborn. Hassir looked her over once and nodded to his companions, who then preceded him to their ship as he waited for her.

Once she caught up, he continued along the stone pier, headed for his vessel anyway. "Any time before dying can be a good time to talk. Now is as good as any other."

"Do you have any plans about how to avoid dying?" She started there, because any other discussion would be worthless if they were dead and unable to execute any other plan they might create.

"Against the Genovin?" He laughed, moved onto his ship, and sat along the railing casually. He indicated toward the railing opposite him, since the ship was narrow enough at the bow for them to be face to face. "They sent thirty ships north because they know we'll decimate them the moment we lay eyes on them. If they board any of the ships of our fleet, that ship is forfeit, everyone agrees on that. But the Earthborn are as shortsighted as they are strong. If we can sink their ships without being boarded ourselves, most of us will come home alive."

"I wonder if they regret killing my parents at this

moment." She said almost casually as she sat on the railing across from him. "Together, destroying the Genovin would be easy for them. Especially if Devon was helping." She sighed and looked up at him. "Assuming we survive, what, if any, kind of alliance would you be interested in?"

"Assuming we survive." He shot back with a grin, clearly amused with her manner. "No matter how long I live, I cannot imagine ever becoming accustomed to the directness of your kind. It does save time, I suppose." He glanced up at the palace, then clearly decided he didn't care if Cadmos was attempting to listen to them or not from the heights. "We've recently acquired common ground. Melyssa killed my grandmother before you were born, after she surrendered to the armies of the Isles, a portion of which was led by your mother."

"My mother was a powerful wolf." Daiva wasn't about to let him drive a wedge between them by talking about her parents, but she wouldn't let him speak evil of them either. "Every wolf around here has been raised to believe that the Reef is full of dogs. Wolves so insane they can do nothing but run around in circles. I am sitting here having a conversation with you, so that must not be true. Devon warned me that you and your people were not to be trifled with. He knew more of your strength than the rest of us. How can we utilize this common ground for both of our benefits? What do you want out of it?"

"The same thing every child of a murdered parent wants, naturally." He glanced away at his crew, and said something under his breath that got a nod from the Skyborn nearby before retreating to follow whatever command he'd been given. "The only problem is, only one of us is going to get the opportunity to see Melyssa's face when she realizes she's about to die."

Daiva turned contemplative after that, since she wasn't sure she wanted to give up that particular opportunity to a wolf she didn't even know.

"Even if she is dead," she continued on, since she would

need to think about who would get to kill Melyssa, "there is still the matter of her mate and her children. It would also mean," she paused as she looked over at him, "that you will have conquered the Isles."

"I have no interest in the Isles." He scoffed and looked around them at the harbor, with its intricate stonework and beautiful statues decorating every available space. It was meticulously shaped by those in the employ of the royal family, and the capital almost sparkled with the majesty of the wolves who lived there. It had been the home of Daiva's family, offshoot of the royal line as they were, for centuries before her birth. It was part of her heritage, but the wolf in front of her looked like he was surveying a dung heap rather than a jewel of the world. "My only interest is in the welfare of my people and the preservation of my territory. Whatever happens beyond the Reef is none of my concern."

"Really." She replied flatly as she stared at him. "Somehow I find that hard to understand. If you really want to be left alone on the Reef, the only way you can ensure that happens is if you can control the forces outside of it. If your only concern is to kill Melyssa for revenge, then even if you accomplish that, you accomplish nothing and certainly not any sort of preservation for your people." She was beginning to wonder if he really wasn't as smart as he sounded when she first spoke with him. "Being ruthless can be a great way to rule, but being ruthless and shortsighted is not going to accomplish anything."

"No, I can't imagine being shortsighted would accomplish much." He didn't seem offended by anything she'd said, and was still grinning as he looked back at her. "How would you proceed, then, if you were in my position and were attempting not to be shortsighted?"

"The only way to get what you want is to align yourself with someone who already has a following here on the Isles, so you might have that. Then you need to work to remove Melyssa *and* her entire family. After that, you would need to establish a leader that you feel you can either trust or who you can scare into doing what you say while you remain on the Reef." She shrugged as she stared across at him. "And upon further contemplation, I think that I would be willing to fight you for the right to kill Melyssa. I cannot simply give you that pleasure uncontested. I don't even know you, and I don't give out pleasures so freely."

"You're Stoneborn. As I understand your kind, you rarely give out pleasure at all." He actually chuckled at the idea of her fighting him for the right to kill Melyssa, but he nodded. "We can do battle for the privilege of claiming her life later. For now, would you agree that a discerning ruler, being aware of the necessity for allies within the Isles themselves, might venture north to visit the Isles himself in search of such allies, even though he truly despises the sight and stink of the place, and has traditionally avoided coming here at all costs?"

"You were summoned here." Daiva watched his expressions carefully. She didn't really think that he actually came here to find allies. Who did he think he would find, exactly? "Did you come here with intentions to speak with someone else?" If there were others planning some kind of revolution, she certainly needed to know about it.

"There are a number of noble families on the Isles who have long been dissatisfied with her majesty the queen. Many of them connect to you or to your late parents in one way or another, but there are a few you may be unaware of." He clearly enjoyed knowing some things that she didn't, but he was only willing to dispense so many secrets at once. "If it were to come to a battle for the right to kill her, you and I would not be the only wolves in contention, though I imagine we might be the last two to survive the conflict."

"I'm glad that you are aware of my strength, then, in the very least." Daiva jumped down gracefully from the railing of his ship. "It is good to know that we are on the same side. Temporary as it may be." She looked him up and down, since she knew that he couldn't possibly be interested in much more than Melyssa's death, despite his attempt to seem like he thought further about the entire issue. She looked around at his crew. "What happens to your Reef if you die? Do you have an heir that you left behind?"

"My Reef will do as it pleases, as it always has." He found the question almost laughable, and didn't leave the railing when she did, staring down at her as she prepared to leave. "As for an heir, no, I am unmated, as is my sister. But upon my death, she would be capable of administering the affairs of the Reef until she produces a Fireborn child or chooses a suitable inheritor from among our other lords."

"Curious." She remarked as she leaned against the railing. "Do you have something against mating as well? Is that too traditional for the Lord of the Reef?"

"Hardly." He glanced over the rest of his crew, who filed past the two of them on their way off the ship, apparently under orders that involved a great deal of haste. Several of them, as before, were in wolf form, running in an organized kind of chaos that did not stop to hesitate or ask questions.

Soon, the two of them were the only ones left on the ship, along with a few Skyborn far away at the stern with their eyes on the bright horizon. "I have nothing against mating, but I have no tolerance for power-seeking, weakness, stupidity, or unwarranted arrogance. The number of potential mates lacking any of these traits is small, the number lacking all of them close to nonexistent, in my experience."

"I see." She responded simply as she thought about what he said before she looked into his eyes again. It was still a little startling to her, seeing his Fireborn eyes and being reminded in a way of the brother that she had loved and lost. "You will not have better luck looking around here. Most here are more concerned about their clothing than they are about gaining strength or knowledge."

"So I've gathered. I've never had any intention of taking a mate from your people." He glanced dismissively at the homes that rose from the shoreline nearby in gaudy and highly artistic edifices, each seeking to outdo the next in grandeur while the ocean spread out at their doorstep as an apathetic audience to their pageantry. "You are small, you are simple, and you have forgotten what we are."

"Are you actually directing that at me?" Daiva narrowed her gaze on the Fireborn. "I am not the deluded wolf that most are."

He didn't respond to the obvious challenge in her expression and her tone, but he didn't look away from her either. The expression in his red eyes was difficult to read beyond their inherent ferocity.

"Perhaps not." He admitted, though his voice was so neutral it was hard to tell whether he was actually admitting the possibility that she was right or he simply didn't care enough to argue the matter. "Convey my respect to your brother, and let him know that my people will accompany his when we depart, in accordance with the queen's wishes. You may also inform him that you will be sailing with me, and you will be fighting alongside my people when we confront the Genovin."

"I do not think that he will let his crew be commanded by you, Hassir of the Reef. I will convey your respect, and the two of you can decide how you will fight." She thought it was incredibly presumptuous that he thought that he could command her brother's people through her, and she certainly wasn't just going to allow him to think that he could.

"I did not say his crew. I said you." He shot back by way of clarification, looking her up and down one more time. "There are other Stoneborn who have accompanied me here. You'll learn what your kind is supposed to be, rather than what these islands have made you."

Daiva wanted to laugh as soon as she realized that he thought so little of her skill simply because of where she came from. "I may not know everything, nor do I have all the skill I hope to one day obtain, but do not underestimate me, Fireborn." She blinked a few times as she balled her hands into fists at her side. "I will sail with you and I will fight beside your people, but only because I agree to do so. Not because you think you can command me."

"As you say." She could hear him chuckle behind her as she stepped back onto the comforting stone of the pier beside the ship. "And my name is Hassir." He shot after her as she began to walk away, and when she turned to look at him again, he was giving her the same enigmatic smile that seemed to be a permanent fixture of his face; before he turned away from her dismissively.

FOUR

Adriana was surprised when she woke to the sound of someone walking down the long stone corridor toward her cell. She blinked a few times when the noise of footsteps stopped, rubbing her eyes to try and make out the outline of the person outside the bars. It wasn't yet morning, but time meant nothing when someone was a slave.

"Yes?" She asked softly and sleepily, since she still couldn't see who was standing nearby in the relative darkness.

"Hope you got enough sleep this time." A ragged voice came back at her, before she heard and felt the bars on her cell door shake at the wolf's presence. "Apparently your lord and master didn't feel like giving you much of a break before he decided he wants you back under him tonight."

She had to bite back a groan when she heard the prison keeper's voice, but she certainly wouldn't complain about being able to see Destin again, and so soon. Adriana knew, though, that it wouldn't be good news, it couldn't be good news, if he was asking for her so soon. "You sound so jealous. Don't be jealous, Miris."

"Right, that's it. That's it exactly." The bars of her cell bent themselves apart with a low whine that made some of the other humans in the cells around her squirm in their sleep, but the huge man in her doorway didn't so much as glance to see who he'd disturbed. Adriana was not a small woman, but Miris dwarfed her in height and bulk, his head well above the low ceiling afforded to the slaves in their small pens.

"If some noble bitch takes it in her head to take me out and use me as she sees fit, I doubt I'll do much complaining about it, that's true enough. But you're not the type I'd be enthusiastic about, and your lord certainly isn't. I like a woman who hasn't already had the fire taken out of her by childbearing. You're too worn out for my tastes."

Adriana smirked up at the large man turned even-larger wolf, unafraid of him even though he could kill her easily if he tried. "Keep telling yourself that, Miris. The inexperienced ones are the ones that whimper and bleed. They have no idea what they're doing." She moved past him slowly, since she didn't want to wake anyone up, but she glanced back at him once. "Maybe that's why you enjoy them. They don't know what they're missing."

Two bars from the cells behind her shot out and caught her across the back for that comment, sending her to her knees on the stone right in front of him, which was clearly right where he'd wanted her.

He crouched down slowly so that he was on eye level with her, hands clasped with his elbows resting on his knees as he looked her over. His eyes had been brown once, she could remember seeing them in the face of a scrawny, hopeful man in the same captive situation she was in. They had taken on a myriad of colors since his turning, the swirling hazel of all Ironborn, but the glint of wickedness and malice in his eyes was altogether his own.

"Your lord is going to sail away tomorrow to pick a fight with the Genovin. A fight he's going to lose. And when we receive word that he's been killed, I'm going to see to it you never leave your cell again."

Even on her knees in front of him, there was nothing that Miris could say or do to remove the defiance in her eyes as she stared back at him. "That's what your Turning got you? A job babysitting human slaves when the real warriors are going out to fight? Here I thought you were meant to put that anger toward something useful."

He stood back up and returned the bars around her to their proper place, since they both knew he wasn't going to do any permanent damage to her. Not yet, at least. "You are far from useful. If and when I do anger the lords of the Isles, it will be for a much better reason than the likes of you."

He nodded toward the entrance of the prison and started to walk away, leaving her on the stone with half a dozen sets of eyes looking at her with a wide spectrum of emotions. Some were legitimately happy for her to see Destin again, others clearly resented her just as much as Miris did, others still seemed not to care so long as the Ironborn wasn't threatening them, and some who were completely uninterested and decided to go back to sleep.

Miris picked up his spear from beside her cell where he'd left it, and continued on down the hall to finish his patrol. "Enjoy your night with your lord, Adriana. It might be the last night of your life you get any enjoyment at all."

Adriana didn't hesitate to get up, even though it pained her to do so. Miris' little act was surely going to leave bruises across her back, but she scurried out anyway. She didn't have to be told where to meet Destin.

She ran most of the half hour between Chainhome and the shore near his family's house and found him there, as she knew she would. "It's not good news, is it?"

"Has it ever been, where Melyssa is involved?" He hadn't been difficult to find, down on the shore stones that were exposed by the low tide. He didn't look away from the water when she first approached, but his spinning thoughts quickly circled back to the idea that it might be the last time he saw her, and he turned to look at her as she joined him. "Ten ships are being sent south tomorrow afternoon with the tide to go teach the Genovin a lesson the queen thinks they need to learn. The wolves from the Reef report that they have at least thirty of their own."

She moved close enough to touch him and ran her fingers across his arm. They might be seen together by the shore, but she didn't particularly care. "I am not going to say goodbye to you. Not now, not ever."

"The Genovin may not give you much choice." He answered softly, pulling her in against him, the warmth of him a sharp contrast to the chill of the rock beneath them. "I knew Melyssa had her sights set on them, but I thought she would at least have the wisdom to wait a few years until we could finish rebuilding her fleet."

Adriana turned and buried her face into his chest, and she inhaled slowly to take in the scent of him. A few tears squeezed out of the corners of her eyes, but she bit her bottom lip to stop herself from crying any more than that. "So all of the things we hoped to have . . ."

Destin made no effort to hold back the tears running down his own face. He knew how futile it would have been. "Don't give me up completely yet." He kissed along her hair and took in a deep breath of her to steady himself against the rising rage and frustration he felt at the impasse of his situation. "Until you see my body with your own eyes, and you watch them lay me to rest inside the ocean, I will be fighting for us somewhere."

When she looked up at him, she took in the sight of his deep blue eyes and kissed him gently a few times before her kisses became desperate. "Is there really no other way?" All she could think about was being left without Destin and living out the rest of her days as a slave or living out only a few days until Miris felt particularly bored one day.

She could see in his eyes that he'd been circling around the same question for hours before she even arrived, without an answer. "We don't have the strength yet to move against Melyssa directly." He kept his voice low, though he knew that wouldn't stop any snooping wolves in the vicinity from hearing him. "If we had another Fulness, maybe two, but there are still too few of us to chance it, and we still have nowhere else to go. I can't risk your safety by defying her. Not yet."

"My safety?" She looked appalled that he would say something like that at a moment like this. "You have to realize this is bigger than my life, Destin. And if you go now . . . I have a feeling that I'm not going to be safe no matter what happens." She shook her head and kissed him once before she pushed her hair away from one of her shoulders, exposing some of her skin. "You are better off biting me and leaving me here."

It was Destin's turn to look appalled, but she could see him run his tongue over his teeth even as he glared at her. "You know I won't do that. Leave you here in the middle of the sickness and sail off not knowing whether you survived or not." His glare only lasted a moment before it softened, since he didn't want to fight with her, about her turning or anything else.

"I've told Taimon and Kaia to keep you at the house as much as possible while I'm gone. If that will even be possible. The guards here can ensure your safety at least. And if anything does happen to me, the two of them will make sure Miris and the others don't get the chance to do you harm while Leander gathers everyone together to move against the queen."

"What is the point of my safety if you're gone?" Adriana's voice trembled as she ran her fingers along the side of his face. "I'm not as strong as you think I am."

"No, you're stronger." He held her gaze before he kissed her until she was breathless. "I'm going to come back, and when I do, I am going to tear these isles apart to make way for us. You just have to be here when I get back."

Adriana held tightly to him afterward as her terrified heart pounded in her chest. Her breathing was quick from both his kisses and her fear, but she didn't want to make their parting any worse for him. "I love you." She whispered, a more dangerous confession than any plans of insurrection, for them. "I will wait for you."

"I love you." His promise was a scrape of his beard against her neck followed by his lips, before he let her go to glance at the ocean. "I don't want you to wait for me yet. Come with me tonight. The ocean may be cold, but I can take you somewhere warm enough to forget about it for a while."

Adriana didn't hesitate to agree, especially knowing that she might never see him again. She didn't want to think about that, though. She wanted to think about every moment he held her, kissed her, told her he loved her. "I'd go anywhere you asked me to go."

He managed a quiet smile as he moved to the water, pulling her arms around his neck so that she could hold on once they were in the water. "You should be careful with those kinds of promises. I've seen some very strange places on these waters."

"I don't care. Even strange places with you are better than being without you." Adriana kissed him several times as she held onto him, but she didn't want to distract him too much while he was leading the way. "Someday we'll be able to explore strange places together, right?"

"I'd like that." He stepped into the water, and the ocean rose up to carry them away, gathering itself around them to sweep them out beyond the shallows. The tide was coming in, and the waves were climbing on the shore behind them, but at Destin's touch, it was as though the flow of the water chose to reverse and drew them out into the depths in the space of just a few breaths.

Their pace didn't stop, carried along as if by some kind of independent-minded surface river until the shore behind them was little more than a memory. The space east of the island was dotted with islands, most of them no bigger than a sandbar, a precious few of them large enough for private residences of particularly antisocial wolves. All such passed them by at a slow march, as if they were giants plodding away with the rest of their bodies beneath the surface.

Destin turned them aside at one such protrusion of

stone, larger than a mere dot of sand, but too small and too barren to be useful as a private residence. There was a large outcropping of stone as an overhang that shaded most of the island, wet sand and sturdy grass covering the space beneath like a carpet. There were a few other smaller islands within sight, including one particularly massive island rising high out of the ocean further east. Still, it was the closest they could come, under the circumstances, to leaving the world behind.

"You said you're going to keep me warm, right?" She held even tighter to his neck, but she knew he had her securely in his arms. "Too bad you can't put a baby in me too. It's not close enough to the Fulness." She knew such things were so taboo that she didn't even know of a half-human/half-wolf child, but they certainly must exist.

"That would only put you even more at risk." He carried her up out of the water, draining it from their clothing with a thought to send it rushing back into the sea behind him. "I would wish the same thing, if we knew more about what would happen."

Adriana wrapped her legs around his waist and leaned in to whisper into his ear. "No one would have to know." She nipped at his earlobe afterward, and ran her nose lightly against his cheek. "I'd be fine."

When the water had been drained from their clothes, Destin set her down and removed the simple sash holding his own in place. There was never much reason for him or any wolf to wear complicated clothing, and it never took more than a few gestures to set them aside. "One day maybe we'll find out. When I come back from the Genovin, when the fight against Melyssa and her family is ended, and we can find some peace for ourselves."

"When you come back from the Genovin, we'll rebel and run away together." Adriana pulled her worn dress over her head and tossed it aside before she closed the distance between them. She ran her hands over his expanse of skin and whimpered softly. They didn't get enough time together. Not like this. Stolen moments here and there, rushed lovemaking, but not many like this. Away from everyone and everything. "Your body makes me dizzy with want."

In his skin, Destin looked mostly human, though his eyes, like all wolves, set him apart. They were a shade of deep blue that had never been seen in humans, but the rest of him was a powerful man in the prime of his life.

His deep blue eyes, however, couldn't take themselves from Adriana's body. His hands followed, taking hold of her hips as soon as she was close, holding tightly as the ocean slammed against the rocks behind him in an echo of his own possessive thoughts. "I can't wait for the day you never have to be far from me again."

Adriana still didn't know how she truly captured the attention of a strong, handsome, prestigious wolf like Destin, but she wanted him for more than one human lifetime. His hungry gaze on her made her even more needy with desire. "We can sleep curled up together. We can wake up every day next to each other." She kissed along his shoulder and down his throat before her hand wandered down to his cock. "I can have you all day long."

"Ambitious." His growl was an approving sound. His fingers went to her neck to tip her chin up to look at him, his thumb tracing her throat as he studied her eyes. His other hand parted her thighs as she took him in hand, his fingertips working toward the center of her to draw her closer against him, one stroke at a time.

She couldn't help the gasp that escaped her lips when his fingertips brushed her sensitive clit, but it only made her stroke him more. "Is it ambitious to want to make love with you all day? Sounds like a dream."

"I know wolves who pass the Fulness that way." He groaned against her cheek, savoring the time with her as he imagined their future. "That first day, following the Rising Night, the whole world feels like it's running, racing toward something it'll never reach. People sleep their fill, maybe grab something to eat if they're lucky and they can slip away from their partner long enough . . ." His grin was a teasing crescent half-hidden in his beard, his touch turning possessive, "and then back to all they desire from each other. I could spend a day like that. Bound up in you, listening to every sound you make."

She whined softly as his beard teased along her face and neck, his teeth teased along her skin. The threat of him biting her was something she felt on an instinctual level, and she wanted it desperately even if he was unsure about it for her future. Her hands continued to explore him, stroke after stroke against her palm. He was so much stronger than she would ever be, so much more dignified and important, and she was just a slave. "How did I get so lucky to have you want me like this?"

"It's not luck that you are who you are." He stroked her one last time and then laid her down in a quick succession of movements, ending with him kneeling over her like the wolf he was, one knee pushing her own apart. "You're not what anyone's made you, you're not what you were born to be. You get to decide who you are, in spite of everything else. That's the woman I love. The woman I want more than anyone or anything else on this ocean."

Adriana was breathing heavily as he loomed over her, and her breasts rose and fell with her panting. "I want you more than my next breath." She desperately wanted to haul him down to her, and her legs opened even wider. "I need you. Inside of me. All over me."

He was not in the habit of keeping her waiting.

Making love to a wolf was a different experience altogether than the other men Adriana had been with. The humans she had been paired with to produce children hadn't been altogether unpleasant, but there was nothing to match the ferocity with which her wolf loved her, and made love to her in turn. The humans she'd been with were after either their own pleasure or, more rarely, hers, but when that was accomplished, their interest went no further.

But from the start, from the way he wound her up and warmed her, toyed with her and teased her, it was clear his intentions with her were both relentless and thorough. If he was being forced to leave her, then he was damn sure going to give her a day to remember him by while he was gone.

As human as she was and as human as he wasn't, it wasn't lost on her how feral he made her and how controlled he was while he teased her. His tongue explored her nipples, her skin, he even kissed his way down and back up again, teasing her with his lips. When he ran his fingers through her folds again, she was soaked from all of his attention. Adriana shivered in pleasure as his fingers made lazy circles around her sensitive clit.

Every part of her felt like she was on fire, waiting for his next touch. When he finally gave her a bruising kiss, she could feel him sliding so slowly inside of her. Adriana broke off the kiss to gasp against his lips. "You're . . . torturing me on purpose."

"I would never."

He would always.

Every chance he got, for as long as possible.

He had worked her body into a frenzy, but his pace was slow, answering the craving in her with satisfaction that felt like it was just a gasp away, a rising threat at the base of her spine, threatening to cascade through her entire body. He knew her body as well as he knew his own. He laid a hand against her neck as he thrust a steady pace into her, watching her eyes, watching her grip tremble as she held onto him. "All day?" He challenged, his blue eyes searching hers. "Is this where I should keep you for an entire day and a night?

Adriana wrapped her legs around him to try and force him to move quicker, but no amount of strength in her body was anywhere near his. She reached up to grip him at his shoulders, but he pinned her hands together and held them with one of his own as his other hand remained at her neck.

"Yes." She whined, unable to imagine any other way that she would want to spend her time, even when he tortured her. Adriana was entirely at his mercy, and he was the only wolf she would ever trust with such vulnerability. "I am whole . . . when I am with you."

The words were all he needed to carry him forward in his life, over any expanse of ocean. He laid himself heavily against her, thrusting deeper, losing another piece of his own restraint as she took all of him perfectly. He could feel her climax coming in her rising cries, echoing off the stone around them and disappearing across the ocean waves. He wanted to keep her exactly where he had her for hours, for days, but more than that, he wanted to see the satisfaction in her eyes, feel the tide crash through her heart all at once.

It didn't take many thrusts before her cries and her body reached a fever pitch, and she arched against the ground where he had her pinned. Her whole body was dizzy with the pleasure he'd meticulously built up, and her chants of "Oh Gods, Destin" were breathy and desperate. It was inhuman, the way he made her feel so good, not only with his body but also his love, and she ached for him in all the ways.

His kisses at her neck as she cried out lingered to savor her, to taste her, taking deep breaths of her scent in the moment of ecstasy. The salt of her sweat was more delicious to him than the ocean that gave him life. "You are incredible, every time." He was breathless with his own need for her, but Destin was nothing if not controlled, at all times.

Adriana couldn't respond immediately, but her hips didn't stop wiggling or moving with him still buried deep inside of her. She wanted his pleasure as deeply as he savored hers, and one day she wanted his pups. One day. "You . . . I want . . . to hear . . ."

He could never deny her what she wanted for long, as hard as he tried. When she had recovered, he lifted her easily against him, and turned to lie back, taking his own turn to stretch out along the moss and the rocks. Drenched as they often were by the sea, they were more comfortable for him than he imagined they had been for her, but best of all was the feeling of her on top of him, the silhouette of her curves against the stars over the ocean.

"You can have all you want from me, Adriana." He whispered her name like a prayer, pulling her down into a heavy kiss as her hips rocked against him. "Oh, take it all. Everything. Everything I have to give you, it's yours. Take it. Take it all."

She was grateful for moments like this, moments where it felt like they belonged to no one else except each other. Adriana watched him carefully as she increased speed and bounced hard on top of him, desperately aching for his climax as she built toward another. "I love you, I love you," Adriana repeated as she watched his face twist with pleasure as he finally climaxed.

Her name echoed over the ocean as if it was a call being taken up by the whitecaps of the waves. At her back, the nearby ocean crashed against the rocks of their tiny island in instinctive answer to their master's orgasm. His large hands were likely to leave bruises on her hips, the rest of him growling out in ultimate satisfaction as she rode his climax out of him.

It took a long time for his heart to return to any kind of normal cadence, and for the ocean to begin to quiet again behind her. Destin's body relaxed against the sea-soaked stone, his touch drawing her down to use him as her bed as they both caught their breath.

Adriana slowly situated herself on top of him afterwards, her whole body feeling very much exhausted but electrified at the same time. There was no way for her not to feel the impact of an Oceanborn's power when he was surrounded by the water at a climax of pleasure. It zipped through her body, foreign as it was, and felt like a strength beyond anything she could ever know as a human. It thrilled and then exhausted her, in all the best ways. "When we get mated someday . . . I can't wait to hold onto that power. Your strength. Instead of just feeling it rush through like sand between my fingers."

"You won't need mine. You'll have your own." His voice sounded certain, reassuring, even though his thoughts behind the statement were filled with worries. That power was on the other side of a great many uncertainties for her. If he returned from fighting the Genovin. If their revolution against Melyssa succeeded. If they made it to some kind of safety. If Adriana survived being bitten by him, and the changing sickness that came after. So many questions. So little certainty.

But on the other side of it all . . . to have centuries with her instead of stolen hours? It was a paradise worth the risk.

* * * * *

Taimon watched from farther up the shore as his brother and Destin's human woman embraced and slipped into the water, headed out under Destin's power toward a more sequestered part of the island where they could say their goodbyes in private. He sniffed at the air with his snout a few times as they disappeared, reassuring himself that no one else was close by and Destin hadn't been overheard, the air still a chaotic mess at Taimon's own insistence.

A couple of the guards came over to take a peek. He said silently to Daiva, sitting beside him on the rocks of the cliff, so still she might as well have been one of them herself. Both wolves watched the situation carefully, their shifted forms affording them private telepathic conversation. *Other than that, nobody is around in either direction. I think they were pretty well covered.*

Good. Daiva moved slightly to turn her head and look at her young and usually wild brother. *It is up to you to watch out for Kaia, and stay close around here so that you will be protected. If you can and it is necessary, save Destin's human. But only if you are sure that you and Kaia will be safe. I know he loves her, but you and Kaia need to be protected foremost.*

Taimon walked with his tail low and his head even lower as they made their way together back to the house. He stole a glance at his powerful sister infrequently along the way.

You really hate her. He said without exactly asking a question. He was never sure exactly what would set Daiva off, and he tended to draw her anger more than anyone else in the family. She tended to ignore Kaia more than anything else, and even though Taimon wanted to be of help and tried as hard as he could to support his siblings, it never seemed to go well. *I think she's nice. She makes Destin happy.*

I do not hate her, I just think she is a waste of his time. Daiva knew Taimon was scared of her, and rightly so. Taimon was more trouble than anything else, and she wanted him to grow out of it quickly. *If he doesn't think she would even survive a turning, then she is not worth his time or his affection. He needs a companion who will last, and one who can support him properly.*

He obviously didn't agree completely with her assessment of Adriana, but he knew better than to contradict her. *Do you really think you can come home? I haven't fought with many Earthborn, but that's because I want to stay alive. There's a reason they've never been conquered before.*

The queen does not intend for us to conquer the Genovin right now, and I don't think we should try. She moved a little closer to her brother, because even though he thought that she hated him, she really did care for him, in her own way. *I am trying to find a way to work with the Reef, and if we can, we'll try to find a way to work with the Genovin. The real enemy is the one we're loyal to.*

He shook his head and scratched at his neck in a mannerism that annoyed even Kaia, since it made him look more like a common dog than any wolf ever wanted to appear. *Fireborn are even worse. It's just a little sad that the Reef and the Genovin are the only choice of friends we have left.*

It is not sad. She let out a small snort to remind him not to act so undignified, especially in front of her. *The Reef has always been known for its power. It's about time Melyssa learned that her fire isn't the only one that burns.*

As confident as Daiva sounded, listening to her didn't make Taimon feel any better about their chances. *I just want you and Destin home safe. That's all I care about.*

I don't know how to comfort you, but you must know that I am not going out on a boat just to die. When I die, it will be on my terms.

That, I believe. A gust of wind blew the heavy door shut behind them a little too loudly when they arrived home, and Taimon flinched at the sound, since he couldn't quite control the wind in wolf form precisely. *If you did die some way you didn't approve of, you'd yell at your own gods to put you back in the world until you got your way.*

I certainly would. Daiva shifted as soon as they were back in the house, and she reached out for her dark gray robes on a hook by the door. She immediately looked around, and by the silence that she felt in the echoes of the house, she knew Kaia wasn't home. "Make sure Kaia doesn't run out like this all the time, Taimon. I'd hate to find her pinned in a corner with one of her dirty, flea-bitten friends."

Taimon shifted as well, but he didn't bother grabbing his robes, yet another habit that annoyed his older siblings. "She likes Earthborn. There's not much I can do about that, I'm sorry to say. And she's not out scratching an itch right now. I can hear her humming in the gardens. She never leaves the grounds nowadays."

"Make sure it stays that way." Daiva looked over at her young brother and shook her head. "As soon as we get home, you need a tutor." She didn't look at him for long before she started up the stairs. "I'm going to get some sleep."

Taimon bowed slightly to her as she left, but she didn't even acknowledge him before she was out of sight. When she was gone, the house was an incredibly quiet place, and Taimon didn't like it at all. The silence meant his family was gone, and it was a huge change from the way the house had been when it was full of family and friends.

All the life was being taken from their family, and for what? For not wanting to live in accordance with the dictates of their king and queen? Taimon shook his head at the thought. He didn't want to live in a silent house without his family. They needed to come home. They had to.

FIVE

Two days of Destin's absence felt like ages to Adriana. She worried about him constantly, even though she knew her worry wouldn't do anyone any good. It was early in the evening when she returned to her cell, and while she knew why they had been sent back early, she just curled up on the scattered hay and waited.

The new shipment of humans had finally arrived, later than normal, but it had arrived. Chainhome had been rearranged in the days prior, the Stoneborn and Ironborn keepers restructuring entire rooms to make the cells fit for two people at a time. Every human in residence knew what that meant. Adriana had yet to be paired with anyone for the breeding season, so she knew she would get a man from the new arrivals. The last thing she wanted to think about was what kind of man was going to be shoved into her cell, but she knew it was a part of her life no matter what she wanted.

The guard on duty was a Stoneborn she had known all her life, by the name of Takas. She could feel him coming down the broad central hall of Chainhome, his steps reverberating through the corridors. It let every slave in residence know that they needed to be on their best behavior. The group of humans shuffled along in front of her cell, mostly men but a few breeding-age females, all with their heads down and eyes darting from side to side, their hands bound in front of them with stone shackles. Some of them had trouble holding up their bonds, much less walking with them.

Takas stepped up to her cell and motioned her to her feet, saying nothing as usual. He looked her over casually, making sure she still appeared physically fit, then turned his attention to the group he'd ushered in. "You." He nodded at one of them, and Adriana could see the young man tugged forward forcibly by the stone wrapped around his hands. "Your name."

The man looked like he was only barely an adult, with shaggy blond hair that fell around his face and the barest dusting of blond hair on his cheeks and chin. He looked barely taller than Adriana, and was neither particularly skinny or well-muscled. He was unremarkable in almost every way except that he looked nothing like any human she'd ever met. He had no scars on his bared upper body, and looked as if he'd actually been well cared for in his life up to that point. "Shian, master."

Adriana picked out a couple pieces of hay from her hair as she leaned against the bars and looked out at the young man and then over at Takas. She thought about introducing herself, but Takas had an even worse temper than Miris and she never knew how to judge his mood.

He looked at the two of them again in succession, then moved to grab one of the bars of Adriana's cell. The stone around the edges moved away from the bars until he could pull it open.

Shian made the first wise decision of his time in Chainhome and hurried inside without being asked or shoved. Takas gave an approving nod as he closed the cell on them both, forming the stone around the bars again once they were sealed inside.

"Move." He growled at the rest of the slaves in front of him, who scurried away down the hall immediately, a few of them shooting glances back at Shian as they went.

The man, for his part, didn't seem any more excited to be in her cell than Adriana was excited to have him there. He stumbled toward the back of the cramped space, and stood against the wall, rubbing his wrists and hands as the stone fell away into pebbles, released from Takas' control. His eyes focused on the small barred window that looked out on the overcast day beyond the prison, but he could see nothing of substance through the iron. "What's your name?" His voice hadn't shaken when he introduced himself to Takas, but it shook in the aftermath of the wolf's presence, and he still refused to look at her.

"Adriana." She spoke softly. She felt bad for the young man, even though she still desperately wanted to be with Destin. Adriana remembered being in his position, being forced into a cell with a man that was much older than herself, knowing the only reason why she was there was to produce a child.

She had been lucky with Piers. He had never mistreated her, and they had been friends, of a sort, for the years prior to his death. Maybe she could be that same person for Shian. Fortunately for her, she was still young, even though she was clearly the older of the two of them. Experience and knowledge could help her make a friend, hopefully.

She went to the corner of her cell where she'd left her uneaten bread and an apple Kaia snuck in the day before, and she grabbed the apple. Adriana looked down at it longingly before she walked over and held it out to Shian as an unspoken peace offering. "Are you hungry?"

He started to refuse it, but took the apple from her fingers after obviously thinking better of it. "Thank you." He didn't eat it immediately, though, since he wasn't actually hungry. He looked up into Adriana's eyes for the first time hesitantly, through the messy strands that hung over his face. His eyes were a bright, piercing blue that momentarily reminded her of a Skyborn. "They gave us food a little while ago if you're still hungry. I don't . . . is this all they give you to eat?" He looked back and forth between the apple and the bread across the small cell in obvious shock and disbelief.

Adriana looked over at the bread and then down at the apple before she looked at him again. "They gave us broth and bread tonight, but I drank the broth while it was warm. The apple was a gift yesterday, but most humans never see them. Not unless you're lucky." She raised an eyebrow and watched him carefully as she took a few tentative steps closer.

"Where are you from?" Adriana reached out and ran her fingers across one of his arms where there was not a single scar. She knew it would make him uncomfortable, but knowing the things they would need to do, touching his arm was nothing in the grand scheme of things. Her arms and hands held their fair share of scars and bruises. "You're . . . you look untouched."

He hadn't been self-conscious about his appearance the moment before, but as soon as she touched him, his pale face flushed and she could see him tremble a little at her inspection. "I um . . . I was raised on the Shield Isle, under the care of Lord Calis and Lady Ressa. I was a slave of their household, with my parents and brothers and sisters."

"With your family?" Adriana was shocked to hear that, but she didn't stop her inspection of him. Adriana looked him over slowly before she lifted her green eyes to look into his blue ones. "You seem extremely nervous. You've never been used for breeding before, have you?"

"No, I haven't." He shook his head with confidence in his answer for the first time, but didn't move away from the wall. "My parents and masters told me my whole life growing up that I would be paired with someone once I had eighteen winters, but I didn't know I'd be leaving the Shield Isle."

"Eighteen?" Adriana was quiet for a moment, since she had to wonder if it was likely that the man hadn't *any* experience at all. She touched the light scruff on his face before she dropped her hand to her side. "Well, I'm sorry you were sent here."

"I just . . . didn't know it would be like this." There was horror in his eyes as he looked around at the cell over and over again. He was obviously having trouble coming to terms with the fact that the two of them barely had enough room to lie down comfortably beside each other. "At home we have our own quarters and we eat what the masters and the army don't want."

"I always heard that Calis was the soft one." She didn't know what it would be like to live underneath the rule of a wolf that would be kind to her, but she was sure she would never know.

Adriana was about to say something else when she heard footsteps again. There was a faint ring of laughter that followed, and while she seemed confident before, she looked horrified in an instant. "That's Chiara."

He looked worried at her expression, but he was obviously more confused than scared. "The princess? I didn't know she lived here?"

"She lives where she likes, and they bring her in for the breeding season." She said softly but she moved closer to him. Adriana slipped her hand into his and gripped his firmly, but not painfully. "Let's back away from the bars."

He didn't let go of her hand as he looked back through the bars. As they waited for whatever was coming, he lowered his voice, since he wasn't sure what to expect. "Why do they bring her in for the breeding season?"

"She's a . . ." She was surprised he hadn't been informed about Chiara or what Chiara could do, but she supposed that maybe that was the design all along. The humans on this island knew about her, but the others wouldn't. "She's a Heartborn." Adriana whispered into his ear and kept her face close to his. "If the new matches seem troublesome, she . . . removes the trouble."

He huddled down a little into the corner of the cell beneath the window with her, listening to the rest of the slaves go silent at the woman's approach. "How does she do that?"

"She . . ." Adriana started to answer, but she went quiet as the woman stopped near their cell.

"She makes people fall in love." A smooth, silky voice answered, as Chiara leaned forward so her face was visible to those in the cell. "Hello, young Shian. I could sense your anxiety all the way down the hall. Why are you nervous? Don't you think you've been paired with a beautiful woman?" Chiara raised an eyebrow, her face almost teasing.

He immediately went pale as the woman looked him over, and even as he began to ask how she knew his name or anything about him, the words caught in his throat at the sight of her. She was like no wolf he had ever seen before, but he could see echoes of his former lord Calis in her features. Her hair was a bright blonde that fell around her shoulders, just above the deep purple dress she was wearing. The dress was a pale match for her eyes, sparkling violet in the darkness. She was so beautiful it was almost painful to look at her. "I . . . yes, my lady. She is b-b-beautiful."

Chiara laughed softly and looked over at Adriana with a smirk, but the smirk didn't reach her eyes. "Looks like you got a young one this time, Adriana. He should keep you busy." She raised an eyebrow and looked at their joined hands. Chiara wanted to remind the human woman of her place, and so she looked at the two of them a little longer. "Show me how well the two of you go together, Adriana."

Adriana knew how Chiara worked, though knowing didn't mean that she was able to protect herself. She felt Chiara's power settle into her thoughts, and did nothing to resist. It would have only made matters worse. She leaned in closer until she ran her nose along the side of Shian's neck and kissed his skin gently. "We could make a strong, beautiful child together." She whispered into his ear before she could stop herself, clearly as bewitched as Chiara wanted her to be.

Shian twitched and shuddered under too many different emotions to settle on any one in particular. As soon as

Adriana was close, his shaking hands settled on her waist, but he didn't respond to her kiss or her whisper aside from turning comically red in the face. "I . . ." He looked back and forth between Adriana and the beautiful wolf outside the cell, fear pounding in his heart at the suddenness of what was happening.

"I'm . . . sure we could?" He said hesitantly, his eyes darting around the room, looking for a way out even if there was no hope of finding one. He didn't want that wolf in his thoughts, and every time she looked at him, he could feel her looking right through him.

Chiara grinned at him and took a deep breath as though she could inhale every emotion he felt all at once. Adriana continued to kiss along his skin as Chiara watched with a raised eyebrow. "Now, now, young Shian, that's not how you return such passionate affection."

His panic soared to new heights as he felt the invasion of the wolf's power in his own mind, but his panic was limited to a distant corner of his thoughts as he turned back to look at Adriana. It was as if the image of Adriana had haunted his dreams for years, the sound of her voice, even the scent of her, something so deeply a part of his fantasies that he couldn't understand why he hadn't realized it the moment he entered her cell.

She was holding him so close, like every wish he'd ever had, granted in a single moment. The world became a different place, just for a moment, and his hands locked onto her waist, no longer trembling or uncertain. His lips returned the attack of her own along her neck while he moved to pin her against the wall of the cell. He had never wanted anyone or anything so much in his life as he wanted Adriana in that moment.

Chiara giggled and glanced back at Miris as the humans enjoyed each other's kisses and touches. It was as if the wolves didn't exist outside the cell at all. "She's been too long without another human male, don't you think?"

Miris was always the first wolf in Chainhome to take

pleasure in someone else's misery, but as he stood in Chiara's presence, everything about him was subservient. He stood in one place, leaning on his spear with both hands, keeping a respectful distance from the Heartborn princess and his head bowed. There were very few wolves Miris feared, but one of them was standing in front of him. "Yes, Majesty. Much too long."

Chiara glanced at Adriana once more and smirked once she saw the young man left marks on Adriana's neck. Without another thought, she stepped away from the cell and moved on to another that contained a new arrival. As soon as she turned her attention elsewhere, her spell on the two started to fade, but she hoped that Adriana would remember what she was up against.

The intensity between them continued for a while before Shian was finally capable of turning his mind around and questioning what was going on. By then his simple slave clothing was in a state of complete disarray and he was trembling all over again, though most of it was at least still in place on his body. He still held onto Adriana, and the sound of their heated breaths echoed off the walls around them. Their breathing mingled with the low ghosts of conversation and cries of various types flowing from the stone cells around them.

"What . . ." he gasped for breath, fear entering his eyes instead of the passion that had filled them before, "what was . . . what did she . . ."

Instead of pulling away, Adriana ran her fingers across the cheek of the strange man in front of her. She wanted to feel guilty because the man she really wanted was out on the ocean, but guilt would do her no good.

"I think that was because she wanted to prove something to me, but also to all the new arrivals. Heartborn can make you think and feel a lot of things that you never thought you would." She met Shian's light blue eyes and dropped her hand to hold his again. "I don't know you, but I think I would rather get to know you on our terms instead of hers."

He didn't pull away from her either, clutching at her hand when she held his, but he didn't stop shaking. Shian's eyes darted between looking at her and watching the iron bars of their cell for any signs of the woman coming back to change him again. "I never knew they could do anything like that. Any of them. Her brother, Lord Calis . . . he's always been kind to us. Never . . . never like that." His hand moved up over her back in a caress that had seemed altogether natural the moment before, but froze the moment he remembered. His fingers moved off her skin slowly, as if they were apologizing as they went. "Will she come back?"

She gave him a rueful smile and a one shouldered shrug. "Most of the time, there are about half of us that struggle to get along during breeding season, so it keeps Chiara busy. Luckily for me, you're attractive. You and I can be friends, right?" The corner of her lips turned up slightly, since she was trying to deal with this situation the best that she could. There were worse men that she could have been paired up with.

Shian nodded nervously, since he had been just as worried about who he was going to be paired with, but Adriana seemed like a kind person. "My parents taught me never to say no to a friend when someone offers to be one. We don't have much, but we can have friends." He offered a hesitant smile, still incredibly nervous, but he was stuck with the woman, and she with him. Even if it was nothing like the life he'd previously known or the life he'd envisioned, it was something, and he wanted to make the most of it.

Adriana squeezed his hand and looked out at the bars for a moment before she led him into the corner farthest away from Chiara or Miris. She sat down on the floor and pulled him down with her before she released his hand. "Tell me about yourself. Tell me about your family and your home. It will help."

He still looked nervous about the wolves outside their cell being so close, but he turned so that his back was pressed along one side of the corner, and hesitated as she moved in close to sit against him. She was a complete stranger to him, and even as fiery as they had been a moment before, he was still nervous about opening up to her.

"Well, I . . . my parents were personal servants of the lord and lady in their household. They helped run their manor, prepare their meals, their clothes, all of it. My mother had nine children. Four of us died before being named. My older brother died last year in an accident." He shook his head, since he obviously didn't want to talk about it.

"My older sisters were paired off to other slaves in our household the last few years as soon as they bled, but my parents managed to keep me around to help them even though they said I should've been sent off two years ago. This year, lady Ressa decided they had stalled long enough, and sent me here. She told my parents they had taken advantage of her leniency too long, and their punishment was that I would be sent away instead of being paired off with a woman on the Shield Isle so I could stay close to my parents."

Adriana could still see his mother's tears in Shian's eyes, and his parents' begging still rang in his ears. But they were separated by walls and bars and miles of ocean, and Ressa had been adamant they would not see him again.

She slid away so he wouldn't be so uncomfortable, but she wanted to comfort him even though she barely knew him. "I am sorry to hear that. I know you must miss them terribly." She sighed and looked over at the bread she previously left untouched. Adriana grabbed it and pulled off a piece to eat. "This island is never going to be like your home, but there are still some things to find happiness in. I'll introduce you to the people worth knowing and people you can trust."

"There are so many humans here." He seemed to settle down for the first time. A little distance from her and a lot of distance from Chiara and Miris seemed to help. "Back on the Shield Isle I saw maybe a few hundred of us over the whole island when running errands for the mistress, but this place is huge. There have to be thousands of us here. I never knew there were so many of us."

"The King and Queen are here. They keep us busy. That's why they have the princess oversee the breeding season." She shrugged, glancing up into the ceiling as if she could look at all the other humans present through the stone. "We're not actually as worthless as they like to make us seem, and the wolves here like to do as little of their own work as possible."

"I just . . . I guess I didn't know what to expect." His fingers twitched over the simple clothing he wore to cover himself a little more, but it didn't seem to help the faraway look in his eyes. "I thought I'd grow up on the Shield Isle and serve lord Calis like my parents for the rest of my life. I didn't even think about what life would be like for us anywhere else." He looked around nervously to make sure there were no wolves lurking outside the door, and relaxed a little more when the hall remained empty. "Have you lived here your whole life?"

Adriana nodded. "I was born here, raised here, never knew who my parents were or even who my siblings might be." She knew the reason why they took the human babies away from their families was so that the slaves would feel connected somehow, and that it might stifle violence, since everyone had no idea if they would be fighting against their very own flesh and blood. "I've had two babies taken from me, and I still don't know if the children I see running around could be ones that I carried and cared for that first year of their lives."

The horror and disgust on Shian's face would have told her plainly that he hadn't grown up on the Queen's Isle, if nothing else had. "I'm sorry. I knew . . . I mean sometimes we would get other children that came in from the other Isles, and my mother or my sisters would take care of them for a while, but I just . . . I guess I never asked. I thought they were just orphans whose parents had died somewhere else." That was purposeful blindness on his part, he knew, but it was still hard to deal with everything he ever thought about the world crashing down with every breath. "So your . . . The man who was here before me, what happened to him?"

"Piers. A couple years ago he died in a fight. Just a brawl while out working that got out of control. He was very kind to me, and when I was a scared, young girl, he didn't have to be kind." She watched his expressions, and suddenly she felt more pity for him than she would for most. He knew something different and better, and that made his loss worse. "I will do my best to be kind to you in turn. I'm sorry this is your future."

He looked around the cell slowly, taking in the sight of the place as she proclaimed it his future. It was uniform grey stone, the bars the same color he imagined the night would be if it could bleed, rust coating them in places, perfect wolf-formed blackness in others. "The wolves on the boat coming here had a lot of fun telling me how hideous a hag I'd be paired with when I got here. How I'd have to work in the shipyard and I wouldn't last a season." He shook his head, trying to clear his mind of their taunts, and reached over to take her hand and pull her a little closer. "I'm glad they were wrong about one of those things, at least."

Adriana laughed softly and tried to convince herself to focus on the new person in front of her. Destin was so far away, and after what Chiara did, Adriana had to be careful about everything. Especially her thoughts and the truth of her heart. She ran her fingers along the outside of his hand and leaned in a little closer. "Maybe we can just start with getting comfortable?" She waited for him to nod before she moved in and snuggled against his side. "I'm glad you don't think I'm too unfortunate looking."

"You're not. At all." He repeated, putting his arm around her and holding her tight, even though he knew she was still very much a stranger. He looked up over her head at the tiny window in the cell, then across the hall at its equivalent in their neighbor's wall, where the light was beginning to turn a fiery orange, headed toward sunset. "Do they um . . . do they leave us alone at night, at least?"

"Yes, they leave us alone at night." Her voice was soft as she wrapped her arm over his chest. Adriana closed her eyes and she took a deep breath as she told herself silently that it was alright for her to be pressed against some strange man. "It may seem like they're all against you, but you and I will be a team. Alright?"

He nodded against her hair, but didn't say anything else for a long time as they sat there in each other's arms.

* * * * *

The daylight faded around them until all that remained to give life to their world were the sounds of their fellow slaves somewhere out in the darkness. Some of them obviously hadn't needed much encouragement from their masters to become more than friendly, and were vocal about it. Some were voices crying on the first night far from home.

Others were singing, and Shian held his head up to listen. The music was low and rhythmic, almost a lullaby but less comforting, in words too distorted by echoes for him to hear clearly. "What is that?" He asked as his fingers trembled again, not sure whether to feel more comfortable or be afraid of something the other slaves were warning the rest about.

Adriana didn't open her eyes, as she held a little tighter to the stranger that was now supposed to be her closest companion. "It's a song of mourning." She said softly against the side of his neck. "They're singing for you and the rest who arrived tonight. They sing the same song when the wolves come to collect the new children every year."

He listened a little longer, hypnotized by the music that was apparently for his benefit. He could see his brother's face in the darkness looking back at him from the life they wouldn't get the chance to live together. Adriana could feel a few tears fall from his thin blond beard against her cheek, but he neither sobbed nor sniffled. Some aspects of being a slave were apparently universal, even under a kinder master. "You don't sing?" He asked when he could do so without his voice breaking.

She shifted her body and gently wiped away his tears. Adriana didn't cry unless she had to say goodbye to Destin, but she could understand the pain of the life Shian had lost even if she had never had something so grand to lose before. "I sing to my children. Only because I hope somehow they'll remember something about me that way."

"Maybe they will." He tried to see in the darkness if she was crying as well and needed tears wiped away from her cheeks, but he didn't see any to be had. He marveled again at the gift he'd been given in his cellmate and companion. "Will they let me stay with you after they're born, or put me somewhere else? I could sing with you."

That made her smile and was also grateful that she had been given someone who was a little more timid instead of someone who would have been overbearing and controlling. "That would be nice. And no, they won't move you anywhere else. You and I are together until something happens to one of us, or if a few breeding seasons go by and we aren't successful together. There have been some people that have been paired together for many years."

Shian couldn't think that far into his own future at the moment, so he shook his head, especially with the mourning song echoing through his thoughts. "I hope you won't regret me being thrown in here with you." He said quietly. "You seem like a good person, and good people don't deserve to be stuck with things they hate."

"I already like you." Adriana gave him a sideways hug. It was nice to have someone to hold onto instead of just curling up on the floor. "This could have been much, *much* worse for both of us. I know some women . . ." She listened carefully, but she didn't hear anyone nearby. "Who enjoy taking new, young men and changing them for life. I don't know what you've already experienced, but I don't want you to be fearful of me or anything that happens between us. It can be enjoyable, and I want it to be. There's so little we can enjoy around here."

"I um, there was one girl back home, we . . . well, we got along pretty well." Even without much light in the cell, Adriana could almost feel the heat rising to his cheeks again, just one more mark of how different his upbringing had been. "So I'm not completely stupid. At least I hope you won't think so."

Adriana couldn't help but laugh, since she didn't think that he was stupid. "You kiss very well. I think you'll be fine." She emphasized her point by kissing him on the cheek somewhat playfully. "So you got along well? Do you miss her?"

He didn't sound like he was smiling when he answered. "She um, we were found one time when we were together, and one of the Lady's friends in the house didn't like it that we were together without having been paired. So she was beaten and I was confined to the house. She hated me after that. Never talked to me, never even looked at me again. So no, I guess I don't, really. I'm sure she was paired with somebody this year."

"I'm sorry." She whispered before she sighed against his skin. "I didn't mean to bring up a bad memory for you."

"Our life seems like a series of bad memories." He said so quietly it was hard to hear him above the continuing hum of the music around them, but he took a deep breath and let out a heavy exhalation that blew her hair back over her shoulder. "I've never understood it. But my father said the point isn't to understand. The point is to accept the world around us and learn to do the best with what we have."

Adriana wanted to tell him that maybe, just maybe, it wouldn't be like that all the time. Maybe they would get away, maybe the both of them could be happy and truly just be friends, but it was too soon to tell and she didn't know him well enough to spill any secrets. She ran her fingers along his forehead and then along his cheek. "I think I got lucky again."

"I'm glad you think so." He leaned in hesitantly and ventured a kiss along her cheek, but then looked up sharply as he heard something dragging along the floor toward their cell. Whatever it was, it stopped every few feet for a while and then continued on slowly.

Before he could ask what it was, a young boy no more than four or five came into sight, two more his size with him, all of them pulling as hard as they could on ropes that were dragging a large box of straw through the hall. The lead boy stopped in front of Adriana and Shian's cell and went back to the box, taking out a few large armfuls of straw and shoving it through the bars toward them before crouching and smiling at them as he hung onto the iron with his tiny fingers. "Hey, 'Ana. Who's he?"

She smiled widely as soon as she heard the familiar little voice, and she sat up to crawl closer to the bars and touch Malcom's little hands. Adriana had spent a lot of time with the young boy, and somehow she felt as though she was a kind of mother to him, even though he looked nothing like her. "This is Shian. He just arrived from the Shield Isle." Adriana looked back at Shian and motioned toward the small boy. "This is Malcom. He's one of my closest friends. Aren't you?"

"Mhm!" The boy nodded vigorously and went to grab another armful of straw while the other children did the same with other cells nearby, making sure everyone had enough to accommodate the newcomers. He then grabbed a thin blanket from a pile in the straw and handed it over as well. "He's not hurting you, is he, 'Ana?" Malcom attempted to look very fierce for a moment as he glared up at Shian, just to make sure.

That made Adriana smile even more, but she shook her head. "No, he has not hurt me. I don't think he will.

Especially now that he met you, I know that he'll be on his best behavior." She glanced over at Shian and then back at Malcom. "You're going to be a strong warrior, aren't you?"

Malcom nodded again, obviously showing off in front of Shian, and his hands tightened around the iron bars of their cell as if he intended to bend them back on themselves. "One day." He said with the depression of childhood impatience dripping through his voice.

Shian laughed, and the sound was deep and genuine for the first time since he'd walked into Adriana's life. "I'll be on my best behavior, Malcom. I promise. Go on, your friends are leaving you, you shouldn't get in trouble for falling behind."

Malcom turned in panic and saw that his friends were dragging their cart farther along the aisle, and he spun back to grab Adriana's hand. "I have to go, 'Ana. See you tomorrow at the ships." He grabbed her hand and kissed a knuckle, then ran off with the others, grabbing more straw and giving it away as quickly as he could.

Adriana chuckled softly as she gathered up the new straw so she could make a pallet that would accommodate the both of them. "I love that boy. I really do. He hasn't been working out on the ships that long, but he's quick and he's an excellent climber. He and I watch out for each other."

Shian helped with the pallet and took one of the thin blankets in the cell to wrap around the straw to hold it in place, before laying out two more on top of it for them to sleep under. "This, at least, feels a little like home." He took off his shirt to lie down on the rough straw mattress, pushing the blanket beneath his head into a sort of pillow as he settled in.

Adriana laid down next to him, but she gravitated to his side again, since she liked being close. "I'm glad something does." She rested her hand on his bare chest. "Don't lose hope. I think maybe someday things will be different."

"Different?" He pulled thin blankets up over both of them, though his movements were still unsteady, since it was the first time they'd even spoken to each other, let alone slept in the same bed. "Different how?"

"Just different. Less . . . brutal and cruel." She knew she was being too comfortable with him, but she was hesitant to pull away. It was easier to jump in with both feet than to think about what was happening and who she really wanted to be with. "Should I sleep closer to the edge?"

"No." He said quickly, reaching out to pull her closer, but hesitantly, since he didn't want her to think he was either trying to tell her what to do or being so needy that he had to have her close. "No, I um, I don't think us sleeping on the edges would make for a less brutal and cruel world. We can use both blankets and be warmer this way."

Adriana smiled and curled back into his side easily. "This is nice. I forgot how nice it was to not be alone in this cell."

He tucked the blankets around them securely and shifted to get comfortable on the straw, one arm around her shoulders and the other wrapped up in the blanket to keep it in place. He resisted the urge to continually look past her at the bars of their cell to see if any wolves were walking by, but he couldn't help listening for footsteps. "I'll try not to be an embarrassment to you with the other slaves. And don't worry, I'm not dying in battle any time soon. I've always been useless in a fight."

She yawned against his cheek before she kissed his face lightly. "You're the first male who has ever told me I won't have to worry about that. It's good to hear. I don't want to lose anyone else."

Shian looked down at Adriana as she said so, even though her eyes were closed, since it seemed like there was more to what she was saying. But she was already half-asleep, and he wasn't going to ask her for more information than she was clearly willing to offer at the moment.

He just leaned down, kissed her hair, and pulled the blanket a little higher around them. He had imagined a number of different possibilities for his first night on a strange Isle, but none of them had resembled comfort or warmth. Adriana deserved her secrets, whatever they were.

SIX

It was strange for Daiva to be on a ship that wasn't her brother's. At first, she thought her brother was going to tie her up and take her on his ship anyway, since he certainly didn't trust the Reefborn with her life. Daiva knew, though, to gain trust she would have to show some, even if she didn't want to.

Most of the ship from the Reef was filled with Fireborn, but she saw her fair share of Skyborn and other Stoneborn like herself. Some of them were more wild and unrestrained than others, but most of them kept their distance. The few who leered at her and tried to test her boundaries or her patience were met with the unpleasant surprise of the stone weapons she carried.

Hassir, for all his congeniality the day before, kept his distance for the majority of their first few days at sea, once he had seen her aboard. He spent most of his time with some of his Skyborn companions aloft in the intricate rigging that accompanied the sleek ship.

For three days they alternated their position with regard to the rest of the fleet. First they would speed ahead of the other ships, showing off their capabilities, before slowing in the middle of the ocean when Destin's flagship was just out of sight. They would wait for the others to catch up and the 'game' would continue. From the way Hassir's Skyborn constantly laughed at the orders they received on the air, it was obviously annoying the rest of the ships, Destin included. Hassir gave no indication that he cared.

For the last few hours, though, they had sailed in tandem with the rest of the ships. Not because Hassir decided to finally comply with orders to sail in formation, but because that morning they had passed the southernmost barrier islands of the Reef, leaving the volcanic crags behind them. Most of the wolves on the ship stood silently on the deck with their eyes trained on the horizon, waiting for any sign of their intended prey.

"You've succeeded in making some of my crew nervous." Hassir's voice came out of nowhere, disturbing her watch as her grey eyes swept the horizon.

He sat behind her on the railing of the ship, beside a barrel of lamp oil. He wasn't looking at her, but was methodically coating each of a dozen knives he wore in the oil and returning them to their sheaths along his arms and waist for later use. The deliberateness of his actions was so casual that he might as well have been preparing a meal or tying up a pair of boots. She had yet to see the man appear anything but perfectly at ease wherever he was.

"Have I?" She was surprised to hear his voice, but she tried her best not to show it. "Good." Daiva said evenly. She didn't want anyone, especially his crew, to be completely confident in themselves. That kind of confidence led to error and oversight.

"When I brought you on board, they thought I was doing so for their benefit, so they'd have some sport along the way." He seemed amused by the smile on his face as he put away one of his knives carefully. "They're also not accustomed to traveling with someone of your . . ." he motioned to the stone weapons she carried with her, which he'd admired the entire trip, "creativity."

"I see." She watched him carefully and raised an eyebrow just slightly as she kept her hand firmly on a blue stone knife that had a transparent and beautiful blade, with a hilt made of the toughest marble. The blade itself was just as fierce and sharp as anything an Ironborn could make. "I only enjoy *sport* on my own terms."

"What terms are those?" He finished with the last of his blades and started walking along the deck toward the prow, a few wolves moving out of his way as he went. After only a few steps he looked over his shoulder at her, clearly expecting her to follow.

Daiva glanced along the horizon once more but did follow after the Fireborn, even though she didn't like that he *expected* her to do so. "If I want it to happen, or I am particularly interested in the wolf. No one has yet forced me, and no one will do so. I originally submitted to be matched by the King and the Queen's choosing, but then they murdered my family, so I do things on my terms."

"Who would they have matched you with, I wonder." He replied without looking at her until they reached the prow, where he stood with his arms folded casually over his chest. His red eyes scanned the horizon along with every other pair of eyes on the ship. "Someone lowborn, I'm sure. Another Stoneborn, perhaps, to appeal to the dignity of your kind, but no one of pure breeding. That would not be a risk they would be willing to take with you."

She couldn't help but scoff, though she knew he was probably telling the truth. It would be dangerous for the king and queen to put her with someone who was of pure blood. Daiva's family was just as pure as the royal family, and her blood could produce some very distinguished wolves, with the right match. Daiva looked him up and down slowly even though he wasn't looking at her, and she wanted to scold herself for being drawn to the Fireborn even for just a thought. She liked their passion, even though the Lord of the Reef seemed very controlled. That also appealed to her greatly. "What they want does not matter to me now."

"Nor should it." A smile spread across his face, but it

was caused by the sight of a sail appearing in the dim haze of the horizon. A cry went up by the rest of the wolves on the ship, beginning with the Skyborn and spreading to the rest of the fleet. "They are as irrelevant as they are short-sighted. They just don't know it yet."

"Yet." Daiva looked out across the water before she looked over at her brother's ship. In that moment she wanted to be with her brother and to fight beside him, but she didn't say anything about how she was feeling. Daiva gripped her knife and took a deep breath. "Let's get this over with."

Hassir nodded and looked over her knives again curiously before he turned to face his people. "I hope you survive this, Stoneborn. Truly I do." He smirked at her and turned his attention to his people awaiting his orders in the rigging.

"Full ahead into them, and tell your gods to wake up and see something worth watching!" His order was met with shouts and howls from all parts of the deck, and the ship lurched forward so violently that it almost threw Daiva and Hassir both off their feet. They quickly jumped ahead of every other ship in the small fleet, their prow pointed right into the center of their enemy's armada.

More Genovin ships came into sight with every passing moment. From the sluggish response of the Genovin in turning to face them, they clearly hadn't been expecting an armada, but they gathered quickly, preparing to face the attack.

Daiva could already feel the water churning in response to her brother's power. Before they even made it close enough to attack, one of the front ships for the Earthborn had been flipped and swept up in an Oceanborn current.

The Reef's ship turned to trap some of the outside ships, and when they got close enough, Daiva reached into one of her pockets. She had small rocks that she instantly formed into pointed arrowheads, and she threw them across the water with the force of a Stoneborn, strength only rivaled by the Earthborn of the enemy ships. She watched carefully as they rained down on the Earthborn, slicing through skin and rigging alike to cut the Genovin to shreds.

The enemy ships were just as eager for a fight as they were, but every time their ship got close enough to attack, it veered away again, circling past the Genovin ships. The other ships from the Isles sailed right into the Genovin, the sea turning to a churning battlefield under Destin's power and that of the other Oceanborn captains of the fleet.

Hassir didn't seem in any rush to fully engage, and his Skyborn kept their ship just out of reach of the Genovin, to the great amusement of the crew. Several Genovin attempted to leap from their ships to attack Hassir's, but either they fell short and dropped into the ocean, or they landed on the deck and were quickly dealt with by Hassir's Stoneborn crewmates.

"Your brother's reputation is deserved." He said calmly beside her as they slid past a few more Genovin ships, leaving most of their companions from the Isles far behind on the other side of the conflict.

"Of course it is." She looked irritated as their ship skirted on the outside, avoiding the heart of the battle. "If your plan was to avoid everything the entire time, then it was a mistake for me to agree to board your ship."

"I am avoiding nothing." He didn't seem angry at her accusation, though, and kept his eyes on the other ships around them. The bulk of the Genovin fleet still urged itself forward into the battle. "I just have no intention of permitting this battle to go on any longer than necessary." He smiled at her again and moved back up onto the prow of the ship, glancing backward at a few lanterns hanging above the deck behind him. A dozen other Fireborn moved out from the hold to the railing along with him, following his lead, and she felt the wind turn the ship violently back into the heart of the Genovin fleet.

They were alone on the far side of the battle from the rest of the ships of the Isles, and their ship was almost laughably small in comparison to even the smallest of the Genovin ships. The Earthborn nearest them were already massing on the decks, waiting for them to get close enough to jump the distance and board. Hassir turned to look at her again, his usual vicious smile on his face. "You may want to take some cover, my lady Daiva."

There was a flash of heat on one side of her, and a brilliant orange glow drew her attention to a growing ball of fire between the lanterns hanging on the deck, doubling and tripling in size as she watched. Portions of it began to siphon off toward each of the Fireborn standing on the railing, swirling around each of them in turn until they were living beacons of power against the overcast afternoon.

The Earthborn on the nearby ships were no longer eager to board, no longer smiling, and their ships attempted to push away from the Reef ship as quickly as possible.

Not quickly enough.

The inferno leapt from the Fireborn in a living bridge of flames between the Reef ship and the dozen Genovin ships closest to them. Every wolf and every scrap of timber was immediately engulfed, and the Fireborn led by Hassir showed no signs of stopping. There was no mercy in their brilliant eyes, and no restraint.

Even though he warned her to take cover, Daiva found herself moving closer to Hassir and the heat shimmering off of him. She wanted to help, but she knew he didn't need it. "Very impressive, Hassir." She spoke from behind him, almost a whisper into the flames.

The other Fireborn assisting him quickly tired and had to step down from the railing to rest, but Hassir was the last one standing on the prow. Fire flowed from his fingertips to catch the stragglers that escaped the initial conflagration. Even when the fire stopped coursing off his skin, it lingered around his shoulders like a mantle of lordship. He wore no jewels or outer ornaments like the king and queen she grew up with, but as she looked at him, she could see the royalty in him. Even if it was of a different kind than she had ever known.

"Pathetic dogs." He sighed and jumped down from the railing to stand near her as he watched the Genovin fleet burn. "The Skyborn will take us through the wreckage once they start going down, and then you can have your fill of them."

Why was watching him brutalize Genovin ships so distracting? Daiva felt betrayed by herself yet again, but she couldn't step away. "It is a shame it takes a Mated pair to partake in something like that." She wished she had been able to feel that power for herself, and to lend her own to his overwhelming firestorm.

He looked away from his work, even as the ship moved forward under the force of a gale into the center of the burning wreckage of the Genovin fleet.

"It is a shame." He took out one of the longer blades he carried and easily ignited the oil coating on its surface into flame. The sharp edge of it hummed along the side of her stone knife. She could feel the flames warming the stone, though it was too strong to be melted so casually. "One day perhaps I'll have the opportunity to witness you bring down a mountainside, and share such a sentiment."

"Perhaps." She mused as she looked down at the flames between them, hungrily engulfing his weapon. "Though I do think you'll be quite busy with the Reef, especially when you take it back from Melyssa."

"Then perhaps the avalanche you show me will have to be her palace falling into the sea." His red eyes danced with dark humor at the thought as cruelty twisted his smile in eager anticipation. He glanced back at the ships approaching before he could continue. "First the Genovin. Then, my lady, we will see about the Isles."

Daiva didn't say anything else as their ship slid past the still-burning ships of the Genovin. She didn't hesitate to jump from ship to ship to wreak more havoc on the survivors. After jumping to a second ship, Daiva was injured from fighting with the weakened Genovin, but she didn't seem to notice the blood or a broken wrist when she made it back to Hassir's ship as he circled back around.

As she returned, Hassir threw fire into the face of a wolf that attempted to follow her back on board his ship. Their passage left nothing but chaos and fire in their wake as they slid masterfully between the ships. Their position at the rear of the Genovin fleet had made retreat impossible for any of the survivors, but that did not stop some from trying. A few of Hassir's Skyborn had fallen from the heights under the assault of their enemies, leaving a few friendly corpses on the deck. Still, the majority of his crew was intact.

As they reached the ships of the Isles, it became obvious that Hassir's ship was the exception rather than the rule. Three ships of the Isles were in various stages of sinking, their hulls smashed out from the inside by the enormous strength of the Genovin Earthborn. Two more were overrun with the enemy, fights still raging on the decks.

Destin's ship somehow was separated from all the others, and there was no sign of him at the prow in his usual place. The ocean still boiled around it, toppling another enemy ship as Daiva watched, but there was no sight of the wolf himself.

"Does your brother always take to the sea rather than face his enemies directly?" Hassir didn't sound pleased at Destin's absence, but the question was rushed and mostly distracted as he engulfed the sails of another enemy ship in flames.

"No." She responded sharply as her eyes scanned every ship within sight that belonged to the Isles. Daiva was alarmed at her brother's absence, but she tried to explain it away. "They can cause more damage if they go to the water directly, especially if they are close to the enemy ships." She did not think that her brother would leave his ship, though, and she gripped tightly to part of the railing that was still intact. Both of them could hear the wood crack beneath her unbroken hand.

"Of course." He said without convincing her that he

believed what she said, but they had too much to deal with at the moment to worry about Destin's location. The remaining Isles forces were still outnumbered by the Genovin. As they joined up with the other ships from the Isles, the survivors of the Genovin managed to surround them on every side. Earthborn leapt from every rail to gain hold on every ship as the fighters of the Isles tried to hold them off.

A pair of Earthborn managed to land on the deck beside Daiva and jumped to their feet quickly as they got their bearings. Fire engulfed one, commanded by one of Hassir's Fireborn, but the second wolf managed to whirl around and land a fist in the chest of the Fireborn wolf that commanded it. Bone snapped and flesh collapsed on impact, and the Fireborn fell backward on the deck as the Earthborn patted out the flames on his arms and torso, turning his sights on Daiva.

She stared at the wolf and quirked one eyebrow as they moved closer to her. Daiva didn't look around, didn't yell or even move until the wolf was close enough for her to reach, her knife glimmering in front of her. Daiva thought about giving him some kind of warning. She thought about telling him he would be better off jumping out into the water, but instead she leapt at him and went after his throat with her weapon.

Just before the knife connected with his skin, what was one blade splintered into several tiny blades, all connected at the hilt which left the wolf's throat sliced into ribbons and bleeding profusely. She pulled her weapon out and stabbed him over and over without making any noise. Maybe he had been responsible for her brother's disappearance, maybe not. He was a convenient target for her rage regardless.

The wolf might have been able to dodge the initial attack, but not her creativity, and his companion met a similar fate as he tried to avenge the death of his friend. Both were laid in a heap on the deck when Hassir looked down at her with an expression on his face that was difficult to read. It wasn't caution or curiosity, but something between the two, and the slight twinge of a smile at the corner of his mouth showed his approval of her skill. It didn't last long before something else attracted his attention and another wolf fell onto the deck consumed in tightly controlled flames. They charred the life out of the wolf without so much as scorching the deck beneath the new-made corpse.

More Earthborn followed, landing together to try and gain some kind of a foothold on the Reef ship. Hassir's fighters spread out along the deck to make for a more difficult target, but the battle was obviously about to take a poor turn for the forces of the Isles. As the Earthborn charged, though, the ship lurched to one side, and half the ocean seemed to crash down on the side with the Earthborn. The water swept some of them immediately off the deck and into the sea, no matter how they struggled.

As the ship began to right itself, they could see a massive pillar of water spiral into the sky, almost as high as the masts of the Reef ship, with Destin at its crest. The water reached out like a living thing to crush the masts and bodies of the Genovin, protecting Hassir's ship, and the few others ships close enough.

His clothing was ripped to shreds and Daiva could see that he couldn't use one arm at all, holding it close to his chest at an unnatural and painful angle. She knew her brother well enough to know that even in peak condition, there was no way he could sustain the kind of spectacle he was undertaking for very long, but he was certainly trying.

She felt slightly comforted that he was alive for the moment, but she wondered if he intended to make it through his final attack. Daiva watched him intently, though she felt helpless as he managed to continue his attack without anyone else's help. There were only a few more Genovin ships that were standing upright, and she assumed some of them had fled.

"We should . . ." Her thoughts were scrambled as she tried to think about what they should do, especially as she watched her brother. "Help him."

The look on Hassir's face as he watched Destin was one of honest admiration, and he nodded in agreement as he pushed himself back up to his feet. He shouted a few orders to the Skyborn who remained in the rigging, and they started forcing back the Genovin ships. Spears and other Earthborn weapons were thrown off their course as they were hurled at the rampaging Oceanborn threat by wild winds.

"I can see why Melyssa and Cadmos declined to kill the two of you." He mused quietly, his voice almost inaudible against the chaos all around them. Destin's assault smashed two more of the enemy ships and scared the rest of them enough to fall back, allowing the Isles fleet the advantage again.

"They'll realize it was a mistake for their reign soon enough." She growled through clenched teeth, both from pain and anger, and perhaps a bit of fear for her brother. Daiva didn't look back at Hassir, since all she wanted to do was to finish off the remaining Genovin and drag her brother back to safety.

The tower of water between their ship and the Genovin began to subside as the Genovin fleet was pounded into nothing by the Isles forces, and Daiva could see the moment Destin finally gave up. He turned in the water to look back at her, the water parting in front of him so that he could get a clear look at the ship, and she could see the relief in his eyes when he saw that she was still alive and relatively whole. His eyes closed the next moment as he lost consciousness from exhaustion, and the column of water he'd used as a weapon fell back into the sea, taking him down along with it.

While Destin might have looked relieved, Daiva felt a surge of panic when he disappeared under the water. She knew he couldn't drown, but she also knew that he was unconscious and she couldn't lose him to the sea that he loved so much.

"Destin!" It was the first and only moment that any of

the wolves from the Reef heard or saw any emotion from her, and she couldn't stop herself from jumping over the side of the ship into the water, though logically she knew she wouldn't be able to find him.

Beneath the surface of the ocean, all was peace in the wake of the conflict's chaos. There were pieces of ships floating everywhere, bodies of wolves falling through the water toward the depths, a confusing jumble of light and shadows that made nothing clear.

She heard it the moment a few other wolves joined her in the water from Hassir's ship, the few Oceanborn along with him on his journey north. Their power resonated in the water around her as they collectively searched for Destin in a few frantic moments. Two of them, though, swam to Daiva immediately and pulled her up forcibly out of the water to keep her from drowning. The water pushed her into the air at their command until it toppled her back onto the deck beside Hassir.

Her wrist was in blinding pain as soon as she hit the deck, but she still scrambled upright to rush to the edge of the ship. She coughed seawater and her wounds stung from the salt, but she still looked for her brother. "Why did they put me back here? He's still out there!"

"You are no use to him drowned." Hassir watched the water as well, no trace of irritation in his voice. The two Oceanborn who retrieved her immediately disappeared again beneath the water at a gesture from Hassir, plunging into the depths to look for Destin. Hassir looked Daiva over as her coughing subsided, then glanced at the ships attempting to retreat in the distance, pursued by the strongest remaining forces from the Isles. "His ocean will take care of him until they find him."

Daiva turned and glared at the Fireborn but her hands fell to her side before she turned her gaze back toward the water. Her tone was even and emotionless again when she spoke. "I do not know why it matters to you if I drown or not. You have your own plan for your victory. Destin and I had a plan as well."

"Plans change." He watched the water for any sign of his fighters returning. "After today, it matters a great deal to me if you drown and if Destin is lost." He looked over at her again and moved to walk past her. "Watch for your brother. I have my people to attend."

She moved a hand to her knife where it was still secured at her side, and she wanted to attack the Fireborn with it, but she remained exactly where she was. Daiva thought briefly about her brother and sister back at the Isles and she knew Destin would want them cared for, but all she could think about was her littermate beneath the waves.

She had lost enough.

Her grey eyes watched every wave in front of her, and she trembled with anger as the water dripped off of her. "Don't you die out there, Destin."

The remaining ships of the Isles clustered tightly as they each assessed their situation. A few were abandoned as they took on water, overcrowding the four ships that remained when all was done, but no survivors from the Isles were willing to board Hassir's ship for the journey home, leaving him and his people to themselves.

Hassir ordered the corpses of the Earthborn thrown overboard without dignity or consideration for their burial. Dola, acting as temporary captain of the Guardian, had commandeered one of the few Genovin ships still floating and loaded it with corpses. A small group of prisoners was permitted to take the macabre voyage home for the last rites of their kind and a warning to the Genovin people.

Hours passed as the debris of the battle was sorted out and dealt with. The ship heading south to the Genovin bearing the bodies of the dead had barely pushed away when Hassir's Oceanborn returned to the ship, climbing up the side and immediately kneeling in front of Hassir.

"He was taken immediately to the depths." They started explaining, with their faces turned down toward the deck. "We followed him as far as we could, but when he reached the deepest currents, he was taken too quickly, we could not keep pace with him."

Hassir growled low in his throat at the news, and stepped up to the two of them with a hand outstretched. They seemed to expect what was coming, but they still cried out softly as he put a hand on each of their bared necks, the skin sizzling where he touched it. The red imprint of his fingers began to blister when he pulled his touch away, still snarling down at them. "A reminder of your failure. Get out of my sight."

Daiva watched as the other Oceanborn moved away, and she felt numb as she realized that her brother was truly gone. She didn't know what it meant, if he was dead or if he would just be carried away to some other land beneath the water, but she did know that it meant that she didn't know if she would ever see him again.

She took ragged, deep breaths of her brother's beloved sea air before she turned her steely gaze back to Hassir. "We have no reason to linger. We should get back to the Isles."

Hassir held her gaze as he nodded, something like sympathy in his eyes, if he was even capable of such an emotion.

He turned to the rest of his crew standing nearby. "You heard her. North."

The rest of his crew scattered to get the ship underway, not waiting to be told a second time or for the rest of the Isles ships to follow.

SEVEN

For days, Daiva kept to herself, mostly because she was trying to figure out a way that she would be able to carry on the plan that she and her brother devised without Destin's help. In the aftermath of their parents and their brother being executed, he had been the real leader of those who remained loyal to their cause. He was the wolf that the people wanted to follow, the wolf that the rest felt loyal to. Daiva was too cold and calculating to create and maintain that kind of loyalty, though she hoped the rest would remain loyal simply to her parents' and her brothers' memories.

The more her family dwindled, the less hope she had left of any success in the rebellion the Isles desperately needed to be whole again.

Eventually, when they were near the capital again, Daiva decided to approach Hassir. Her eyes were as emotionless and calculating as ever, but it was clear she was strained and wasn't as even-keeled as she wanted to be. "There were a lot of things we vaguely spoke about and I believe we intended to discuss directly if we survived the Genovin. I need to know what you intend to do now, and if you still intend to involve me in your plans."

He was in his accustomed place near the prow, standing by the railing to watch the world flow by. It was a rainy and dismal afternoon, and most of the other Fireborn were belowdecks where they could stay dry and warm. It didn't seem to bother Hassir.

He stood with a lantern beside him, the flames dancing between his fingers and up his arm idly as his eyes scanned the horizon, but he turned to look at her as soon as she presented herself so bluntly in front of him. Before he answered, he looked over her shoulder at one of the other wolves nearby on watch and dismissed him with a quick gesture of the flames. The wolf hastily moved into the rigging to keep watch from there instead, leaving the two of them alone.

"My intentions have not changed in a hundred years, from the moment I was forced to kneel to Melyssa as a young wolf and watched her throw my grandmother's body in the ocean. My intentions are to destroy her and her mate, and to do so in a fashion that will break the Seven Isles and free my people from outside rule."

He spoke as bluntly as she had, the fire of his resolve evident in the steel of his expression. "To do so, I cannot attack them directly. She will retreat and sacrifice armies in my path and be gone before I can reach her, like the coward she is. The attack will have to come both from within and from without if I am to break the Isles completely."

"Do you believe I can assist you in that?" She didn't know what kind of confidence he might have in her or in her family's followers. Especially since he had seen her in a moment of weakness.

He was clearly wary of answering the question at all, but rather than giving her a straight answer, he gave her another question. "Your parents were well-loved by the inhabitants of the Isles. Reports have been that your mother drew the affection and loyalty of many wolves in her service and in the commerce of the Isles. She was even known by some of my own people on the Falls, which is how I first came to know of your family. How much of that loyalty survived her death?"

"Almost all of those who would have followed them in life are still loyal to my parents' memory and their plans. I am concerned that without my brother they may not have as much confidence in me, but I do not intend on giving up on what my parents started. If I do, then I'm resigning myself to becoming as much a slave to the Isles as any human already is."

"Almost all." He didn't sound like he was pleased to hear that phrase from her, but he moved on anyway. "What are your people, then? Oceanborn like your brother and your parents? Or did the loyalty of her people extend to the common elements as well?" He knew there were very few Fireborn on the Isles, and the other elements were simply more numerous everywhere but the Reef.

"There is a large amount of Oceanborn, yes. They have been the most repressed by the queen's rule, even though you would think that Calis would be the wolf to reach out and support a fair share of them. There are many others, though, and every kind of wolf is represented. Except for two, of course. One of my parents' closest friends and confidantes is a Heartborn who is still extremely loyal to my family."

He made a disgusted expression at that, and his lip curled. "Loyal to your family and one of that traveling troupe of their kind as well?"

"Traveling troupe?" She thought for a moment and she shook her head. "No, no, he does not associate with Ellis' people. He's mated to an Earthborn, in fact."

That only deepened the disgust on his face, but he brushed it off afterward as he shook his head. "So long as you trust his loyalty and he's capable of being useful, that is sufficient." He was silent for a while as he pondered the information she'd given him about her people. Hassir knew he had far greater forces than she did at his command, though the diversity of the people of the Isles and the fact that she could work easily from inside the capital itself was promising.

"After our work here in the south, Melyssa will feel confident that she has dealt the Genovin a crushing blow. She will wait for word from her ambassador to their kingdom, which may be months in coming. After that, she will continue to threaten them until next summer, when she will claim they have not met her demands and will order an invasion of the Genovin lands themselves. Once she does so, I will have the necessary pretense to bring my armies north into the waters of the Isles to await her fleet without arousing her suspicions. When the attack comes from within, my own fleet can rise up from the south, and leave her and all those loyal to her with nowhere to run."

Daiva nodded as she carefully considered the details of his plan, though her head still wasn't able to come up with the answer that she and her brother had been battling all along. "You may not care about this, but it's a question that needs to be asked. Those who fight from within, where will they go? What will you do with the Isles afterward?"

He hadn't considered that question either, but he shrugged as he glanced south. "There are many islands of my own Reef which are uninhabited where wolves may make a home for themselves if they wish to do so. The Fireborn, Skyborn, and Stoneborn like yourself who fight with us may come and make a life with the rest of us if they prefer, and if they are capable of surviving our way of life. The others may live on the Falls. But regardless, if they inhabit my lands, they will live by my rule."

"Of course." She accepted his answer, partially because there would be no other answer. "On behalf of my people, then, I offer an alliance to bring down the king and queen of the Isles. I will ready the people to act in accordance with your plans."

"Let them be *your* plans." He corrected almost gently, a smile working at his mouth that was cautiously optimistic. "No sane wolf of the Isles would follow you if they knew they were also following me."

"They're not really all that sane if they're going against

107

the royal family anyway, but as you wish." Her tone was as gentle as it had ever been, though no less straightforward. "That was all I needed to know. I needed to know how to proceed." She almost added, 'without Destin,' but decided to keep that to herself as she took a few steps backward, clearly leaving the conversation at that.

"Your brother was not a rash captain." Hassir said as she started to turn away, having never moved from his place. "He did not make decisions lightly, especially those of great importance. Every report I have heard about him remarked on his methodical nature. Perhaps that was part of growing up with a Stoneborn sister."

"I am certain that it was a large part of his methodical nature. I always made sure he was aware of all of his options. If I let him make decisions on his own, he was far too emotional a wolf by nature." Daiva hated talking about her brother in the past tense, but she also had to accept the truth she had in front of her.

"What I mean is that he chose to save you." Hassir said quietly, though the harsh depth of his voice was still evident. "Knowing that he was the heir of your parents' legacy and the leader your people would look to, he chose to save you rather than himself. He held you in enough regard to know that you could lead your people in his absence and be trusted with their care."

Daiva nodded, though she did not understand why the Fireborn ruler was taking time to express what her brother did or did not intend by his sacrifice. From everything that she had seen of the wolf, she assumed that he cared little outside of being able to burn something to ash whenever he wanted to. "I will not let him or my parents down. I do not think they ever expected anything great from me, it was Devon and Destin they pinned their hopes to, but I will exceed everyone's expectations."

That elicited a broader smile from Hassir, and he nodded in agreement. "I believe you will." He stared into her eyes for a long moment and looked her up and down once, the fire still dancing along his arm as it had been throughout the conversation. It gave him the chance to soak in the power of his own element just as he seemed to be taking in the image of her standing in front of him.

He truly hoped she was right. It would be a pleasure to watch her become what she desired. "I believe we will be excellent friends, lady Daiva. Now and hopefully for many years to come."

She raised an eyebrow as he looked her over, and she wished she had an answer as to why he was evaluating her all of the time. He agreed to an alliance, she did not know what else he could possibly wonder about concerning her. "You remembered my name this time, lord Hassir." Daiva decided to return the evaluation with a look of her own, though she was fully aware that she looked him over because of her attraction toward him and no other reason. Daiva remembered what he said about who the king and queen would have paired her with, and it had her thinking about his own lineage. It was every bit as royal as her own.

"I will not forget it." He said with a final chuckle, and turned slightly to face the ocean again, nodding at her broken wrist. "Have a care for that hand. It may wrap itself around Melyssa's throat someday soon, should you somehow wrest the privilege of her death from me."

Daiva glanced down at her wrist, though when he turned away, she knew the conversation was nearly over. "Whenever you are ready to battle me for it, I will not hesitate."

"When you are well enough, perhaps. There is very little enjoyment to be had in the defeat of a crippled enemy." He turned his back on her, but the last she saw of him was his smile and the easy air of nobility that hung around him.

The fear that flowed from his crew as they stole glances in his direction to make sure they were following his commands was palpable. He stood as still as a Stoneborn against the railing, and the only movement that showed he was alive or conscious was the constant wave of fire flowing around him with the currents of the wind over the sea.

EIGHT

Adriana, like all of her fellow captive humans, heard it from the prison keepers when the ships had returned from the battle. She heard there were fewer returning than had been sent out to fight, and it made her nervous. Apparently they returned victorious, which she knew had to be because of Destin, but all she really cared about was seeing him again.

It had been pleasant spending time getting to know Shian, and he was as sweet to her as she was kind to him. But he wasn't Destin. They still hadn't made the leap that most of the breeding couples had taken, with the season having begun, but she was glad about that. Adriana just wanted to see Destin before the Fulness. Then and only then would she worry about what she was supposed to be doing with Shian.

A day had passed since the return of the ships, and Adriana was hoping that Destin would find his way to her. As sunset neared, she found herself looking toward the water and hoping over and over again that he would sneak up and steal her away from the work of the day. A few times, she thought she saw him, but it was just a deceptive break in the waves.

The sun hadn't yet found its way down over the horizon

by their return to Chainhome, but Shian was already asleep, as he had been the day before, and the day before that. The hard work of their assignment building ships for the royal navy was taking a toll on the young man, but he had complained very little, and then only to Adriana.

Even so, he had taken the first opportunity that presented itself to collapse on their shared pallet upon returning to their home. That day had been particularly grueling, as their taskmasters pushed them to work harder and faster upon receiving word that only six of the ten ships that had been sent south had returned, and all of those in poor repair. The Isles needed more warships, and quickly.

When the great iron gates to the prison house opened far in the distance, Adriana could hear the sound of the hinges like distant screaming, and a clang as they were closed again. Two sets of footsteps came up the hall toward her at a slow, even pace, until she could see two figures approach. Both figures were dressed in plain, unadorned brown robes with their hoods pulled up, mostly covering their faces.

The shorter of the newcomers, whose matching brown beard she could see inside the hood he wore, slowed as he approached her cell. He clasped his hands in front of him before taking a few steps closer to the bars.

"You are Adriana, I presume?" When he spoke, his voice was incredibly soft, and soothing in a way that immediately made many of her aching muscles relax, just at the sound of her own name. His expression and his tone were otherwise unreadable, but he didn't move to approach the cell any closer.

"Yes, I am Adriana." She replied as she tried to see as much of the figure as she could, but it was difficult in the dark. "Who are you?"

"I do not believe we have met, though I have heard a great deal about you." He reached up and slowly put back his hood, revealing a soft face that looked immediately friendly and warm in ways that were difficult to explain. When he lifted his eyes to meet hers, though, all warmth fled in the face of instinctual fear.

Violet eyes.

"My name is Leander. I've been a friend of Destin and Daiva's family for a very long time."

Adriana backed away from the bars slightly, since she hadn't known that there were other Heartborn lingering around the Isles other than Chiara. She stared at the wolf for a moment with her words caught in her throat before she found the courage to speak. "Did . . . did Destin send you?"

"Not precisely." He took a step back from the bars as well, respecting her fear of him, and methodically sat down on the stone floor of the hallway facing her. He leaned forward with his elbows on his knees to speak with her, gesturing to the floor on her side of the bars if she wanted to be seated. "I have news of him which you should be aware of. As one who loves him, you have that right."

"News?" She moved forward to grip the bars, but she slid down the bars to the floor, since she knew that if Destin wasn't there in front of her, something had happened. "Is he hurt? Did he get captured?" Her voice was already shaking. Somehow, in a society that made it almost impossible, she had found a way to get close to a wolf and to love him more than anything else in her entire world.

Leander cringed under the flood of emotion from the human in front of him, but he soaked it all in for a few breaths before he opened his deep purple eyes and spoke again. "During the battle with the Genovin, he overturned the ocean itself, by all reports, and drowned half the Genovin fleet with his own gifts. Afterward, by Daiva's own witness, he was exhausted, and fell unconscious back into the ocean. Others of his kind searched for him for hours after the battle was won, but they could not find him. They said he was swept away in the deep currents of the ocean. He has not been seen since."

Adriana wasn't exactly sure how to respond, especially since it felt like the Heartborn had put a knife through her heart. It sounded so final. "But that doesn't mean he's dead. He's . . . he could still come back."

The Heartborn nodded, obvious sympathy in his strange eyes. "That is Daiva's hope, and I knew it would be yours as well. The mistress over the waters of the Reef, the lord Hassir's sister, has ordered her people to be on watch for him as well, should the ocean carry him through her territory."

She let out a tiny sigh, and glanced back at Shian's sleeping form before she looked at the Heartborn again. "How did you know? About me? Is it obvious?"

He shook his head and kept his voice down as he answered, since he hadn't taken the time to check the minds and hearts of those close by who might overhear their conversation for malice. "I am occasionally called upon by your lord and Daiva to supervise their younger siblings when they cannot do so themselves. On one such occasion, you and Destin returned to the veranda on the shore."

He allowed himself a smile, and the warmth of his intentions and regard for Destin's family was a tangible sensation running through her. He felt her emotions at a depth that only Heartborn were capable of experiencing. "My senses have always been far-ranging, and a connection such as the one that you and my lord share is not easily ignored for my kind, especially at the times of its renewal."

When he smiled she felt comfortable smiling a little bit as well, though she was still trying to convince herself that Destin was alive and he *would* return to her. Even though the news that the Heartborn brought to her might indicate that she should not hold such high hopes. "Will you . . . if they find . . ."

"Of course." He answered hurriedly, though his smile weakened a little at that thought, since he knew how unlikely it was that Destin would resurface anywhere among the Isles, if he ever returned at all. "I know they will not stop looking for him. He is too important to be lost if there is still a chance of him being found."

Adriana's smile faded as quickly as it had surfaced, and she looked down at the floor before she closed her eyes. "Thank you for telling me. You're kind to do so. I . . . I should . . ." She opened her eyes again and looked back at Shian, who looked peaceful even though she knew every part of him was probably still aching from all the back-breaking work. "Maybe this was what they wanted all along. What they planned."

"I can promise you that it was." He glanced up at the woman in brown robes near him. After a quick, silent conversation to which Adriana was not privy, he returned his attention to her. "The blame for Destin's death needed to be placed on someone else, to draw supporters of their family back to the king and queen and set the entire kingdom against the Genovin. They will never do the work of eliminating an enemy if there is someone else to do that work for them. That is true for wolves both inside and outside their own kingdom."

"You know, I'm not the only human who respects Destin." She spoke very softly, though she was sure the Heartborn could hear her. "Once everyone finds out about this, there will only be more unrest. I'm not the only one who thought that maybe Destin would change the world as we know it."

Leander's eyebrows narrowed over his nose, and when he spoke again, it was with a voice that Adriana could only hear in her mind. Destin had described the silent communication of wolves while out of their human form to her before, but he had never mentioned the ability of a wolf to do so while still appearing human, and the sensation was more than a little unsettling. *What kind of changes did you and the other humans have in mind?*

Adriana wasn't sure how to respond to the wolf in a similar manner, but she was under the assumption that if Chiara could read her thoughts, then the wolf in front of her could as well.

The man in here with me, Shian, came from Calis and Ressa's island. He was raised with his family. He knows his parents. He was given a bed that was more than a few pieces of straw, and food to support his hard work. He also said that he has never seen so many humans in one place as he has seen here. I imagine most of us would follow a wolf to the bitter end if we were promised just a little more . . . dignity.

Leander clearly understood her thoughts and the intentions inside her, but the expression on his face was sad as he looked back at her. He glanced around at the rest of the humans in the immediate vicinity. *You may someday be turned, and lead a life at Destin's side, should he return from the sea. But the rest? What life can humans ever have beside wolves? What could your entire number, your entire race contribute, in a war of our kind? You would be consumed like dry leaves in a fire.*

Yet, for some reason, this entire island needs all of us to function. She said with more defiance than she intended to reveal. *We hunt for your food. We tend to your every need, your homes, your fields, your ships, your families. If we're so useless, why do you breed us like rabbits?*

Just because you are useful does not mean you are powerful. He still wasn't convinced, even by her defiance, but he respected her spirit. *For this world to be changed, it will take force, and that is something you cannot match when fighting against wolves, of any kind.*

You are wrong. She narrowed her eyes at the wolf in front of her. *If you intend to support Destin's plan, then why would you refuse our help? How could it possibly hurt to include us if we want to fight?*

His look softened, and he shook his head, since he knew she hadn't understood the basis for his objection. *My kind, and Chiara's,* though the shared identity between them clearly pained him from the look on his face, *feel death in a way that I can't explain to you. All death is the severance of ties with others. An enemy you can no longer hate, a child you can no longer love, because they have been taken from this life. I have no desire to see any more lives lost than will already certainly be the case if Daiva's plans come to pass. You and the other humans, numerous as you are, will be nothing but a diversion in any war of wolves, and a diversion quickly dealt with.*

She scoffed and slid away from the bars slowly. *Maybe you are close to Destin's family, but you're just as much a wolf as all of the rest of them.* Adriana shook her head and moved closer to Shian, clearly quite irritated with the entire conversation. *We are more powerful than any of you give us credit for, especially in large numbers. You'll see.*

Perhaps I will. He stood up at that, since clearly the conversation was over, but he stepped back over to the bars again, wrapping his fingers around one as he whispered to her. "Be safe, Adriana. I hope I return soon with better news."

Adriana looked back at him once before she crawled back onto the mattress and laid down against Shian. It hurt to think that she might never get the chance to be so close to Destin again, that she might not hear his steady heartbeat beneath her as she could hear Shian's. Shian unconsciously wrapped his arm around her and held her close, and she let out a shuddering sigh as she fought tears. If Destin wasn't alive, then all of her dreams about a life outside her cell died with him, and instantly, she could feel her heart breaking.

Leander bowed his head against the bars for a moment, but then reached back and put his hood up again. He tapped the bars one last time in farewell, then moved away with the woman who had accompanied him into the prison house, the two of them walking shoulder to shoulder toward the exit.

I was not aware such arrogance existed in humans. I always thought that was a distinctly Fireborn trait.

Once they were out of Chainhome, the woman immediately pulled down her hood, since she didn't like the idea of sneaking around. She was a stunning young-looking wolf with honey-brown eyes that shined with her adoration for the wolf next to her.

I knew there had to be a reason why Destin would care about a human so much. She shrugged and reached out to grab

Leander's hand, since she knew he craved contact almost constantly and she was more than happy to give it to him. *Maybe we do underestimate them. The rest of wolfkind underestimates Earthborn too, and you know how many times I've protected your attractive backside.*

Only because you found it attractive in the first place. He put down his own hood as well, since he'd only hidden himself because he knew he would frighten the humans with his passing, and he hadn't wanted to do so. *They may be useful when the time comes, and I know Adriana will do what she can now to stir them all up against their masters. But I don't have much hope of their odds. I'll let you gloat when you're proven right.*

She paused for only a moment on their path to pull him in for a quick kiss before they continued onward.

They headed to visit Dola and Gale so Leander could talk to Dola about what happened and what Dola's opinion about whatever was going to happen next. Daiva had been very tight-lipped, but they both knew that Dola would be more talkative. *I was hoping that maybe you and I would find some way to the Genovin kingdom and talk with someone before an attack happened. It would have been nice to get some kind of connection there.*

I don't think any of the nobles among the Genovin would be very receptive to anything we have to say anymore. Not after the slaughter they endured at Destin's hands. Even moreso when they find out about the Reef's involvement. That facet of Daiva's plan wasn't something that everyone was privy to yet, for reasons Leander could understand, but it still complicated things greatly for their cause.

Daiva had to get help from somewhere.

Marella, Leander's mate, was an odd match for a Heartborn, but she liked to think that her personality complemented his own. He was always so serious and contemplative, even though he was just as kind and compassionate. She was mostly straightforward and playful, but she was smarter than most Earthborn, even if she played the part of simpleminded so everyone would always underestimate her.

Leander had seen through her game the first time he met her, of course, but she was glad for it. It brought them together, and as soon as she had convinced him to kiss her, she'd never let him go. *We don't have a lot of options, or a lot of time to find options.*

No, I don't suppose we do. He stopped them for another quick kiss, taking a moment afterward to savor the feeling of his mate so close against him before they proceeded away from the heart of the capital. They walked toward the center of the Queen's Isle where Dola and her mate lived. *Do you believe he can come back? Could you, if you were lost to the earth for so long?*

I believe Destin can, yes. Could I? She thought about it for a moment and squeezed Leander's hand a little bit tighter but careful as always not to hurt him. *I don't come from a royal line like Destin, or a family as pure as yours. I don't know if I could come back, but for you, I would die trying.*

He squeezed her hand and basked in the devotion he constantly felt from her. It sustained him, in ways that were a mystery even to himself sometimes, but he was grateful for it with every beat of his heart. *He will come back for Adriana, if he is able. I just wish we knew how long that was going to take.*

Marella looked back toward Chainhome and shook her head slowly before she looked away. *I fought alongside Piers and the humans that died those years ago. It's going to be complicated. Human pairs get complicated.*

I'm sure he knew it would be complicated the moment he allowed himself to fall in love with a human. Leander still didn't have much regard for humans or their lack of gods-given abilities, but he did know that their emotions and their thoughts were just as valid and clear as any wolf's.

The man they've paired her with is young and inexperienced, but seems to be a decent human. He won't give Destin any cause to kill him because of his treatment of Adriana. But Destin has to come back first. Leander was trying to be hopeful about that outcome. He just couldn't delude himself into thinking it was a foregone conclusion. There was too much to be done to rely on something so uncertain as a wolf coming back from the dead.

* * * * *

The great estates belonging to the nobility of the Isles were clustered along the eastern shore of the Queen's Isle, with some few stretching inland. Beyond them, Leander and Marella walked through the great marketplace of the capital, a broad plaza filled with wolves from everywhere in the known world. There were Earthborn herders from the Isle of Eagles selling what remained of their livestock, Stoneborn artisans from the Reef with cups and jewelry of such intricate design it dazzled the eye. Forestborn from all over the Isles and from the Falls to the south presented the fruits of their own efforts. There was even a low stall of Ironborn keeping mostly to themselves, offering cutlery and other implements of their creation.

Leander waved at several of the wolves in attendance through the market and received knowing nods from several others. A contingent of Forestborn weavers was immediately saddened at the sight of him, freshly remembering the loss of Destin, but Leander could feel that the captain's absence would have no effect on their loyalty.

The same was true of a group of Stoneborn in attendance from the Shield Isle offering the stone from their quarries. Their expressions were more stoic and dispassionate, but Leander could feel the rage just beneath the surface, waiting to escape. He allowed each of them to feel just how deeply he agreed with their sentiments, then moved on beyond the market into the more open lands outside the capital proper.

I wonder how many we lost. Marella glanced around the wolves, actually grinning at her own friends when she passed by them. *Daiva is well respected, but not nearly as well loved.*

Those we lost, if we did lose any, must have been following Naisa and Kensin for the wrong reasons, if their loyalty was lost with the death of those leading us. The Oceanborn believed in a world without Melyssa's insane tyranny. Their loss does not make that world impossible. He knew he didn't have to preach to Marella of all people, but it was still good to remind himself of the same things sometimes. *Even so, those who have always followed Daiva are some of the key fighters we will someday need. Her appeal among the Stoneborn is unmatched by any other wolf, even Ciula. Who is even less easy to love.*

I hope it's enough. She held Leander's hand firmly, but she was always aware of her unnatural strength so that she wouldn't hurt him. *It would be nice to be around some people who didn't think you were crazy for loving and mating with an Earthborn.*

I was crazy. He grinned over at her and squeezed her hand teasingly as they walked. *I still am, most of the time. But I occasionally allow you to set me straight when I've gone too far.*

I'm just lucky that I'm beautiful and youthful. You might've looked me over otherwise. Marella caught sight of Dola and Gale's home and she grinned before she looked at Leander again. "You know, it might be contagious. Wanting puppies."

"Don't even start." He gave her a playful shove toward the house. He could be as rough as he felt like being with her and still never do her harm, Earthborn as she was, so he never held himself back with her. In any way. "We have centuries yet for me to put you through that kind of abuse. Our time for little ones will come."

"But they are so cute!" She argued as they got close enough to hear the little yips and barks from inside. "I can make it happen, you know. I know how vulnerable you get around the Fulness." She pinned him with a shameless smirk. "And I know you like it, even if you try to convince me that you don't."

"It was never a question of me liking it. Resisting you was never my strong point. Temptress." He smacked her playfully on her backside as they waited after Marella knocked loudly on the ceramic door. Their house was one of the stranger dwellings Leander had ever seen, but the two of them seemed to enjoy it well enough. The door they stood at was set back into a hillside that covered most of the subterranean house.

On the crest of the hill, there was a brick tower built several stories high so that its heights could catch the winds that constantly blew above the nearby foliage. Smoke was rising from a chimney set into the earthen tower, and Leander hoped it was a portent of a delicious meal to come.

He was starving.

NINE

As soon as the door flew open, Marella was attacked by the three puppies, which had her laughing. She picked up the biggest, the Earthborn, kissing his nose before she looked up at Gale. She and Gale had been close friends for a long time, even lovers once, but ultimately they both wanted something more exciting than another Earthborn to roll around with.

"Looks like you have your hands full." She leaned in a little bit and inhaled deeply. "We have excellent timing, my love." She looked back at Leander with a grin. "Smells like Dola has a meal cooking."

Leander growled with appreciative hunger and got down on the floor to play with the two smaller pups. Gale stayed back and watched, towering over everyone else in the room with an ease uncommon even among Earthborn. Their earthen home was built with extra-high ceilings and doors just out of consideration for Gale, who stood head and shoulders above even Leander, who was generally tall in his own right.

Most Earthborn tended to shake the ground when they walked just as a way of intimidating those around them. With his bulk, Gale didn't even have to do so on purpose. For all his bulk, though, he never had the heart to become a soldier, content to let Dola carry the military responsibilities of the family while he remained at home to protect their property and their young children. "Couple of boars I brought in last night. They've been roasting most of the morning."

"Smells incredible." Marella gave the little Earthborn pup another kiss before she put him down. The pup went racing toward his siblings and pounced onto Leander as well. "How's Dola doing?" She glanced toward the other side of the house, though she knew that the Skyborn could hear the conversation if she wanted to.

Gale's normally open smile dimmed, and he shook his head. "She's been better. We all worshiped the captain, Dola most of all. The queen tried to appoint someone else over the Guardian, but her crew rebelled and threatened to tear the ship apart before they let it be captained by anyone but Dola. I think she realized they would have done it, too. So she came out for an official visit and appointed Dola a few hours ago. Didn't stay long, of course."

"I doubt the queen is in any state of mourning over the loss of the captain." Marella sighed as she looked between Gale and Leander before she continued. "We gave his human the news, and of course she took it as well as expected. What we really need to focus on is what happens now."

Dola stepped into sight and spoke immediately. "Daiva wants us to work with the Reef, and that's what we will do. I'm sure that Hassir has some kind of plan in action."

"Maybe. I don't know that we should trust the Reef, but I understand why she went for their help. We do not have a lot of options." Marella looked at the tiny pups and sighed. "We need to find a place where we can all go after this. The Reef is no place to start a respectable life."

"And the Genovin are not precisely friendly, especially after this attack." Leander said from the floor, blowing in the face of the small Skyborn pup and laughing along with the puppy's excited little barks. The third puppy was content to rest up against Leander's side and watch the other two play at the moment, her deep blue Oceanborn eyes taking in the conversation around her without comprehension. "That leaves us nowhere but the Reef."

"The Reef is a great place for Earthborn to starve." Marella shook her head and sat down next to Leander and the pups. "And I'm not raising a family on the Reef."

"The Falls, then." Gale said, even though he knew it wouldn't make anyone in the room happy.

"Right." Leander said a little too sharply, looking up from the floor at all those present as he scratched behind the ears of the Oceanborn sitting calmly in the midst of the discussion. "Leave the Isles as refugees and settle in the very first place Melyssa or her followers will bring their war if we leave any of them alive. The Falls are not an option either."

"We can't wander forever." Gale said quietly, since he had no intention of fighting with their allies. A few servants of the household moved through the room carrying some of the trappings of dinner, and as they stood in the main room, a few other wolves came in from other parts of the house. All were members of the Guardian's crew, come to be with Dola and each other in the wake of Destin's loss, but all the faces of those who gathered were intent on the same goals as the rest of them. "And no matter how successful we are, if we stay, we are doomed. Melyssa has too many followers and too many connections with the rest of the nobles of the Isles. We need ground of our own."

"I have heard of other islands nearby." Dola motioned to their table so that Marella, Leander and Gale would take a seat. She put a bowl of her own milk on the floor, and the pups immediately scurried toward the bowl. "I don't know what any of them are like or who might inhabit them, but there are places out there. We just have to find them. Nowhere around here will be safe."

Marella glanced over at Leander as soon as they sat down at the table. *What about your suspicions about Daiva and her interests in the Lord of the Reef?*

He shook his head subtly as they sat down, looking over at his Mate. *That is Daiva's business. She'll share it with everyone else when she sees fit, and I trust her not to let it complicate her plans. She understands better than any of us what's at stake.*

I hope you're right, and she keeps her interests separate. She's never really had any interests before, has she? Marella looked down at the plate set in front of her, and took a few slow bites to avoid being engaged in any other conversation outside of the private one with her mate.

"So then who do we send out who won't attract Melyssa's suspicions?" Gale started in on the meat without any apologies, growling his satisfaction at the taste with a few appreciative looks at Dola. The other conversation around their potential island homes died down as soon as Gale spoke, and all the other wolves of the crew looked to him and Dola for their opinions.

"Whoever we send will make Melyssa suspicious. It's her nature." Leander interjected, even though no one was looking at him. "It's also how she's stayed in power for this long. Before we send anyone or do anything, we need to know, beyond any question, who is with us. That's the only way we're going to know what we're capable of."

"I'd like to think everyone here enjoying this meal is with us." Dola looked around with eyebrows raised. "Or I should have started poisoning the wine?" She smirked and the rest of them chuckled, though everyone continued to enjoy the meal. "Destin talked about other islands close by. I can take a small crew and go looking under the pretense that we are looking for Destin. He's not going to surface until he is ready to do so, but the queen won't deny us one more look."

"And she might even be happy about getting you away from the Isles for a while." Gale said quietly, since he obviously wasn't looking forward to her leaving again so soon, but he understood the pragmatics of the plan.

"She won't give you the Guardian just to go look for Destin." One of her subordinate Oceanborn spoke up, named Tiven, through a mouthful of boar meat. "She'd piss herself with glee at the chance to replace you with one of her cronies there, even temporarily."

"She *will* give me the Guardian. It's my ship until I'm dead or Destin returns. Queen or not, she's not going to cause an uprising within her victorious crew over a ship." Dola looked over at Gale since she knew he didn't want her to leave again, and she didn't want to leave either. But for the future of their family, they had to find a place to live. "She will want to keep a close eye on Daiva. Most of you will need to stay to protect her."

"Her eyes can be diverted from time to time." Leander answered, since he knew he would be one of those left behind. Heartborn were very little good to anyone out on the open ocean. "I've already given Daiva some advice on how to minimize Melyssa's suspicions following the captain's disappearance. I believe she'll follow it. So long as we can encourage the queen to keep her mind on her ambitions concerning the Genovin, she will have less opportunity to concern herself with us."

"It's too bad about the Genovin." Marella said softly as she took another bite from her plate. "They would have helped us, you know. Wouldn't you say, Gale?"

"They would have tolerated us." He took a drink from his glass of the wine that was passed around along with the meat. It had been his homeland long ago, after all, even though he had long since turned his back on it. He still remembered it mostly with fondness. Mostly. "For the chance to stick any kind of thorn in Melyssa's paw, they would have tolerated us and tossed us out at the edges of the southern wasteland and ignored us. But yes, they would have helped us, if you call that help."

"Well, that's slightly better than being on the queen's list of who she wants to kill next." Marella reached out and placed her hand on top of Leander's. "We shouldn't act until after the Fulness, right?"

He squeezed her hand and nodded his agreement. "No, it would be best to have that behind us before anyone heads out to sea again." He looked around at the rest of those present who gave their agreement, and sighed as if that concluded the plans. "Once you've gotten past the Shield Isle on the way to the Reef, move west, outside the shipping routes between here and the Falls. No one ever has reason to go that far out to sea, so you should be left alone."

"I will remember that." Dola picked up a puppy yipping at her feet. Landon, her Earthborn pup, was never quite satisfied with just milk anymore. She pulled off a piece of meat from her plate and she handed it to him before she kissed the top of his head. "I'm not exactly eager to leave home again so soon anyway."

"None of us are." Tiven chimed in again, echoing the sentiments of everyone else around the large table. "But the chance of a new home is worth leaving the old one for a while."

"Only for a while." Leander lifted his glass of wine, a gesture that was repeated by everyone else around the table before everyone downed their contents and the buzz of conversation was taken up all around.

His purple eyes scanned the faces and lips of all those in the room for a while in silence as he smiled at some joke Gale made about how hungry Landon was all the time, then he squeezed Marella's hand and looked across the table at Dola. *You did well to invite everyone when I was going to, but there is no one here you need to worry about. Or if there is, they're hiding their intentions so well I can't detect any disloyalty in them. Which I find unlikely.*

One can never be too sure. Dola sighed and fed another piece of meat to her eager pup. *Other than Gale and Destin, you are the wolf I trust most. I just needed to know for sure that I would be traveling with wolves that wouldn't end up killing me and tossing me out to sea.*

That I can't promise. But the Guardian is a sturdy ship. I don't think you'll have it rocking in the water to such an extent that you make all of your passengers sick this time. There was one voyage in particular early on in their friendship that Leander would never let her live down. The passengers on that ship had most certainly wanted to kill her and toss her in the ocean. Destin stopped them, explaining that she was a young Skyborn from an incredibly powerful line, and she hadn't yet quite learned to control her skills. Leander had been one of the wolves most nauseated at the time.

I have learned just a bit more control. Dola set Landon down on the floor and he whined at her feet until he decided to run over to his father and beg for more from the big, burly wolf instead. *They're so little still. I hate leaving them.*

At least their eyes are open. And if they're beginning to crave meat, you know they're close to being fully weaned. He smiled down at the little Oceanborn who had hopped up onto the bench beside Marella, and held out a piece of meat for her himself, once he got an approving look from Gale to do so. *Once we find a new home, we'll need a lot more of these, living out of touch with the Isles or anyone else.*

I added my fair share for now, three will hold me over for a while. You're older than I am, you should join in. Dola teased Leander in return.

Clearly you've been talking to my mate. He grinned over his newly-refreshed glass of wine, then looked back and forth between Dola and Gale for a moment with a thoughtful look in his eyes. "The captain's human mentioned something you should be aware of, though I don't know how much bearing it will have on how we decide to move forward."

He put his cup down and listened for a moment to make sure other conversations were going on unhindered, since talk of the captain even having a human that he preferred to all others wasn't something he wanted broadcasted abroad. "She said they would want to help when the time came. The slaves. Everyone knows they have no love for us, of course, but she seemed to think they could be of some actual use."

"Interesting." Dola thought about what he said. "I suppose it can't hurt our cause, not that I think they would be much help."

"The queen has used slaves in other battles before, hasn't she?" Marella looked over at Dola with a shrug. "They can't be completely inept."

"She's hand-picked fighters before." Gale volunteered, sounding intrigued by the idea. "Sometimes given out Turnings as a reward for valiant service. It's not a completely worthless idea. And they have numbers if nothing else."

"Something to keep in mind, certainly." Dola nodded slowly. "When the time comes. Will you continue to visit Destin's human, Leander?"

He shook his head as he took another bite of the boar, the beast was delicious and he was easily sated, especially in human form. "If there is any news she needs to be aware of, I will, but otherwise there's no need. She's been paired for the season, so she'll likely be bearing soon and will have enough to worry about."

Dola winced when he said that, since she had been aware of her captain's intentions. "He was hoping to get her away from Chainhome before that happened. He's never been the jealous type, but he didn't want to share the love of his life."

"No one does." Gale said with a growl and a possessive look that swept over Dola with a slight rumble in the ground beneath her feet. "If we find a place to run to, we should be able to verify our numbers and our plans by the spring, after the humans have their offspring. That should give us plenty of time to prepare and to find the captain, if he's able to be found."

"We don't have a lot of time, but we have enough." Dola said softly, though she fixed her eyes on her mate. "I think we have discussed enough for now. Let's enjoy our meal and think about the coming Fulness before we get ahead of ourselves."

Leander looked back over at Marella when Dola said so, and just smiled. *Don't go thinking too hard, over there.*

Aw, please? Marella looked at Leander with a visible pout on her beautiful and plump lips. *We might die, the least we can do is enjoy our Fulnesses together . . .*

There's always a chance that we might die. The least we can do is plan on living. He grinned back at her and took another bite, chewing slowly to savor the feast. *We'll see.*

I don't like that answer. Marella got up from her chair and went to sit on Leander's lap, which actually got a few chuckles from the rest of the wolves around the table. "You know, this one is quite stubborn. I didn't expect that when I agreed to mate with him."

That got a laugh from all around the room, and every set of eyes turned to look at the two of them, which produced a shiver from Leander that Marella could feel in her own body. So many connections between those in the room and Leander himself firing at once was a rush of power that he sometimes had difficulty even holding onto, and it all flowed right through her by way of their mated connection. "Hearts are stubborn things. Even the earth shakes every once in a while without anyone giving it a reason. Hearts take their own time making up their mind about things."

Marella leaned in closer and then rubbed the tip of her nose against his slowly. "Anything I can do to help you make up your mind? You've already been fed a delicious meal."

"I'm always up for seconds." He brushed his lips against hers teasingly, everyone in the room still laughing at them. All the couples present moved a little closer together, caught up in the power of Leander's own emotions for Marella. It was a subtler kind of power than shaking the room or turning the ocean inside out, but no less powerful or persuasive, and Leander was old enough that he didn't even have to try.

Marella sighed as his lips teased hers, and she barely had a chance to kiss him before Dola spoke up.

"I have puppies running around here, don't get that started in here. Go on, take your kisses and take it outside. All of you."

There was more laughter all around, and some couples actually took her orders and ran, after bowing to Dola as the mistress of the house and thanking her for dinner. They stayed fairly close around the house, since night was falling and most of them would sleep on the floor or in their own element nearby, but Leander and Marella were two of the last to leave.

"We'll be heading farther inland to make our preparations for the Fulness, but we'll see you the night after." Leander bid Dola a hasty but polite farewell on their way out. "I'll see who else in some of the inland villages can be counted on while we're passing through."

"Sounds like a decent enough plan." Dola pointed toward her door and a strong breeze whipped through, pushing the both of them forward. "I see the look on her face. Go on, then. You better satisfy that ambitious Earthborn of yours. I've got one of my own to worry about." She smirked and looked back at Gale.

"They take a lot of work." Leander laughed along with her and headed out with an arm looped around Marella's waist.

He hoped it wouldn't be the last time he saw his friends alive. He hoped that Fulness wouldn't be the last he'd have the chance to spend with Marella. He hoped Destin was alive somewhere and would come back to them.

He hoped for too many things, but that was all any of them had left. Plans, anger, loss, friends, and hope.

TEN

After a shortened day of work, Adriana took Shian's hand as they walked back to Chainhome. They both knew why shortened days of work existed, though neither of them had tried to push their relationship to the point where they used them as intended. They kissed, they cuddled, they talked and hugged, but Adriana knew it wasn't enough. If they didn't start doing things as they should, Chiara would be back to haunt them.

Fortunately, Shian had learned about Destin, even though he thought she was unwise to give her heart to a wolf. For her part, Adriana mostly kept her thoughts regarding her captain to herself. He was stronger than that.

As soon as they got to Chainhome, there was a meat stew waiting for them inside their cell. Another incentive to do what they were supposed to do.

"Is the work getting easier?" She finally asked as she chewed on a piece of bread. "I can tell your arms are getting stronger."

He sat down and immediately started rubbing at his arms with something that should have been a laugh, but lacked the strength to actually sound like one. "Are they? It feels to me like they're getting weaker. All they do is hurt." He groaned and shook them out again, trying anything to get the ache to subside. It didn't help that he also had several small cuts along his forearms from instances where his hands had slipped on the wood he carried through the work site. They were wrapped in bandages that prevented him from losing too much blood, but he dreaded taking them off. "Tomorrow they said I'm being reassigned to the sails, since they've decided I'm useless anywhere else."

"You are not useless. You just aren't used to this type of work." She jiggled a stone loose from the wall and pulled out a small clay pot before she moved close to Shian. Without asking, she unwrapped his bandages and gently rubbed salve from the little pot on every place that started to bleed. "Kaia gave this to me, so I know it will work well. She's meticulous even if she's a little crazy. And working on the sails won't be so bad. Malcom will be there."

"Oh good. I have as much value as a kid. I feel much better." He hissed in pain a few times as she worked on his arms and tended to the bandages, but the salve did seem to numb them quickly, even if it also left his arm full of tingles and strange sensations. "You should save that stuff for when you really need it. I'll just go out and get a few more of these tomorrow."

"You need it. That's enough of a reason to use it." She re-wrapped another part of his arm and kissed his cheek gently. "I'm trying to take care of you. Is that alright with you?"

He smiled under the kiss, but his emotions on the subject were complicated at best. He had grown fond of Adriana in the days they'd been together, and he knew, even if she was in love with a wolf, and a high-profile wolf at that, she was still a good person, just as kind as she was fierce. But knowing that she was in love with a wolf made it harder for him to know exactly what he should be feeling for the woman at all. "I didn't see you for most of the day, are you alright? Of the two of us, I'm a lot better at whining when something hurts."

"I'm alright." She looked down at herself, and while she

had some cuts, she'd certainly suffered a lot worse. "They ease up slightly on the women who are supposed to be bearing children." Adriana spoke softly before she finished tending to his wounds. "Shian, I think . . ." She moved a little bit closer to him and sighed. "This doesn't have to be awkward between us. I'm sorry that I made it that way."

Footsteps moved along the hallway outside their cell, and Shian moved to help her put the salve away in its hiding place before anyone else saw she had it. By the same instinct, he moved with her to sit on the straw mattress they shared and leaned back against the wall.

Shian drew her into his lap so that the overseers of Chainhome could see that they obviously weren't having any problems being close to each other. It felt good to have her so close, and she could feel a slight tremble in his hands whenever he touched her that had nothing to do with how sore they were from the day's work.

"Tell me about Piers, the man you were paired with first, before . . ." he still wasn't sure exactly how to talk with her about her wolf, since just talking about humans having any kind of legitimate, loving relationship with their captors was still completely foreign to him, "before your captain."

Adriana draped an arm around the back of Shian's neck as she pressed herself close to him. She kissed along his neck to keep the momentum moving. "The first breeding season after I bled, I was paired with Piers. I didn't know anything about him, except that he was a lot older than me." She shrugged and smiled just a little. "He taught me some of the fun things first. He taught me how to kiss. He taught me how to caress and entice. He was gentle, even though he was a big, strong fighter. He always told me it was because I was so pretty that he wanted to treat me right so the affection between us was real. And it was."

"So did he . . . I mean, the two of you could have been separated whenever they wanted, he could have been moved, they could have given him another female to be with . . . how did you deal with that? I know it's not like we have

135

much choice, I just . . ." he stumbled and stuttered most of the way through his words, wanting to return the affection she was showing him, but not sure how.

The sound of footsteps outside continued to spin him in circles about his situation. He thought of what he wanted for her, what she wanted for herself, what their masters wanted for both of them, what Shian wanted for himself. None of them aligned, and they never would. "That's not a life, having the things that should matter most to a person dictated by some Stoneborn shoving people into cells."

"This is as much of a life as most of us get." She kissed him again. "Piers and I loved each other, even though the love meant something different to both of us. He told me I stole his heart, and I just wanted to make him happy."

Even as she said it, she realized the way she was affectionate with Shian had changed since she had been with Piers. The way she rested her face against his, it was like she was already a wolf, at least in spirit. "Piers and I stayed together because we were successful together. We wanted it that way. They don't pull pairs apart unless they can't get along or they can't conceive." She finally kissed his lips and wrapped her legs around his waist. "You are the only person I have now. We are friends, and I know that every day, I love you just a little bit more. What more can people in our position hope for?"

He wasn't completely inexperienced, that was obvious from the way his hands moved easily to push her dress up to her waist, but his eyes never left hers. "We can *hope* for anything. We have that much freedom, at least so long as there are no Heartborn around." He pulled her down into another, more heated kiss, more than any they had shared under their own influence. "She's not here right now, and I don't want her to make us into something we aren't going to be. I hope . . ."

He hoped for a lot of things, and had hoped for even more before being sent off to the Queen's Isle. Most of those hopes were starting to feel like unremembered dreams as he tried to look back at them through the haze of work and stone and chains that was the backdrop of his new life. But he still remembered the only hope that had ever mattered to him. Hoping to find someone he could share what little life and freedom he was given with, for as long as possible.

His life with Adriana was nothing like he had envisioned it would be, and he wondered if she was even the person he would have chosen if he'd had the choice. But as she'd said, she was the only person he had, and he was lucky to have her. "I hope you're as happy with me as you were with Piers. Someday, if not today."

Adriana slowly tugged off his shirt and tossed it aside so she could run her hands over his skin. When she spoke, it was between heavy breaths. "I *am* happy with you, Shian." She gently pushed his shoulders so he would lay back on the mattress with her still sitting on his waist. "You mean a lot to me already. And I'm going to show you how much I want you to forget the harshness of this new life of ours. Just for a while."

* * * * *

It was Miris' turn to be on watch out in front of Chainhome for the afternoon, and he didn't even condescend to look in the eyes of the slaves passing by. Not long ago, he would have been one of them, coming home every night to whatever female they left for him and working through the days as one of the carpenters building the ships for the royal fleet. His eyes had once been a brilliant green. Now they were as mottled and confused in color as his life had become ever since his turning.

Before, his sister would have been coming home with him from the shipyard. Not any more.

The Stoneborn on the other end of the long ramp leading up to the prison kept her silence, as always, preferring to work with the pile of rocks she always had sitting beside her on watch. She made them into small trinkets or animals or some such that Miris couldn't have cared less about. None of it mattered.

As the sun began to set, he could feel some of the other Stoneborn behind him begin to prepare for the first night of the Fulness, closing up the prison house of the humans so that no one could escape. Ostensibly, it was also for the safety of the humans inside, but every human knew, and Miris still knew, that it was just to keep them contained during the days when wolves were most vulnerable.

He should have gone in and assisted in making sure the bars of each cell were secure against escape, but he truly didn't care. Let them escape if they wanted to. Fewer rats to watch.

He turned and raised an eyebrow at the sight of Chiara and her entourage coming up the ramp toward him, a few guards shadowing her as always. He dropped to one knee, since he valued his life and his sanity, but his instincts did not extend to his mouth. "Cutting it a little close to the Fulness, aren't you, Highness? Or just hoping to get a little taste of what most of these rats are up to before the first night?"

"Breeding season is my favorite time of the year." Chiara responded with a grin as she looked Miris up and down. "I'm not concerned about the Fulness. I've always been the adventurous type." She looked at the other guard, a Stoneborn female who couldn't help but shake her head at Miris. "Are you bitter because you're jealous of some of those noises coming from inside?" She turned her gaze back to Miris. "It was easier for you to find partners when you were human, wasn't it?"

"Well it helps when they're delivered to my room." He didn't get up from the stone, some of the metal around his leg still ringing upon impact as if to act as a strange kind of cushion between his knee and the ramp. "They always left me the sickly ones, though, it seemed like. They weren't much good at actually surviving the birth of the children I gave them. I kept telling them I needed a good, strong bitch who could actually handle me, but no one seemed to listen." He shrugged nonchalantly without looking away from Chiara's fascinating eyes.

"Don't expect that to change." She moved closer to him. "No one listens to me either, unless I make them." Chiara grinned and reached to run a hand along his arm. "You seem so dissatisfied with your position. Are you not happy with the way things ended up? Is this not the reward you hoped for?"

"No one gets a reward in this world just for surviving." He wasn't bright enough to keep his mouth from running, but he was smart enough to always be afraid when she reached out and touched him. He had seen all his life what the woman was capable of when she reached into the mind of her victims, and she wasn't a wolf he wanted to be on the wrong side of.

His eyes flicked past her to the guards of her retinue, and she could feel the surprise run through him to see not just Earthborn and Stoneborn among them, but an Ironborn like himself as well. "You may not have a problem with my kind, but that doesn't go for everyone else in the kingdom."

"Your kind fascinates me." She ran her fingers along some of the metal on his arm. His arm was familiar to her, but she was certain he didn't remember her from before. It was safer for him that way. Often, though, she desperately wanted the nearness of someone familiar. "Tell me, Miris, what is something that you want but you don't think you can ever get?"

His mind answered before his mouth did, for once, and she could see the simple fantasy with brilliant clarity, since he had gone over it so many times.

He and his sister had wanted to be turned, find mates, serve the royal family in whatever capacity they thought best, live in a comfortable home, come and go as they pleased, and be respected in wolf society for their service.

He wanted to live to the incredible old age that wolves

were capable of, with friends and his woman or whatever women he chose to keep close, and die in some respectable way before he reached the decline of his life and withered away.

He wanted to be a wolf and have a wolf's life, but he was stuck between the world he'd wanted to escape and the one that would not accept him. He had no illusions that that fact would ever change.

"Not much point talking about desires if they're not going to happen, is there, Highness?"

"You are deliciously complicated, my friend. I used to be that way once." She looked at the metal he had on him once again. "Do me a favor, will you?" She leaned in close and tapped on her ear. "I always wanted to see an Ironborn at work in a different way. Take your best metal and put it through my ear." Her guards moved closer, but she held out a hand to keep them away. "Both ears. If it feels good, I promise to reward you for your work."

He glanced at her guards when they moved in closer, but she could feel that it wasn't fear that prompted him to do so. The moment they made a threatening move, he was immediately looking them over and deciding how he would kill each of them.

The Ironborn was closer to the back of the group, so he would deal with him last. The Stoneborn would try and use the ramp against him, so they needed to die first. He'd lay their bodies out as obstacles for the Earthborn behind them to give him time to put a spear through both Earthborn, then stand and deal with the Ironborn carefully.

The entire plan moved through his mind in an instant before they obeyed Chiara and stepped back again, but Miris didn't forget it, and kept watching them out of the corner of his eye.

When she didn't move away, he shrugged and looked down at the metal coiled around him in a variety of ways. Most of it was iron taken in bits and pieces from the bars of the cells inside Chainhome, but he'd also managed to steal a few scraps of silver that he kept wrapped around his wrists beneath the rest of his armor.

A small, sharp tendril of it broke off from the rest of one of the bracelets and coiled around his finger like a tiny snake. He let her watch it coil as he moved in close enough that his body was pressed against one side of her own. Her perfectly styled hair was brushed roughly away from her neck, drawing a few more growls from her guards. All their anxiety did was amuse Miris. He tilted her head to one side and looked down in her eyes, the silver poised close to her ear.

"This is going to hurt." The growl against her ear wasn't exactly a warning. It felt more like a promise.

She smirked in a way that made her look as crazy as her reputation said she was. Chiara raised an eyebrow as her violet eyes held his hazel ones. His eyes were so familiar but the gaze behind them proved he didn't remember. "I've suffered worse."

He nodded to say that he believed her, then held her head forcibly in place while the silver pierced her ear not once, but twice in rapid succession, coiling through the outer edge of her ear in a quick spiral before the ends shaped themselves into a tiny representation of an actual snake, with a pointed tail and small indentations for eyes above infinitesimal fangs.

It was more violent than beautiful, but he seemed satisfied with himself as he let go of her chin. He brushed past her to the other side and did the same, knowing she could see his handiwork through his own eyes by way of her witchcraft. "Everything you hoped it would be?" He let go of her when he was finished, without moving away.

Chiara reached up and touched the metal, and when she pulled her hand away, she could see droplets of her blood on her fingertips. "Perfect." She looked back at her guardsmen. "Whatever metal he wants, you will deliver it to his home." She demanded before she turned back to Miris. *I have one more task for you, with a higher reward.* Chiara reached out and ran her finger down his chest to make sure she had his attention.

Hearing her speak into his mind shot him right back to his days as a slave, especially to one instance in which she had thoroughly convinced him to be desperately in love with a woman who had been the single most unpleasant cellmate he had ever endured. It wasn't a favorite memory. *Anything in my capacity, Highness. I'm as much your property now as I was then. Even more now, maybe.*

Chiara leaned in and whispered into his ear as she pressed herself into him. She missed him, even if he didn't remember her. "Watch Destin's human closely. If anyone comes to visit her, I want to know who and when. If anyone helps her, make sure no one else knows about it except me. If she's comfortable, she's more likely to make mistakes." Chiara kissed along his jawline before she stepped back so that he could look into her eyes again. "Will you do that for me?"

Miris had no lingering fondness for Adriana, just as he knew Adriana had no fondness whatsoever for him. While there was a hint of reluctance when it came to spying on his former companions inside Chainhome, it evaporated quickly in the crashing reminder of his place in the world and the opportunity in front of him to improve it.

"With great pleasure, Highness." All he'd seen of Adriana's cell in recent days had been her and her new breeding season companion, and he hadn't noticed any other visitors. With Chiara's instruction, though, he would keep a much closer eye on it.

"Good." She looked back at her guardsmen and gave him a warm smile. "Helon, you will take Miris' place here tonight." She looked back at Miris and beckoned for him to follow. "Why don't you spend the night with me?"

When he looked back at the guard who was set to replace him, the man didn't seem particularly bothered about being relegated to watch duty over Chainhome. Helon stepped up to take Miris' place, outfitted in much better armor and bearing some of the most beautiful weapons Miris had ever seen from his own kind.

He was hesitant to accept at first, but he picked up his spear from where it leaned against the stone and he bowed slightly. "As you say, Highness." He was still her property, after all, just as he'd said, on that night and on any other.

ELEVEN

Hours later, as the night took over, Adriana was pressed up against Shian's side beneath the blanket they shared. She was breathing heavily and her hair was lined with sweat near her face, but she didn't seem to care. She kissed Shian's cheek as they laid there and listened to the howls that often accompanied the beginning of the Fulness.

"Some things don't change." He moved the blanket to cover her a little more to keep her warm. His eyes were on the small window that opened into the outside world. Only a few stray beams of light from fires or the nearly-full moon were visible through it, leaving them otherwise in darkness. "Back home, the prince would have us all sealed up in a lower room of the manor with food and water for each of us for three days. I usually slept the whole time just to keep from hearing the howling."

"Hopefully this is preferable to sleeping." She teased as she nudged at his side.

She could feel the chuckle that went through him, and he moved to kiss the side of her neck where he had recently learned she was most sensitive before lying down again. There were a few bits of bread left over from their dinner, and he reached up over his head to grab one piece, stale as it had turned. "Have you ever been out there? During the

Fulness nights, I mean?"

"Only once, and I think Destin wanted to kill me for it." She shook her head and ran her fingers through Shian's hair slowly. "He came back from a battle just before the Fulness, and he was so injured that I couldn't leave him. It was strange, watching him shift against his will, but I didn't leave his side. He refused to see me afterward for weeks, but I didn't try to stay out again after that. It really is too dangerous for us out there."

He clearly agreed with that, and nodded against her hand as his fingers worked their way up and down her back. "My brother and I snuck out once a few years ago before he died. We climbed to the rooftop of one of the watchtowers, since we figured we'd be safe up there while all the wolves were running on the ground."

He shook his head. "We weren't. All the Skyborn lookouts who weren't level-headed enough to stay at their posts ran through the watchtowers like they were late for their duties. The wind threw me off one of the roofs and landed me in the ocean, which wasn't much better." He had to laugh, even as dangerous as the memory was. "It was close to morning when I finally got back to shore, and luckily one of the kinder Earthborn in the household found me and dragged me home. My parents just about murdered us for that."

"I guess we're all a bit curious about what it's like out there." She snuggled in close. Adriana felt comfortable and warm next to Shian, and she didn't want to lose that by thinking of anything or anyone else. Not now. "They never come running through Chainhome, so I suppose it means we get to enjoy these days together. Without work or wolves prowling about."

"I'm certainly not going to complain about that." He let out a deep sigh of contentment and actual relaxation for once. "This would be the time, you know." He turned toward her, his voice dropping so that he was sure only she could hear him. "Like you were talking about to that other wolf who came by before, about all of us helping with whatever they're doing. The Fulness would be the time to do it. All of us out of here at the same time while all of them are doing nothing but running crazy? That sounds like decent odds to me."

"You're right, this would be the best time. That's probably the real reason why they keep us all locked up." She ran a finger along his eyebrow before she looked into his bright, clear eyes. "They can't really use their elements against us when they're wolves."

"They can't?" He flinched once as something outside of Chainhome cracked, but though the sound was as sharp as a lightning bolt, it didn't seem to be close or to affect the rest of their prison, so he relaxed again. "It certainly seems like it to look at them."

"They're just wild animals at this point. Sure, they're faster, stronger and more brutal in their wolf, but they're still just animals. They usually can't focus enough to use their element effectively." Adriana ran her hands over Shian again before she closed her eyes and turned her head away from the window. "It's not the kind of thing wolves talk about much. I'm sure they don't like to think about being this out of control if they can help it. You grew up without a lot of other humans around. Makes sense you wouldn't know that about them. No reason to worry about them now, though."

"I have a hard time imagining a life where we're not worried about them. Ever." He turned toward her and kissed her slowly. "What would that even look like? Humans just doing everything for themselves with no wolves around? I feel like we might starve within the first month." He laughed at how ludicrous the idea was to begin with. Wolves were everywhere and controlled everything.

"I used to dream of a place like that." She murmured against his skin as she yawned, since she had used a large amount of her energy rolling around with Shian. "I think it has to exist somewhere, don't you? A place just for humans?"

"Maybe." He shook his head, doubtful, and pulled the blanket up over her shoulders, kissing one of them to settle her a little more into sleep. "But so far as I've seen, the world belongs to wolves, and us along with it. If I ever run across a place like that, though, in dreams or otherwise, I'll let you know."

Adriana was grateful for the kind of man that Shian was, especially since he was kind to her and others would not have been. Especially knowing the truth about her and her association with the wolves. "If we do make a baby, I don't want to lose it." She admitted sadly. "I never wanted to lose any of them."

He knew it was the purpose of them being thrown together, but hanging around the fostered children running around Chainhome for the past few days taught him very quickly that losing children was a way of life for them on the Queen's Isle. "If your friends succeed, maybe we won't have to. We can find a place to raise it as our own, like my family did."

"You think so?" Usually she was the confident one, but after losing a pregnancy and giving up several babies, she wasn't ready for the idea of losing another. "I hope so. I want to keep any children I have." She kissed his cheek. "You seem like the type who would be a good father. A loving father."

"I would try." He promised, though he flinched beneath the covers at the sound of renewed howling outside. "If we ever get the chance. You'll be a good mother, nobody who's ever met you will question that. You take care of people. It's something you seem to be really good at."

"I hope you're right." She pressed one of her hands lightly against his ear and she draped one of her legs over his torso underneath the covers. "Don't worry about that out there. Let's just go to sleep."

He ran his hands lazily up and down her back and along her side to lull her to sleep, even humming once in a while to drown out the sound of the wolves running rampant outside their window. They were tunes his parents sang to him as a child, and though he knew Adriana was anything but a child, the sound of them was still comforting.

* * * * *

Adriana didn't generally have any trouble falling asleep, and it wasn't long before her breath evened out against his shoulder. He could feel her steady heart against him, as they laid together more closely than they had before, with nothing in the world to separate them except what was intangible and potentially lost forever.

Sleep evaded Shian, though, and some infinite stretch of darkness later, he disengaged from Adriana and stood up beside the pallet, taking care to ensure that she was wrapped up tightly in the blankets to stay warm. He didn't bother putting on clothes, just paid a visit to the chamber pot in the corner of the room and stood at the window looking out at the world.

Most of what he could see was the ocean, stretching away untouched against the dark horizon, but there was a strip of shoreline that fell within his vision just at the edge of the window. Dark shapes played along its sandy expanse, running after each other either in play or in a battle for their lives, it was hard to tell which. Dirt and pebbles from the shore flew everywhere as they passed, and as one wolf attacked another, even the ocean rose up to assist in the fight, the incoming surf twisting around one wolf's ankles to send him yelping onto his side. Other groups ran in every direction, either oblivious or uncaring, burning off the urgency the moon called up in them by running themselves blind.

The world had gone insane only a few scant paces from where he stood. The moon was at its height in the sky, shining down over it all and apparently proud of its achievement.

It wasn't a safe world. It never would be. It wasn't a

world he wanted to be a part of, but it was the only one he'd ever known. Just once, he wanted to go to sleep in a place where he didn't have to flinch in the night and fear the power of the animals walking around him. Adriana wanted to keep her child and raise it herself. That didn't seem to Shian like such an outlandish dream.

He looked back at Adriana asleep across the cell from him and sighed, walking across the space to the bars separating them from the hallway. Up and down the corridor, men and women were asleep, some entwined, some not, but all sleeping through the madness outside. He knew the corridor went on for hundreds of cells, thousands of people all chained in one place waiting for the end of the Fulness to come when they would return to their servitude outside.

Adriana's friends had to succeed. No one deserved to live in a cage.

He returned to the pallet and slipped beneath the blanket behind her, leaning her back against him as he made sure they were both adequately covered by the meager blankets. She would be safe and warm if he could ensure it. Their children would not be orphans. Not if he had anything to say about it.

* * * * *

I promise I didn't this time! Taimon protested to Daiva as they ran along the shore, keeping back behind his older sister, with Kaia running nearby beside him. *Seriously, I wasn't gone that long. All I did was go in and grab a couple bites to eat from the roast they had, that's all!*

You always have a story to tell, Taimon. Daiva replied with a growl, though she didn't even look behind at her siblings. *I have my paws busy, you know. The Lord of the Reef has been gone the entire Fulness, and so our lives might well be on the line. I don't have time for your foolishness.*

It was roast chickens. Seven of them. It was not *foolishness.* He defended as they ran, but he still kept his distance and sniffed the air. *They give off a pretty distinct scent, and I'm sorry, but I'm still not getting any of it.*

Kaia was wise enough to keep quiet, but she sniffed the air as well. She didn't smell any chicken, but she did smell something else. When she paused and Taimon and Daiva kept running, she ran a different direction, only to run into a very large wolf. *Miris? What are you doing around here?*

He was walking at a relaxed pace, and his scent was mixed with someone else's, but it was a little difficult to place at first sniff. *Just . . . running for the Fulness.* He seemed very satisfied with himself, and less mean in general than he normally was the other times she'd encountered him. *What are you doing out and running unsupervised? I thought your sister would have chained the two of you up somewhere by now.*

Chained me up? Kaia growled at the very idea as she watched Miris closely. He looked almost drunk, and she thought it was very strange. Especially for him to be away from Chainhome. *I am not uncontrollable. I can handle myself just fine.*

Can you? He let out a snorting laugh. He stepped up closer to her, towering over her even in wolf form, and prowled around her once, sniffing at her fur a little too intimately for relative strangers. *I doubt that. But I'd like to see you try.*

Kaia whipped around quickly, on the defensive. She'd never been technically allowed so close to a male during the Fulness that wasn't one of her brothers. Although she'd been risky before without permission of course. *My sister is looking for the Lord of the Reef. Have you seen him?*

He laughed at the question and shook his head. *No, I haven't seen anyone tonight. Absolutely no one, except you so far. What does she want with the Reef?*

I don't know, I never know what she wants. Kaia circled around him again and she took another sniff just to try and figure out what had altered his mood. *You seem to be in control. I'm impressed.*

I'm always in control. He snapped at her once with his teeth out of instinct as he advanced on her. He'd had a few Fulnesses when he'd first been turned when the moon had turned him feral, especially during the High Night, but he'd adjusted to his state fairly quickly, as turned wolves went. *Unlike some bitches I could name. I've seen you out on the Fulness before with your Earthborn lovers when you didn't think anyone was watching.*

Don't act so jealous. She snipped with a soft growl as she ignored his snapping at her. *You better get out of here. Daiva will be furious if she finds you snooping around. Unless you're here for something else.*

What else would I be here for? He gave her a grin that she could feel as he looked her over, his thoughts a little more obvious in wolf form than either of them should have been comfortable with.

Be that way, then. Kaia was the worst kind of flirt and she knew it, especially because he was right about her Earthborn tendencies, but she liked a male that could throw her around easily. *Just get out of here before she smells you.* It was her turn to snap at him before she went running after her siblings. Destin would kill her if he knew she had been anywhere near Miris anyway, and Miris was trouble that she didn't need.

Taimon found her first as she ran after her siblings, but she could feel the panic in his thoughts. *Where did you go? Daiva just destroyed a street going berserk looking for you!*

She needs to calm down. I thought I saw someone snooping around. Kaia looked back to find Miris gone before she looked at her brother again. *You both take the fun out of the Fulness.*

It'll take all the fun out of life in general if she kills us. Let's not tempt her about that, alright? She's been a lot snappier than normal since Destin disappeared, and I've been dealing with most of it. Just stay close.

He ran with her for a while before they found Daiva again, and Taimon was glad to see his sister visibly calm when the two of them came into sight. *She went to take a piss and forgot where she was. She didn't get far.*

Yes, silly me, I got lost. Kaia said sarcastically before she looked at their sister again. *Can we just go home? Your friend isn't here, he's probably up at the castle with all the other snobby wolves.*

Daiva looked in the direction of the castle before she looked back at Taimon and Kaia. *Go directly home and do not leave the house. Do you understand me?*

Taimon stopped as if she'd struck him, and didn't get any closer. *I'll take Kaia home and then come back and find you. You shouldn't be out here on your own.*

Kaia needs someone to watch over her, or else she'll end up pregnant by some Earthborn before any of us even know what happened. I will be fine, Taimon. I just need to find Hassir.

He still looked like she had beaten him with the words instead of just speaking them into his mind, but he nodded. *I'll do as you say. But be safe, Daiva. You're all we have. Please.*

I will not leave you unprotected. Daiva brushed her fur against Taimon's before she pushed him toward Kaia. As soon as they were off and running, she headed toward the castle.

Halfway to the palace, she saw the bonfire.

The wolves around the bonfire sat in a circle, with a huge ring of stone at their backs that had obviously been prepared earlier that day, making the place a massive firepit a few dozen paces across. Wolves were perched on the stone, some of them scratching at it restlessly or fighting with each other while their Fireborn counterparts inside the ring sat motionless, facing the flames. There was a kind of reverence to them that she could see as she approached, one wolf or another from time to time leaving the stillness of their posture to walk through the flames. They shivered in the fire as if standing in some kind of rainstorm, enjoying the caress of the heat along their fur without being consumed.

She didn't move close until she saw the red fur of the wolf she knew she was looking for. When she spotted him, she walked around the large fire slowly. *Do you always hide from your friends during a Fulness?*

I had business to attend to with which you were not involved. He responded from his place near the fire, turning his snout slightly to look up at her. His fur made him difficult to see against the stone, lit red by the firelight already, but he was easy to pick out from among his fellows. *Do you always seek out allies to plot rebellions instead of honoring your gods on the Fulness?*

I honor my gods all the time. The Fulness is my own. She growled at his insult, since she was even more upset he now openly admitted to being involved in other business without her. *I received information that Chiara was out and about this Fulness. You would not have had 'business' with a Heartborn, would you?*

Does that possibility trouble you? He seemed amused as always by her, and turned to step out of the bonfire circle, moving toward her at a slow lope until he reached the stone circle. He leapt to the top with ease, coming up only a few paces away from Daiva. The Stoneborn between them wisely moved away along the ring to give them space. *You have a very limited understanding of Chiara if you believe she is high on our list of concerns among the royal family.*

I know she has a particular taste for Fireborn, and I know she likes to be the keeper of information, even if she doesn't share it with the people you would expect. Daiva didn't back down as he approached. *I am not interested in challenging Chiara, but I will, if it is necessary. You disappeared. That does not inspire trust.*

I have no interest in inspiring trust. Not in the way you wolves of the Isles seem to mean the word. He got up closer to her before he moved off the stone ring away from the fire. He moved as usual without waiting for her to follow, though he knew she would if she wanted to continue the conversation.

None of his people moved to accompany him, all of them busy with their own contemplative worship. *Trust here seems to mean people believing they have some kind of connection that can be relied upon. Something that gives people a debt and obligation to each other. The kind of trust I want in an ally and a friend is that I know your desires and you know mine, and each of us can be relied upon to act in accordance with those desires. That is the only kind of trust that matters to me.*

Desire is fickle. It is like your fire, able to burn down to embers or blaze uncontrollably. Desire can change in an instant. I need something more reliable than desire, Hassir of the Reef.

I am more than fire. He stopped a distance away from his people, on a rise overlooking the sandy shore dropping away at a long slope toward the sea, hundreds of wolves running rampant along its expanse. *Just as you are more than stone, otherwise your desires would be incapable of changing at all.*

Daiva hopped up and walked closer to him than she ever dared to be close to a male during the Fulness. Kaia was careless, but Daiva never had been. *My entire life and the future of my family depends on our alliance. If your other business is with the queen, at least have the decency to tell me to my face.*

He allowed her to stew in her own worries a while longer as he examined her face and the feelings he could observe from her thoughts. She was a tightly-controlled woman, but the stress of the situation would have undone almost anyone else. The fact that she was still filled with such determination and courage in the face of her own undoing was impressive to him, along with so much else about her.

The only business I have with the queen is the unfinished matter of killing her, which I have already made clear to you. My business of the last few days has been a series of administrative affairs concerning the exports of the Falls, which continue to decrease per my own orders. The lords of the Isles are understandably upset about that. Also concerning the strange survival of my ship in the face of the annihilation of several others. A matter I have been defending to many of the other nobles of your kingdom who sought to use that fact to draw my loyalty to the Isles into question before the queen. Also a number of lords here who have Fireborn daughters they were hoping I would take as a mate so they might gain prestige in the eyes of their lords. So yes, I have had business, none of which pertained to you.

Daiva was silent after that explanation, and she fixated a little too long on the idea of Fireborn females being thrown at him before she looked away from him. *I appreciate your explanation.* She took a deep breath of the night air before she backed away slightly. *I just needed to know that we were still allies before you headed back to your home.*

I do not owe you explanations. He said with a flash of the distant fire in his red eyes. *And in the conflict to come, I will not justify my actions or my lack of action to you or anyone else. I will act as I see fit at all times, to preserve the freedom of my people and to bring about the ruin of Melyssa's family. At every turn, that is what you may expect from me, and from all those loyal to the Reef.*

He crossed the small distance she placed between them, so close to her their snouts were almost touching before he sat on his hindquarters to speak to her. *I met your brother once, when he visited the Reef to taste our life there. I am told that you were close to him before he was murdered. But close as you may have been to him, you do not understand fire as he did. It may seem fickle and temperamental, moving one direction and then another. To someone who does not understand its nature, it seems more made up of chance than purpose. But understand this: fire is capable of only one thing in the entire length and breadth of its existence. It burns. It knows nothing else and cares about nothing else. That is what I will be, so long as this alliance between us lasts.*

Even though she felt that he was close to her to challenge her, to make her feel as though she would need to step back, she didn't move. *I, like you, will always act as I see fit for my own family and my own people.* Daiva stared into his glowing eyes and she moved a fraction of a step forward. *And you are right, I know less about fire than I think I do. But I am willing and eager to learn.* There was another pause before she let out a slight breath against his fur. *Did you decide to take a Fireborn mate?*

Hassir shook his head, but didn't move away from her even as she got closer. *Blisteringly stupid females fit for nothing grander than lighting candles for better wolves to see by, all of them. It has also never been the practice of my ancestors to mate with another Fireborn, with some exceptions. The Skyborn and Stoneborn who live under my rule have always lived more peacefully when they feel they are represented in some way by their Lord or Lady's mate.*

Daiva still wasn't sure what he thought about her, except that he seemed to find her either amusing or irritating in one way or another. Before she could stop herself, though, her thoughts betrayed her. *Would you consider me?*

She could feel his smile more than she could see it, the thorough amusement with her that was a constant fixture of his thoughts boiling to the surface in his emotions as they passed between them. *Why do you think I required you to fight on my ship during the attack on the Genovin? I have been considering you ever since you came up to me after the meeting of the captains.*

Interesting. Daiva was surprised he had been evaluating her for so long, though she was glad he was so particular and he took his time to judge every aspect of her. She had certainly evaluated him, though she had not thought of him as a potential mate until recently.

It was a smart move for both of them, she felt, even though she knew Destin would not approve. Their parents had mated for love, and Destin would have wanted her to do the same. It was not who she was, though. Love was different for her, and it would have to develop much later, if at all.

We would make an excellent match, and I know whatever children we could produce would be rare and valuable. You and I are from very distinguished lines of wolves. Even though she had been standing close to him the entire time, she finally allowed herself to take a breath of his scent. Being restrained and controlled all of the time, especially during the Fulness, was not easy.

He circled with her as she moved, the two of them pacing around each other with an entire world of untouched possibility between them. *Many of your people have no place on the Reef. Your brother may be able to remain with proper instruction, but your sister would be best fostered on the Falls, though she will be a target there for retribution from the royal family if we succeed. This match will prove complicated for many of your people in the same way, if pursued.*

Both of my siblings will be well guarded until I am certain that they are capable of protecting themselves. She watched him circle, her own fur bristling a bit against the heat she could feel both from him and his fires nearby. *I realize there would be complications, but I believe that there is more to gain between us than would be lost.* Daiva moved so that she could brush her fur against his when he passed her. She wasn't going to let him continue to circle her like prey. She was more than that. *It is a smart match.*

He stopped when she brushed against him, and stayed close to her afterward, looking slightly down into her grey eyes to watch for her resolve. *It is a smart match.* He finally agreed, and she could feel the satisfaction rippling through him that she had been the one to come to him with the idea that was already on his mind. *It is also one that the royal family will act to oppose as soon as they learn of it. The moment you declare that you intend to be my mate, they will find an excuse to kill you before it becomes a reality.*

Daiva was not the sentimental type, and she knew that Hassir wasn't either, but she lifted up her snout so that she could rub it against his lightly. In a way it was so that she could learn his scent better, and in another way, it was claiming him for herself by marking him with her own scent. *I don't care for official declarations, and we need more time before they try to kill us.* Daiva licked the side of his face as the influence of the Fulness wore on her with his closeness. *If this is what we want, there is no reason to wait or hesitate.*

I am answerable to the elders of my people. He returned the affection, heat resonating from his fur and moving in waves that almost scorched down her back and legs. *It is customary when the master of the Reef or its waters takes a mate that the members of my court be notified and given the opportunity to challenge my decision before it is carried out.*

Challenge the decision? I would like to see them try. Daiva shivered at the feeling of heat along her fur, and she growled appreciatively, despite herself. *Then we can only hope it takes Melyssa some time to figure out what has happened. Otherwise, it might not be easy to gather those loyal to us under her watchful guards.*

She'll hear nothing. By the time my trade business here is finished and I leave with my people at the new moon, I will have them believing that I am considering Chiara as a potential mate. He seemed amused by his own plan, and took another deep breath of the scent of her, committing it to memory just as she had his own. *It may be some time before I am able to return to the Isles. My kingdom sprawls out along the water. It will take time to gather a force I feel that I can trust to prepare for an assault of this magnitude.*

Now that a decision had been made, Daiva was not so quick to let him move on with his plans. They were her plans too. *Chiara.* She exhaled another growl, this one possessive, since she did not want to share with a Heartborn. *You will go alone, then? Back to the Reef?*

He could feel her disappointment in the notion, but he didn't rise to it. He didn't move away from her either. Hassir reached out to lick once along her own neck, the sensation just as scorching as the rest of him. *Does that disappoint you?*

Yes. Daiva was never so careless as her younger sister during the Fulness, and so now with the temptation literally burning in front of her, she did not want to resist. Daiva growled again and nudged her face into his fur before she nipped at his neck. *I want to see my future home, to know what the Reef is like, now that we are in agreement.* Even though at the moment, she was clearly more interested in something else.

He let out a low growl she could hear in his thoughts was the equivalent of the deep chuckle that so often accompanied his presence. *The moment you set foot on the Reef, you will understand it. I cannot say the same of many wolves, even those who have lived there all their lives.*

His words flowed together in her mind in a jumble of images, not quite memories, but a communication of his perceptions as clear as his thoughts could paint them for her. Through his voice in her mind, she could see a jagged plain of stone stretched out beneath a fiery sunset, not a single form of life visible in any direction. Every hill and valley gave way to some new danger, some new test of endurance or violence.

Small prey lived on the scant grass that grew in the crevices of the stones out of the heat of the sun, slipping from shadow to shadow. Larger predators covered huge swaths of land searching for a single meal, with wolves hunting them in turn. In the middle of the barren plain, a single stone tower rose up to vanish in the darkness above the world, a single wolf prowling its corridors as it kept watch on its territory, awaiting all challengers to its claim.

All over the Reef, it is the same. My people claim what they can hold, and hold only what they are strong enough to conquer.

Is there anyone there waiting to challenge me to claim you? She continued to keep her fur pressed into his, though she was starting to wonder if she would be able to resist much longer. Daiva didn't have pups running around, but she did not know if the Lord of the Reef did.

A few, perhaps. Hassir didn't seem particularly concerned with the idea, and growled again before he shoved her over in the shadow of a tree and stood over her, his teeth nipping at her neck a few times as the same kind of hunger moved through him that he could feel in her. *No one of consequence. You will be doing your future kingdom a service by killing them if they are stupid enough to confront you.*

I would gladly be of that kind of service. She was glad that it was clear that they both wanted the same thing in that moment: each other. Daiva challenged him right back, which immediately turned the standoff into something much more violent and yet intimate at the same time.

Most of her life, Daiva had forced herself to hold herself back. Especially from intimacy during the Fulness.

With Hassir, she made no such attempt.

TWELVE

When the sun finally rose over them, Daiva and Hassir were two of the first wolves to greet it in their copse of trees near the beach. Neither of them had slept, and when the sunlight touched them, their human forms returned easily, both of them settling in to relax where they had fallen in a mixture of sand and scrub grass.

For his part, Hassir looked just as well-contented with himself as his thoughts throughout the night had suggested, and he leaned back against a young sapling with one hand around Daiva's shoulders and the other running through his hair.

"The stone ring will remain intact through the remainder of the Fulness if you would prefer to return there to rest for the day." The words felt almost forced, but only because the two of them had spent so long cherishing their most basic and animal aspects. Anything so human as showing consideration for each other's welfare felt entirely foreign.

"I'll be close by." She ran her hands over his skin, since it was strange for her to see him back in his human form. "I would enjoy spending the rest of the Fulness with you." It was the first time she had made herself any kind of vulnerable to a male during the Fulness, but all the rumors had been quite true. Intimacy was so much better during the

Fulness.

"Our gods are yours as well. Some of them, at least. You are more than welcome in their company." He clearly wasn't in much of a hurry to go anywhere, as he brushed back her dark hair to see her face. She was a beautiful wolf and a strong woman, and he thoroughly enjoyed both parts of her. "If you conceive this Fulness, my people here in the Isles will notify me, and things will have to progress more quickly. That would not be ideal, but it is not a possibility that worries me."

As soon as he brushed back her dark hair, she quickly leaned in and captured his lips in a violent kiss. She didn't let him free until her cheeks burned. "Nor me. For the first time in my life, I am more than glad to take the risk." She looked him up and down before she looked into his blazing eyes. "You are the match I need. I have no doubts."

"That's what I admired about you first." He ran his fingertips in a single caress that started along her cheeks and worked its way down over her neck and shoulder, tracing the curve of her side to her hip and the leg that was still stretched out over him. "Most wolves have perfected the art of appearing as though they fear nothing, as though they know precisely what they are and what they want. Very few truly do. Nothing seems to make you question your place in this world. I respect that."

"And you know exactly what you want, and how you intend on taking it, with no regrets and no hesitation." She growled her satisfaction even in her human form. "Though do not think for a minute that I will just give you the opportunity to kill Melyssa. You will still have to battle me for it."

That made him laugh against her hair, and he kissed her neck afterward. "One war at a time. I will fight that battle with you when you are mine. Not before."

Daiva smirked, which was a rare sight in itself, before she started to pull herself away slowly from him. They needed to spend their day recharging from the night before. She glanced over at the circle made of stone once before she looked back at him. "I am curious." She mused as she looked toward the smaller fire afterward. "Would you take me through the flames?" Her brother Devon didn't like doing it, helping her walk through fire, but she wasn't afraid to do so.

That broadened his grin to mischievous proportions as he allowed her to help him stand, and he only took a moment to stretch from the way they'd been tangled together for most of the night. Hassir started walking back toward the stone circle without answering her. Most of his people were still asleep in various places around the area, a few men and women half-buried in the stone as they rested for the day, a large number of Skyborn sleeping completely exposed to the cool morning breeze both on top of the stone ring and just outside it away from the fire.

Within the ring, the fire had expanded from where she had last seen it the night before, but burned lower, with wolves sleeping soundly on stone pallets throughout. Wood was still piled high between the pallets to fuel the flames, carried in by the Stoneborn who were still on watch. The heat was already suffocating just standing on top of the ring, but Hassir breathed it in hungrily as he took Daiva's hand. He willed the flames not to harm her, though that hardly lessened the heat she could feel from them.

Daiva gathered all the strength she could from the heated stone beneath her feet, and she let out a groan of contentment when the stone shifted slightly underneath them. The heat that rushed past her from the fire caused her skin to flush, but it also had her holding tighter to Hassir. Though she couldn't explain it, the flames created a reaction of arousal in her that no sane female would have enjoyed.

He gave her a moment to adjust to the feeling, then moved along the stone with her until they reached the steps that had been formed for them to descend into the firepit. He squeezed her hand as they stepped down together, the heat increasing with every breath.

"I don't know how much your brother told you when he returned home from his time among my people," he said without looking back at her, picking his way carefully between the sleeping bodies of his people to allow them to rest as they saw fit, "but my court stands along the caldera of one of the great fountains of the Reef. My people and I make these shrines every time we visit the Isles in order to make this place the tiniest bit hospitable."

A sheen of sweat already covered Daiva's body, but she just looked around at the flames, fascinated as ever. Daiva reached out to touch one, since she had full trust in Hassir that he wouldn't let it burn her. "He didn't talk about the Reef when he came back. He was unconscious for days, and when he finally woke up, he ran off, and eventually ended up dying for sticking his seed into Chiara."

She looked around at the sleeping wolves and shivered slightly as beads of sweat rolled down her bare back and down the center of her chest. "There was something about the Reef that he knew he couldn't handle. That was the only time my brother avoided anything, when he knew he couldn't defeat it." She stepped up and kissed Hassir again, her skin slick against his. "I'm not afraid." She emphasized when the kiss broke.

There was no sweat on his own skin, but his body was every bit as heated as the flames that licked along her skin. The sweat evaporated from the line it had formed along her spine in a rush of vapor that set her nerves tingling, but the heat still didn't scald her as he walked her into the heart of the bonfire. His power moved through her to claim her, for the time being, on behalf of the flames around them. They would no more burn her than they could him.

"The reason you aren't afraid is because there is nothing and no one in this world who should not fear you." He growled with the voice of the fire around her echoing his sentiments. It curled in patterns of sensation along her legs and around her hips in ways that reminded her of an Oceanborn's touch, playful and yet much more dangerous coming from a Fireborn. "There is nothing about the Reef that you cannot handle. Or any other place in this world I have any knowledge of, for that matter."

Daiva gasped softly as the flames licked up her skin, and she held even tighter to Hassir. The sensation felt so thrilling, so daring and dangerous, she never felt so hungry for another wolf in her life. She jumped up and wrapped her legs around his waist, unable to stop herself from attacking him.

In the midst of the kiss, he laid her down on her back against one of the stone pallets that was shaped in the middle of the flames. They were surrounded on all sides by a wall of red and orange light and heat, the grey of the new day hanging over them like the ashes that would remain when the fire died.

Daiva was a woman who could match him in every way, who knew no fear, and would fight the wars he intended to fight. In all his scheming about how best to take his vengeance on the Isles, she had never once entered his mind, but he could not have conceived of a woman so perfectly suited to his needs as the one beneath him. He would do whatever was necessary to keep her by his side, and with the help of her people, he would have everything he had desired for nearly a century.

But first, it was going to be a very pleasant Fulness.

THIRTEEN

The Fulness and the new moon came and went, and Hassir departed the Isles with the rest of his people. There was a strangely comfortable farewell on the dock as he left, between and the royal family. Chiara was a part of it to see him off, but as he boarded his ship, it was Daiva's eyes he sought out in the crowd.

When she returned to her home that night, there had been a fire left burning in one corner of her estates that once belonged to her brother Devon, which the servants informed her they had been incapable of extinguishing since a wolf broke through the gates earlier. They weren't able to describe the wolf in question, but the fire continued to burn for a solid week before it finally fell to ashes.

Autumn storms rose and fell over the Isles in quick succession from one Fulness to the next, making chaos out of the final harvests before winter set in, but work all along the Queen's Isle continued unabated.

After the Fulness following Hassir's departure, a mated pair of Skyborn from the Reef arrived and presented themselves at Daiva's service, claiming that they were sent to tutor her younger brother on the orders of lord Hassir, as a gesture of gratitude for her service aboard his vessel against the Genovin.

A few days later, they began sending messages south on the winds on Daiva's behalf, updating Hassir on her progress in the Isles. They continued to do so for two more Fulnesses, though everyone involved was just a little disappointed that Daiva turned out not to be carrying Hassir's pups after the Fulness they spent together.

The moon waxed and waned, and still there was no sign of Destin.

After a particularly exhausting day of lessons for Taimon, Daiva left her younger siblings momentarily as she went to speak with the tutors. They had taken quarters high in the Skyborn perch on one of the towers she had built for the estate.

Left aside with Taimon, Kaia had herself wrapped up in several layers of clothing as she looked out at the bleak waters while the cold air whipped at her skin. Winter had settled in over the last months with a vengeance. "Daiva has been spending more time with your tutors recently. Do you think she's taken a liking to Skyborn?"

Taimon gave a laugh that resounded from the heights of the tower to echo out across the water, then calmed himself as his outburst got a glare from Daiva and the other two Skyborn. "Not in a thousand years. I can't see that. Even those two, stoic and condescending as they are." Taimon hadn't exactly taken an immediate liking to Hadria or her mate, mostly because they reminded him daily, sometimes hourly, of just how far behind in his studies and the practice of his element he truly was. "I'm actually surprised she's allowed them to stay this long. She hates guests."

"She must enjoy torturing you that much." Kaia smirked and moved closer to the edge of the tower overlook, where she took a deep breath of the sea air. "I saw Destin's human again yesterday. Adriana."

Just the mention of her name was enough to wipe the smile off even Taimon's happy-go-lucky face. Four Fulnesses had come and gone since Destin's disappearance, and even Taimon, by far the most optimistic wolf in the family, had begun to give up hope that their brother was simply having trouble finding his way home.

Dola had departed shortly after the first Fulness of their return, just before Hassir, and had similarly not been heard from since. There had been whispers, begun by Melyssa, of Dola being accused of treason in stealing one of the ships of the fleet for her own use, but no word of her had come in from anywhere in the known world, making it impossible for Melyssa to even prosecute a case against her and her crew.

The single mention of Adriana was enough to bring all of the events of the past few months roaring back to Taimon's mind, when he was normally so talented at keeping them out. "Where did you see her, down at the shipyard? I thought they already closed up there for the season?"

"She looked like she was cleaning up the site." Kaia fidgeted with the blanket around her shoulders and she looked at her brother again. "She's going to have a baby. I could tell."

Taimon was confused by that, since if it was already obvious that a human was going to have a baby, she'd already been pregnant for some time. Humans took much longer with their offspring than wolves, for some reason Taimon didn't pretend to understand. "You didn't talk to her?"

"No, I . . ." She dropped her voice a little bit lower and moved closer to her brother. "I think there are wolves watching her. Wolves like Miris. I was going to take some more apples to her, and Miris asked me all these questions."

"What kind of questions?" He reached out a hand to try and calm the winds around them, which was the exercise his tutors had set him to that morning. It was incredibly difficult, since Taimon felt like it was working against his nature to make the wind blow less. They were high enough that it was a constant force, but Kaia was cold, and that was reason enough for him to try and keep it still. Not that he could manage it for very long, but he was trying. "Why would they interrogate you about a slave? Destin's not here anymore."

Kaia didn't know why anyone would ask her questions, all she knew was that she was being asked. "When Miris catches me, he asks me why I'm being nice to Adriana and no one else. He asks me why I bring her things." She shivered again, but eventually she snuggled into Taimon's side, even though he was still trying to control the wind. They were littermates, after all, and since birth, it felt natural to huddle together and stick together. "I think they think that Destin is coming back, that he's playing some kind of game with them or something."

That thought actually made Taimon laugh, though it was half-hearted at best. The wind did begin to slow around them, and Taimon felt proud of himself as he managed to divert the wind around the tower rather than completely stopping it as he'd been trying to do. That was much easier. "I wish that was true, even if that's never really been Destin's way of doing things. Everyone knows you and me are the sneaky ones in this family. Father too, but, well . . ." he shrugged, since obviously their father wasn't sneaking around about anything anymore. "It's good that they're still so afraid of him, though. I hope they stay that way."

"Even if he comes back now . . ." Kaia wanted their brother to come back, desperately, but she didn't want him to come back only to find that his human had moved on. "It will break his heart."

Taimon made a face down at Kaia. "She's carried three other babies before, it's not like she was ever going to be devoted only to him. If he had been worried about that, he would have taken the risk and just taken her from Chainhome in the first place. Kept her here to work around the estate." He shrugged, since Kaia admittedly knew Destin better than he did. "Besides, if she is bearing, they'll leave her alone more than they otherwise would, which he would be happy about. So there's that, at least."

"Why can't *we* take her out of there?" Kaia ignored her brother's expression and continued to try to find ways to make Destin happy, even if he was possibly dead. "We can take care of her better than they will in Chainhome. That would make Destin happy, wouldn't it?"

"Maybe. But it would also make them a lot more suspicious that he's actually here and we're hiding him for some reason. I think." Taimon didn't have their older siblings' mind for strategy and planning, and even though he wanted to help Adriana for Destin's sake, it didn't seem like a good idea to him. "We can ask Daiva and see what she thinks."

Kaia wrinkled her nose and shook her head. "Daiva will say no. She doesn't care about humans, even the one that Destin loves." Her shoulders slumped and she pulled away from Taimon. "Maybe I can ask Miris questions about why he asks me questions. Maybe he wants Adriana for himself. Even though I don't think he likes her, as pretty as she is. For a human."

Taimon started to tell her it sounded like a good idea, so long as Daiva was alright with it, but he stopped himself before he mentioned Daiva again. Daiva would just kill that idea before it started as well. Neither of them were ever involved in anything to do with the family's business or the deep plans that he knew Daiva was always working on with the rest of their family friends.

They were young, so Taimon understood being kept in the dark, but Daiva would always consider them young if they did nothing to act otherwise. They weren't *children*. They were just young wolves. "That's a good idea. You should talk to him. Just make sure you do it somewhere public, where other people can see you. I don't want that Ironborn getting any ideas."

"Miris? Getting ideas about me?" She laughed and shook her head before she tucked her hair behind her ears. "He has told me many times he thinks the only thing I'm good for is picking weeds." Kaia shrugged nonchalantly. "He's even more difficult now after his sister died. And I liked her. She was the one who introduced me to several of my Earthborn friends."

"I don't want *them* getting any ideas either." Taimon said with a pointed look over at her. She had generally been good about not associating with anyone on the Fulness in the months since Destin's disappearance, but that didn't stop her the rest of the time. "You know Daiva's never going to give her permission for you to mate with any of them, and Destin wouldn't have either."

Kaia scoffed, since she didn't care as much about Daiva's opinion as Taimon did. "What does Daiva know about finding a mate? She can't even find one for herself. I don't want her picking mine, she'll pick someone boring and old."

"Probably." Taimon chuckled, then shuddered at the thought that crossed his mind. "And probably some Stoneborn or something for me. That would be awful." He shook his head violently and lost his concentration on the wind around them, which resumed with a vengeance as if it was angry about being held back for so long. "Anyway, you should talk to Miris. See what you can find out. Just don't tell Daiva until you survive and you get some good information."

Kaia nodded and grinned before she kissed her brother on his cheek and moved away from his warm embrace toward the stairs. "I'm glad we agree." She gave her brother a wave before she headed down the stairs and disappeared. She could get information, especially from Miris. All she would have to do would be to convince him to be nice. For once.

* * * * *

Miris wasn't outside of Chainhome when Kaia arrived, and very few of the slaves were still inside for the day, which made it much easier for her to leave some fruit for Adriana. One of the Stoneborn guards informed her that Miris had been reassigned part of the time to work as an overseer at the shipyard assisting the other slaves with the finer details of the metalwork for a ship that was nearly finished.

When she got there, he was easy to find in the mass of humans going about their tasks. He was out at the prow of the ship, working on fashioning a battering spike to stretch out ahead of the ship. It was still crude and there was a great deal of detail still to be done, but it was in the shape of a man with both fists extended forward, his body contouring to the curve of the keel beneath the prow. The face above the fists was one of the only parts that had yet been completed, and it was a look of rage that gave the entire ship an angry demeanor. Miris was working alone on the hands, shaping them with care to make them look as accurate and as brutal as possible.

Having been raised around ships, Kaia had no problem getting around, even if it was a ship that wasn't in the water yet. She had brought a small basket of food as a peace offering, especially because she knew Miris had a favorite sweetbread made from a particular fruit that wasn't found in many gardens.

"Hungry?" She asked from a short distance behind Miris, since she didn't want him to haul back and smack her for coming up behind him.

He did flinch, but only because he'd been intently working with his element for so long undisturbed. When he looked back and saw her with food, she could see the instant suspicion on his face, but he moved to one side on his platform to make room for her beside him. "Always." He gave her an inquisitive look as she made her way up the scaffolding to him, though, and he made a few more small adjustments to the iron while he waited. "They've got you running food now?"

"No, I made too much." She lifted up the thin piece of cloth over the basket and pulled out a large piece of the bread for him. "It was Destin's favorite. I walked by Chainhome and didn't see you there, so I thought I would bring it to you here."

He looked over the bread for a moment and raised it to his nose to sniff it first before he broke off a piece and took a bite. She had his attention completely diverted from the work, so he rested his elbow on his knee as he chewed slowly, obviously savoring it. "So what do you want?"

Kaia took a small bite for herself, and she was pleased with the taste. She was dedicated to learning how to make delicious meals with the plants she could grow, and she was well on her way. "I want to know why you pay such close attention to Adriana." Kaia decided to be blunt instead of coy, mainly because she didn't think that Miris would respond well to an attempt to weasel the answer out of him. "Destin has been gone for a long time now. Why can't you just leave her alone?"

Her directness seemed to amuse him, and his face twisted into a smile as he chewed the bread he'd taken. "Apparently it wasn't just Destin who was in love with her from your family." A laugh rumbled through his chest deep enough to send a thrum through the platform they were sitting on and right into Kaia along with it. "I keep an eye on her because I'm smart enough to do as I'm told, unlike some people I could name."

Kaia glared at him but raised an eyebrow and offered more of the bread. "You? Do as you are told?" She took another bite for herself and looked out along the rest of the ship. "That does not sound like the Miris I heard about. Did they give you a collar with those eyes, or you just decided to be the submissive type?" When she looked back at him she knew she was poking at a sleeping bear, but she didn't imagine he would actually hurt her. "I didn't think you were old and boring already."

His smile disappeared at that kind of jab, and the platform they sat on shook slightly as Kaia heard a chain far below them rattle suddenly. It snaked up through the air and wrapped itself around her ankles and throat, binding her against the rope on her side of the platform making it immediately difficult to breathe. The chains around her ankles wrapped up farther around her calves as the rest of the strand crept upward, waving through the air in time with Miris' own thoughts, considering what to do next. "If your mouth were a little less pretty, someone would have beaten it off you by now, has anyone ever told you that?"

She gasped when the chain wrapped around her and caught her off guard. Kaia's heart pounded in her chest with panic, but she was not going to let him bully her even though she couldn't exactly stop him. Kaia took short, choppy breaths as he constricted her throat, but she tried to convince herself not to panic any more than she already was.

"Whatever they're giving you, is it worth it?" Kaia didn't know what he knew, but she did know she couldn't trust him enough to tell him the little she did know. "I don't know . . . what information that you . . . are fishing for, but it isn't going to . . . help you." She fixed her green eyes on his hazel ones. "Don't help them."

He considered what she said for a moment in silence, and the chain began to loosen around her neck. Not enough to allow her to move, but at least enough to let her breathe freely. The free ends of the chain moved to her wrists, wrapping along her skin slowly to bind her tighter, almost playfully.

"What reason could there possibly be for me not to do as they want?" He looked around at the shipyard, hundreds of slaves moving in urgent rhythm around the ship, carrying wood, sanding seams, breaking their backs at the behest of their lords. "This world and everyone in it, even you and your high and mighty family, belongs to them." He moved closer to her on the narrow platform and sat with one leg on either side of it just as she was, her ankles caught together tightly beneath it. He took another piece of the bread out of the basket and popped it in his mouth without looking away from her. "Even slaves know that."

Despite knowing that she wouldn't get free unless he

wanted to let her free, Kaia wiggled and struggled a little against his chains. She wondered if he was enjoying the show, but he only looked wickedly amused. "I don't belong to them. And you don't have to, if you don't want to. You're one of us now, and clearly you have the power to take what you want, when you want it." She looked over at the bread and back at him. "You didn't have to chain me up to eat the rest. I would have given it to you." Kaia chewed on her bottom lip and sighed. "You have to believe that there is something better out there than being a slave, even when you're a wolf. You're better than that."

The look on his face went from one of cruel entertainment to something subtly more dangerous, but he didn't say anything for a long time. When he finally moved, he slid along the platform until he was pressed right against her, his chains loosening just enough to give her the hope of escape without the actual possibility. She could see every one of his piercings up close, metal curling its way in a tight spiral down the outside of one ear and another jutting through one eyebrow in a vicious spike. The bright hue of the copper only darkened the bronze of his skin in comparison, and contrasted with the myriad of colors swirling through his eyes.

"And what if I'm not better?" He growled against her, the richness of the sweetbread on his breath almost against her lips.

"I think you are." Kaia's heart pounded harder as he held himself against her, but she knew he was only trying to intimidate her. Miris had never once indicated he was in any way attracted to her or interested in gaining her attention. "You didn't work this hard to be this powerful just to be someone's dog. You want something for yourself. And you should."

He didn't move away from her, and left his huge hands on her thighs where they came to rest, searching her pure green eyes to see just how sincere she was in what she was saying. He finally moved a hand up to her neck and considered squeezing for a moment, just to hold onto the ease with which he could end her life if he wanted to. Just as his fingers started to dig into her neck, though, he moved away from her, and the chains wrapped around her slid back down to the ground below where they came from.

"Thanks for the bread." He turned back to his work. "Go back and live in your made-up world, little flower. You'll figure out where we really are soon enough."

Kaia rubbed at her wrists and her neck as soon as she was free from his death grip, and she wondered if they would bruise. She sighed as she started to walk away, but she paused and looked back at him. "I need to practice my skills, you know. Could we make a practical deal, at least? If you make me some jewelry, I'll make you some hot meals."

He seemed intrigued by that notion, even though it made him laugh when she asked for jewelry. "There are a dozen Ironborn smiths in the marketplace every day. Why do you want jewelry from me?"

"Because you don't make anything to sell in the marketplace. Whatever you make will be unique." She said it as though it was obvious, but clearly he didn't think so. Kaia pointed at what he was working on before she showed up. "I don't know many Ironborn that would take that much time to put detail on a ship. That makes me want to see what else you can make." She shrugged and moved a little further away from him. "You tell me what you want to eat, you bring me something beautiful as payment, and we both benefit."

He glanced back at the figurehead he was working on when she indicated it, and then back at her, watching, as always, for any sign that she was joking with him or making fun of him. He was accustomed to that, but she didn't seem to be, as far as he could tell. "We'll see."

"Alright. Goodbye, Miris." She was hoping he would agree so she would be able to practice more of her cooking, but now she doubted he would show up at all. Taimon was not reliably home, and neither was Daiva. It was difficult for her to make meals for herself. Kaia glanced back at him once but continued walking away, rubbing at her arms and neck. So much for helping Daiva, or anyone else, for that matter.

Miris watched her go, so long as she wasn't looking at him, his mind running over the Forestborn's words the entire time. Even when she was gone, he looked down the trail she'd taken, her timid voice still echoing in his ears, until he shook his head and forced himself back to his work.

When he was nearly finished, he called for water, and had to laugh at the slave who was sent to deliver it to him. "So you *can* do something right once in a while." He took a cup from Adriana and waited for her to pour for him, the sweat still running off his face even though there was a distinct chill to the air with the season. He'd pushed himself hard for the past two days trying to finish the figurehead, and it had taken a toll on him that he tried hard not to let anyone see.

Adriana wanted to throw the whole bucket in his face, but instead she just poured the water slower into the cup. "What are you babbling about?"

"I heard about what happened the other day with the sails. I probably would have been on your side. I'm sure they looked much better cut right down the center." He laughed into the cup as he drank and then held it out for her to pour another. "It's good that they have you working at something more up to your talents now."

"I really appreciate it when someone recognizes my skills." Adriana quipped. He clearly didn't know the whole story about the sails, or the truth, but Miris never could be bothered with the truth. She was disappointed that she wasn't able to be close to Shian and Malcom, but the fact that her belly was just rounded enough to show the growing baby inside of her meant she was now going to be taking care of tasks that she loathed.

"Well, pretty soon, the only skill that matters will be your ability to lie around and get fat." He lifted his second glass in a toast to her belly and downed it quickly. "As I remember, you're *very* good at that." He considered a third cup and then decided against it, handing it back to her just as she went to start pouring. "How's it been these past few months, being back with your own kind after spreading your legs for a wolf for so long?"

"Is this how you keep yourself satisfied? You need someone else to tell you stories of what they do and how they do it so you don't feel so alone at night?" She glared at him and dumped a little bit of the water over his feet. "I know you were always disappointed we were never paired together. You are lucky, though, because there is no way you would compare to an Oceanborn."

Once he had her riled up, if anything, Miris looked even more satisfied with himself, and with life in general. "If there was ever a moment when I wanted you, Adriana, I'd have had you the moment I was turned. I still could, if you decided to tempt me into it one of these nights. Bearing or not."

"Tempt you? Why would I tempt you? You don't know how to please a woman, only how to break them." She looked him up and down once before she shook her head and took a drink of water for herself. "Shian knows what he is doing. I have no complaints, nor any need for *you*." She touched her tiny bump with intention. "Clearly."

Life felt normal when Adriana was railing at him, and he was glad for it. The entire conversation helped to clear his head from just a few moments before, and already he felt like his day was improving. "I suppose once you've dropped that child, weaned him, and it's no longer your concern, you'll have to get busy finding another wolf to wrap your legs around. Maybe the next one you decide to take for yourself will actually enjoy you enough to turn you."

Adriana knew he knew how to hit the sore spots and to hurt her even though she wished that he didn't. They had known each other far too long not to know some things that they shouldn't know. "There is only one wolf for me."

"Yes. And he's dead." He let the word cut through her

with all the force it rightly possessed, not moving from his place on the platform as he watched her reaction closely to see if she gave any indication of the queen's theories of Destin's survival being correct. "That's a reality you and the rest of his family should face sometime soon."

Adriana's eyes always burned when she thought about Destin being dead, even though she didn't want to believe it. Her hands curled into fists at her sides, and she remained quiet for a moment before she responded. This time it was in a lower tone, though still sharp and even. "Is there anything else you require, Miris?"

He shook his head slowly, looking at her with something that almost approached respect at the fact she'd been prudent not to give in to whatever anger he knew he could draw from her with a single word. "Not at this time, Slave." He turned away from her and went back to work on his figurehead, which was almost finished to his satisfaction.

* * * * *

It was a long day that only seemed to get longer after she had confronted Miris. His words stayed with her, even though she didn't want them to. Adriana worked the rest of her day quietly, and she was dismissed before Shian and Malcom because of her current physical state.

Adriana laid on the straw mattress in their cell and looked up at the blank stone overhead as she ran her fingers across her belly. Every now and again she could feel flutters from the baby, and while it was exciting to feel again, all she could wonder about was if Destin was dead or alive. If he was alive, wouldn't he have found a way back to her by now? Wouldn't he have sent her a message?

It was well after sunset by the time Shian came back, but there was still enough light left coming in through the cell across the hall for her to see him clearly. Adriana wondered for the tenth time just how the boy she'd met four months prior had so quickly turned into the man standing in front of her.

He had his share of cuts and scars all along his arms and chest, acquired quickly and often at the shipyard, but those scars covered arms and a chest that had lost all trace of childhood. He was still skinny and lacked the bulk of men like Miris or even the powerful form of Destin that she'd come to love, but he was clearly fit and up to whatever task their masters set before them. His blond beard had come in fully, a sharp contrast to his former self, since his former masters had preferred that the unpaired slave boys remain clean-shaven as a mark of their youth. His hair still fell in shaggy waves around his face, but only his eyes retained their youthful gleam. The rest of him had clearly become a part of the life they lived.

"Who came by with these? Kaia?" He picked up the small bag of fruit tucked away near the bars of the cell and held it up for Adriana to see.

"She must have snuck them in." She said softly, but she went back to staring at the ceiling. "I'm not feeling very hungry, you can have whatever you like. Eat it all, if you want."

He did a double-take at that, but he was silent as he took the fruit to the far corner of the cell where it could be hidden from the guards along the foot of the mattress. He carefully peeled one of the citrus fruits and tossed the peel out their tiny window to destroy the evidence of its presence before he went back to sit beside Adriana on the pallet, offering the first section of the tart fruit to her quietly despite her original refusal. "Anything you want to talk about?"

She sighed as she sat up slowly, and she took the piece of fruit from him, but instead of eating it she just held onto it and leaned into him. "How have you felt about everything since you arrived?"

His expression turned confused, making him look much younger than he had finally started to appear. "Everything is kind of a lot in one question. What do you mean? How have I felt about what?"

"Well, us, I guess. You and me."

He still wasn't sure what she was looking for by the question, so he hesitated for a while as he chewed the piece of fruit. "I . . . don't know. A lot of things. Mostly I'm grateful that you're you and not someone else. You've made pretty much everything about being here tolerable." It wasn't the first time he'd told her so, which made him even more confused about why she was asking. "I feel like we get along pretty well, I suppose? Did I do something? What happened?"

"You didn't do anything." Adriana kissed his cheek and felt a flutter in her stomach before she let out a short chuckle. "Well, you did do something, I suppose." She took his hand in both of hers after she set aside her piece of fruit. "I just worry that I haven't been fair to you. That keeping us at a distance is hurtful to you because of my other feelings."

He gave her a slight glare and took a bigger bite of fruit, since he was hungry and he wasn't going to let a conversation they'd had several times keep him from enjoying a luxury like fresh fruit. "I don't think there's ever going to come a time when I'm able to look you in the eye and say it isn't incredibly strange that you're in love with a wolf. You already know that. But I've known your feelings since almost the first day I got here. It's not like I had any illusions about this. Or about us."

It had been almost two months since they'd even been intimate with each other, since that was around the time Adriana had been absolutely certain she was carrying a child, having not bled for over two Fulnesses. As much as they enjoyed being with each other and staying close at night, it had been something that once existed between them and had left a strangely awkward gap in their lives. Even so, they had continued to work and take care of each other while Adriana dealt with the telltale signs of her early pregnancy.

"I'm not him." Shian said for what was almost certainly the hundredth time, but all resignation, sadness or anger, if any had once existed to begin with, had been drained out of the words, leaving them as nothing but fact. "And I'm never going to try to be."

"I wouldn't want you to be." She continued to hold onto him as she paused in the middle of her words. "If he was alive . . . I would know it by now." Adriana fought tears and squeezed Shian's tighter before she lifted up her eyes to look into his. "Do you think that you could ever love me after all of this?"

"After all of what?" He knew she constantly felt as though she had put him through some kind of terrible ordeal in living with the ghost of Destin around their lives, but Shian had never seen it that way. All he saw was Adriana. She was the one who still lived with a ghost.

He squeezed her hand and reached up to open her mouth for her, popping in a piece of the fruit to force her to eat. "When this baby is born, I'll be here to help you with it, take care of you while it grows and learns to walk, and then when it's weaned and they come to steal it from us, I will be here to cry with you. I'll be here for as long as that is the pattern of our lives. And even when it isn't and someday either I die of my own stupidity or they move one of us, I'll still be grateful for you. And I'll still love you, even if I know it isn't the way he did."

Adriana sniffled as she swallowed the fruit before she moved to sit in his lap. Destin was gone. She didn't want to believe he was dead, but if he was alive, she would have known about it. He was gone, and she was the only one holding onto someone that wasn't there. "I love you too, Shian. I don't want there to be anyone between us. You're all I have left, and you've been wonderful to me."

"You make it pretty easy." He cradled her in his arms, glad as always to have her close, no matter how complicated their situation was sometimes. "Is it because we're getting close to finishing the Striker? Is that what got you all turned around today?"

"Maybe." She buried her face into his chest with her tears. "I never wanted to believe he was dead. But I know I need to move on. And I'm lucky to have you here with me."

Shian ran his fingers through her hair even though he felt guilty that his hands were still so dirty from the day's work. He knew the gesture calmed her, though, so he continued anyway. "I've heard of three wolves in all my time as a slave that people actually seem to like. Well no, four, I forgot Kaia. Everyone seems to like her. Two were my old masters, Calis and Ressa. The other is your Oceanborn. I've never heard slaves talk about a wolf the way people here in Chainhome talk about him. I still laugh every time Malcom tells that story about the day he almost killed Miris."

She tried to laugh as she thought about the story, but now she knew there would be no one to protect her from Miris, and there was a part of her that did not care. "Destin . . . changed me. My whole life."

"Love does that to a person." He kissed her cheek gently, since he knew his life had been changed by Adriana too, even if it wasn't the same as what she had with her Oceanborn. "If he's gone back to his ocean, then he's not far away. Just outside the window."

She knew he was doing his best to comfort her, but Destin was always going to feel far away. Somehow they had missed the opportunity to find a way to build a life together. Adriana kissed Shian's jaw before she sighed against his skin. "Will you hold me until I fall asleep?"

He nodded and returned the kiss before he sat her back on the pallet. "Finish some of this fruit first while I wash up. You two need it more than I do." He moved the bag closer to her before he headed to the side of the cell next to the bars, where a bucket of water and a harsh cloth was left for them to bathe with. He stood naked in the cold darkness against the bars of their cage and scraped away as much of the day's drudgery as he could manage. He barely even noticed his own shivering anymore, as the cold air dried him and he made his way back to their pallet, looking forward to sleep.

Adriana ate because he asked her to, and as soon as he

laid down, she cuddled closer than she had in the last couple months. She pulled the blanket high on both of them and she actually kissed his lips lightly, which she hadn't done since they had last been intimate. "Sweet dreams, Shian."

He was surprised by the closeness, but he returned the kiss gently, not wanting to push anything between them after a discussion like the one they'd just had. "You too, 'Ana." He didn't use the nickname often, since the only person who seemed to use it with her was Malcom, but it signified who she was to him. The closest person he had in the world, his best friend, and the one person still in his life he would do anything to protect.

FOURTEEN

The first thing he remembered was the darkness. The depths of the ocean were as much a home to him as anywhere he'd ever been, but he had rarely visited the truly deep places of the world before. Far from land, far from family, far from the changing day and night that held sway over the rhythm of his life above the waves. The darkness of the depths took everything away at once. Time, memory, hope, even fear. All that remained was the abyss, and the peace of the depths unbroken by sound or sight.

He could feel things moving in the water, crawling or gliding along the ocean floor he'd fallen to while unconscious. Some of them seemed to know him, seemed to recognize that he was a god among them, a master of the only world they knew, and that he was not to be disturbed. It took time for him to find and subdue some of them and find them palatable to staunch his hunger after having been senseless for so long.

The journey to the surface took days, though he had no means of counting them. Life beneath the waves was much like the islands above, sparse and disconnected, with ages of open water between them, but deadly and violent when it finally appeared. Even when he finally reached the surface, the night sky above him gave no indication of his whereabouts. The horizon was an unbroken shell of black around him, the nearly-full moon glinting off its surface to mark its difference from the sky.

Exhaustion took him that night, and the Fulness took him the next, twisting his mind in the vast expanse of water and reducing him to nothing more than another denizen of the endless expanse, hunting, killing, searching, never finding.

He was a powerful wolf, from a powerful line, and capable of great feats within the purity of his element, but the constant saturation of its presence worked in him to erase the pieces of himself that remembered any other part of his life. His home, the people he had loved, the life he lived on dry shores, all were pushed aside by the urgency of the power to which he had been born. The first Fulness overtook his being. The lost days that followed buried all that he had been beneath a never-ending torrent.

He knew hunger and he knew power, the one satisfied by the other. He needed nothing else.

When land finally did appear in his perceptions, it was like seeing the ghost of a former existence, faintly remembered and deeply suspect. His prey had gone to hide in the shallows where it thought he would not follow, but once he had finished his meal, he took in the sight of the rising slope beneath the filtered sunlight above, and the place where the ocean floor met the ocean's crest intrigued his addled mind.

The water followed his will without command, too much a part of him to do otherwise, bearing him up to rise with the tide. Destin's paws bore the weight of his body again for the first time in the incoherent life he could remember. When he left the water and blinked the ocean from his eyes, the shore he found himself on was empty, the tree line over a hundred meters removed from the surf.

Something tugged at his mind as the water dripped from his fur, something he knew he should remember, something he should feel. As the sun beat down on his black and gray body, he crested the slight hill that stood between the sea and the rest of the island he'd landed on.

There were strange structures built along the tree line in orderly rows that resembled nothing in the world he'd recently left. The 'something' continued to batter the back of his mind as he watched creatures walking on two legs between the structures, going about the business of their lives and making sounds that carried through the air in different ways than sound had traveled through his former ocean world.

He didn't know them, but he was supposed to know what they were. He didn't recognize their faces, but he knew what faces were . . . knew what those things they walked on were called . . .

Destin stumbled back along the slope of the beach out of sight of the settlement, convulsing with the memories that had been pushed back by the insistence of the ocean's power for too long. They were too much for him to take in all at once, too much to realize he'd lost. Too much . . . too much . . .

Destin shifted back to human form for the first intentional time in over four months, and fell on his face in the shade of a bush near the rise, his legs incapable of holding his weight any longer. He lifted his face toward the unseen people on the other side of the hill and opened his mouth to cry out for someone, anyone, but no sound came out. His deep blue eyes closed and his body went limp, as his lips soundlessly shaped themselves around Adriana's name, and the world went dark again.

FIFTEEN

It was late in the afternoon before anyone made it out to the water's edge, and it was an older woman who was alone, carrying a basket to gather some seaweed. The older woman stared at the human form for a moment, and then she looked out at the water for any sign of a boat or ship and saw nothing.

Slowly, she approached and sat down in the sand next to the naked man. He was clearly alive, at least, his body visibly shivering with shallow breaths. She reached out and touched the man's shoulder and shook gently. She didn't know if he was injured or if she should try to move him, but he didn't seem to be bleeding or broken.

It took her several minutes to rouse him at all, and when he did show signs of regaining consciousness, the arm she was shaking flinched a little. Destin similarly pulled away from the danger, rolling away along the sand, but stopped and grunted against a few stones along the beach as he struggled to get his bearings. His limbs shook as he came up to full consciousness, but he hadn't even managed to open his eyes yet as he pushed himself to his hands and knees.

"Whoa, careful there." Her voice was silky and comforting, as though she was meant to tell stories and sing lullabies to help soothe people into serenity. The woman moved closer to him and pulled a shawl from around her shoulders and draped it over him. "It has been a long time since I've seen a young body like yours. Better get that covered up in a hurry. Are you alright?"

As his mind caught up to his body and began to wake, he brushed the sand from his eyes, still breathing heavily and shuddering as the shawl laid awkwardly around his midsection. His hair and beard were wild from being at sea for so long, and they were still matted with sand and fallen leaves from the bush. He started to calm down as he fully opened his eyes, invisible behind the curtain of his unruly hair.

"Where am I?" He attempted to say, sputtering a few times before he finally got all the words out. His voice was dry and cracked from long disuse, but it was still intelligible, if only barely.

Instead of answering him, she grabbed a water pouch out of her basket and held out the pouch. She remained close, though she eyed him carefully. His strangely colored hair and his otherwise young stature had her on her guard, since she was fairly certain what kind of man she was dealing with. "I have a feeling you are a long way from home." She reached out and brushed a little more sand off of him. "Mine, however, is not too far from here. Do you think you can make it if I help you?" She wasn't about to give him any more information than she needed to until she was sure of what and who she was dealing with.

He took the pouch from her numbly, but as soon as he saw what was in it, he shuddered again and handed it back to her. He'd had too much of his element for far too long. He needed to come back to himself before he could return to it. "I can try." He didn't flinch away when she started to brush him off, and finally managed to stand upright, though he was shaky at first.

His balance improved quickly, though, and he got most of the sand off of him and his hair out of his face before he remembered her request and tied her shawl crudely around his waist to cover himself. It did nothing to hide the rest of him, though, and the rest of him radiated power. He wasn't a particularly tall man, but he was powerfully built and had obviously worked for what he gained. Destin had arms that looked like they could wrap themselves around a ship's anchor and haul it up single-handedly. For all the obvious physical power he possessed, though, he still shook as he attempted to follow her up the low incline one hesitant step at a time. His eyes were still a little hazy with whatever he had gone through to get to the beach.

When he did not take the water and she was able to get a better look at him, the woman was more careful around him. She helped him to her small home anyway, and once she was inside, she set him down on her bed. It was soft from her accumulation of animal furs over the years, and he could hear a fire crackling across the room. There was a half-eaten loaf of bread on the table that she offered to him, wondering if he was hungry instead of thirsty.

Once he got a better look at her, he could see that she was a much older human than he was accustomed to seeing. Her features were beautiful even though they were well worn and there were wrinkles in her face. It was clear that she had been a very attractive woman in her youth, and it had mostly carried with her in her age. Her eyes were clear and bright, a warm, light brown in color. Her hair was like Destin's, except it was peppered by age, white in several places. "You'll be alright here."

He took the bread and ate a single chunk of it quickly, sighing in contentment at the taste as he visibly relaxed. It was something completely unknown of the ocean, and that fact on its own made it precious to him at the moment. "Thank you." He was starting to shake a little less than he had when she found him, and after another bite of bread, he managed to look up at her eyes. "My name is Destin. I'm sorry that you had to find me this way."

"My name is Elyra." She returned, as she continued to sit by and watch. "I don't mind coming up on a naked man, so long as he's attractive. And not bleeding. It is a lot more work if they are bleeding." Elyra smirked before she got up to find him some suitable clothes to wear. "You're a wolf, aren't you? Oceanborn, by the look of your eyes."

The fact that she had to ask confused him, until he began to look closer around the house. It had none of the trappings of homes he was accustomed to, no access to the roof for Skyborn, no customary plants in the windowsills to make the space hospitable to Forestborn, and barely any stone used in the house's construction. Even the stones lining the fireplace were rough-hewn in a way that was almost jarring to his eyes, stacked together as well as they could be made to fit and pasted in place with what looked like baked mud. Even Chainhome had been built by Stoneborn to be smooth and safe from the elements. This place had no such protection.

"Yes, I am." He decided there was no point in lying about what he was, and he had no desire to do so in the first place. "And you are human. Where are your masters?" His voice had no malice to it or accusation, only curiosity, since he thought it was strange that a human would be left alone to build their own house and stoke their own fires.

Elyra chuckled softly as she shook her head. She pulled out some clothes that would be too large for Destin, but she held out the shirt and pants to him anyway. It had been a long time since she had any reason to keep men's clothing around, but she kept them from her brother. "I am human. And I have no master. I take care of myself pretty well." She smiled at him before she looked back toward the fire. "There is a stew in there, do you want some of that?"

The only other human who had ever dared to laugh at him had been Adriana, but Destin found the experience both strange and strangely comforting. It got a slight smile from the edge of his mouth, but he shook his head. "The bread is more than enough for now, thank you." He pulled on the simple clothing quickly, and took a moment to appreciate the care that had gone into its construction, the careful stitches and the well-worn fabric from a thousand washings. It was more comfortable than most of his own clothing back home, even if he had to tie the pants tightly to make them fit and the shirt hung off him loosely.

"It seemed cold outside for the afternoon." He felt sheepish just asking the question, but he was still trying to get himself oriented. "Has it been . . . I mean . . . what season is it? The last day I remember it was approaching the Fulness just before the equinox."

"My, my. You were adrift for a long time, Destin." She sat down on a small stool once he declined the stew, and she motioned for him to sit back down on her bed if he was still feeling tired. "There have been three more Fulnesses since that one, and we are not far from the next one. It is getting quite cold now." She raised an eyebrow as she continued to inspect him. "How are you during the Fulness? I might have to trap you in here, it would be too dangerous to let you roam free around here."

What she said was so completely backward to anything he had ever conceived of that it took him a few moments to register what she'd said. A human? Trap a wolf? During the Fulness? That made no sense.

"In general, I am fairly level-headed. Though these past few months at sea . . ." he shook his head and rubbed at his eyes, still adjusting to being human again after spending so much time steeped in his element.

"So long as there are a few days between now and the Fulness, I should be well enough to maintain composure. But if those are your requirements, I will of course abide by them, as your guest." He was coming to realize quickly that he was among humans, with no signs that a wolf had ever even been a part of the home's existence. It was an unsettling feeling.

"This island is a home for humans." She could tell he was still confused, but she expected him to be after hearing how long he had been at sea. "There are very few wolves on the island, and those here are connected to their humans in one way or another. Some of them help protect us, but we mostly take care of ourselves. During the Fulness, they stay contained so that the rest of us can go on with our lives. I've seen what Fulnesses are like elsewhere, and nothing gets done when wolves are enjoying themselves like that." She paused. "I don't mean offense when I say that."

"Of course." He said automatically, since he had been raised at court, after all, and having good manners was considered the height of good breeding among noble wolves. "Have you ever heard of the Reef? The Genovin kingdom? The Seven Isles?" He had no way of knowing how far he had drifted when he was at sea, or where he was in the ocean with relation to his home. If he was in a place almost without wolves, he couldn't possibly be close.

"Oh yes, I have heard of them all." She ran her fingers through her long hair. "I was once a kept human of an Oceanborn like yourself. He was a wolf of the Seven Isles, but no one of real importance." She gave him a small smile. "He was kind to me, at least. Most Oceanborn have kind hearts, I've always thought."

"Most." He agreed, since his opinion of his own kind was rather high, on the whole. "Not all." He continued taking pieces of the bread she'd given him until it was gone, still taking in all the details of the simple but comfortable home. "How did you all come to be here, then? If you were once kept on the Isles?"

"My brother and I, along with a few other humans, managed to escape because my wolf was so trusting of me. I gathered supplies for a long time and we escaped during a Fulness many years ago. My brother has since died, but we expanded our people here by gathering slaves from all of the closest islands. The Falls, The Reef, The Genovin, The Isles. Over time, we've created our own home here. Some of our smallest children have never interacted with wolves at all."

He was amazed by the simple story she told him, just because what she was suggesting was something no wolf, and certainly no noble, had ever even considered as a possibility before. There had been small slave escapes over the years, a family here and there, sometimes as many as a few dozen at once escaping and heading out to sea, but they had always been dismissed as fools who couldn't possibly survive away from their masters.

Yet here Elyra was, with however many others she had gone to save, apparently healthy and having lived a great deal longer than most humans generally did on the Isles. She looked like she was in her decline, whatever that meant for humans.

"If the lords of the Isles knew about this place, they would not tolerate it." He didn't sound angry about what she'd said at all, and there was a note of something like fear in his voice, on her behalf. "It's a wonder you've managed to go undetected for so long, if you visit those kingdoms so often."

"You, like all of them, would not even think that a place like this could exist. I am one of few who live so close to the water, but if the wolves come after us here, they will find a stronger resistance than you imagine." Elyra did not want to reveal to the wolf how many humans she would estimate, but she knew they were safe. "This is a large island, though it is too small for any of the wolf kingdoms to care about conquering it. And there is a feral Oceanborn population off the opposite coast from here, to the southwest. They mostly live in the water by the whirlpool there. Between those wolves and the whirlpool, no ship wants to get close."

"Now you're talking about ghost stories." He said skeptically, since he'd grown up on homespun stories his parents had told him about the great eye of the ocean, a whirlpool of such fabled power that it was both the source and the end of all water that covered the world, a vortex which allowed nothing to survive.

"Am I?" She chuckled and shook her head. It had been a long time since she had had a proud wolf in her company. "I'll show you myself once you are well. Then we'll see who is telling stories."

The confidence in her reply and her laugh made him second-guess himself, and he had to give the woman another long look, but she seemed to be telling the truth, as she understood it. Either way, he wasn't going to argue the point with her. "If it exists, I would like to see it." Even if there was such an act of nature in existence near the island, it didn't help him get home. If months had passed, then he was sure everyone on the Isles believed he was dead. Taimon, Kaia. Adriana. Daiva, if she had survived the remainder of the battle. "I need to return to my people. My family will have given me up for lost by now."

"I don't think you are ready to go home, but I won't stop you if you want to go." She got up from her stool. "I can't give you one of our boats, though. If you want a boat, I'll help you make one. Otherwise you're going to have to swim back."

He could understand that, especially from a human who clearly wasn't interested in having anything to do with wolves. He nodded and took a deep breath to try and steady his still-shaking hands, the power running through him still far too much to allow him to rest completely. "I'll start work on one as soon as I've rested, then. After the Fulness has passed, depending on how close it is."

Elyra looked at his shaking hands, and from probably too much experience, she knew that he needed to be put to work in order to burn off some of the energy pent up inside of him. She pointed toward her door, and then she looked back at him. "Maybe you can help me with something."

When she led him to the outside of her small house, he could see there was a stream that ran down out of the trees past her house and several others in the small settlement. There was a deep well dug at a distance from the stream with people standing around it, looking at the two of them in instant suspicion as they walked.

Destin just tried to stay close to Elyra as they approached a wheel that was set in the stream but wasn't spinning as it should to move the water onto a wooden channel that fed the well. "I can't quite figure out how to fix our water wheel. My brother made it, and he was the one who kept it up. Can you get it working?"

Destin looked around at all the curious and fearful faces that surrounded him first, but they seemed to be holding back out of respect for Elyra, so he approached the wheel cautiously. It was a fairly simple design that he was familiar with, but he was careful to stay out of the water as he inspected it. "Any of you here carpenters?" He looked around, since he certainly didn't expect a woman of Elyra's years to be chopping at wood.

"I am." A man said defensively as he stepped forward with a small axe in his hand, obviously prepared to defend himself if necessary.

Destin didn't miss the instant dislike in the man's eyes, and just crouched by the wheel looking up at him. "My name is Destin, friend. What's yours?"

The man didn't seem to like being called friend, but he answered anyway, his fingers tightening around the handle of the axe. "Beylan."

"Well, Beylan, these spokes have gotten twisted, probably during a frost. Most of the flats are starting to rot out too. You should replace as many of them as you can, and try to lift it out of the water when you expect a freeze. It'll keep them from going twisted again. Once they're replaced, it should spin just fine." Destin got up and brushed off his hands, watching the man to make sure he understood, but Beylan seemed to grasp what he was talking about.

Destin nodded and headed over toward the well, treading carefully between several of the people, who got out of his way as he approached. The well was almost completely drained, and he could feel the water down at the bottom, a good sturdy stone basin that was impressively deep for being so close to shore.

"As for this . . ." he said quietly, turning to look at everyone gathered before he extended a shaking hand toward the stream.

Young and old alike screamed and staggered back out of the way as the stream arched up over their heads, rising completely out of its basin into the air.

The ribbon of water curled up over the roof of a nearby house, clearly panicking the occupants, before it condensed itself into a point and funneled down into the well steadily. His hands shook less and less as he drew the entire contents of the stream into their village well, until he could feel that the cistern was almost full.

He capped it off right at the brim of the stones set in place to surround it, and moved his hand again to return the airborne stream to its proper channel. He stepped over to it to ensure that it was running properly and there was no danger of it flooding its banks because of his intervention, then released it from his hold, allowing the water to settle to its previous course before he turned to Elyra. "I hope that helps."

Elyra was one of the few who did not respond in fear, and she nodded as soon as he was finished. "Thank you, that does help. Sometimes I forget how useful an Oceanborn can be." She smiled at him and looked around at the people watching. "I'll keep him under careful eye. He swept in from the ocean, and he'll leave when he is able."

The people started whispering amongst themselves and walking away, but they were all still watching the wolf with careful glances. "This is sure to get the rest of the Elders talking." She chuckled again. "Did that help you too?"

"Some." He admitted as he looked at the woman with new respect. For someone who professed to have lived most of her life away from wolves, she knew a great deal about his kind. He flexed and relaxed his fists several times, enjoying the feel of exercising control over himself and his element again. "Elders?"

"The leaders of our city.'" She looked around again. Most people had disappeared, which left the two of them alone again. "We don't have masters, but we still need leaders and some kind of way to govern this many people. I'm one of the Elders, so I'm not too worried, but the rest don't always agree with my methods." She looked at the water wheel and then at Destin. "Come with me, I will show you the walls of the city. Maybe it will do you some good to walk for a while."

He wasn't sure why she would want to do that when she was so reticent to tell him much about her people, but he nodded and waited for her to show him the way to follow.

As she stepped away, though, Beylan moved to block Elyra's way with a sidelong look at Destin. "I'll go with you. You shouldn't go walking the trail to the city alone with the likes of him."

"He's been polite, Beylan. It's like I told you before, they are not all bad. It is impossible for all of them to be bad." She didn't turn down Beylan's offer, though, as they walked. "You should know that all of the guards will know of your presence here. There will probably be a weapon trained on you at every turn. If you aren't as polite as you seem to be, they'll kill you in a hurry." They headed down a rough path that became paved as they went inland, and as more trees appeared around them, it was obvious they were being watched.

"Well . . ." Destin turned to give Beylan a slightly amused look that clearly didn't amuse the carpenter himself, "I do usually prefer it when people tell me in advance that they want to kill me. It makes life simpler."

"I thought so." Elyra smiled and continued to lead the way.

It was well over an hour's walk through the dense forest to get to the city buried deep within. As they got closer to the wall, there were more and more people. All of them humans. The air had taken a distinct turn as they walked, and she saw Destin shiver slightly as they went. She had to wonder if it was still because he had too much of the ocean running through him or if it was actually because of the cold. "How did you find us?" She eventually asked, mostly because she knew he didn't find them on purpose.

"I didn't, really." He was looking around at the people on either side of the trail as they walked, some of them out tending to orchards subtly woven into the fabric of the forest, some of them fishing in the stream as it ran parallel to the path they'd been on for well over an hour. "I was involved in a battle between the Isles and the Genovin. During the battle, I was knocked unconscious and fell into the sea. I've been drifting ever since."

"Who were you fighting for?" She asked as they walked and she paused momentarily to catch a piece of fruit from the people tending to the orchards. It was the last they would get before it turned much colder. Elyra held out the fruit for him to take if he was interested, even though it wasn't plump and perfect as it would be if it had been grown by a Forestborn. "We had a few people arrive from the Genovin a few Fulnesses ago. They said that the islands were preparing for war."

He took the fruit, and even though she could see the judgment in his eyes at the inferior quality of it, he still nodded his gratitude as he bit into it. "I fight for my family." He wasn't willing to give away his origins so quickly, no matter how gracious the woman had been in offering her hospitality and her protection. It had occurred to him along the way that he might be following her into some kind of trap despite her assurances that he wouldn't be harmed. "And I can honestly say I have no idea where they are at the moment. A lot can happen in four months."

"We aren't going after your family, Destin. We don't go looking for wolves." She stopped on the path when towering walls came into sight, and she pointed at them in the distance. They were surrounded by trees and deep forest, but somehow there was a giant wall in the middle of it all. "We probably should not get any closer."

"You mean *I* shouldn't." He gave her a look, then turned back to the wall. He took in the sight of them slowly, his eyes flicking along the high wooden structure in amazement that such a thing had been made entirely by humans. It went on as far as he could see through the trees in either direction, with a broad space cleared of trees all around it. The humans who had arrived on the island had staked an obvious claim on the ground, and were just as obviously prepared to defend it. He saw several individuals moving along the top of the barrier armed with bows and arrows, keeping watch over the dwindling afternoon. "You're right about one thing, certainly. No one from the three kingdoms would ever dream humans were capable of anything like this on their own."

"Why do you say that? Being your slaves is what gives us the skills to do all of this." She waved at a few more people before she looked at Destin again. "Don't you think humans have any worth at all?"

"I said no one from the kingdoms would think you capable of this. I didn't say I wouldn't." He took in the sight of the wall for a while and then turned back to her. "Back home, I was the overseer in charge of shipbuilding operations for the queen of the Isles. I've worked with humans for probably almost as long as you've been alive. I know what you're capable of, I've just never seen you work on your own before, without our direction."

"Well, we are quite capable, I think." She assured him as they both stared at the wall. "To be honest, I didn't know all this would come out of my desire for human freedom. It was only a group of ten of us that escaped, and now there are so many. It still amazes me."

"I have to wonder what this place will be like when it's stood as long as the Isles, then." He looked over the wall again and watched one of the gates open, doors that were large and heavy enough that he imagined they would give even an Earthborn a difficult time to tear open. The walls wouldn't stop many other kinds of wolves that really wanted to get in, but Destin was just glad they had any kind of protection at all. "And do you still go to the three kingdoms to rescue slaves?"

"About twice a year, yes." Elyra said with a nod. "We

would like to go more than that, but it is hard to get in unnoticed and to get away without getting hurt. We've lost good people too many times."

"With those kinds of risks, I'm sure." He said contemplatively, then turned to look back at the trail they'd traveled. "If there are any more wells that need filling, I'm happy to help. Otherwise, I think it's best if I go back to sleep for what may be several days."

"We could use a little more help with the wells, but let's go back to my home. You can sleep there as long as you need."

Beylan moved to walk with Elyra as Destin lagged behind at a glare from Beylan. "Helpful or not, Elder, you can't keep an animal in your house."

"You know my history, Beylan. I had a wolf in my bed for the longest time. I can handle one in my house. Maybe he can help us."

"We don't *need* their help." He growled back at her, even though he knew he was speaking out of turn. "That's the whole point of us being here. To live without them. Not to mention, if you let him go back to the Isles, he'll bring their whole fleet back here to undo everything we've done."

"The point is to live here *free* of them. I keep telling everyone that it is impossible to live in a world without them. They are more numerous than we are, and they aren't easily ignored." Elyra looked back at Destin before she looked at Beylan again. "I will figure out what to do with him so that we are safe. If I have to, we'll knock him unconscious and drop him out at sea again. He won't know where to find us."

"That might work, if he is telling the truth about having just drifted here in the first place." Beylan clearly didn't think that was the case, but he wasn't going to argue with Elyra any further. "The moment he shows the first sign of being anything but helpful, he dies. He has to, for all our sakes."

"Is that an order of the Elders? I don't remember going to a meeting today." She gave Beylan a challenging glare. "If anyone is threatened, then he will be contained until he is dealt with. I am sure there will be a meeting about what to do soon."

Destin stayed silent through the exchange, still not sure why the woman was taking his side, unless it was some kind of lingering gratitude for her treatment at the hands of her former Oceanborn master. Even then, Destin certainly didn't want to push that kind of generosity too far. The sky had turned the grey shade of winter above them as they headed back toward the coast, and Destin cursed a few times under his breath when he saw that snow was beginning to fall. Even on dry land, he couldn't quite escape his element.

When they returned to the village, he saw that most of the occupants had retired to their homes for the day, though he still saw a few pairs of eyes peeking out of windows and cracked doors as he returned to Elyra's house. Beylan gave him a parting glare before heading to his own house, but said nothing else. So long as Destin was aware that he wasn't welcome, that seemed to be enough for him.

"Thank you." He said as soon as he was back in the house with Elyra, moving to help her put more wood on the fire, since she was moving one log at a time and, though he was tired, it was at least something he could do.

"I saw the state you were in when you washed up from the water. I know you didn't end up here on purpose, and I know no wolf would go through the dramatics of putting on that kind of show." She was grateful for his help with the fire, and once he added more wood, she spooned out a bowl of stew for herself. "I don't know what to expect from you now, but I'm willing to give you a chance. That's what we give everyone who sets foot on our shores. A chance."

"I won't waste it." He promised as he sat near the fire across the room from her, letting it warm him. "How many years have you seen, Elder, fifty? More than that?"

It was strange for her to hear this stranger call her Elder, but she didn't stop him from doing so. "A few more than that, but not much. You aren't accustomed to seeing a human like me, are you?"

"A few, but not often." Humans were incredibly short-lived compared to the lifespan of most wolves. Destin knew that an old wolf like Melyssa or Cadmos would have seen six or seven generations of humans in their time. He himself could remember knowing young slaves around his household growing up who had grandchildren back at home. "Are your children or grandchildren here on this island with you as well?"

Elyra shook her head and took a bite of her stew and chewed it slowly before she answered. "I had several children that were fathered by the Oceanborn who kept me. After they were born, though, they were always taken. I'm sure I don't have to explain to you the reason why."

"No." He said sadly as he started to relax, though he could still feel the ocean running powerfully through his veins. "I'm sorry. I wish they could have been taken to a place like this, rather than the place we both know they were taken instead."

"My Oceanborn had a particular love for intimacy during the days of the Fulness. It was inevitable, I am sure." She took another few bites of her stew as she watched him carefully. "I'll show you where you can find the wood you will need once you are well. Unless you decide to attack someone, then they won't let you live to escape."

"Yes, that point has been well made." He sighed, but couldn't blame her for her attitude toward him or that of the rest of her people. "I know that you have no cause to believe me when I tell you this, Elder, but I promise you that I will do nothing to insult your trust, so far as it goes."

He stood up and undid the laces at the neck of his shirt, pulling it off over his head and folding it carefully before setting it aside. He began to finish undressing in order to shift, then remembered what she'd said earlier and left the room, coming back a moment later in wolf form bearing the carefully-folded pants between his teeth. He set them down on top of the shirt and went to lie down with his back to the fire. She could see his deep blue eyes staring into the darkness in the corners of her home, his thoughts far away.

She stared at him as he laid there by the fire and her own memories of a past life came rushing back. Elyra felt bad for him, even though she didn't know why she should, since she barely knew him. "Sleep well, Destin."

He looked up when she said so, and just nodded to her as if to return the sentiment. He kept his eyes on her for a long while without moving, then looked around at the space. He couldn't speak in wolf form, and she was hardly a wolf to be able to understand him mind to mind, but there was something between jealousy and respect in his ocean-blue eyes as he looked around at the space. She had seen the same emotion there earlier when he was taking in the sight of her home for the first time, and there was something behind it that he wasn't saying.

He clearly wasn't going to be any more forthcoming that night, though. Tomorrow, he would begin working to build a boat to take him home, and within a few days, he hoped to see Adriana again. He just hoped she was well when he got there, and that he was able to find this place again. She would love it in such a place. And she would be safe. He hoped.

SIXTEEN

Kaia was sitting in front of a large fire and wrapped in several blankets, but she still felt ill as she watched the flames. "I hate winter." She whined as she remained unmoving. "Everything is dead and it makes me feel ill every time. I hate it."

"I know." Taimon said from across the room, trying to keep the warm air from the fire centered around his sister. "But not everything is dead. We're all still here." He shrugged, looking down at himself, since he obviously wasn't hurting as much as she was during the cold seasons. "Some of us more than others."

"Not all of us are still here." She replied softly as she pulled the blanket a little tighter. "When Devon was alive, I could snuggle against his fur in the winter. He never seemed to mind." She sighed sadly. "And Destin . . . He made me laugh so I would forget how cold it was." Kaia found herself sniffling and tears rolling down her cheeks. "And he never let me cry. He took my tears off my cheeks." She knew her siblings didn't need to hear all of her stories, but winter always depressed her.

A hot breeze immediately ran past her cheek, blowing away her tears with Taimon's equivalent of a joke, but it didn't help her mood. "You need to spend more time in your garden and less in front of the fire. That's the only thing that's going to help you."

"It's dead." She pulled her knees up to her chest under her blankets and rested her chin on her knees. "I don't want to spend time out there."

"Enough of your whining." Daiva finally snipped as she got up from her chair where she had been reviewing some documents. "You are a Forestborn, this is a struggle of your kind, but not a death sentence. Destin and Devon are gone, but you are not. Stop whining."

"And you are cruel and heartless." Kaia shot back, still sniffling. "Do you even miss them? All you do is run around plotting and planning, and for what? Destin was trying to do it for love. Devon tried to do it for a different future. What is it you want, other than a fight?"

Daiva stared at her younger sister and tapped her fingers on her stone chair before she gathered the documents nearby into a pile of large tree shavings. She got up, tossed it all into the fire, and looked back at her siblings. "I have things to do." She turned her attention to Taimon specifically. "Make sure she eats."

He nodded obediently, and went to grab a few pieces of fruit that were dried during the growing season and had grown by Kaia's own power when it was at its height. They had plenty of food stockpiled to last them until the spring, mostly because of Kaia's work for them during the summer, but that wasn't really the issue.

"You're wrong about her, you know." He sat back down next to Kaia, hoping as he did that the current snowstorm would abate soon and allow the world to at least pretend for a while that it wasn't cased in ice. "She fights for love too, just in a different way than Devon or Destin did."

"Love? Who does Daiva love other than herself?" Kaia looked over at Taimon. "How can you say that? You see her. She doesn't even talk about Destin. It's like she wants to forget him completely."

"Destin is the reason she wants to break this world in

half." He kept his voice low, since he didn't want Daiva to hear him talking about her. "And Devon, and our parents. They're the reason she's been on a mission ever since the battle with the Genovin. The only way she's ever going to rest, ever again, is when they're all dead."

"She was there, every time." Kaia said softer, but she was still angry. "Why didn't she do something? Why didn't she save Destin?" Kaia knew her sister was one of the strongest wolves she had ever seen. Why didn't Daiva ever do anything to stop their family from being killed off?

"Because she's a wolf, not a goddess." He had asked the same questions before, and felt the same kind of guilt. Like Kaia, he hadn't been there when their family was killed, either time. "Just don't tell her I said that. I think she forgets sometimes."

Kaia wasn't convinced their sister was kinder than she thought, but she munched on the dried fruit quietly for a moment before she slid closer to her brother. "How do you know she's doing this for them? How do you know she's not doing it for herself?"

"Because Daiva never does anything for herself. Not once that I can recall, as a matter of fact." He looked up at the window as he tried to remember any instances at all, but nothing came to mind. "When our parents were alive, she served them and backed up Devon every time he would let her. After that, she sailed with Destin whenever he left, and fought with him. Since the Genovin, she's been running up and down the Queen's Isle meeting with everyone she can find who might support us and making certain of their loyalties. Not to mention the fact that she's been taking care of us, since Destin isn't here to do it anymore."

"Taking care of us means she trapped us in here as soon as she got home. She doesn't trust us. Why can't we do anything to help? I tried to reach out to Miris. That didn't work. He doesn't care about himself or anyone else." She sighed dramatically after she finished talking, since she hated feeling trapped or stymied.

Taimon held his peace. He felt the same way, but the difference between them was that he had always been comfortable being limited. Growing up, it had been more than clear that the two of them were destined to live in the shadow of their older siblings. Not just because they were younger, but because they were lesser elements. It made society at large discount them, and Taimon had never questioned that.

"There's going to come a time when Daiva's going to finally bring us in on her plans, and when that happens, we need to be ready to help." He looked at the window that Daiva had mostly sealed up, but which still couldn't quite keep out the sight of the storm outside, snow falling in harsh waves. A few flakes made it into the room with every breath, but the hot air from the fire immediately turned them to a puddle near the window. It only made him miss Destin more. He'd have kept out even that much of the outside world. "No one's doing anything in these storms, though. Whatever Daiva has in mind, it's going to have to wait until spring, just like us."

Kaia didn't move away from Taimon, and while she wanted to shift into her wolf to be warmer, she knew it would be painful, since she had to preserve what little energy she could maintain for the Fullnesses. "I can't wait until spring." She kissed her brother's cheek and rested her head on his shoulder. "I hope it gets better by then."

"You know, you say that every year." He joked with her gently, poking at her side through the furs she had pulled tight around her body. "And every year it does. I'm seeing a pattern here."

* * * * *

Adriana was glad to be inside on such a blustery day, and she was glad that Shian and Malcom were working inside too. There were only a few slaves outside because of the conditions, and she felt sorry for them and grateful at the same time. When she had finished her basket-weaving, she set the large basket aside and snuggled into the extra blankets they had been given until Shian arrived.

He and Malcom were sent earlier that day to work in one of the larger chambers of Chainhome, cutting the reeds and the wood to make the baskets the rest of the slaves were working on. He'd been out a few days prior during a lull in the storms to cut the trees themselves, and it had been grueling work. Even within the stone walls of their home, though, and with all the activity racing through the halls, Shian's cheeks were still bright red when he came back near nightfall, and his skin was icy to the touch.

"These are beautiful." He commented as soon as he came in the door, looking over the stack of baskets Adriana finished on her own after being left alone all day with the supplies. "They had us cut plenty more for tomorrow and the next day, so it doesn't look like we're going to be sent out anytime soon."

"Hopefully they are sturdy as well as beautiful." She grabbed one of his freezing hands and pulled him over to their bed. There was warm soup waiting for him and she didn't want it to get any colder. "Come. Eat."

He allowed her to warm his hands for a while, until feeling returned, then started eating the soup quickly. They hadn't been given anything else all day, but he was accustomed to that. He took his meals where and when he could get them, and always preferred it when he could share it with Adriana. "Still kicking like it's trying to escape?"

She smiled and nodded as she sat close to him and kept rubbing along his back to try and warm him up while he ate. Adriana looked down at her ever-blossoming belly. "Yes, still kicking. Do you want to feel? He always gets excited when you're here."

He handed her the stew, hoping she would take some more of it, and laid a hand on her stomach with a smile. "Did your others kick like this too? It's a wonder you don't have bruises showing through." He lifted her dress to take a peek, since he knew it would make her laugh, then put it back down again quickly.

Adriana did laugh, and she leaned in to kiss him afterward before he went back to eating more soup. "No, the others weren't like this one. This one is pretty special." She really did believe that, especially because she knew how excited Shian was to be a father. He would be a wonderful father. As much as he was permitted to be. "We still haven't picked a name."

That dimmed his smile a little, and he took his time with his next bite before he answered. "Will he get to keep it? I mean, after his first year?"

"Yes, they keep their names. Wolves don't care about that, and they don't want to take the time to rename them." She kissed his cheek, then kissed the tip of his nose. "Don't be sad. It's too cold to be sad and shivering both."

"That's true enough." He finished the soup and set the bowl aside where Malcom or one of the other boys would be along to collect it later. "I don't suppose anyone came by with an apple or two." He didn't expect anything of the kind, since Kaia hadn't come by in weeks, as soon as the snows started, but he still hoped.

"No, I'm sorry." She wanted to think that Kaia stopped coming because of the cold, but she also thought it could be because Kaia simply didn't care about her now that Destin was dead. "I wish there was more for you to eat. Liliana gave me more bread than usual because she thinks I have two babies in here."

She moved away to bring the rest of the bread to him, but then cuddled close again. Adriana was always eager to be close to him when she could, being as affectionate as possible. She already loved Shian, and every day she was convinced she was a little more *in* love with him. It wasn't the same as what she felt for Destin, but that didn't matter and she couldn't dwell on it. Destin was gone.

He took some of the bread, but it was gone quickly, leaving them with nothing but the sound of chattering teeth echoing through the corridors around them. He tucked the blankets around them where they huddled against the wall. "It's alright. I'm not that big a man, it doesn't take much to fill me up. If anything, I'd be more worried about Liliana calling you fat. I don't think I would take that. Especially from her."

"Do you think I'm fat?" She said with a smirk as she poked at his side playfully underneath the blankets. "You can tell me. I can handle it. I try to be as beautiful as I can manage . . ."

"I prefer you a little rounded." He said with another poke of his own and a kiss to the side of her neck. "I'm the one who made you that way, so it's not like I'd have any right to say much about it even if I didn't."

"That is quite true." She smiled at him and slid into his lap so he could envelop her in his embrace. Adriana kissed the side of his neck in return before she wrapped her arms around his midsection. "I'm glad I have you, Shian."

He adjusted the blankets around them and sighed as his body began to warm up after the long day working with the raw materials for the baskets. Over the last few months, it seemed like everything in the world had turned cold around him, except Adriana. On the voyage to get to the Queen's Isle, he had envisioned a life of servitude and solitude, but in spite of everything else that was expected of him as a healthy young man, he couldn't find it in himself to be unhappy with the life his masters had given him. Not so long as Adriana was in it. "I'm glad you have me too. I'm not interested in being had by anyone else, certainly."

Adriana tucked her head under his chin and ran her hands slowly along his chest in a continued effort to warm him up. "I think we should name the baby after you."

He shook his head with a chuckle. "No need to curse the child like that. He'd be better off with some variant of yours. Darian, maybe."

"Darian?" She shook her head and she thought carefully as she chewed on her bottom lip. "What about girl's names?

Just in case." She really thought it would be a boy, but she didn't have any proof either way.

"I knew a girl named Danna once." He shrugged and laughed beneath her kisses, his hands moving down over her legs to warm her skin, since his hands had been under the blanket long enough to be comfortably warmer. "Might be a little awkward to have a daughter named that, though, considering she's one of the few other women I've had besides you."

"You probably shouldn't name a daughter after a lover." She laughed before she kissed him yet again. "What about Shanna?" Adriana had warmed her hands by that point, and she slid them under his shirt to caress along his skin.

"Shanna's a good name." He relaxed under her touch and smiled down at her. "Hopefully she'll like it, if it is a girl."

"I still think it's a boy. But we'll have to think of another name later." She spoke softly into his ear before she kissed him a little harder. "I need to make sure you stay nice and warm."

"You're the one doing the hard work here and taking care of a growing baby. I should be the one who does the work to keep you warm." He moved to lay her down on the pallet they shared, which was a complicated adventure of keeping the blankets warm around them. "And you don't have to make sure I stay nice. I try to be that way on my own."

Adriana's cheeks got warm as soon as Shian took control, and her heart pounded a little harder in her chest. They had spent the last several months keeping each other warm with amorous activities, and they were definitely in tune to each other's likes and dislikes. "We'll . . . take turns keeping each other warm, then."

SEVENTEEN

It had been several months since Daiva had watched Hassir sail away back to his Reef. Now that he was returning, it was hard for her to contain her excitement.

She was waiting on the beach for Hassir's ship, even though it was still snowing. It was a light snow, but it still gathered on her robes as she stood and waited for the ship to pull into the shore. A part of her wanted to run toward the Fireborn on the ship that she had claimed as her own, but she took careful, measured steps toward the boat and only sighed a slow breath of relief as soon as he came into sight.

The months since they'd seen each other had not changed him, at least not in any way that mattered. Like all the other Fireborn on the ship, he was dressed the same in the middle of a snowstorm as he had been during the late summer when they had first met, cured leather pants and a simple leather vest trimmed in black fur, his torso and arms bare against the cold.

Daiva watched the other Fireborn on the ship disembark first, every snowflake melting as soon as it made contact with their skin. For Hassir, though, the snow never even had a chance to reach him, disappearing as it hit some kind of invisible aura of heat all around his body, leaving him perfectly dry and untouched in the white haze of the world.

"My lady Daiva." He said with a smile and a growl, obviously satisfied that she was alone on the dock to greet him. He hadn't announced his coming to the king and queen, or to anyone else besides the Skyborn tutors he'd sent for Taimon, and it was a mark of how much he could trust her that she was the only one who had come. "It is good to see you again."

She smiled right back at him, and took a step closer as she debated how to greet him but then decided to step in and pull him into a hungry kiss. As soon as they were kissing she felt more relaxed, growling quietly in a rumble through her grip on his vest.

He grabbed a handful of her robes as she held onto him and returned the kiss just as hungrily, her entire body flooding with warmth and an immunity to the cold around them at his touch. "I missed you as well." He growled back at her once the kiss broke.

He maintained his hold on her afterward, a promise in his red eyes of what was in store for her later on, but clearly he had other business before they could get to a more proper reunion. "I'm curious, how long has it been since you killed someone, my lady? Since the Genovin, or have you had something to amuse yourself with since my departure?"

"Unfortunately, there are not as many opportunities to maim or kill here in the Isles as there might be elsewhere." She remained close to him, pleased that he held onto her robes as though he already owned her. That kind of possessiveness made her want him even more. "I do not recall killing anyone worth noticing since we fought the Genovin. Why do you ask?"

"I wanted to make sure you were properly bored before I supplied the cure for such a condition." He stepped slightly to one side so that she could see his ship again, though he didn't look away from her. He didn't need to. He knew what was behind him.

He could feel the heat of the wolves behind him even as they stood and glared at Daiva to try and intimidate her. Hassir knew his chosen mate well enough to know how futile their attempt would be, but they wouldn't have been Reefborn if they hadn't tried. There were two females standing behind him, both of them Fireborn, neither of them happy, glaring at Daiva with steam rising from their bodies as the snow hissed upon contact. "Daughters of the council members I told you about before. They are of the opinion that you are unworthy to be my mate."

Daiva raised an eyebrow as she looked past him but then she turned her attention back to Hassir. "So they intend to kill me?" She said it simply, as though she really only needed to clarify what was about to happen. Daiva looked at the females again, one of them scorching the wood of Hassir's ship as she clenched the side of the boat. Just to infuriate them further, she moved close to Hassir again and kissed along the side of his neck slowly. "Have you ever taken either of them as lovers?"

"No, but several of my subordinates have. They're reported to be adequate." He obviously didn't feel strongly on the subject. His grip on her robes remained through the kiss, and he similarly enjoyed her possessiveness. He truly appreciated a woman who knew what she wanted.

"Too bad. It would have made me enjoy their deaths just a little bit more." She ended her kisses along his neck with a nip to his skin before she stepped away. "I am a busy wolf." Daiva said loudly with her attention on the two females still on the ship. "Unless you've changed your mind about your intentions, it would be best for you to state them plainly so that we can get this over with."

Some of the other wolves nearby began to back away to the edges of the broad stone pier, but Hassir walked with her, crossing his arms over his chest, intending to watch what unfolded from the closest possible vantage point.

The two women stepped off the boat at her challenge, and she could see that neither of them was eyeing the other with any kind of suspicion. Clearly they decided to set aside their own differences in favor of killing an Isles bitch, so they could sort out their own competition later on their own terms.

"The one on the left is Sakala." Hassir informed her from just behind her shoulder. The woman was taller than Daiva, but leaner, with hair the color of bright gold, braided in a tight spiral down her back. "Stoneborn parents, litter of three Fireborn. She's killed both her siblings already in the past few years to ensure her inheritance of her parents' estates."

He gestured dismissively to the other wolf stalking toward her, with short silver hair cut in a close halo around her head. She was a fairly small wolf, and Daiva could tell by the way she moved that she was young, but there was a kind of madness in the girl's eyes that went beyond the usual savagery of Fireborn. "The other is Minsa. Mother is a Skyborn, never claimed by a father. Only survivor of her litter. Abandoned on the Burning Shore when she was a child and only recently returned to court."

"Are you going to tell her about our favorite foods too, my lord?" Sakala growled at him, clearly unhappy that they weren't being permitted to introduce themselves to the woman they intended to kill.

"It's only fair we get to sum you up the same way, I think." Minsa added, hanging back a little behind Sakala. "Water-eyed parents, only survivor of your litter after you let both your brothers die in front of you. Is that about right?"

Daiva looked the female up and down once before she decided to speak. "You have your version of the story, and I have mine. It will not matter to you what my version is." She clenched one hand into a fist until a few of her knuckles cracked. "That estate of your parents', do I get to claim it once you're dead?"

Sakala visibly bristled at that kind of insult, and Daiva could feel the heat off them both, but as she opened her mouth to respond, Hassir answered for her. "Our laws are fairly clear on that point. Sakala is the heir to her parents' property, and since they're nearing their decline, it's unlikely they will have any more children. Sakala's killer will have the right of inheritance she currently possesses."

"Sounds perfect. I need an estate for my siblings once we are mated." She replied to Hassir, though she still wasn't looking at him. Daiva shrugged off her robes so that she was only in a thin dress underneath, but she knew that she would rip through it once she necessarily had to shift during the fight. A large stone jumped up from the beach into Daiva's hand and she tossed it up playfully. "Who wants to die first?"

Hassir leaned in to give her a last kiss on the neck to wish her well for the fight, and then she could feel the heat of him recede slowly as Sakala stepped forward, not even bothering to look at Minsa as she did.

"Once you know you're about to die," the woman said as fire gathered through the air, streaming from the lanterns on the ship to trail along the ground on either side of her, "I would be grateful if you would show yourself in your wolf. Your pelt will be a warning to any others who would come between me and my lord."

"I would be grateful if *you* didn't. The last thing I want is your hideous fur laying around in my house, especially when I come between you and your lord." Daiva twisted the stone into a few amorphous shapes in her hand, familiarizing it with her touch. "In fact, I plan to do many things to your lord when this is finished that you will never have the opportunity to do yourself."

Without any further warning, Daiva shaped the stone in her hand into something that looked like a blade, and threw it as hard as she could at the woman's shoulder. They had come for a challenge, not a dance, and Daiva would fight dirty if it meant that Hassir was still hers by the end.

It glanced off Sakala's shoulder, and Daiva could see that she'd drawn first blood, but then the woman's fire became her own weapon. She unleashed at Daiva with a scream that sent the snowflakes around them flying in all directions. Her fire wasn't the generalized inferno that Daiva had seen Hassir produce. It was more like a focused stream of flame that glowed a menacing red, devouring the snow between them even as the storm began to intensify again.

Daiva didn't hesitate to shift immediately, ripping through her dress as she did so, but she went running after the Fireborn underneath the stream of fire. She threw herself on top of Sakala and knocked her backward, but the stream of fire caught her fur. Daiva immediately rolled off the dock and into the sand, putting the fire out before she jumped back up and into her human form. She pulled pillars up out of the ground through the sand that marched quickly toward the dock, spikes appearing and headed toward both Sakala, Minsa and whoever else was stupid enough to get in the way.

Sakala had shifted as well, into a wolf that was admittedly one of the more beautiful creatures Daiva had ever seen, in startling gold that reflected the light of her fires and seemingly nothing else. The flames she claimed held tight around her as she watched the stone march closer, and she found what she hoped was the quickest path off the dock to get to the sandy beach beside them.

The way the Isles bitch had pulled so much stone directly out of the ground and warped the pier so much in so short a time was shocking. Even with Stoneborn parents, Sakala had never seen someone use stone so quickly and effectively. She had been expecting slow strength, endurance, not the kind of rapid ferocity she was getting from Daiva. Sakala shifted again and knelt in the sand, sending wave after wave of fire toward the Stoneborn in front of her as she tried to stay away from the stone spikes. She knew that she was on the defensive, and she hated it, but she needed to rethink her strategy.

Unlike some other wolves, Daiva didn't play games when she fought. She remembered the way that Devon was killed, the way that her parents were slaughtered in front of her. It had been a game for Melyssa, and the taunts from Melyssa still haunted her. Daiva didn't care to prolong someone's death, even if they had asked for it. It had been months since she had seen Hassir. The fact that she was fighting for him so soon after seeing him again made her even more vicious and ferocious. She wanted him, and she did not like being challenged for what she wanted.

With the Fireborn still scalding her with flames at every chance, Daiva decided to go for a more direct approach. She pulled up a pillar right behind Sakala and ran after her as fast as she could, pulling out her special knife as she ran. It was held by a leather strap to her body, so even when she shifted, it didn't drop away like her clothing.

Sakala was caught off guard both by the column right behind her and by the fact that the Stoneborn seemed oblivious to the fire she was running through. Most of her opponents avoided the flames until Sakala could box them into a corner where they had no escape, where she could roast them alive and be done with them, but this Stoneborn . . . Sakala turned to reposition herself again, attempting to regain the tactical advantage in the fight with a final blast of fire in Daiva's face. She ran headlong into one of Daiva's pillars and was dazed for a moment, but it turned out to be just a moment too long.

Daiva pounced on Sakala the moment she was given the opportunity to do so, and she laid the Fireborn flat out on her back in the sand. Just as Daiva was sure that she was going to get blasted in the face with fire, her knife made contact with Sakala's throat.

There were burns all along Daiva's face and arms, but she hardly noticed as she kept the female pinned. "I told you. He's mine."

She took the knife and nearly cut off the female's head with the depth of the slash beneath her chin, and she got up quickly. Her blade was still dripping with blood at her side when she fixed her sight on her next battle. "One more to go."

Minsa was crouched on the edge of the dock looking down at her when she turned around, and the small woman was smiling in one of the most demented expressions Daiva had ever seen on a wolf. She actually laughed once, a high-pitched, almost whistling giggle as she laid her hands on the stone edge.

"Thank you. I never really liked her." The fire burning near Sakala hadn't been extinguished immediately upon her death, and Daiva couldn't move quite fast enough before it jumped from Sakala's dead hands to Daiva's knife, seeming to disappear inside the blade. In moments, though, the heat had clearly spread through the stone, and it was superheated against her hand before she could even draw a full breath.

Daiva growled loudly when she had to drop her own beloved knife, but she dropped the blade and shifted again in one swift movement. Daiva wasn't going to be intimidated or toyed with, and she wasn't going to allow herself to be forced onto the defensive. As long as she could move, she could run, and she would run after her enemy instead of away from them.

She bolted toward the crazed Fireborn, hoping to push her closer toward the water. There was plenty of stone in the shallows, but nothing for Minsa.

Minsa did scramble back at first, incredibly light on her feet as she avoided some of the obstacles that Daiva had thrown up earlier in the fight. In wolf form, Minsa knew Daiva couldn't directly control the stone beneath them, and that was certainly preferable to Minsa at the moment.

"Have you ever been to the Reef?" She asked in a light-hearted voice, as she turned human again for a moment to tumble past Daiva as she charged, putting her back on the landward side of the pier, walking backwards toward the shore. "It's a wonderful place. You would really enjoy my home on the Burning Shore. There are all kinds of wolves like you there."

Her footprints along the stone left orange marks as she

walked, and the fire in the stone only grew from there as it had grown in Daiva's knife; until there was an entire strip of the pier that was molten rock, just barely solid under its own weight. The pier shifted uncomfortably all along its length at the structural implications, but clearly Minsa didn't care.

"Wolves like me?" Daiva inquired loudly when she shifted back into her human form. She glanced at the molten rock that looked like its own river in the middle of the sand, and she headed out toward the water anyway. Once her feet were in the water up to her ankles, she stared at Minsa as massive boulders started to emerge out in the water.

As they slowly gathered up out of the water, Daiva's whole body shook with the amount of energy it took, but she shaped the boulders without even looking at them. They bent slowly into something that looked almost like a spout, and when the waves crashed over them, the water shot further off the rocks and onto the shore. The molten stone that Minsa created sizzled and steamed against the cold winter waters, but Daiva remained at a distance.

Her tactic certainly kept Minsa's molten stone at bay, but Minsa herself remained out of reach as well, as the orange glow of her power continued to creep over the beach for dozens of paces in every direction. The surf would cool the stone in one place for a while, but it continued to resurge afterward, brighter and brighter with each repetition.

"Wolves like you!" She answered with a smile, running her hands lovingly over the molten stone surface that her power created. "Insane Stoneborn who have no conception of where they belong. Fire belongs only to itself."

She looked at Minsa and pointed in the direction of Hassir before she decided to move out of the water and closer to her enemy. "That fire belongs to me." As Minsa stroked the molten surface lovingly, Daiva's hands twitched and shattered it in her face, throwing every piece up into her with as much force as Daiva could muster. She was getting tired, but she was still pushing as hard as she could. The water made her feet ache with cold, but Daiva didn't look away from her enemy.

The explosion of stone beneath her took Minsa off guard, and the supposedly-safe zone of molten rock she had created for herself clearly no longer held the sense of security it had the moment before. She stood back up with a few specks of liquid stone on her neck and torso, still just glaring at Daiva for the insult she'd just endured. The pure anger in her eyes manifested a moment later in white-hot flames bursting up from the ground all around her, born of the lava she was standing in. Minsa shifted into the small silver wolf she was, and leapt for Daiva's throat along with many of the flames she had called up, no longer interested in humiliating the Stoneborn with her lack of control over her own element, but interested only in blood.

Daiva let Minsa reach her without trying to dodge the wolf, and she wrapped her arms around the tiny female even though she was instantly engulfed in flames as well. Stoneborn were second only to Earthborn in physical strength, and she found a way to wrap her burning hands around Minsa's neck and tackle her to the ground. She could hear bones cracking, and even when she shifted she was able to sink her teeth into silver fur, but it was hard to tell what damage she was doing and what was being done to her in turn.

When the frenzy of the moment passed, the fire around her died, and the first thing she could feel was the spray of the ocean on her singed fur, both soothing with its coolness and biting with the salt in her several wounds. Her teeth had a difficult time dislodging from the spine of the female beneath her, cracked and torn as it was between Daiva and the sand, but Minsa was no longer moving, and the magma she left behind slowly returned to its normal state without her intervention.

Hassir walked toward her across the burning stone, hands swinging casually at his sides as he looked over the damage both to Daiva and to the dock around them. His people gathered to watch as well, but they all kept their distance. "Can you walk?"

She took several deep breaths in her wolf form before she shifted back into her human form and slowly attempted to get up. It took her some time, but Daiva was not about to accept help even from Hassir after fighting as hard as she did against the two females he'd brought with him. Her own blood, mixed with Minsa's, dripped down her body, and there were burns covering her skin, but she did not make a sound of complaint. "I am grateful there were not three. I do not know if I could have survived three."

"You could have." He said with confidence as he turned to walk with her, leaving the rest of his people behind on the ship. The snow was falling so thick that their presence and any evidence of the fight had been hidden by the storm, and he intended to keep it that way. "My people will take my ship back out to sea and wait for my summons. I remember your home being close by, is that correct?"

"Yes." She moved away from him momentarily to fetch her discarded robes, though they were wet from the snow and the spray. It was only when she put them on that he saw her wince, but that was the only show of pain that she allowed herself before she made it back to his side. "My home is close. My parents were Oceanborn. They built their home by the sea."

As she pulled her robe back on, he picked up her personal blade, still obviously heated from Minsa's attack, but the fire didn't bother Hassir. At his touch, Daiva could see the blade cool by degrees, and when he knew it was safe for her to handle, he moved close and returned it to the sheath at her side for her. "Good. I also assume your sister is a capable enough Forestborn to have a remedy for your burns on hand?"

"Yes, of course. There is plenty for my needs once I get back to my home." She finally allowed herself to look over at him as they walked, and she let out a heavy breath, since she was glad he was there with her and he was hers. "There is also a meal prepared, if you desire. There is little to hunt in this season."

"I'm sure it will be sufficient." He reassured her as they walked. She could feel the heat of him as she had before, but he didn't reach out with it as strongly as he had upon greeting her, allowing the snow to fall on her burnt skin to soothe it as they made their way down a broad stone avenue that ran near the coast away from the dock.

"You should know that your killing of Sakala is no light thing. The estates which belonged to her family comprise several small islands along the western edge of my kingdom. They are currently inhabited by mostly the slaves of her family and by a few wolf overseers of the lesser elements, but they are substantial in their own way. If you meant what you said about housing your brother and sister there, they will be comfortable."

"I meant what I said." She nodded as she thought about Taimon and Kaia, and though they wouldn't like to move away from the home they knew, she cared about their safety more. "I will not leave them here when I go to the Reef with you." She looked over at him and met his fiery eyes with hers, which only drew her a little closer to him again. "Other than that, her land does not matter to me. She stood between us and our plans. No one will stand between us."

"No, they will not." He reached up and put a warm hand along the back of her neck, one part of her body that was not singed or bleeding from the fight. The touch didn't last long because he knew she was weakened, but it was clear he had no interest in being away from her.

When they reached the gates of the estate and were admitted by the Stoneborn guards, Taimon was already headed down the front steps of their home at a run toward her, with Kaia not far behind. "What did you do?" He yelled the accusation at Hassir, and Daiva could feel the cold air around her already whipping itself into a frenzy to go along with her brother's mood. He looked just the slightest bit like Destin in that moment, but without the power or gravity behind his tone or the threat in his face to actually back up any promise of violence.

"He did not do this." Daiva responded firmly but softly, since he reminded her of Destin and she couldn't help but feel a tiny bit of emotion, especially while weakened. "There were two Fireborn females that intended to get in the way, and I killed them." She looked at her brother and sister, and back at Hassir. "Let us go inside where it is warmer."

Kaia was already shivering as she stared at her sister, calm as ever but burned and bleeding, and she shook her head. "Isn't he from the Reef? Why do we want to let him in the house if his people did this to you?"

"Because he is my intended mate, and I do not want him to stand out here in the cold when there is a meal waiting for all of us inside the house."

Taimon took the longest of anyone present to process what Daiva said. "He didn't . . . he's . . . you're going to . . . he's your *what?!?*" He exclaimed a little too loudly, his voice echoing off the walls surrounding their estate and shaking great piles of snow loose from the roof of their house. The snow came crashing down around them and Taimon had to jump out of the way of some falling icicles.

Taimon was already apologizing as he followed them back into the house and shut the door, but the look of confusion remained on his face, even though Hassir looked only amused. "Kaia, run and grab whatever burn salve you've got left. From the looks of her, she's gonna need all of it."

Kaia was still just as shocked as Taimon, and she ran off as she was told to get the salve, but not without looking back at the Fireborn several times as she ran. Her sister was going to mate with someone? Someone from the Reef? Destin would not have been happy with that, that was for sure.

Daiva pulled off her robes and took a moment to inspect what damage happened as a result of the fight. She went closer to the fire with her knife and seared some of the deeper wounds closed without making a single noise. Apparently her appreciation for fire had been more than any

Fireborn could have predicted, especially those who thought they could scare her with it.

After her deeper wounds were closed, she took a wet cloth brought by a slave and wiped away some blood. The burns she would have to tend to last. Taimon and Hassir were still in the room as she tended to her wounds, but she did not look up once. "Taimon, this is Hassir, Lord of the Reef. I have told you about him. You did not mishear me outside, I am sure. He is my intended mate." When she finally looked up, she looked into Taimon's eyes. "I do not know why it takes such an emotional response from you to generate that amount of power. You should practice to get that kind of result with your tutors."

"Oh. Sure. Fine. I'll do that. In the meantime, if you want another outburst like that out of me, you can get it! Any time you want!" He shouted again, echoing painfully through the house, since he had been surprised himself when he had managed to produce that kind of effect out of doors. Taimon wanted her to know that, emotional response or not, he was serious about being in shock. "And yes, I know who he is. Why do I know who he is? Because *everybody* knows who he is! Because he's from the Reef! The place even Devon wouldn't go to stay, because they all lose their minds as children and then laugh while they watch their sanity burn to a crisp!" He turned quickly to Hassir with a hand up, his inborn manners not forgotten. "No offense intended. Family business. You understand."

Daiva put one hand up to her ear and then she continued to stare at her brother. "I said I wanted you to practice with your power. I did not say I wanted to bleed from my ears." She blinked a few times and sighed. "Devon did not want to go to the Reef because he was too ambitious for the Reef. He wanted more than to live in his own element and to fight amongst those at the Reef, and look where that got him." Her look softened slightly, especially when Kaia came back into the room. "Hassir and I make a good match. The best that I could ever find for myself, certainly, and he is going to help us do what Destin wanted us to do. What our parents wanted us to do. Dethrone Melyssa and Cadmos."

"For what? So we can enthrone him in their place?" Taimon lowered his tone slightly, but his voice still boomed through the room at his uncontrolled outburst.

"What if you were enthroned in their place, Skyborn?" Hassir responded, finally joining the conversation as Kaia began to tend to Daiva nearby.

"Me?" Taimon gave a short, breathless laugh before he realized that the lord of the Reef wasn't likely to possess much of a sense of humor. "Why would I be the one taking their place? I'm not a prince, we're distant, *distant* cousins to the royal family, and besides, I don't want . . . no way. No way would I ever want that."

"No, of course you don't." Hassir said with a shrug and a smile. "Then why would I?"

"Because you . . ." Taimon could have sworn he had an answer to that question when he started speaking, but he trailed off incoherently, a hundred different insults running through his mind that he immediately considered were probably a bad idea to hurl in the direction of a Fireborn.

"I am lord of the Reef." Hassir restated pointedly. "My interest is in my own kingdom. Once Melyssa and Cadmos are dead, these Isles may do as they please. They can sink back into the sea, for all I care. I want them dead and I want my kingdom left alone." He nodded at Daiva. "Your sister and your people are capable of helping me accomplish that. So that all may benefit."

"Destin and I planned this revolution together." Daiva said in a tone that was as gentle as they would ever hear from her. "Once Hassir and I are mated and this begins, you and Kaia will go with Leander and Marella until everything is over, and then we will set up our life at the Reef. The Isles are not going to be our home anymore, and we'll be better for it. I do not want to see any more of my family die because Melyssa is terrified of our bloodline and our legacy."

Taimon was silent as Daiva laid out the next steps of

their plan so simply, looking back and forth between her and Hassir several times as Kaia tended quietly to Daiva's wounds. "You and Destin planned this together, but you couldn't trust me and Kaia enough to tell us what you had in mind before you brought your Fireborn into our house?"

Daiva hissed as Kaia rubbed the salve into her skin roughly, but she did not say anything to her sister. She had expected both Kaia and Taimon would be angry with her. "I knew that Chiara had her spies questioning Kaia all of the time, and I did not know if she would set her sights on you now that Destin is gone. I could not risk what she might pull from your minds, and I didn't want you killed because of it."

Taimon still obviously wasn't satisfied with that answer, but he realized that Daiva was the final authority in the family, and there was only so far he could push his protests before she grew even more angry with him. "You're going to need time to recover before anything else happens, so whatever plans you've made, I hope they can wait." He looked her over again and then looked over at Kaia, since he trusted her opinion more than anyone else's in the room. "What do you think, two, maybe three weeks? At least until we're past this coming Fulness."

"The burns won't fade for a while. They're deeper than they look." Kaia said when she slathered on a little more of the salve before she stepped away. "You should make sure you're healed before you go mating with a Fireborn, sister." Kaia moved to stand by Taimon and sighed in defeat as she started to walk away with him. "I don't think I'm hungry any more."

Daiva wanted to protest as they walked away, but she knew from the beginning they would not be happy with the plan because they were not included in it. Daiva wished that they could understand that they weren't ready to fight in something like this, and keeping them away from the information was the safest route. Instead, she let them leave before she turned toward Hassir. "I am glad you are here."

"As am I." He replied quietly, then waited for her to get up and accompanied her to her rooms. He didn't help her up and did nothing for her, but he did take her robes as she shuffled them off, and stood beside the beautiful marble slab that rested in the center of the room as her bed. "I am going to partake of the meal you mentioned, and then I will have Hadria send for your Heartborn friend Leander. Considering the storm, it may be some time before he arrives, but I'll come to wake you when he does, and we may begin finalizing our preparations."

"Of course." Her voice sounded tired as she went to sit on the edge of her marble bed. This was not the kind of welcome she intended when she thought about Hassir's arrival, but ultimately they were partners. Their plans and preparations had to continue. "Eat as much as you like. I'll be here."

He put out a hand and rested it lightly against the bottom of her chin as he looked down at her, standing between her knees at the edge of the bed. "As will I. Every time you wake or sleep, from now until the day someone finally claims the Reef from me along with my life."

He leaned down and kissed her almost gently, mindful of her burns. Through the touch, she could feel Hassir's own power moving through her, in a kind of taste of what was to come at the time of their mating, when the essence of who they were would be inextricably joined. The presence of his power made the burns feel just a bit more bearable, a bit more familiar, but could not take them away completely.

She needed rest, she needed to heal, and she needed strength for her body to be capable of doing either. The fire in his veins that fueled his life moved into her, to warm every end of her body in comfort. His power continued to churn inside her even after the kiss broke, like a living thing that had taken up residence in her blood and bones.

"Sleep well, Daiva."

EIGHTEEN

Destin was awake before most of the other inhabitants of the village on the shore. As soon as the rest of them stepped out of doors, they could hear him working down by the water's edge, sanding and scraping endlessly at the hull of the small vessel he'd made for himself.

The way he worked made many of those in the village nervous around him. As soon as he began each day, he worked with the ferocity of a demon until the sun went down and there was no more light for him to see by. That morning was no different, especially since that day was the day the entire village knew he intended to depart.

As he worked, he continued to curse himself as he had done for the past month of his stay among the humans, on what he had learned they referred to as the Free Isle. He had fallen asleep in Elyra's house and had not woken again until the Fulness several days later, when he'd found himself caged in the house for the night. In the morning, the humans found nothing damaged and nothing out of place besides Destin in a different corner of the room than he'd been in before, so he was permitted to run free on the High Night, though he noticed most of the village locked themselves indoors while he hunted for his meals.

The month following had not improved his mood or his

frustration, as winter storms ripped through the island and blanketed everything in snow and ice, including the trees he had hoped to use to build his boat. The ice was hardly an issue for Destin, but it had rendered the wood unworkable, at least for the time being.

The work had progressed slowly, and he had been forced to pass a second Fulness with the humans just as the boat neared completion. It had warmed him, though, to rise on the first morning of the Fulness and see several of the humans working on the boat for him while he was unable to do so. He knew it was mostly because they wanted to speed him on his way, but he appreciated their help nonetheless. With the Fulness past, he hoped to be on the move even before the sun set, but there was still much to do by way of gathering supplies he would need for the journey home.

When he saw Elyra coming down the beach with a small basket, he wasn't surprised. He stopped in his work long enough to smile up at her, and ran a hand through his hair to get it out of his face. He looked a great deal more human than he had when he first arrived on her shore, but there was still something undeniably wild about the man that didn't go away even when he was in skin instead of fur. "Good morning."

"Good morning, Destin." She approached him with the basket and a similar smile. "You look like you are quite ready to find your way home." Elyra held out the basket, which was heavier than he thought it would be when he took it from her hands. "There is dried meat and fruit in there to last during your trip. The bread might last you a day or two."

He looked over the basket twice as he crouched on the side of the ship near her. "These are from your winter stores." He said with concern in his voice. "Any winter that starts as early as this one will last longer into the spring. You should hold onto these for yourself."

"I will be perfectly well without them." She replied without any hesitation. "You have helped me in a lot of ways, Destin. This is the least I can give to thank you."

"I think permitting me to share your fire and your home for two Fulnesses is more than enough thanks for anything I've done." He had helped as best he could in their small community during the time he'd been with them. He cleared the snow from the entire settlement and packed the ice so thick around some of the common areas that it actually insulated them from the cold, but such things had been nothing more than a trifle for him in the face of the hatred he could feel from all of the humans nearby every day. "I am the one in your debt, Elder, not you in mine."

She looked over at his boat and back up at him before she spoke again. "I am sure your family will be glad to see you. Do you have everything you might need?"

"Almost." He yanked a rope into place and looked over his work to make sure it would hold. There were just a few items he needed to secure before he got on his way, but there was something more pressing he wanted to be sure of before he left. "Beylan's daughter brought over some bread for me this morning as well. I'd like to talk to you about something, if I may. Will you share it with me?"

"Of course." She nodded toward her house. "Let's go where there's a fire to keep us warm." After he secured his boat, Elyra walked with him back to her house and they sat down at the table. "What's on your mind?"

He settled into the chair and broke the bread, dipping his own in the small plate of fruit preserves that came with it. "I'd like for you and the rest of the Elders to know something about what's going to happen when I go home." He chewed slowly, his eyes lingering on the bread as if it would answer his uncertainties about the future in front of him. "I'm going home to start a war."

Her eyes widened slightly, but she didn't react otherwise, since she did not know what that would really mean to her. Or what he thought it meant to her. Their island was not about to get involved in a war between wolves. "I see. Why do you want us to know about it? There is no way that we can help you with that, and no one would want to."

"There is one way. And I hope you will want to." The rest of the bread remained untouched between them at his announcement. There had been secrets behind his eyes since he arrived. In the hesitation, she could see them forming themselves into words finally ready to be shared.

"If you came from the Isles, then you know of Chainhome. Or perhaps you lived there yourself at one time. You know how many humans live there as our slaves. There are easily more than a thousand there, and thousands more throughout the rest of the Queen's Isle." His fingers shook slightly with the weight of the plans he had in mind, but he was committed to his purpose, more than ever before. "I mean to free them, if they wish to be free. And when my people and I go to war with the Queen, any humans who wish to leave will leave the Isles with us."

"You mean to free them." She repeated slowly since she had a hard time believing that he would be able to accomplish what he proposed. "And I assume when you say that you will free them, that means that you don't intend to keep them as slaves of your own. Why?"

"Because I love one of them." He said simply, though it was one of the first times he had ever actually admitted as much to anyone but Adriana herself. "And there are complications regarding my relationship with the royal family which prevent us from living in peace beneath their rule."

"You're starting a war with your own kind over a human?" Elyra could hardly believe her ears, but she let out a chuckle as she sat there across the table from him. "You know, if you had mentioned that after you arrived, I think a lot more people around here would have liked you." She shook her head slowly as she thought about what he was planning to do. "So where do we come in? Are you going to bring your human here and leave her after a war? That does not seem likely."

"No. I intend to bring them all here." He watched her

carefully as he spoke, watching for any signs of anger or rejection in her expression. He knew he was asking a great deal of her people to accept strangers, but he also knew from a month of experience that her people were serious about saving as many humans as they could. He was telling her that he could accomplish in a single revolution more than they could hope to accomplish in decades of picking off slaves from one island or another. "All I ask is that you and the other Elders consider permitting me and a small group of my followers to remain here for a time afterward, until we are able to find a new home for ourselves elsewhere."

"We will gladly take everyone in and do what we can. I am certain that there will be those that argue against wolves coming along, but if you can bring us that many humans, then you deserve a temporary home here." Elyra reached out to touch his hand lightly. "Do you really think you can do it?"

He was grateful in that moment that she'd been kept by an Oceanborn so many years before, because he didn't have to explain the tears that escaped his eyes as she agreed without hesitation. He had grown to respect and admire Elyra for everything she had helped to make of her world, and he was glad to have someone like her on his side, no matter the opposition he knew she would face from the other Elders or the opposition he would face from the rest of the Isles upon his return.

"They believe I'm dead, and for all I know, my siblings may be dead already as well. But as soon as I can bring my people together from all the Isles, they'll know otherwise. Yes, I believe I can do it."

Elyra actually smiled at his tears and picked up a small cloth off the table and slid it over to him. "Your human is lucky. Wolf or not, there are not many people in this world who would start a war for the one they love."

"Starting a war is not going to be the hard part." He nodded his thanks for the cloth, but he didn't need it, the water droplets disappearing in his beard or otherwise quickly fleeing his face once the moment of emotion passed. "Finishing it will be." He took in a deep breath and glanced at the window before looking back at Elyra. "You believe you can convince the other Elders not to kill us on arrival?"

"As long as they are convinced you will leave and leave us in peace, then they will be flexible. I have a lot more power than I like to show." She smirked. "I don't know how they would think that you will hurt us if you bring humans to us. Don't worry about what happens when you get here, just worry about getting here."

"I'll do that." He promised quietly, reaching out to pat her hand once as he stood up slowly to leave her home, walking the short path between her door and the broad shore. It wasn't as though he had anyone else in particular to say goodbye to in the village, so he just stood by the side of his boat for a moment and looked the place over, hoping to see it again soon. "Thank you, Elder."

He stepped into his boat and pulled up a few of the braces that kept it in place, as he saw a few of Elyra's people beginning to gather up the shore. He wondered if they wanted to see him go with their own eyes so they could be sure he was gone. He gave them a wave that only a few of them returned, then turned to face the sea and took his accustomed place at the stern.

The ocean rose calmly from where it lingered at a safe distance, a portion of it swelling up the beach like some kind of rapid high tide, until a large pool of it gathered around the boat. The remaining braces fell off as it righted itself in the water, and Destin held on for a few moments just to make sure that nothing was wrong, even though he'd tested it previously just to be sure.

Once he was satisfied that the boat was at least provisionally seaworthy, he relaxed a little against the short railing of the stern, and the pool of water he'd called up from the ocean swept him rapidly off the sand and into the waves. He looked back once to see Elyra again, but once he'd given her a final wave, the sea rose behind his boat and plunged it into high speed across the surface, skipping almost like a stone under the power of the ocean pushing it along.

The storms of the winter were far from over, and Elyra's companions had been able to give him only the most rudimentary instructions as to how they normally navigated between the Isles, but he knew that he would know familiar waters when he reached them. If he reached them.

He shook his head to put all such thoughts out of his mind, and narrowed his eyes to focus on the horizon, and the home that was too many days away for his taste.

"Great mother beneath us," he whispered into the spray kicked up by the waves he worshiped, "see me safely home, and help me set to right all that has been done to my family and your children. I have never dishonored you, nor will I ever. Give me safe passage, that I may continue to make my home upon your shoulders."

He closed his eyes for a moment, hoping that his gods were listening, though he knew better than to expect certainty one way or the other. All he could do was hope, but hope was enough.

* * * * *

After a solid day of mostly sleep and a meal or two, Daiva was fully recovered from her burns and injuries in the fight for Hassir. She sat up slowly from her marble slab, which still had an imprint of her body in it. It moved beneath her like water, bending and rippling with ease, but once she got up from the marble, it instantly went rigid behind her.

Daiva stretched lazily as she headed toward a small table in her room where there was always a pitcher of water, but as soon as she noticed someone else was in the room, she momentarily froze. Hassir was in a chair by the fire, and it appeared he was reading over a communication by parchment before he tossed it into the flames.

"You're here." For some reason she thought he would go back to his ship, even though he mentioned staying back with her until they saw everything through. She hadn't expected him in her room. Daiva didn't move to cover her nudity, most wolves rarely did, as shifting in and out of their wolf form was more work with strict modesty. There was no reason to hide their skin, as they never hid their fur. She proceeded with quenching her thirst and moved to brush out her brown hair and plait it to keep it out of her way. "I suppose you did say you would stay."

"I did. But you would have been forgiven for forgetting, given the state you were in at the time." In the style of many of the wolves of the Reef, the only clothing he wore was a wrap of simple black cloth at his hips that was tied at one side, falling around his calves. It settled around him as he stood and approached her, his eyes tracking over her body to look at the various sites of her more prominent injuries from the day before. "You appear well-recovered."

Daiva looked down at herself as well, though she didn't feel any aches. The burns had healed completely, and any cuts or bruises were also similarly gone without a trace. She reached up to her shoulder, and the worst of her burns had healed as well. "Nothing a warm bed of marble cannot repair. Unless perhaps I lose a limb."

"That would be an impressive feat. I've never seen restoration on quite that scale, with any element." He stepped closer to her, following her own look to her shoulder as if he was there to give his own inspection of the results. "I have rarely seen anyone fight with the skill you showed that day. Who was your instructor?" He raised one hand to her shoulder, brushing aside some of the light stone dust that I settled on her skin so he could continue his inspection.

"My instructor? My father, if I can give anyone credit. My parents were more peaceful people than I am. Rebels, they did raise, however." Daiva watched curiously as he inspected her. "If you're looking to judge me on my physical attributes, I can answer any questions. I was not raised in a harsh environment, but before Devon's death, I went frequently among Stoneborn and Earthborn to fight in a pit, and won more than I lost. Devon and I used to go together, Destin would be there to drag us home if needed. Otherwise, I'm healthy and have no reason for concern regarding reproduction, if that is also a curiosity. I have no children, so that has not yet been tested. We did risk it when you were here before."

"I have no concerns on that score. Everything I know about you, either directly or by reputation, convinces me of your honesty on all counts. If you had any concerns that would render you a liability to me and my continued rule of the Reef, I believe you would have made them known long before now."

He walked around her for the inspection, his hand never leaving her skin as he considered her. "As for your ability, you proved that on the docks, in my eyes. Word of that challenge will spread through the Reef when those who witnessed it return home. My people will know by reputation that it would be a mistake to challenge you."

"I expect that they will test it again, regardless." His touch was warmer than the rest of the room, and more than once it sent shivers down her spine from the way his hand traveled a path along her skin. He could feel and see that her body was defined enough to show strength, but she also had curves at her hips, and thighs that were not merely skin and bones. Daiva had more softness than she had tight muscle, which also made her very different from her younger siblings. Taimon and Kaia were taller, thinner, but they were still much younger. Daiva had the body of a female who chose to look the way she did, strength and curves both.

"And you will destroy them as you destroyed the challengers on the docks." He sounded entirely confident in her abilities, coming around to stand in front of her again. "Once we are finished with Melyssa and her sycophants, of course. First things first."

"First things first." She agreed as she met his eyes momentarily before she stepped up to him. "Are you inspecting me or are you actually teasing me?"

"I am appreciating you." He corrected, grinning as he met her eyes. "Something I intend to do frequently and for extended periods when we are mated and we have returned to the Reef." His hands were warm as they rose to her neck, brushing her braid back over her shoulders. His thumbs rubbed along her jawline to tilt her head back.

"Too often, even my own people feel the need to retreat after they've been threatened. To recover. For you, I imagine if Melyssa had walked in here even the moment you were ready to collapse, you would have done away with her." The red of his eyes was dark enough to resemble blood in the dim lighting of the room. His eyes dropped to take in the full sight of her in a slow sweep that was as scorching as his touch at her skin. "I enjoy that about you."

His perusal and praise at the same time was more than enough to ensnare her attention for a very different reason. She reached out to run a hand over his exposed chest, but her touch didn't have heat like his. At least not a Fireborn type of heat. "Typically I prefer some opportunity to strategize. But if I have learned anything between my two brothers, it is best to employ simple strategy, then dive in wholeheartedly."

"Enthusiasm does sometimes have a way of making up the difference for a lack of opportunity to plan." He stepped into her touch, kissing her with warmth in his lips as if to wish her the very best of mornings, taking his time to celebrate the fact that she had woken up rejuvenated.

She made a small noise of pleasure as he kissed her, but she wrapped one arm around his neck so she could hold him in place. Daiva ran her other hand slowly across his side. "Our mating will start a war. I better enjoy you now while I am not currently fighting to kill Melyssa."

His body was already responding to her as she held herself against him. He let go of her only to pull aside the knot on the fabric at his waist to toss it aside on the floor, his eyes never leaving hers. "You are welcome to enjoy me whenever and however you wish, both before and after our war. When the killing starts, I do prefer to remain focused on the pleasure of that, rather than any other."

"I like that about you. I appreciate your focus and drive to complete what you set out to do." Daiva kissed his lips again before she let her hands explore further, now that he was also naked. "Enjoying you during the Fulness is one thing. Enjoying you now means I have a little more control." She bit down on his shoulder, but not hard enough to break skin. "If you burn me, I don't mind. Sometimes Fireborn think they need to hold back. I don't want that."

"You're not the only one with more control away from the Fulness." His hand warmed as it cupped her breast, his fingertips nearly scorching the skin, but stopping short right at the edge between pleasure and pain. "When we are mated, and you share my power, I will have you in the middle of a raging inferno, and you will feel only me. Until then, it will have to be your element for our bed."

Her breast throbbed in the best way, which compelled her to answer his promise with a kiss that nearly bruised. He definitely had the power to burn her alive, but she was the one who had the power to break his bones with no effort at all.

She pulled him back to her bed, and when they collapsed into it, it was as soft as water. He laid back and she threw herself on top of him. If she wanted to, she could trap him in the marble and take complete control. She considered it as she licked and nipped her way across his skin. "Is it possible to torture the Lord of the Reef like this? Or are you immune to being tortured by pleasure?"

"I've known wolves who consider themselves immune to pain. I pity any who consider themselves immune to pleasure." He laid back as she had placed him, lingering with his arms along the stone as if giving her the opportunity to shackle him if she was so inclined. When she didn't, he propped himself up on his elbows just enough to be able to watch her and her progress.

Daiva made her way down his body to take his cock into her mouth, and while she greedily laved up and down, one of his wrists found itself encased in hardened marble. It prevented him with one hand, but she only acted more excited when he gripped her head with his other hand, his fingers digging into her scalp. When she popped off, she licked slowly around the head. "I've been entirely wrapped up in the rebellion. I need this."

"There should never . . . be more work than pleasure in life. Even for those who rule others." He didn't fight the stone that bound his wrist, but he growled in pleasure as her stone bed moved to support him so he could watch what she was doing to him. The woman's confidence was breathtaking in the best of all possible ways. "The celebrations . . . of our victory . . . will last a lifetime. A lifetime to which I am very much looking forward."

"Your heir will be the ruler of the Reef, and Melyssa's time as queen will not even be a memory." Daiva didn't resist or struggle even when his hips bucked against her mouth, but she did punish him by sucking harder and yet not allowing him to reach climax. When she pulled away again, even against his hand in her hair, a tendril of marble whipped out to bind his other wrist. "Now you're really caught. My lord."

"I've been in worse positions. Certainly less pleasant ones." He didn't struggle against his bindings any more than to test the strength of them, the commitment and solidity of the stone. "I would say that you have me at your mercy, but I know you well enough by now to know that you have none."

The marble reclined a little and she straddled him again, her knees at his waist as she slowly lowered her body against his. Her breasts pressed against his chest and she ran her nose against the column of his throat. "I will confess that I prefer your company to your distance."

"Good." He growled his approval as she explored him at her leisure. His skin was a blanket of scars, like many wolves she'd known, scars were true testaments to the challenges he had endured and survived. Only the deepest injuries would leave scars at the rate wolves could heal. "I have no intention of taking you as Lady of the Reef only to leave you behind when I move about our dominion. You should accustom yourself to my company."

"Excellent. I vastly prefer the notion of fighting at your side. I wouldn't tolerate being left behind." Daiva bit his skin in a few more places before she slid herself down on his rigid cock. Daiva cried out as he filled her completely, her arousal quite obvious as she slid up slowly. Going slow was torture for her when she just wanted to fuck him wildly, but now that she had control, she wanted to keep it. She also knew that they wouldn't have time to savor each other in the coming days. This was her chance.

The heat of him suffused every part of his body, steady and inviting under every touch. He laid his head back against the stone under her control, molding itself to every contour of his body to let her have every bit of leverage against him she liked. "You told me not to hold back about burning you, yet you decide to be gentle with me?" He lifted his head enough to give her a challenging look through the growl in his chest. "Harder, my lady. I am not fragile."

"I'm savoring. And teasing. There is a difference." She leaned down to kiss him, but afterwards she had his lip between her teeth, and she bit hard enough to draw droplets of blood she then licked up. "Don't tell me what to do." The marble gripped his backside along with his wrists before she straightened up and stared into his dark ruby eyes but she did increase her pace and fervor although she didn't give him any opportunity to touch her. He just had to watch as she rode him.

Even restrained, the lord of the Reef was never powerless. The harder she rode him, the more of his power moved through them both, scorching through her veins, as foreign as it was to her nature. The recuperating sleep she'd had in stone was one thing, but his own power afforded no such rest, no such contentment. It wanted more, always and everywhere, from him, from her, from the world. It was a demanding, bottomless resource offering a sip of itself to be tasted.

His wild Fireborn energy demanded, and she gave in. She never liked to be out of control, but in the moment, all she could think about was chasing her climax on his cock. Daiva released his hands because she wanted his touch, but she didn't look away as she gripped his shoulders. Her grip was definitely bruising his skin, but she couldn't stop now. She was so close to climax that she was groaning with each thrust.

When his hands were free, all he did was encourage her further, grabbing her hard by the waist to pull her into him roughly. His hands were a sudden rush of heat against her hips, scalding her skin with the rush of power between them. His own climax was becoming a pressing need, driving out all thoughts of teasing or holding back. But even as his own power flowed in her, he could feel her Stoneborn nature settling him, helping him to hold back for as long as she wished to savor him before they both took what they wanted from the other.

His scalding touch only heightened her pleasure with the stinging against her skin, and she couldn't hold out. She arched back slightly on top of him and he could feel her body lock up like a vise around him. Daiva grabbed onto him and kept thrusting her hips against him so she could prolong her pleasure. Just when she thought she was coming down, he slid his heated hand between them and his hot fingers against her clit had the marble around them cracking under her cries of pleasure.

"More." He commanded, locking eyes with her as hers lost focus, his other scalding hand gripping her thigh as her legs shook under waves of pleasure.

Even if she didn't want to bend to his command, her

body had other ideas, and no one had given her the kind of pleasure Hassir was capable of. Her hands still gripped his shoulders but he could feel her hold back from breaking his bones, only just so, as his touch sent her through another intense climax. Her fingers dug into his skin and drew blood, but every time he burned hotter, she loved it even more. He could brand her skin and she would moan his name.

The frenzy of her pleasure, her strength, the way she shook as she rode him, was enough to send him into his own orgasm. He wasn't shy about his own cries of pleasure, Daiva's name roaring out of his throat to echo off the stone of the house she had built for herself and her family. She was powerful, and demanding, and he loved every moment.

The floor cracked beneath them, as well as a few walls, but she would worry about mending them later. Once the inferno of pleasure had torn through them both, Daiva collapsed gracefully on top of him, dripping in sweat, extremely relaxed and satisfied. Other than sex with Hassir during the Fulness, this was the best thing she could ask for. Not only were they compatible in goals and ambitions, but clearly they were compatible lovers. "That was . . . absolutely excellent."

Hassir relished the way she clung to him even after their shared climax, the pleasure and the power of it lingering in their bodies by way of the shared connection. Some things remained instinctive in both halves of their dual nature. The way she writhed against him in satisfaction had the stone rumbling beneath him in time with the growls in his chest. "You conquer in this as you do everything else." The compliment crackled from him like the low coals of a bonfire, his hands moving constantly over her back to excite and soothe the muscles along her spine.

She basked in his compliment, feeling more confident than ever that they were a match made in perfection. Daiva slowly stretched out on top of him before she met his lips with a languid kiss. "Let's do that again. Then prepare ourselves to kill Melyssa and her family."

D. Brumbley

NINETEEN

Adriana wanted to growl like a wolf as soon as she saw Miris was on guard again, but she was getting too big and she was too tired to put up much of a fight. She glared at him when she passed by, since she couldn't just ignore him. "Back again, I see."

"I just can't get enough, you know that." He was sitting off to one side of the platform that guarded the gates of Chainhome. A link of the gate swayed to hold itself in front of her to prevent her from entering. He never could get enough of making Adriana's life miserable. "You smell like piss. Been assigned down at the tannery this afternoon, or are you just that terrible at holding your bladder when you look like you're about to pop like a ripe melon?"

"My bladder works just fine. Are you sure you aren't the one that smells like piss?" She swatted at the chain in front of her. "Let me pass. You wouldn't want Chiara to catch you antagonizing a female who is about to give birth. Then she might have to punish you like everyone has been talking about. How do you like being her sex toy, anyway?"

"It's a pretty good life. I'm glad you asked." The chain swatted right back at her hands, smacking her on the knuckles to chastise her without moving to let her through. "There's something to be said for a woman who knows what you want from her the moment you want it."

"Don't be fooled. The more time you spend buried inside her, the more you become her pet. What you think you're going to get from Chiara is beyond me. She doesn't think any more of you than she does any human in Chainhome. Are you going to let me pass?"

He was quiet as he considered that, but it still didn't seem to faze him at all, and he shook his head at her. "The reason why I'm beyond you, Ana, is that I understand how this world works, and you never have. I'd have thought losing your lover would have taught you that, but I guess you must not have missed him that much in the first place."

"He's dead." She replied sharply as she grabbed onto the chain that continued to wave in front of her face. "You remind me of that all the time. What else is there to say about him?"

"Apparently not much." He shrugged and let her pass finally, since there was no point continuing to torment her if she was so dense she couldn't understand what was wrong with her.

When his sister died and he lived, Miris had lived as a silent shell for months, the sister who had been his one true friend his entire life stolen from him by chance and her own hopes. He could still feel the anger of her loss inside him every day, though Chiara was the only one who'd ever even known what it was that made him so angry most of the time.

Adriana, on the other hand, had lost the man he'd heard her profess to love, heard her claim he was her entire world, and had moved on within weeks to a barefaced boy. She'd spent her days since the captain's disappearance laughing, buried in the boy's arms night and day, and it made Miris sick just to look at her. "Get inside where it's cold. It's where you belong."

"Maybe once everyone is inside, you can crawl in your cell for old time's sake." Adriana took a deep breath as soon as she was able to get past Miris, and closed her eyes so that she wouldn't cry. Why did he have to torment her about Destin? He had lost someone dear to him too, didn't he know how horrible it was to be reminded day in and day out? Especially when she had Shian to think about, and Shian needed her.

Shian was already in their cell when she arrived, and one of the Stoneborn nearby let her in, sealing up the bars behind her. He was sitting up against the bars, since the lamps were out in the hallway and he could feel the meager heat from them on his back as he mended one of their blankets. "Is everything alright? They didn't tell me where you were."

"I'm fine. I'm sorry, I was held up by Miris." She looked over at the bucket of water, and she knew it would be cold but all she could think about was that Miris said she smelled horrible. She pulled off her clothing quickly and grabbed a rag.

He wasn't sure why she was so intent on getting clean in such low temperatures, but while she cleaned herself off, he took her dress and laid it aside to be washed, then got out her second one, since they were only ever allowed to have two sets of clothing. He put out one of the blankets as well, for her to dry herself off with, since he knew she'd need it. "I thought he was off with Chiara tonight. The Fulness is coming up, isn't that normally when she comes by to take him off our backs for a while?"

"I wish she would." She rubbed her skin raw before she sighed and shivered from the cold air hitting her wet skin. "Do I smell horrible?"

That immediately confused him, but it wasn't the strangest question anyone had ever asked him. He got up and went over to her and gave her an obligatory sniff, but then leaned in and kissed her freshly-washed shoulder. "No, you smell fine to me. Is it me? I was messing with some of the sheep herds earlier today."

"No, I . . . Miris said . . ." She shook her head and grabbed a blanket to dry off. "I'm sorry. I don't know what is wrong with me today. It must be because of the baby." Adriana gave him a weak smile and kissed him gently before she continued to dry herself off. "They will be bringing the food around soon, I'm sure."

He helped her dry off, since he didn't want her to freeze, then helped her quickly into her dress and his spare pants just for good measure to keep her warm. Once she was dressed, he went with her back to the bars of their cage to sit with their backs toward the pathetic fire that was burning too far away in the center of the corridor for light. "Just ignore him. I haven't said more than three words to him since I got here, and he generally leaves me alone. Maybe eventually he'll do the same with you."

"I don't think that will ever happen." She leaned into Shian, then looped her arm with his as she snuggled close. "I can't believe your pants don't fall off of me. That's a bad sign."

"Hey, I like those pants." He said with a chuckle, moving so that the warmth of his breath would help to defrost her hair as he spoke. "One of my favorite people made them for me."

"I'm glad I'm one of your favorite people." She smiled up at him and closed her eyes again. "I think this baby is going to take over my spot, though. You spend an awful lot of time telling him or her how much you love them."

"Yes, well, if my experience of babies back home is accurate, I'm going to spend a lot of the next year telling him to be quiet, so don't worry, it'll balance out eventually." He put a hand along her stomach as if to say hello to the little one, then put his arm around Adriana to keep her warm. "No one's taking over your spot. This cell isn't big enough for them to throw any more women in here for me anyway."

Adriana gasped as if she was scandalized by what he said. "What? More women? Is that what you want?" She jabbed his side with her finger before she laughed against his arm. "You are a greedy man."

"Well, clearly I'm a very useful piece of property for our masters when it comes to getting women pregnant. All I'm saying is that I could understand if they were to put a few more in here with us." He chuckled and shook his head. "No, that I could not handle. Not the life for me."

"Aren't you the confident, studly man?" She moved into his lap as she usually did and then remained close against him for warmth. "What life would you choose, if you could choose it?"

"Wow. You *have* had a rough day." He smoothed her hair back over her ears and pulled the mostly-mended blanket up over her back. "You mean what would I do with my time if it was mine? Or what kind of work would I choose to do?"

"Yes. Let's suppose that tomorrow they let us out and we could do whatever we pleased for a solid week. What would you want to do?"

"Besides sleep by a fire somewhere?" Just the thought made him feel colder, so he brushed it aside. "I think I'd like to go work in the palace, actually. Running errands for the royal family, running messages, summoning nobles to meetings, things like that. It would be interesting to just . . . know what's going on. Be in the middle of things but not the target of things for a change."

Adriana knew how she would want to spend a week away from Chainhome, but she didn't say anything about that. There was no reason to want the impossible, not now, not anymore. "Sleeping by a fire sounds pretty good."

"I'm sorry. I'm no Fireborn." He said with a laugh, and kissed along her cheek. "Are you still feeling alright? After the night you had a few weeks ago . . ."

"Thank goodness you are not a Fireborn. I *do not* want to sleep by a Fireborn." She held tighter to him and nodded, though she was still so grateful for his concern. "I'm alright." Adriana ran a hand along her stomach slowly. "I think the baby is eager to come out and meet you, though."

"Just as long as it isn't too eager. I don't want this to be the first place it sees. They should've taken you up to the

birthing halls already. I still don't know why they haven't."
It was warmer there, and the slaves were much better cared
for in the days before and immediately after their children
finally arrived. Spring was right around the corner, but the
world was still much too cold a place for an infant to survive.

"Because wolves like Miris think that I'm lying in order
to get up where it is warmer." She sighed as she ran her hand
over her stomach again. "I don't want to be alone up there.
I want to be with you."

"Well *I'm* certainly not going to birth anything. I
wouldn't survive anything like that and you know it."

"I am hoping for a quick birth, but they never go
according to any sort of plan." She shivered a little bit, but
he just held her tighter to his chest. "I think for now,
though, I'll try to get some sleep. It's hard to get any rest
once the kicking starts."

He moved with her toward their pallet, and smoothed it
out for her as much as he could before he laid down, waiting
for her to join him before he tucked the blanket around
them as always. He sighed deeply once they were lying down
and she was against him, since the world went back to
feeling right as soon as the blanket was closed around them.
"I keep telling him to be kind to his mother. I hope he
listens."

"He usually does if you keep your hand there." She
moved his hand so that it rested on the side of her belly.
"And it keeps me warmer."

Keeping Adriana warm had become one of his primary
goals in life, and he kissed the back of her shoulder to let
her know that he took his duties very seriously. Shian's
fingers traced lazy caresses over the fabric of her dress as
the two of them drifted off to sleep.

The primary sound that could be heard over the howl of
the winter wind outside was the clink of Miris' footsteps as
he walked the halls of Chainhome, trading off with the other
guard standing watch by the gate to inspect the prisoners for
any signs of trouble. He passed by the fires slowly, since the

weak watch-fire that they kept burning did nothing to dull the edge of the wind. Being inside, however dismal and lonely most of the cells were, was still preferable to being outside alone.

When he finally returned to relieve his Stoneborn companion, the wolf gave him an accusatory glare, clearly aware of how much Miris had dawdled in returning to his post. Miris shook his head and sat by the fire, his eyes on the long ramp that led up to the prison. He scanned the surroundings every few minutes just to make sure he kept watch on everything moving in the middle of the night. When he was satisfied there was nothing close, he reached into the bag at his side and drew out the contents, going to work on his most recent project by firelight.

He had switched the watch back and forth with the Stoneborn three times when he came back out and noticed a shape down at the water's edge that hadn't been there before. It was too small to be a proper ship, but Miris wondered if some fishing vessel hadn't washed ashore in one of the storms, or been run aground by the wind. He looked at the front gate of the prison and gestured at the iron bars to close, sealing the place shut in one piece of solid metal before he made his way down the steep incline to investigate. If a wolf had died of their own stupidity, he'd be damned if he wasn't going to have the privilege of being there to see it.

As he approached, his spear held non-threateningly in one hand, he could see the boat had actually been moored, after a fashion, and tied up against the rocks tightly. He got close enough to look down at the boat directly, looking for any sign of a passenger or any belongings left behind; only to have a tendril of water creep up right below him and slap him lightly across the face before falling back in the water.

Completely alert, his spear held ready for a fight, Miris whirled, looking for the source of the jab. If someone was picking a fight, they had picked the wrong night to do so, and the ocean water was incredibly cold.

"Alright, who is it?" He growled into the darkness, looking back along the path from Chainhome and seeing no one. "If you're looking to dance, then come right on out and let's do it, then!" He growled low in his throat and turned his spear in every direction, since he had no idea of the direction the threat might come from, or even what form it would take.

The outline of a body disengaged itself from the stone and stood calmly on the path between Miris and his post, hands out to the sides and the hood on its cloak down.

"Do you know me, Miris?" The voice from the figure said quietly, even gently, as it took a few steps closer. "I'm glad, for my own purposes, to see that they still have you guarding Chainhome, though I'm sure there are other assignments you would prefer."

It wasn't in Miris to be fearful of anyone or anything on first sight, but in that moment, he made an exception. The voice belonged to one of the few wolves he had ever learned to both respect and fear. Except . . . that wolf was also dead.

"Captain?" Miris' voice shook slightly as he hung onto his spear tightly, looking around to see if he'd been ambushed alone or if the Oceanborn had others with him.

"Good. Your memory is still intact, along with the rest of you." Destin descended a few steps along the path so that Miris could see him clearly, his hands still clasped in front of him as he did so. "I've come back from the dead, but it's not a talent many wolves come by naturally. I would not advise testing that notion by defying me right now."

Miris stayed completely still as Destin approached, and finally managed to stand up straighter, planting his spear in the ground beside him as he tried to appear less terrified than he was. All he could see flashing before his mind was the way the ocean had looked the day Destin had drawn it up to swallow him. He'd been battered, bruised, and had broken several limbs that day under Destin's assault. It had taken weeks to heal and get himself back in a condition to do anything for himself. All because he had made a single disparaging comment to Adriana.

If Destin knew what the last few months of his absence had been like, Miris was as good as dead.

"Is my family alive?" Destin asked sharply as he came to stand within a few steps of Miris. He was easily within reach of the Ironborn's spear, but didn't seem concerned about his own safety, only that of his family.

Miris nodded numbly, his mind still racing over the fact of the Oceanborn's survival. "Y-yes. Sir. Kaia, Taimon, Daiva, still alive. I um . . . I haven't seen Daiva around for a few weeks, but the other two, yes, fine. They stay mostly at home." Except for when they came out with bread trying to make some kind of strange alliance with him, but he left that part out.

"And Adriana?" Destin's tone was even sharper, almost daring Miris to insult the woman when Destin hadn't seen her in more than half a year.

Miris gulped before he answered. "Also alive. She's inside." He glanced up at the walls of Chainhome and left out the rest of the pertinent facts about Adriana's condition. Miris certainly wasn't going to be the one to tell the captain about that. He preferred living.

"Good." Destin visibly relaxed once those details were certain again, and looked away from Miris at Chainhome almost wistfully.

Miris contemplated the fact that it was an opening, a chance for him to kill Destin quickly without the Oceanborn even having a chance to defend himself. He could cut the wolf's throat and deliver his head to the Queen. That would earn him the eternal respect of the royal family, to know that Destin was dead for certain, no longer have to worry about . . .

"I need your help, Miris."

The depth of Destin's tone took Miris completely off guard, and banished the thoughts of murder that had inhabited his mind the moment before. No wolf ever spoke to him that way. None of them ever asked for anything, besides one in his memory, and that one was not the Queen whose favor he'd been contemplating.

"My help?" As if they were friends? As if Miris had any reason to be loyal or helpful in any way? "My help with what?"

"Just your help. With many things, I'm sure, before this is over." Destin turned back toward him, closing the window of opportunity to attack him without warning, and closed the last distance between them.

Miris could see that the months since the man's disappearance had hardened him, whatever he'd been through stripping some of the pride and vanity of a noble wolf from his expression. He was changed in some way that Miris couldn't quite understand at first glance.

"Your sister said something once that she thought I didn't hear. She said the only thing either of you ever wanted was to live a free life." Destin was shorter than Miris, and smaller, and he was dressed more like a human than a wolf. Nothing about him was intimidating, but he still didn't seem to fear Miris as he stood close by, looking up into the bigger man's face with a searching question in his deep blue eyes. "Is that still the kind of life you want?"

A hundred sarcastic answers leapt to the front of Miris' mind at the question, especially since it was his instinct to lash out whenever someone mentioned his sister, but all of them fizzled on his tongue before he could speak them, Destin's question hanging in the air between them, expecting an answer.

"Yes." The word surprised even Miris, but he couldn't take it back once it was given, so he bit his tongue and kept silent.

"So do I." Destin said quietly, nodding his agreement. "Help me. Work with me. Fight with me, and that is the kind of life we will both find at the end of this."

Kaia's words continued to echo through Miris' mind as he listened to Destin's invitation, and it was her voice that plucked through his heart, the taste of the bread she'd brought him still sweet on his tongue. She had said that he deserved a better life. Was it true? Was it even possible? She had certainly thought so. And if Destin was alive and asking him to fight . . .

Miris finally nodded, his fingers clutching the spear in his hand once as if praying to the metal itself to strengthen him. "Alright. I'm your man. But whatever you're going to do, you'd better do it fast. The moment they see you coming, you're as good as dead."

"I intend to." He reached out and put a hand on Miris' shoulder by way of gratitude for the choice he'd made, and turned back toward Chainhome. "I need to get in to see her first, then I'll go back to see Daiva and the others."

Miris moved with him back up the slope toward the entrance, still reeling from the choice he'd made, but he tried to focus on the moment at hand rather than the greater implications of what he'd done. "You need to remember, when you get in there," he said as they got to the gate and the iron bars unwound themselves for Destin's benefit. "It's been nine months, and everyone pretty well gave you up for dead after three."

Destin knew what he was probably going to encounter inside Chainhome, but it didn't change anything. He still had to see her. "I know. I gave myself up for dead for a long time as well." He looked around to make sure no one else would see him enter, then stepped through the bars. "I won't be long."

As was normal for Adriana in recent days, she shifted uncomfortably in her sleep. She remained close to Shian, though, since he was the only thing that would keep her warm in the cold cell. She could hear someone walking down the hall toward her cell, but she barely opened her eyes even when it sounded like they stopped on the other side of the bars. There was no reason that anyone would need to wake her at this time of night.

Destin stood by the edge of the cell in silence, drinking in the sight of her, the blanket over her rising and falling regularly, her teeth not shivering in the cold the way his own wanted to.

She was safe, and she was warm. Two things he had hoped she was, every moment that he'd been away from her. His lips twisted in a silent prayer of gratitude to his gods that his desires for her had been heard, and laid a hand against the bars of her cell.

He took some time to inspect the face of the boy behind her as she slept, wishing he was a Heartborn so that he could know exactly what kind of man he was. Had the man mistreated her? Had he been kind? From the way they were huddled together, Destin hoped that he had treated her well. If not, he would kill the man and that would be the end of it.

The washing-water that had been sitting in the bucket allocated to them had long since begun to freeze, but it slid up into the air easily at Destin's command, leaving its container behind. It flowed out of the cell through the bars to spiral in the air above the low fire burning in the center of the corridor, growing warmer by the moment as it took in the heat of the flames.

When it was warm enough to be comfortable without scalding, it flowed back through the bars of the cell toward one of Adriana's arms that had escaped the warm confines of the blanket while she slept. The water moved down to run itself from her elbow up to her wrist in a slow caress, flowing up over her palm and each of her fingertips to wake her gently, as if it was beckoning her attention toward the bars of the cell.

Adriana groaned softly at the warm feeling along her arm, and she opened her eyes slowly to look at herself. Was she bleeding? How could she be bleeding? She felt that her arm was wet, so she sat up slowly and looked down at her clothing to see if the rest of her was wet, because she did not want to go into labor in her cell. She was careful not to wake Shian, and when he mumbled something at her movements, she caressed his cheek lightly and kissed him gently on his cheek to assure him that everything was alright.

Adriana got up slowly to dry herself off, and when she did, she looked out her cell. She was sure that she was seeing a ghost or imagining something, except that there was a stream of water in the air between her and the iron bars of her cell.

She felt sick, she wanted to cry, but she put her hand over her eyes and shook her head slowly. It wasn't real. She was dreaming, she had to be dreaming.

"He's dead." She whispered to herself over and over, because it was the only way to make the vision of him go away.

"I can understand you thinking so." His voice was low, rumbling through the stone and the bars softly enough not to disturb Shian or any of the other sleeping slaves, just barely loud enough for her to hear what he was saying. "I thought so too for a long while, but I was glad to be proven wrong."

Adriana let out a choked sob before she uncovered her face and found some way to move closer to the bars. Tears streamed down her face at an unstoppable pace as she looked at him through her blurred vision. "Destin? You're . . . is it . . . ?" She reached out through the bars, but it was difficult to reach far with her stomach in the way.

His hands were warm in spite of the cold around them as they took hers, harder and more calloused than she remembered them. Her tears lifted off her cheeks as soon as they fell, discarded so that they couldn't make her any colder than she already was. "I'm so sorry, Adriana. I'm sorry that it took me so long to find my way back."

She couldn't find words for the emotions that she felt. He was alive. How was he alive for so long and he couldn't get to her? "I . . . I didn't . . . You . . ." She held his hands as tightly as she could between the bars, but she wanted to get through them, she wanted to hold onto him. "Can I come out?"

He looked pained at the question, since he wished she could. "I have Miris dealing with the other guard. I'll be able to come and get you out soon." The bars were far enough apart that he could lean his forehead against hers and kiss her once, but it was still a very limited kind of contact. "I've missed you so much."

She didn't want him to go, and she didn't want to be separated from him, especially in that moment. "You've been gone so long, I . . ." She looked down at herself and back at Shian. "So much has happened, Destin. I . . ."

Destin nodded, since just one glance at her had renewed his anger at himself for having been away from her for so long. "Has he hurt you?" He asked as he met her eyes again. There was a particular kind of violence that Adriana had seen in Destin several times over the course of knowing him, which had only ever shown itself when she was threatened in any way. At a single word from her, Shian's life would end, without hesitation or remorse from Destin.

"Hurt me? No, never." She stared into Destin's blue eyes that she loved so much and she shook her head slowly. "No. He loves me." She felt a different kind of pain then, since her love for Destin had not lessened at all, but she loved Shian too. She was not *in* love with Shian, but she loved him and she cared for him deeply. "I love him too."

Of all the emotions that could have crossed Destin's face at that statement, it was relief that she saw, and he squeezed her hands as he held onto her. A sigh escaped him that warmed the space between them, and he leaned down to kiss her hands once, just because they were the only other part of her that he could reach. "Maybe my gods do listen to me once in a while after all."

"What?" She pulled her hands back slowly, since she was angry he was relieved that she loved someone else. Why would he want that? Before he left, he couldn't bear the thought of someone else touching her, or that she would be intimate with someone other than him. "You wanted this?" What happened while he was gone? Had he left her behind and found some sort of other life without her? She was the one that thought he was dead, not the other way around. So many had been convinced of his death. "Why did you come here to see me if you wanted to be rid of me?"

"That is not what I meant!" He whispered harshly through the bars, reaching for her hands again. He had just returned to her, he certainly didn't want to be rid of her. "When I came ashore, it had been four months since I last knew my own name. The snows were about to start and I knew what that meant here at home while I was gone, and there was nothing I could do to change that. All I hoped for while I was working to get home was that you were alive and safe."

The tears hadn't stopped flowing from his eyes since he appeared, even though they were only visible as brief flashes in the darkness between them. "It will never come as a surprise to me that someone loves you. Or that you love them. That's who you are."

Adriana's expression softened immediately and she went back to gripping his hands again desperately. "I love you." Her voice cracked with emotion. "I am still hopelessly in love with you. What am I supposed to do now? Nothing has changed. Shian and I are paired together, and I would protect him with my life. This is my life now."

He nodded because he understood, and pulled her into a kiss that lasted long enough to silence the rest of the world around them, if only for a moment. When it broke, he remained close to her, with his cheek against hers, even if it meant the rest of his face was resting against the cold iron bars of her cage.

"The island where I came to land is populated with humans. Free humans. I've seen their city and met a few of their leaders." He kissed her cheek and pulled back enough to look in her eyes. "Miris tells me Daiva is still alive, and I know that if she's still alive, she's still angry. You told me once that if the time ever came when we were ready to fight, you could prepare the rest of the humans here for what's coming. Do you still think you can do that?"

"I . . ." She looked down at herself and wondered what in the world she could possibly prepare anyone for when she was so close to giving birth. She would need more help than she could give. "I will do whatever I can for you, Destin. I will try."

"Just spread the word, quietly, for everyone to be ready to move when the time comes. And that they'll know it when it does." He squeezed her hands and kissed her again, sighing against her cheek. "There's a long, shallow beach that runs along the southern coast of the island, white sand that stretches for miles in either direction. The sun rises over one end in the mornings and sets over the other end at night. Some of the people live just beyond the first hill. They watch their children run up and down the beach in the afternoons when the sun has warmed the sand, making necklaces out of the seashells the children bring back to them." His voice was wistful as he spoke about it, reaching up to caress her cheek, his palm warm against the chill of the night.

She was crying again as she thought about it, and she nodded against his touch. "I can keep my baby? We can be together?"

He nodded in return, and kissed her again as if to seal the promise. "Yes, we can. We just have to get there." That was the hard part. It was always the hard part. But she could feel the urgency in his voice and in his touch. The patient, methodical, hesitating Destin was gone. Whatever the ocean had taken from him, it had taken that as well.

Adriana moved one hand to hold onto his robes as she kissed him a few more times through the bars. "Please come back. I can't lose you again. Please." She was still crying, and for the first time, she allowed someone to hear the desperation she felt for so long. She had tried so hard to be the strong woman he wanted her to be after he was gone. She tried to be strong for Shian, but Destin could hear how broken she really was.

"I don't fear Melyssa." He looked her in the eye, wiping

away her tears again. "If the ocean tried to kill me and failed, I certainly have nothing to fear from her and her family. We will come through this, and we will be together." His hands moved down over her arms to her hands, lacing his fingers with hers. "I love you. Don't be afraid."

She gripped his hands tightly and she nodded. "I will be brave for you. I love you. I love you. I love you." She felt like she couldn't say it enough, and she knew he was still going to pull away and leave her in Chainhome again. She hoped that he would actually come back.

He stayed there with her in the darkness and let the silence pass around them both, the faint breathing or snoring of the other slaves all around the only sound moving through the walls.

The hall was empty in either direction, but eventually the distant echo of iron doors closing sharply moved through the corridors, and seemed to wake Destin from the dream of being back with Adriana again. He sighed at the sound, and kissed her again as a prelude to his goodbye. "I'm going to stay as far out of sight as I can, but it's only a matter of time before they find out that I'm alive. Tell whoever you trust. We'll be gone from here soon, and you'll never see another chain again if I have anything to say about it."

Her hands were trembling as he said his goodbyes, and she felt physical pain when he pulled away. She gasped softly before she started to cry again. "I will wait for you."

TWENTY

Kaia was sleeping by the fire in the great room instead of her own room, mostly because her own room always felt much colder. She was sleeping in her wolf form for once, so her ears perked up immediately when she heard the doors creak open. Everyone was already home, there was no one else to just let themselves into their property unless they were attempting it by force. She didn't know who would be attempting to break into their house, but she knew a Stoneborn and a Fireborn who would do something about it. She shifted immediately and started to yell. "Taimon! Daiva!"

A few of the guards of the household burst out of their quarters along with a scramble of movement from farther away in the expansive estate. Taimon came down the stairs first from his tower room, but Hassir and Daiva weren't far behind him, all of them in wolf form for speed after the panic in her tone.

All of them followed her look to see the doors beginning to open, though whoever was on the other side of them was having to exert quite an effort to get through them, heavy as they were. Taimon went immediately to Kaia's side protectively, but Hassir and Daiva crept up closer to the door cautiously, growling at the prospect of an unexpected and unwanted guest.

Finally, the board on the door snapped under the strength of the intruder, and both doors swung open wide, letting in a blast of cold air that set everyone in the room besides Hassir immediately shivering. The snow outside swirled in front of the single figure who had appeared at first, but once he'd regained his balance, every flake that had drifted into the house retreated back outside, leaving him framed against the flurry of whiteness headed into the darkness.

Destin put up a hand to brush his hair back out of his face and looked over everyone in the room with a sly smile. "You should really start sealing that door with stone at night. That board can't even keep an Oceanborn out."

"Destin!" Kaia shot across the room, having pulled on a robe hastily while they watched the door. She jumped onto her brother and wrapped her arms tightly around his neck. "You're alive! You're alive!"

He grinned at her embrace and growled as he returned the hug, lifting his smaller sister off the floor in the process. Taimon wasn't far behind and joined in on the hug without waiting his turn, but it only made Destin laugh even harder. He kissed both on the cheek before he let them go to look them both over, reassuring himself that they were truly alright.

"You got taller." He had to tilt his face upward to look at Taimon without letting go of Kaia.

"Well, you were dead. What was I supposed to do, stay shorter than you?" Taimon shrugged as if growing had been the logical thing to do.

Daiva stepped away from Hassir for a moment as she went to her brother, and Kaia dropped down and stepped back, as did Taimon. Only when her other siblings had stepped away did a single tear fall down Daiva's cheek as she stared at her brother. "I am so glad I was wrong."

Destin couldn't stop smiling, but there were tears freely streaming down his face as he stepped up and pulled his sister into an embrace as well, even if she wasn't generally the type. "I'll try not to force you to admit that too often in the days to come. I've missed you, sister."

Daiva embraced him and held onto him longer than she normally would allow before she stepped back. "I've missed you too. I did not know, for a while, how we would go on without you." She looked back at Taimon and Kaia before she looked back at Hassir. "Some things have changed in your absence."

The smile was gone from his face for a moment as she said so, and he followed her look to the Fireborn, who wrapped a piece of dark red cloth around his hips brought to him by one of the household servants. Destin's eyes narrowed on the wolf, but Hassir wasn't moving to attack or escape.

"Lord Hassir." He said to acknowledge the man, still clearly unsettled by his presence. "Things *have* changed quite a bit if he is our guest. Not that he's ever been unwelcome here, of course." He treaded carefully, since he didn't know what the situation was at the moment, but his words only got a grin from the Fireborn.

Kaia hadn't been allowed to say anything to anyone, and now that she had someone she could tell, no one could stop her. "They're going to be mated. You got home just in time for the show."

Destin's eyes went wide at that, but he looked back and forth between Hassir and Daiva to examine the expression on their faces. Seeing no denial from either of them, his eyes rested on Daiva, but he thought for a while before he spoke. "You're certain?"

"Yes." She went to Hassir again. "We are a good match together and we work well together. I could not find a better match, and I am not going to go looking. Hassir is who I have chosen, and he has chosen me."

Destin had considered many different scenarios to which he might have come home. He considered what the world would have been like if he had come back and been alone, his family and Adriana all gone somehow. He had considered Daiva having died in the battle against the Genovin, leaving Taimon to try and keep the family and its friends together. Or Kaia doing so in the absence of all others.

But the possibility that Daiva would have chosen a mate had never even occurred to him. The reality of it standing in front of him, and the look of absolute assurance on Daiva's face, was enough to set his whole world spinning all over again. When he was certain no one was joking about such a serious matter, he looked to Hassir again. If Daiva was going to take him as her mate, then Destin was sure the man knew what they were planning. "You and the Reef are with us, then?"

Hassir nodded, glad that the Oceanborn caught on as quickly as his reputation had described him. "As soon as we are mated. Many of my people have been waiting nearby for weeks, as have your own. We will move against Melyssa before the next Fulness."

Destin was impressed, but he couldn't stop himself from smiling just a little at the obvious eagerness in the man's glowing red eyes. "Good. So long as you're aware that if anything happens to my sister, you will drown in your own blood."

Hassir only seemed amused, and he nodded. "I expect no less a fate."

"That's it?" Kaia mumbled to Taimon, since she wanted and expected that Destin would talk some kind of sense into their sister. Hassir was crazy.

Destin smirked as he overheard the comment, looking over at his younger sister as he folded his arms across his chest. "Yes, that's it, Kaia. Daiva knows what she's doing. I trust she'll fill me in on her reasons a little more specifically later on," he said with a pointed look at Daiva that called for a more private conversation at some point in the future, "but I also trust that she wouldn't make this kind of a decision without giving it the weight it deserves."

"I don't think you would be saying that if I brought home somebody to mate. Somebody like . . . Lamson. Or Jared." Both Earthborn that Kaia had spent her time with, but that no one seemed to like.

"No, you're absolutely right. I wouldn't be saying that." Destin agreed completely, receiving a nod from Taimon to second his opinion. "I may have been away for the most of a year, but you haven't aged that much. You're still young, and it will be several more years before I want to hear the word 'mate' even mentioned with regard to you. Or our brother."

Daiva nodded in agreement before she looked around carefully and gratefully at her family. It was a miracle that Destin had returned to them, and she was so very grateful to have him back. "The ceremony will take place tomorrow. I still need someone to stand as my witness and protector." She said to Destin, since she didn't truly trust anyone else to save her life if Hassir left her to die. She wasn't really concerned about that, but it was still part of the ritual.

Everyone could see the anxiety on Destin's face as he nodded his agreement, still glaring at Hassir to make sure his point was made. "Who is witnessing for you?"

"My sister Asira was notified just after the last Fulness. If she appears, she will stand for me. If not, then no one will." He shrugged, appearing unconcerned about his own life and the very real possibility of his death at Daiva's hands the following day.

"No one?" Daiva replied with a note of surprise, since she did not expect him to trust her so much already, but it made her happy to hear he did. It was just further proof that she had chosen the correct wolf to be her mate.

"No one. Even Asira's presence is more of a formality than an actual safeguard." He smiled over at Daiva, and while the expression might have been actually sweet coming from another wolf, from Hassir it seemed like just another kind of malice, even if it was an exceptionally intimate one. "If you wished me dead or thought you had something to gain from killing me, you'd have done it already. You've clearly had the opportunity."

"I would rather keep you alive." Daiva responded with her own kind of smirk. It was enough to make the rest of them uncomfortable to watch, even though wolves were never known for their privacy.

"Ew! Stop!" Kaia backed away. "You two don't even know how to be romantic and it still is disgusting to watch." She shook her head as she covered her eyes with one hand. "I guess it's my job to fix the door now?" Kaia rushed to the broken wood doors, though she wasn't sure what she could manage, since it was dead wood.

Taimon went to help get the doors back into place, while Destin went to greet some of the servants and the guards of the household that appeared at Kaia's original cry of panic. All of them knew him, and some of them shed tears along with the rest of the family at his reappearance. Once the door was fixed, the guards returned to their posts and the servants returned to their beds, leaving only the family members themselves to catch up in the great room.

He was interrupted incessantly by both Kaia and Taimon as he recounted the events of the past months from his perspective, but eventually he managed to give them the entire story. Hassir seemed particularly interested in the location of the Free Isle, until Destin caught on to his reasons and assured him that it was well outside the farthest reaches of the Reef. Once that was established, the rest of his account went quickly, though his brother and sisters were just as incredulous as he had been at the existence of an entirely human society.

Once he was finished, it was Daiva's turn to bring him up to date on all the happenings in the Isles while he'd been presumed dead. He listened quietly until she was finished, his mind spinning with everything that Daiva had coordinated in his absence, but he didn't second-guess or contradict a single move she'd made. "So I assume Leander will be in attendance tomorrow? Along with all the other captains?"

"Yes. They will all be there." She confirmed with a nod. "Leander is mostly supposed to keep Chiara from ruining anything, if they get wind of it beforehand. It has been kept very private, however, we intend to announce it publicly once it is over. We want to distract Melyssa in every possible way."

Daiva was always thinking about how their plan would play out, but foremost in her mind at the moment was her mating ceremony. She knew that if her parents were still alive it would be something else entirely, a celebration, but she also knew they would have concerns about letting her mate with Hassir. Even though she missed them, she was proud of the decision she had made. "With the Reef's assistance, this will end in our victory, Destin. I know it."

"So long as the tide stays with us." He sat back in his chair and sighed at the expanse of what was in front of them. "And so long as everyone does their part. Which includes Melyssa and her family playing into our expectations."

"There is only so much planning that can be done." Daiva looked confident, regardless. "We have planned as much as can be planned. Now it is time to fight."

Kaia was sitting closest to Destin, and she looked up at him from where she sat on the floor next to his chair. No one had asked, but she was curious. "I visited Adriana until the winter came. Is she alright?"

Destin reached over and ran his fingers through Kaia's hair briefly before pulling her in to kiss her forehead. Trust Kaia to be the only one who thought to ask about Adriana. "She seems to be well enough. She should be delivering soon, the way she's talking. The boy she was paired with has been treating her well, by her own admission. I visited with her briefly on my way here."

Kaia could tell that Daiva did not like the fact that Destin went to see a human before coming home to his family, but Kaia just smiled after Destin kissed her forehead. "I like seeing how much you love her. I hope I have that someday.

Except probably not with a human." She chuckled and shrugged. Maybe her brother liked being with a human, but she was much too wild for human men. "We'll get her out before her baby comes, right?"

"That depends, I suppose." He looked back over at Daiva, since her plan had a very specific timetable, and very little about it had factored in the humans at all. "On how quickly everything unfolds once it's begun."

"They won't wait long." Hassir finally chimed in. "If it were just myself and Daiva, our mating would have been enough to provoke them into action on its own. But once they also see that you are still alive, they won't waste time."

"Then neither will we." Destin stated simply, since Daiva was right, it was time to fight, whatever form that took. So long as their people had gathered, as Daiva reported, to witness her mating ceremony, there was no longer any reason to postpone what needed to happen. "Tomorrow at sunset, then."

* * * * *

Life in Chainhome taught Shian to wake up at the smallest disturbance, just as a means of self-preservation. More than once, one of the guards decided to let the slaves sleep as long as they liked, and savagely beat those who didn't wake up when they should have. So when he heard a woman screaming in pain far away, he immediately jolted awake. He clutched the blanket and looked around hazily to find out what was wrong, especially when he didn't immediately feel Adriana nearby.

Adriana was already awake and tucked away in the corner of their cell. Her back was against a wall and her legs were against the bars of their cage. She looked over at him when he woke up, but she felt like she was disconnected from her body. Adriana couldn't say anything, all she could do was stare at him as the screams echoed around them.

"Ana?" He asked hazily, still rubbing the sleep from his

269

eyes as he sat up on the pallet. "What's going on? Who is that?"

"Someone is having a baby." She replied softly as she rested her head on one of the bars. "I can't tell who it is." There were so many slaves that Adriana knew she probably wouldn't even know the woman. "I keep waiting to hear the cry."

It certainly didn't sound like things were going well for the woman, whoever she was. Shian had only heard a few women laboring before, and those had been under much more comfortable circumstances. The sound was haunting, drifting down through stone and iron until it was like the distant wail of the wind rather than a human woman.

He got up and took the blanket over to Adriana and wrapped it around her shoulders and legs to keep her warm. A few months before he would have yelled at her for not taking the blanket with her when she got up, but he had since learned how futile it was to do so.

"Is it always like that?" He sat down near her, listening for the baby's cries along with her. "I mean, it's getting close to spring and a lot of you are getting close to delivering. Is it going to be like this a lot pretty soon?"

"Yes." She looked as though she was about to burst into tears when he moved to sit next to her. Adriana leaned into him and rested her head on his shoulder instead of the bars. "It sounds like that a lot of the time. It also depends on the birth. Some are worse than others."

"Do yours normally go quickly? I mean, have they, before?"

"The first one took a terribly long time. At first I thought I could handle it, but halfway through I was calling out for Piers. He actually came and stayed with me. Not very many men do that." She explained quietly as she looked up at Shian. "You do not have to do that."

"I'll be there if you want me to be. You know that." He had assumed he would be there with her if he was permitted to be, just to encourage her and be there for their baby. "The guards already know I'm not going to be much good for working when that happens, I'll be too worried about you."

Adriana was quiet at first, but she nodded slowly. "You should be there for our baby." She took a deep breath before she moved a hand down and entwined her fingers with Shian's. "I need to tell you something."

He thought from the screaming in the background that she was worried about her own delivery coming up, but it felt like something more in her tone. He squeezed her hand tightly and held it in both of his to warm her fingers. "Tell me what? Is something wrong?"

She moved just enough so she could whisper into his ear, since she was afraid someone else might hear her. "Destin is alive. He came here to see me." She was trembling as she admitted Destin came into Chainhome, but her grip on Shian's hand remained strong. Just as she had been afraid that Destin would not want to hear about how she cared for Shian, she also didn't want Shian to pull away from her either. They were going to have a baby together. They cared for each other, loved and supported each other. She couldn't bear to think of losing him either.

Shian felt like the entire world turned upside down with that simple phrase, and even though his mind reeled at the possibility that her lover was alive after more than half a year missing, he trusted her word. If she said she saw him, he believed her.

"That's . . ." he was torn with too many conflicting emotions to even respond at first, and he shook his head in disbelief. "That's incredible." It was the only thing he could think to say, but his thoughts raced. Destin's survival changed everything between them. Would alter everything about their relationship. She felt his grip tighten slightly as a new possibility moved through him, that her Oceanborn wolf would kill Shian for having been with his female in his absence. But nothing about Adriana's description of the wolf had given Shian the impression that he was dangerous. At least not to his friends. "Where has he been this whole time?"

"He wasn't able to talk to me very long, but after the battle with the Genovin, he was lost at sea for a long time." She pulled back to look into Shian's bright eyes for a moment before she leaned in and started whispering again. "He found an island of humans. Humans who are free."

Destin surviving at sea for months was believable. He was an Oceanborn, and Shian had heard some slaves and even a few of the guards theorizing that Destin would return someday when it suited him, to rain havoc down on Melyssa and her family. He had taken on almost legendary status for having actually been good to Adriana and a good captain. But an island filled with free humans? That was beyond belief. "That's just a children's story, Ana. People have gone looking for it for generations. They never return. There's nowhere wolves can't touch."

"Why would he lie about that? Especially to me?" She shook her head and turned so she was facing him as she gripped both of his hands. "He's going to get us out of here, Shian, and take us there." Adriana moved his hands so they rested on the sides of her protruding belly. "And we can have our baby there."

"Us?" Even if a place like she was describing existed, and he had his doubts, he certainly didn't think Destin would want him there. "You, certainly, but why would he help me?"

She squeezed his hands, but her eyebrows furrowed, since she didn't like the way he was thinking. "I am not going anywhere without you, Shian." Adriana let go of one of his hands so she could put her finger under his chin. She wanted to look him in the eye. "This baby is our baby. Your baby. I want you with me."

He didn't tell her what first came to his mind, but just nodded instead, accepting what she said, since he knew she meant it. Being with her, though, was greatly complicated if her lover was alive. "Then I'm with you. It's like I told you before, I'm on your side, whatever happens."

Adriana leaned in and hugged him tightly, even though it was awkward because of the giant belly between them. "I know it is complicated. But I still care for you, and I want us to be free and happy. The rest will work out when we get to the human island. It has to."

TWENTY ONE

Daiva and Destin were alone as they walked to the large stone pit where she and Hassir were going to be mated. The place had been made by Stoneborn generations before, but no one was certain of their intent. Some of the servants of their household had spent part of the afternoon filling it with firewood for the ceremony.

It wasn't until they were nearly there that she finally turned toward Destin and broke the silence. "I'm not afraid. No matter what happens here, or with the king and queen, or anything after. I've seen too much death to fear it."

Destin was covered from head to toe with a thick cloak of plain, unadorned brown fabric that preferred slaves sometimes wore. The hood came down over his face enough to cover his eyes as they walked. No one gave him a second look. The time would come to announce his survival to the lords of the Isles, but it wasn't yet.

"It's not dying that I fear, I don't think. Not anymore. What I feared when I was gone, when I finally came to myself on that island, was being separated from you, and Taimon and Kaia. Not being here for you when you needed me. Now that I am," he turned to give her a look and a smile from underneath the hood, "whatever happens, it's what we've fought for together, and that's worth it."

Daiva gave her brother a small smile and looked toward the pit, since they were nearly there. "I know you don't understand this, and I know you might not agree with my choice, but I'm grateful you did not try to stop me."

"Just because I don't fully understand your choice doesn't mean I can't respect it." He'd been quiet about his opinion ever since finding out that she had chosen Hassir, of all people. "You know your mind, and I can tell that you know Hassir. I may not understand your choice of him, but I can certainly understand his choice of you. A man like him wants a fierce queen by his side, even if he never calls himself king. You will rule the Reef in precisely the manner it needs to be ruled, and more importantly, to me at least, I believe you'll be happy there."

She nodded in agreement. "I did not think of him as a potential mate at first. He said he was evaluating me from the moment he met me. I am glad it worked out this way." When they got to the edge of the pit, she looked down at the enormous pile of wood waiting for Hassir's flames. "Do you think mother and father would be proud of us?"

"I think they would approve of us not acting foolishly, or rashly." He looked across the pit at a few wolves already in attendance, casually milling about the edge of the pit as if they had no idea what was about to happen. He knew all of them, and the sight of them made him smile. "I believe they would be proud of us for not giving up the fight after their death."

"I can agree with that." She went to the edge before she looked back at him once more. "Enjoy the show, brother." Daiva jumped over the edge and down into the pit without another word.

One of the others milling about came up to him after Daiva jumped in, smiling at Destin with eyes that were nearly the same color as his own. "You know, I think it's rather entertaining that they would pick two Oceanborn to oversee this entire thing. Maybe they want us to put out the fire when they leave."

Destin was surprised to have someone he didn't immediately recognize come up to him so abruptly, but he smiled back at her once recognition set in. Where Hassir's red hair was always kept cut close to his scalp, Asira clearly had no trouble wearing hers longer, even if it was pulled back in tight braids popular among wolves of the Reef. She had the same regal presence and the same sharp features as her brother, made even more striking by the beautiful contrast of her eyes.

The two of them had only conversed only a few times, under less than ideal circumstances, but he remembered her all the same. "Or perhaps we're the only two wolves in creation who are capable of putting up with the two of them. I find that just a little more likely."

"You're probably right." She turned her attention to her brother as he joined Daiva in the pit. Asira watched as Daiva went up to Hassir, then raised an eyebrow before she looked back at Destin. "They're possibly the most perfect pair I've ever seen. How much of this do we need to watch, exactly? This tradition is more rigidly upheld around these parts than it is at the Reef. You don't find many wolves at the Reef who care to wait around for a mated pair to be finished with each other."

"Even we don't typically wait quite that long." He had stood witness to several mating rituals before, most notably that of Leander and Marella, but each was different depending on the wolves involved. "Once it's clear they're both likely to survive, they are typically left to finish with each other, as you say, on their own terms."

He looked away from Daiva at the rest of the wolves in attendance, some of whom had just wandered in from their everyday routine once they'd seen the gathering commence and realized what they were about to witness. Some of Asira's Oceanborn guards kept the rest of the populace from getting anywhere near her or Destin, but the crowd was growing quickly as the sun drew closer to the horizon. "By the end of this, at least one member of the royal family will be in attendance, and then we begin in earnest."

"I can give you one guess as to who will find out about this first." She watched the crowd. "This is what Heartborn live for."

Daiva approached Hassir when he made it to the bottom of the pit, and she looked around until they were face to face. "I would like to go first." She said without really giving him much room to speak against her request. "That way your fire will burn later into the night."

He approached her without actually touching her, though it was difficult with her standing so close. She could feel the typical heat in the air around him, the rush of power that accompanied his presence at all times, but none of it moved through her as it so often had in recent days. Restraint was necessary for a mating, but it was a quality they both possessed in the extreme. "As you say."

She removed her robes and threw them onto the pile of wood. Daiva would not need them again for a long time, and she knew they wouldn't make it past any blaze that he would ignite anyway. There was something in the gesture, and the look she gave Hassir afterward, that announced to those gathered that the ceremony had begun, without saying a word.

She looked up past her intended at the pit around them. A single raised hand beckoned some of the stone away from the walls slowly, as she thought about what she would build. She plucked the pieces and held them in the air over the two of them as shower of pebbles rained down, but not a single piece touched Hassir. Even with boulders floating over his head, he did not look worried.

Her eyes remained on the pieces as they fell to the ground behind him at her command, shaking the ground underfoot. She walked over to the boulders and molded the stone without touching it, since it wouldn't drain her energy as quickly if she was doing it by hand. It was harder and more draining to resist the touch, but she worked methodically on her task.

It didn't take long for Hassir to see what she was making, and she looked back at him over her shoulder with a grin. "Do you think they'll be insulted that I decided we need a couple of thrones?"

"I'm sure they will be, and they should be." He seemed pleased with her choice, though, and looked over her work in progress with approval. He remained on top of the huge pile of firewood, just waiting to let it catch as he watched her construction grow. "Our thrones in the Reef are simple things, but it is death for anyone to occupy them besides you and I. I think it is fitting that these be just as overgrown as these Isles themselves."

"I hope when Melyssa sees them, she realizes they are bigger than her own." Her laugh was a low, throaty growl, rumbling through the pit in time with her work until she was sweating from the exertion.

After she finished with the intricate thrones, she turned her attention upward. A crowd had gathered all around the pit, so she started to pull out pieces of stone from the walls to create ledges for viewing. The event was meant as a spectacle, after all.

Eventually she had to shift to expend her energy quicker, and the stone took on her pawprints as she passed. She exerted her will on the stone basin they were in without any conscious control over what form that exertion took. She had to be rid of all of it. Almost enough of it to kill her.

After running around in her wolf form for what felt like far too long, it finally caught up with her. Daiva became too tired to move from all the sculpting and pushing herself, so she curled up on the stone next to his yet untouched firewood. She took deep, labored breaths as she ignored the stone beneath her fur calling out to her, begging her to change back into her human so that it could revitalize her.

She clung to her wolf form as she waited until she would be forced back into her human form either to die or to be saved by the wolf who would be her mate. Remaining in her wolf was against every instinct she had, but that was the nature of the mating ceremony. The bonding of it came from emptying themselves completely, in order to be tied to someone else.

Whispers began to run through the onlookers. Tradition dictated that in the moment of crisis, Daiva's witness should have come forward, to help save her life if her chosen mate decided to abandon her. But Destin held his ground. Daiva trusted Hassir, and so he would do the same, though it killed him to watch his sister's form writhing on the stone, her dark fur a spot of obvious pain against the pale stone in the dying sunlight.

Hassir took a few steps down along the carefully-piled firewood to draw closer to Daiva, but he didn't seem to be in much of a hurry. The stone pit around them had been transformed into a massive gallery that was a clear mockery of the royal palace in the capitol nearby, and Daiva had fallen in her wolf directly in front of the beautiful thrones she had sculpted for them both.

When he reached the edge of the firewood, he stepped down lightly, and knelt near her at arm's length, looking down in her grey eyes as her life drained out of her. She saw only vicious concentration in his red eyes, rather than the sympathy or the compassion she might have seen from anyone else in her family.

Hassir leaned down with one fist pressed against the bare stone of the ground as he looked at her. "You told me once," he said in a voice so low that only she could hear him, "that you wished to know what it was like to share in my fires. To feel what it's like to consume a piece of the world, to understand its destruction." There was reverence in his voice when he spoke about his element that had been almost completely absent from every other communication they shared, and she could see him clench his free fist as he waited for her to truly reach the edge of no return. "Soon you'll have your wish."

It was a struggle for her to lift up her head, but she brushed the side of her muzzle against his face before she laid her head back down. She could feel her heart beating heavily in her chest, and it took most of her strength to stop herself from whimpering in pain.

She would not be weak, even if she was dying.

Dying in battle was another thing entirely, the battle, the blood, it was enough to keep someone moving until the bitter end. This, this was different. Every beat of her heart, every breath was painful as she let herself die in the quiet. It was terrible, but she knew it had to be worth it. Hassir had to be worth it. There was no other option.

From the rim of the pit around them, Daiva could feel the thoughts and wishes of those who had attended in their wolf form, their minds reaching out to her to support her, encourage her, push her to the very edge of her own endurance. The stone beneath her was still in motion at the instinctive expenditure of power while she laid on it in her wolf, a slab of the world rising slowly with her on top of it, as if the stone itself was reaching up and begging her to take the power it could offer her.

She wanted to tell him to wait just a little bit longer, to wait until it was almost too late, but she couldn't move, and she knew she didn't have to. He would wait. He wanted their bond to be the strongest it could be, and so he would wait. Daiva blinked slowly as she watched him until she couldn't keep her eyes open. She took a few shuddering breaths, until it truly looked like she nearly took in her very last.

When he reached out to touch her, she could barely feel it through the pain radiating through her at the loss of power from her own element. She couldn't feel it when he picked her up in both his arms and carried her a few steps away to lay her down on a closely-packed pile of the firewood to remove her from even the last shred of contact with her stone.

All she could feel was the cold around her as he withdrew both his touch and the warmth of his power from the air around her. In her mind, she could hear the screams of outrage from the rest of the wolves around the pit at what he'd done. Many of her own followers panicked that it appeared he actually intended to allow her to die, several of them considered jumping into the pit to intervene.

Unable to sustain her wolf form any longer, Daiva's body shifted on its own back into her human even though it would do her no good. She was away from her element and unable to reach it even if she wanted to. Her heartbeat was thundering in her ears, louder than the onlookers above. She could hear herself dying to its desperate cadence. No other pain in her life compared, blinding flashes of blurred vision blocking out even a last view of the pit. All she could feel was her own life slipping away, and Hassir's own power somewhere nearby.

As soon as she shifted, Hassir could see the spasms taking hold of her that would eventually stop her heart if she was left powerless for too long, but still he didn't move. With every labored heartbeat, he could see Daiva's body grow weaker and weaker, until even the shuddering began to slow, her life giving up on the possibility of continuing without help.

Out of the corner of his eye he saw a few wolves actually leap down into the edges of the pit in an attempt to save Daiva's life. Hassir knew that even if their help had been required, they would have been too late. She was too far gone for them to reach her in time. But not for him.

He leaned down with one hand bracing himself on the wood beneath her, and looked down into her eyes. Hers had since glazed over with the pain she endured, and he smiled. "My lady." She could see the flash of his teeth like a spark about to be set to tinder.

Hassir laid a single scorching hand on her chest and fire exploded through her in a tumult of power that was as unrestrained as the very first time she'd seen him fight against the Genovin. The entire pit ignited at once under his command, but the two of them were unburnt in the midst of the flames.

Daiva felt Hassir's power fill her, consume her, and it felt as though she was on fire from within, flames burrowing through her muscles and scorching her bones. She couldn't help but gasp as it filled every fiber of her being, and once her heart was beating hard in her chest for an entirely new reason, her vision cleared.

Daiva looked up to see Hassir looking down at her while the entire world around them was aflame. She smiled at him, even though it was weak while her body drank in every bit of power he could share with her. "I . . . hope Destin didn't jump in."

"No." He reassured her without removing his touch or stemming the flow of power between them. "I considered destroying those rash enough to do so, but I left them unscathed. They will need a way up out of the pit, though, when you can provide that."

"I'll let them worry about that for a while." She took several deep breaths as she shivered underneath his flaming touch before she pulled him down into a kiss in the middle of his bonfire. It would be his turn after she was restored, but she wanted to take advantage of feeling alive again.

Destin breathed a final sigh of relief even as the fire blossomed out of Hassir to engulf the rest of the pit. He crossed his arms over his chest as he watched the fire and tried to catch any glimpse of his sister inside. He was sure Hassir had saved her, but seeing evidence of her alive would vastly improve the day for him. "He has a penchant for drama, your brother."

Asira shook her head as she watched her brother's flames climb upward, but she smiled as she felt the familiar heat from the flames against her skin. Oceanborn as she was, she still appreciated the warmth, especially because it kept her close to her brother.

"He chose her for her strength. You and I both know that. He would not settle for anything but the strongest mating bond. The longer you wait, the closer to death, the stronger the bond." She turned and looked at Destin for a moment. "Love and emotions meddle with deep mating bonds because no one can wait and watch the other person suffer for long enough. They wanted this, and they won't ruin it by being afraid."

"I don't pretend to be an expert on the subject myself, of course, unmated as I am." He didn't mind conceding the point to her, especially once he caught sight of his sister and her brother through the flames. Daiva was alive, he could see that much for certain.

Once Asira caught sight as well, she went back to lounging on the ledge that Daiva created. The stone was now heated from underneath, so it felt nice and warm against her back as she relaxed against the smoothed stone. Asira looked up at the sky as they waited for Daiva and Hassir to emerge for the second half of the mating. "Are you worried that your admirer will come looking for you?"

She'd been told, briefly, about Chiara and her apparent obsession with the males in Daiva's family. There was a story there about Chiara that no one seemed to have all the details about. "I can see how these events could make lovers out there especially interested. These ceremonies are romantic, even if it's a surly Fireborn and a cold Stoneborn."

Her question prompted him to look around at all the wolves gathered along the rim, but he didn't have to look for very long. There was a small group almost directly across the pit from him and Asira which was given a wide berth by the rest of the onlookers, and Destin's heart sank a little in spite of himself at the sight. "She's already here." He said quietly, nodding slightly in the direction of one of the two wolves in attendance who was wearing purple robes, illuminated in dazzling shades by the fire below. "And she's not alone."

Damos stood behind his sister with a smile on his face that nothing could diminish, even the thought of how absolutely furious his parents would be when he and Chiara returned home later to confirm what they witnessed. "I wasn't aware that Hassir or Daiva even possessed emotions." Damos removed his hand from Chiara's shoulder and stepped a little closer to the flames so he could see her face, his own mate's hand clutched in his, though Bethalyn remained behind him. "Are they as entertaining to you as other wolves, sis?"

Chiara couldn't peel her gaze away from the two wolves below even when her brother looked over at her, and she took slow and steady breaths as her violet eyes took in the mating ceremony. She couldn't see much through the flames, which was fine with her, but what she could feel was better than most things she felt in her life. Mating ceremonies were the strongest bond that wolves could make, and it had the capability of making her feel more drunk than any wine. "Yes, they are. Most other ceremonies aren't as meaningful as this one. These two would die for each other, and that is a lot, considering they barely know each other."

"As I would die for mine." Damos said with a smile back at Bethalyn, devotion bright in his deep red eyes. Mating ceremonies always stirred up memories for all mated wolves of their own bonds, and Damos was no different. "Though living seems like much more fun, if you ask me."

Chiara turned and looked back as Damos' mate snuggled close to him, and she smiled as she looked at her brother once more. "That's how it should be. Mates should be willing to do whatever it takes to make each other happy. I am pleased that you are pleased, dear brother. As our parents will undoubtedly be *thrilled* to hear that they can go to war with the Reef. Again."

"Better the Reef than the Genovin, at least for the time being." Damos had been looking forward to a fight with the Reef for a very long time, and was excited about the scene in front of them, just because it meant they were closer to that kind of assault. "They have to know this is a provocation we won't be able to ignore."

"I don't think they want us to ignore it. Especially with this kind of show." Chiara watched as Daiva and Hassir emerged from the flames, since she knew it was only halfway complete. She looked into the fire, her thoughts conjuring images of another Fireborn, one she had trusted and devoted herself to, even though she had not mated with him.

It was easy for her to get lost in the memory for a moment in the sound of the crackling flames, recalling what she had wanted, what she had felt . . . but the memory was quickly overtaken. It was replaced by the memory, equally sharp and clear in her mind, of her own mother tossing every single one of her newborn pups over the edge of a cliff. A truth she kept to herself, to keep her remaining loved ones safe. "They want to provoke us." Chiara pushed away the thoughts and memories. They weren't helpful. Especially with a war brewing. "Especially Hassir."

"Hassir has been allowed too much freedom for too long. It's been almost a century since the Reef came under our control. He needs to be reminded of his place. And mother has been wanting to remove him ever since it became apparent that he is no longer as willing to kneel as he was when he was younger." Damos watched as Hassir disengaged from Daiva with a last kiss, and began climbing to the top of the still-blazing wood pile. "We need reliable control of the Reef and of the Falls in order to be able to move forward when the time comes."

"Reliable control of the Reef?" Chiara wasn't exactly sure how her parents expected to accomplish that, especially after the things Devon had told her about the Reef, but she decided not to say anything more about it. If her mother wanted something, her mother would set the world ablaze until she had it. This time, though, Chiara wondered how far her mother would be able to go. "I hope, for your sake, that Malis and Calis have thought this through more than mother has."

"I'm sure Calis has. I'm just as sure that Malis hasn't." He snickered at the thought of their hard-headed Earthborn brother. "Calis has his plots and his plans years ahead of all the rest of us, you know that. Except perhaps Father. If mother succeeds, he and Calis and Ressa will be much of the reason why."

"I am sure you are correct." She decided to sit at the edge of the pit and enjoy the rest of the show. "Gods know they can't depend on me."

Down in the pit, the fire drew back from the edges of the burning wood, leaving blackened, half-burned pieces behind as it condensed itself around Hassir. Daiva was left at a distance from the fire, seated in the throne she had sculpted for herself on the edges of the pit.

The world turned darker as the fire in the center of the pit dwindled, until it was a single tiny flame held in Hassir's hand. When everything in the pit seemed to have fallen silent, he raised the flame into the air and it lifted away from his hand, putting distance between himself and his element.

The small sliver of fire turned to a streak of light as it rose, flying in a ferocious circle around the edge of the pit and making most of the wolves present take a cautious step back. It burned a few feet in front of the onlookers, as if racing from face to face to take the measure of those in attendance.

Both of Hassir's hands were outstretched, weaving the flame in intricate ways that were unclear at first. As the moments passed and the fire intensified, it took on the shape of chains, one large link at a time, stretching around the pit. He stood with Daiva at his back, and slowly turned as the chain completed itself in front of Chiara and her brother with a glare from Hassir.

All eyes in the pit turned to the princess and prince and the standoff between them and Hassir farther below. No one spoke, and the only sound in the area was the whisper of the wind and the roar of the flame itself around the edge of the pit. The flames strengthened themselves as Hassir poured out his power, until the chains burned white hot and most of the onlookers had to draw back from the heat, though no one could look away.

When the light was finally blinding and the robes of a

few wolves caught fire, Hassir pointed at Damos directly. The Fireborn prince hadn't moved away from the edge, but Bethalyn had to step behind him to shield herself from the heat. With a look of defiance between the two Fireborn men, the chains all around the pit shattered in a thousand pieces, the flames flailing around the open air over the pit, freed from their constraints in a frenzy of color and light.

Daiva wanted to pounce on Hassir just for that entire show of dominance, but she remained on her stone throne and watched. She stared up at Chiara and Damos after the flames fell, and gave them a mocking nod from her place.

As Hassir shifted to burn more of his energy, Chiara looked at her brother again, though now she was standing behind him and at a short distance from the pit. Her Heartborn capabilities allowed her to converse telepathically with ease, especially so close to a mating ceremony. The bonds of relationships gave her strength, and this in front of them was a feast of power for a Heartborn. *What did you say about controlling the Reef?*

Damos clearly wasn't happy about what they'd just seen, but he shook his head at his sister's question. *Destruction is a form of control. Maybe the least preferable kind, but in the case of the Reef, I believe Mother will make an exception.*

Chiara watched as Hassir's power faded slowly, and she knew that if she wanted to, this moment could be a moment where she could turn the tides. Hassir would be weakened nearly to death, Daiva distracted, and between her and Damos, they could destroy them both.

But the Hassir and Daiva also knew that. It was as if they were daring the royal family to act. Chiara's eyebrows knitted as she tried to untangle the mystery in front of her. They knew a mating ceremony would draw her attention, that it was a provocation, and they would both be at their weakest. Ripe to be made an example of. Chiara moved to look over the edge again, staring down at Hassir as she spoke to her brother with her thoughts. *I wonder what has made him so bold right now?*

Good question. Damos answered as he began looking around at the other attendants. Many of them had broken into conversation about what they witnessed, and he could feel the anger and resentment focused on him and Chiara, even without being able to read their minds himself. Even so, he was accustomed to being hated, even if he didn't feel he had personally done anything to deserve it.

Perhaps because they're surrounded by all the friends of Daiva's family. He noted the different faces he saw, wolves of every element who had either sailed with her lost Oceanborn brother or had been known to be friends of her dead parents. The only face he didn't recognize at first was Asira's, but he placed her after a moment's thought, laughing at the fact that the woman had attended with a slave standing at her side as if he were her equal. *Friends won't make the difference. Not once Mother finds out about this.*

Daiva watched the edge of the pit until she saw Damos turn away with his mate and his sister, though she wondered if his mate would have even tagged along without his sister. She turned her attention back to the red-furred wolf prowling around in the pit and she smiled at him. "I do not think they liked your show."

The growl that answered her sounded almost like a cat's purr, and he glared in the direction of the departing royal children. He lifted his snout and breathed fire toward them, which raised a cheer from many of those present that echoed in Chiara's wake. It was the last flame he was capable of producing, and the entire pit went dark, growing cold with each passing moment as the heat faded from the stone and ashes left from his demonstration.

Hassir remained on his feet as he paced, his paws leaving the stone behind him tinged orange as he passed, but even those tracks cooled as Daiva watched. As a Fireborn, Hassir was accustomed to being the repository of vast amounts of power, but he weakened quicker than a wolf of a lesser element would have when that energy was gone. Soon the stone no longer reacted to his touch, and Daiva could no longer feel the air turn warm in his presence, but still, he struggled to stay on his feet.

Daiva got up and sat at the edge of the still-smoldering pile of wood, which could at least catch fire again when she completed the bond. She trailed her finger through the ashes as she watched him every bit as closely as he had watched her. When he finally stopped moving, he sat down as if he had always meant to sit, and she smiled at him when she looked into his dark red eyes.

"Stoneborn power is very different." She knew he couldn't answer her out loud while in his wolf form, so she continued. "Yours came into my blood as violent as the flames themselves, but my power is more subtle than that. It creeps in at first until it grabs ahold of everything and turns it into strength."

At that description, he forced himself to take a few steps and cross the distance between them, sitting again as he reached her. Hassir brushed his face against her leg, letting her know he was looking forward to understanding exactly what she was talking about.

He shuddered once in the midst of the touch, though, and barely caught himself before he collapsed on the stone at her feet, shivering both with weakness and with the cold, which was completely alien to his nature. She could hear his teeth chattering even though he had tucked his head in an attempt to make sure no one else in attendance could see him weakened.

Daiva pulled some of the stone from the floor to cover them with a shelf overhead to keep him mostly obscured from view. Hassir deserved his privacy and dignity. She laid down on the stone floor next to him as she watched him shiver and shake. He could feel the stone ripple beneath him like water, her way of reminding him that she was still there. "I'll wait until the very end. We deserve that."

He had strength enough to nod, even shivering as he did so. Hassir forced himself to look up into her eyes so she could see he was still there with her. Night had fallen while they were in the midst of the ritual, and within the stone, the world was absolutely dark besides the glint of the remaining light from their eyes.

He reached out one paw toward her as the silence of the stone fell around them, undisturbed by the respectful mass of wolves above, waiting and watching to see if the lord of the Reef survived. Small sparks lifted from his fur as he looked back at her, weak and frail and fleeting. She could see his eyes focus on her face every time there was the smallest scrap of light, as he expended the last of his energy just to keep the image of her locked in his sight.

The last of the sparks died almost before it appeared, and he shifted with a gasp, his entire body shivering against the stone. As panicked as his body became, though, his face was a mask of stoic resilience. His teeth gritted against the agony of the cold to keep them from chattering, but he couldn't even lift his face from the stone. Hassir's fingers clawed at it, desperate to extract even the last hint of warmth to sustain him, but there was nothing to be had.

Daiva watched him carefully until even the desperation of instinct began to fade in weakness, his breaths coming as shuddering gasps of starved life. It was the razor's edge of life and death, an emptiness of self that made it possible for them to belong to each other.

Her hand reached out and touched him. She could not give him the warmth he was seeking except by what her own body could offer, but she could give him strength. Her hand slid up his side slowly as her power trickled into his body, not the raging torrent his own had been in her, but a steadying progression of unbreakable force. The world beneath them began to tremble and crack, but she draped herself over him so that her power would reach every part of him. His shaking stopped completely as he felt the strength of the world's own bones seep into limbs, Daiva's life bound up inextricably with his own.

He had spent his entire life around Stoneborn. He thought he understood their strength, the majesty of their abilities, but the sheer force of what Daiva added to his nature was beyond anything he had imagined. Hassir's arms locked around her with a strength he had never possessed, but he knew Daiva was still stronger by far than he would ever be, and there was no way he would do her harm.

His power was hers. Her power was his. Their power together was greater than it ever could have been for either of them on their own, and he growled in satisfaction as he felt life return perfectly in all his senses.

"You are mine." He growled against her ear, both in possession and in satisfaction, the heat of his body returning under the slow build of her power.

"And you are mine." She growled back at him, as she held onto him tightly. The stone beneath them shifted so that it rolled them back toward the pile of mostly-burned wood. She wanted him to be close so that whenever he was strong enough to ignite it, it was there. Her stone came up and snaked behind him, latching around both of their legs pressed together and caressing Hassir's skin as though he was a new lover.

He had been born with the ability to sense the fire all around him and manipulate it to his will, taking in its power for his own and releasing it as he saw fit. It was an entirely different experience to feel the stone in the same way. It wasn't his element and never would be, but he knew it, understood it, could feel it in ways that he had never comprehended before, because it belonged to his mate.

He moved to be more comfortable against the bare stone, and kissed her once before he put out one hand and barely touched the half-burnt wood around them. Once the first specks of remaining tinder caught fire from his touch, the flame spread in a flowing spiral around them, until the entire pile was consumed again and they were ringed around by heat, supported by pure stone.

As the newly mated wolves enjoyed the shared power between them, the violence of their joint nature, Asira leaned back on her elbows and sighed. "Well, they both survived." She smirked at Destin as she started to stand. "Are you ready for what comes next?" As soon as she was standing, she reached out a hand to pull him up.

There was cheering around them as she pulled him to his feet, as everyone celebrated the fact that they had both survived, and Destin nodded once he was standing on his own. "I am." He took in a deep breath to steady himself, since what came next was a gamble on their part, relying on Melyssa's own paranoia and insanity to act in favor of their family.

He looked over at Leander across the open pit of fire and nodded once. The Heartborn returned the gesture, and one by one, everyone present began to turn toward him and Asira. Leander's subtle touch on everyone's mind drew their attention without exerting any other influence, and most of the wolves present were confused as to what exactly had distracted them about Asira standing with a slave.

Destin reached up and undid the strings that held the cloak around his shoulders, then threw back the hood and allowed the cloak to fall around his feet as he turned to look around the rim of the pit. Beneath the cloak, he was wearing the deep blue robes of an Oceanborn, and he took a few steps closer to the edge as every eye in the gathering widened in disbelief.

His name went through the group in a hushed prayer, and a few among them cried out "Captain" in recognition. Destin's eyes swept everyone present, letting the revelation of his survival sink in for a moment before he spoke.

"My sister is now the Lady of the Reef, and I am still your captain." He smiled at some of those in attendance, Dola particularly, as he saw even his Skyborn friend shed a tear. "Notify Her Majesty that she is permitted one night, this night, to prepare herself and her household. In the morning, their reign over us, and over the Reef, is at an end."

Several wolves went off whooping and hollering, howling and growling, but Dola was still there as most of the crowd dispersed from around him and found her way to

Destin. "Decided to come back to us after all, Captain?"

Destin grinned at his old friend and pulled her into a warm embrace. "You didn't think I would actually stay dead, did you?"

"I'm glad you didn't." She hugged him tightly and stepped back to her usual place just a few steps behind him. "Melyssa tried to take the ship, but I kept her under my care for you."

"Good. Send a few of your Skyborn and however many others you think will be necessary to hold the ship through the day. As soon as word reaches her, she'll start sending her people to try and take the fleet." His mind raced through the plans for the day to come, and he knew it wasn't going to be easy for anyone. "I need you with me for the assault on the capitol. As soon as I find Leander . . ."

"Right here, Captain." Leander came up behind them, Marella right beside him as they greeted Destin, clearly ready for whatever came next.

Destin smiled as he embraced them as well, holding onto Leander afterward. "Between now and morning, I need you rallying everyone you know is even considering fighting with us, and rounding up all their children. Take some of the Forestborn with you and shelter them somewhere in the countryside north of Chainhome. I don't want you or the little ones anywhere near the fighting. Taimon and Kaia can help you."

Marella looked over at Leander with a smirk, since she knew he enjoyed being around children even if she hadn't yet convinced him they should have their own. "See? Even the Captain wants to encourage us. In his own way. Right, Captain?" She looked over at Destin again with the same smirk, lighthearted even when the world was on their shoulders. She was friends with his sister for a reason, after all.

Marella's bright attitude never ceased to make Destin smile, and he nodded. "Once we get where we're going, I fully expect the two of you to have it overrun with pups in a matter of years."

"Sounds like fun to me." Marella's grin brightened further as she put her hand on Leander's arm. "Let's go get started, then. Children are even harder to round up than ants, especially pups." Marella glanced at Dola. "Do you think Gale will want to come with us or go with you?"

Dola opened her mouth to tell them to tell him to go with them and keep her pups safe, but she knew he would never agree to it. She looked at Marella and then Leander. "Keep a close eye on my pups, will you?"

"Both eyes." Leander promised, and put a hand on Dola's shoulder to make sure she felt the promise as completely as the power of a Heartborn could make it. "We'll see you both on the other side of this. Captain." Leander turned and nodded slightly to Destin before he ran off, headed toward the nearest homes of their friends.

"Tell the other captains to gather at my estate." He instructed Dola as he turned back to her. "Daiva and Hassir will be back there shortly. A few hours before dawn, we'll begin moving into position, but I want everyone close by in case Melyssa decides not to wait for sunrise."

"I'm sure she will wait." Dola started to back away so she could get to work. "Melyssa tries to find a way to avoid getting her paws dirty if she doesn't have to. She'll try other ways to end this first."

"Whatever she tries, there are too many of us now for her to avoid us or dismiss us." The group around the pit was still massed and waiting for Dola's instructions, and it made Destin smile. Daiva had done incredible work in his absence, in bringing so many people from all over the Isles to the Queen's Isle one or two at a time, in preparation for what was about to happen. "I hope it's enough."

"It will be." Dola sent a blast of cold air at her captain playfully before she turned her attention to the serious attack ahead of them. "All of us have much to fight for." Dola ran back toward the pit, leaving her captain more or less alone. Asira was there, but no one paid her much mind, since she was from the Reef.

"My brother and I fight together. I hope you don't mind having another Oceanborn bumping around on one of your boats." Asira added as Destin looked at her again.

"Not at all, so long as you stay out of my way." He smiled over at her, since he liked the woman, against all his preconceptions about wolves from the Reef. "If you have any others with you, then I need you and your people dealing with the Queen's fleet and her own Oceanborn loyalists. When we leave this place, we are not interested in being followed."

"Do you think I want her in my waters? I do not think so." She gave him a nod. "I'll see you in the water. Captain."

He took a last long look around the pit and smiled as everyone else began to hurry away to their own preparations. It was a moment he'd been dreaming of every day since his parents had been killed, and he spared a glance at the palace, rising in the distance.

Destin didn't know if Cadmos was a powerful enough Skyborn to have heard his challenge personally, but he certainly hoped so. It was going to be a long night and an even longer day to come, but Destin knew they were prepared.

There was just one more stop he had to make before the morning came. He turned away from the pit and started off northward, immediately forgetting all fears of Melyssa or the army he knew she had at her disposal. He would face them all and more for Adriana. She was worth the fight.

TWENTY TWO

Cadmos sat back in his throne with a single eyebrow raised, the firelight all around the room glinting off his sharp features as he took in the message just delivered. He found it difficult not to laugh, not because the situation was funny, but because the threat was so absurd, even with the news of Daiva mating with the Lord of the Reef. "Only hours mated, and they think to take us in an insurrection?"

"That's not all, Highness." The favor-seeking Skyborn in front of them knelt with his face near the floor, his light blue eyes flitting back and forth from one member of the royal family to another. "Her Oceanborn brother has returned. Destin, the captain who was lost in the battle with the Genovin. It was he that issued the threat, not the lady Daiva."

"Too busy enjoying her new mate, I'm sure." Melyssa sat quietly at first, which was unsettling for all who were nearby. She knew it was too good to be true to believe Destin had died at sea, especially since his parents had remained an intolerable threat for too long in the first place. "We'll worry about Daiva and her Fireborn after we worry about her brother. He's the most important threat, first and foremost."

"How many are with him?" Cadmos asked as he looked

at the side of the chamber, where Chiara sat alone and conspicuously silent. It was her constant behavior for the past year since she'd actually returned to the Queen's Isle from her temporary banishment.

"They're difficult to count. They move around so much . . . I don't really know. Somehow I didn't even know he had returned." She let out a melodramatic sigh, since she knew she should at least sound disappointed in herself.

No one else in the room seemed amused by her melodrama, but Damos answered anyway, since he at least still wanted his parents to think well of him. "The most recent estimates of our spies place them at almost two thousand, but it's difficult to say precisely. Leander's mate keeps killing our spies whenever he discovers them."

"Those pesky Earthborn." Chiara replied with a click of her tongue. "Well, what in the world are you going to do now? And what would you like me to run off and do for you? I am at your command."

Cadmos wasn't any more amused by her playfulness than anyone else, but of all their family, he understood her position best. He was no Fireborn, to be taken in by her pokes and prods. "Your duty has always been Destin, daughter. It has been for the past decade and more. Why, with an insurrection brewing, led by him, would you think that would change?"

"He hasn't cracked in the past. But I will do as you ask. If I can keep him distracted, things will not go well for his followers. That's your assumption, right?" Her tone was bored, even subjects like the rise and fall of her family seemingly no more important to her than the weather. "I'm not even sure he is interested in females, but I can try my best. That's what I do well, right, mother? I seduce."

"Just do as you're told." Melyssa snapped and growled at her daughter. "We've raised you in comfort and as a princess, the least you can do to repay us after your treachery is to do what we have asked you to do."

"She was already punished for what she did." Damos

stepped in to her defense, though he didn't move from where he stood. She could feel how deeply Damos disagreed with what had been done to Chiara, but there was nothing he'd been able to do to stop it. All he could do was defend her when the chance arose. "There's no need to continue reminding her."

"Heartborn always need to be reminded." Melyssa's expression softened temporarily when she turned toward Damos, her youngest and favorite child. "We need you here, and she needs to go. Do not get wrapped up in this."

Damos bristled at being commanded what not to do, especially when his sister and only surviving littermate was involved. But he wouldn't go against his mother's wishes, everyone knew that. He'd done so only once, and even that had been with Chiara's help. He turned to his Heartborn sister and sighed. *He shouldn't be difficult to find. Or to detain. Do this successfully and they'll put the past behind them. You know they will.*

I wish I could believe that. Chiara smiled at her brother and took the time to move closer and kiss his cheek. *Keep yourself safe.* She looked into his eyes once before she backed away and headed for the doorway. "Mother. Father. I hope Destin's howls of pleasure will appease you."

Cadmos rolled his eyes and put his head down in his hand for a moment, irritated with their daughter as always, but still unable to do anything more about it. Chiara had long since passed beyond even punishment. He was surprised she had even accepted her assignment. "It would have been easier for everyone if he had remained dead."

"I wasn't aware you had a preference for things being easy, Father." Damos said defiantly as he moved to face his parents and await their instructions. "Otherwise, you would never have become a part of this kingdom in the first place."

"True enough." Cadmos admitted, since there was no point in denying it and giving Damos the satisfaction of having provoked him.

"We do not need to argue amongst ourselves." Melyssa looked back and forth between her mate and her son. "What about your brothers? Have they been alerted to come here and to meet with us?"

"They've been alerted as to what's happened, yes. I sent a Skyborn to speed word to them as soon as we heard about Daiva and Hassir being mated." Damos shrugged. "But Calis is a day's journey south at least, dealing with the salvage of some trade ships on their way to the Dreaming Isle, and Malis was overseeing prisoner transfer and execution on the Banished Isle yesterday. There's no telling whether either of them will get the message in time or be capable of returning by morning even if they did."

He knew their parents found his brothers more reliable when it came to the important matters of the kingdom. He knew they were right to do so, but the fact that they immediately asked about Malis and Calis before giving him his own duties for the coming battle was still irritating to him in the utmost.

"Let's hope they get here in time." Melyssa clipped with irritation, even though there was nothing to be done about the distance between the problem and her other sons. "Damos, you will lead the army, then." She turned her fiery gaze back on him. Melyssa did not want to lose her precious son so soon, though, and she wanted to be involved. "If it gets to that point. I will be with you."

His mother's assignment in the absence of his brothers didn't help him feel as though it was any indication of confidence, but he nodded anyway. "I look forward to it. I'll make certain the capital is secured by morning." He looked back at his father. "They will not have staged so public a demonstration without support from the Reef. There have been no reports of ships landing in the past few days from the south, so they must still be waiting farther out to sea."

"Leave them to me." Cadmos said confidently, actually smiling at Damos, since he was proud of his son for thinking along such lines. "You worry about the land, and let me worry about the sea."

"What do we do about the Oceanborn?" Melyssa said referring to Destin, since she was at least confident enough that their daughter would bring him in, even if that meant that they had to fight Daiva and Hassir afterward.

Cadmos shrugged. "He was presumed dead once, let him be presumed dead again. We'll keep him here underground until Chiara has what she needs from him."

Melyssa nodded slowly. "We should have destroyed that family a long time ago."

"Well, had we sent Chiara to Destin two years ago . . ." Cadmos shrugged, since that was an old argument between them, and not one that he felt like having again.

"Regardless, their revolution is in the air for the time being. We must at least appear fearful, or all the worms will not wriggle their way out of their hiding places to be exterminated in the morning. Gather the army, set everyone in their place, but let it appear, at least, as though we are truly concerned. Afterward, we will sift our way through the dust that remains and see if there are any surprises among the dead."

TWENTY THREE

Chiara meandered her way from the palace toward Chainhome, since she knew Destin would not go back to his home and put his siblings in danger once he had reappeared from the dead. She was both surprised and impressed he had remained hidden so long, especially since she had been at the mating ceremony, but she had been incredibly distracted. She wasn't disappointed, though, and she wondered how she would handle the situation once she found him.

Chiara smiled as she approached Chainhome and saw Miris was on guard. She raised an eyebrow slightly when she noticed that he was working on something small and seemingly delicate in his hands. Since when did Miris have any association with anything delicate? "You look like you are concentrating a little too hard there, dear Miris."

He was startled, since he had indeed been focused on his work, but he didn't try to hide it once she'd seen it. "That's . . . possible, Highness." He turned to bow slightly, then stood rather than remaining in his seat. "Been working at it for several months here and there, but it's not quite finished yet."

"Interesting piece." She glanced at it once, but it was clear that she didn't actually care about it. Chiara had enough shiny things, and even if Miris had been working on something for her for months, it wouldn't change the fact that she was unable to make any choices for herself except for who she would enjoy from one night to the next. Devon had been too rebellious for her parents, and Miris would be good enough for no one. As long as her family didn't see him as a threat, they would leave him alone. "Has it been a quiet night?" She reached out and ran her fingers along the length of his arm.

"Up here, yes." Almost no one had come by Chainhome for the entire night he'd been there, but he didn't try and pretend he didn't know why. "I heard about what happened down near the capital. With the Lord of the Reef." He nodded toward the door. "Destin's human went up to deliver this morning and her lover with her. Haven't heard any more about her since I was relieved on watch. I don't know if the Captain knows about that or not, but I expect he'll be along soon if he's only got until morning."

"You're an interesting wolf, Miris." She ran her touch down from his arm along his side before she leaned in and left teasing kisses along the side of his neck. He was her type when it came to intimacy, but otherwise he was just fun to play with. She couldn't and wouldn't allow herself any more than that. He was interesting because he didn't seem to care about his own life any more than she cared about her own. "You know I'm here for Destin, but you don't seem to care."

"Is there a reason why I should?" He asked without returning the intimacy at first, since he always liked to make her work for it, at least a little. She could feel his attraction to her even with the first touch, that was never in question. "I have nothing to gain if he and his friends succeed in what they want to accomplish. Nothing to lose either, maybe. But neither do you, really."

"You have enough to gain, even if you don't see it." She chuckled against his skin, and she continued to tease with a few nibbles as she pressed herself against his side. Chiara could sense that Destin was nowhere near Chainhome yet, so she had time to kill. "I'm just here for the show." Chiara kissed underneath his chin and let out a soft breath afterward.

You know more about me now than anyone else, Miris. Isn't it terrible that it still doesn't give you any power? I'm as useless to you as every one of those slaves in there. Her relationship with Miris had started out as simply physical, but nothing with her was ever as simple as physical attraction. His perspective about their world was too similar to her own for her to help enjoying the connection between them. He was one of a few people left who she trusted, even if she had relieved him of some memories of the depth of their connection. He was better off not remembering everything. It kept him safe.

I know better than to go looking for power. He grabbed her by the front of her robes when she began to pull away. He'd always been rough with her, but that was only because he knew she wanted him to be. *I'm not interested in power. Or in war. What I am interested in, you're no good for at all. Never have been and never will be.*

What is that, Miris? Her violet eyes locked onto his hazel eyes, and she just smiled up at him as he handled her roughly. *Love? You're right, I'm not good for love. Maybe once I was, but not anymore.*

I've got no interest in love. He scoffed at the idea as he thought back over all the couples he'd ever known who claimed they loved each other, and who had all been broken in one way or another. *All it does is kill the ones it claims. Just like it killed you.*

Am I dead? She pulled out of her robes he had within his grip just enough that it exposed her skin underneath when she leaned in to kiss him. Chiara bit his bottom lip hard, tugged at it slightly between her teeth before she broke off the kiss. *I feel alive right now, but you're probably right.*

I probably am. He took advantage of her own eagerness, as always, but he didn't push things between them, since he was on watch and she obviously had other business as well.

I've only ever been interested in peace. Which is not something you have a talent for, Princess.

Peace? It will never exist. That's not how power works here. She enjoyed his touch on her skin, and she wished she had enough time to enjoy him fully. *We're similar in most other ways, Miris. I enjoy your company. Even now, even when I know what is going on in your thoughts.*

He tried not to react to that, but it was a useless instinct against a Heartborn, especially one that had woven herself so completely into his mind over the past few years of their association with each other. He wouldn't go so far as to call it a relationship. *Yet you're going to do nothing to stop me.*

I don't know what's going to happen. She shrugged, but she remained close to him afterward. The closeness was addictive, even with someone like Miris, a wolf who most others avoided. *There's no reason to stop you. It's like you said. I have nothing to gain, and I'm dead.* Chiara blinked a few times until she shivered from his still wandering touch. *And what you don't know . . .* She gasped softly as he pulled her close, and she decided to whisper into his ear instead. "I was a part of this plan once before." He knew more information once. But she had ensured he wouldn't remember.

She was right, he hadn't known that, and he admitted that it surprised him, but he didn't pull away. "If you were involved with the Captain before, then why fight him now?"

"I was never involved with Destin." A wave of emotion burned through her, but she tried not to focus on the source. "You know, Heartborn, though supposedly a sign of purity and royalty, are not much different than Ironborn. We're meant to behave, to do what we are told, and to stay away otherwise." She took a deep breath and pulled back slowly. "It's only a matter of time until someone actually kills me, but until then, I'll continue to enjoy the game. Right now, I'm to seduce Destin, though he is quite resistant. I have two wolves I care about in this world, and as long as they're safe, I'll do as I'm bid."

"Two?" It was a commonly held notion that the only

person Chiara had given half a thought to after returning from her brief exile had been her brother Damos. The other wolf certainly wasn't either of her parents or her other brothers, whom Miris knew she hated viciously, so that kind of declaration confused him. "Don't pretend you actually care what happens to me, Highness. We both know you're not that sentimental, however much you do seem to like the earrings I gave you."

Chiara smirked as she kissed his jawline and shook her head. "I care about what you do to me, but you're not demon enough to win my heart, Miris. The pieces that remain now belong to another dark-eyed wolf."

He had no idea what that meant, but he knew if she wanted him to know, she would have told him. He did, however, see movement on the trail leading up over the barren stone that surrounded Chainhome on all sides, and he knew it was probably Destin. "There's your Captain, Highness." His eyes turned back to her as she lingered in the entry of Chainhome itself. "I'll send him in for you. And if your world is still standing by sunset, perhaps you'll think to remember how agreeable I've been to you, and be of a little more use to me in return, eh?"

"I'll make sure you're taken care of, Miris. But always remember that a Heartborn can't be relied on to keep a promise." She righted her robes and slipped into Chainhome. Chiara went to wait by Adriana's cell, even though Miris told her that Adriana was with her lover in the birthing rooms. She leaned back against the cold bars of metal and waited.

Destin went up to Miris and moved past him quietly, the two men exchanging a quiet nod on the way by and no more. They had come to an understanding the night before and there was nothing more that needed to be said.

Miris started to open his mouth to warn the captain on his way by, but he stopped himself before he actually produced any sound. He had no way of knowing if Chiara was nearby, and if she was, he was no match for her. She could twist him inside out and make him do anything that came to her mind. He had to pick his battles, and as his mind raced through the likelihood of what was to come that day, he decided that fighting Chiara directly was not the kind of battle he was going to pick.

He sighed as he looked back toward the dark hallway within Chainhome, and headed off down the ramp. He was abandoning his post, but that was the least of the offenses he intended to commit against the royal family that day.

Destin made his way down the hallway quickly, but as silently as he was able, past all the sleeping bodies of the slaves, huddled together in their cells for warmth. The thought occurred to him that it was the last night Adriana would ever have to spend in such conditions, and it brought a smile to his face.

When he got to her cell, he recognized the orderly way she kept the scant possessions slaves were permitted. Her pallet was pressed against one wall, close enough to feel the pathetic warmth of the fires in the walkway, kept barely bright enough to keep the slaves alive. The stink of the place was worse in the summer, but the winter wind had stripped and sterilized most of the foulness from the air.

Even without it, though, the place felt like a tomb, and the sensation wasn't helped by the screams echoing off the stone and warped by the echoes until they might as well have been the howl of a distant wolf. They faded into abrupt silence as he came to a stop in front of Adriana's cell and narrowed his eyes, trying to pick out her form in the dark. "Adriana?"

Chiara was just past him in the darkness and as she leaned against the cell, she almost felt bad for him when he leaned in to look for his absent lover. Chiara knew Adriana was alive and well, though she was in pain from her progressing birth. "She's not there. Neither of them are."

Destin was immediately on the defensive at the sound of Chiara's voice, but he didn't move away from her. She was no threat to him physically, even if he knew better than to underestimate her in any other way. "Where did you take them?" He growled across the space, though he wasn't sure why he bothered. If she was there waiting for him, then she wasn't going to give up their location easily. She might have even killed Adriana already and was waiting to gloat.

"I didn't take her anywhere. She disappeared earlier in the day to go give birth to her tiny little rat." Chiara sounded bored, but being so close to Destin made her tremble just slightly. The memories he invoked were hard to ignore. "I still don't understand why you didn't turn her when you had the chance."

There was no point trying to lie to a Heartborn, especially one that knew him and his situation as well as Chiara did, so he didn't even try. "Because while she is human, she is nothing to your parents. They would ignore her so long as I didn't make it obvious how valuable she is to me. Your father would have jumped at that opportunity, if I'd taken her to keep for myself over you. If I'd turned her, they would have found an excuse to kill her, if they even felt they needed one."

"But now, because you didn't, she died in childbirth after living a horrible life here in Chainhome. Are you sure you still made the right decision?" She moved closer to him so that he could see her, and while she knew he physically had the strength to kill her quickly, she had the power to stop him if he tried. "Her human lover has now been moved to a different female. I do, however, have her child. If you are interested."

Her words froze him on the spot more effectively than all the wind and ice outside the prison, and he looked back and forth from one of her eyes to the other, trying to see some flicker of truth or falsehood within them. "You're lying."

"Why would I lie?" She lifted an eyebrow and she stared into his deep blue eyes. "Even if she hadn't died in childbirth, I was still sent here after you, which means that I was instructed to get rid of anything in the way. I would have been required to kill her if she didn't die, so the end result is the same. She's dead."

He expected the royal family to come after him directly again as soon as he'd revealed publicly that he'd survived, but he had to give them credit, he hadn't expected them to act quite so quickly. He couldn't process the news that Adriana was dead. If she was, he knew he wouldn't care what happened to him in the coming day, so long as it ended with his family safe elsewhere. He would return to the ocean and let it take him, for good.

"Why are you even here, Chiara?" There were years of history behind the question, behind them both, and he made no effort to hide the different layers of his curiosity from her in his mind. "You know how this ends. For me and for you."

"They still want us to do what they've always wanted us to do." She looked him up and down once, and even though it wasn't the Fulness, she wished that she could just get it over with already. "They also think that they can squash your rebellion by getting rid of you, which I don't think is the case, but who listens to me? After spending a lot of time with Devon, I know how many wolves support your family." She moved closer to him still, but she didn't try to reach out and touch him.

"They held me in place as they took each of my newborn puppies and threw them into the ocean. Malis held me so tightly I thought my arms would break off, but nothing hurt more than the feeling of each of those lives, ones I had grown and created, being snuffed out when they hit the stones or the water below. You can't imagine that kind of pain, Destin. I'm here because whatever future I still have left, I never want to feel that ever again."

The rage that rose up in Destin reminded her, just for an instant, of the passion that his brother Devon had possessed in such vast quantities. It was even directed the same way, in a kind of instinctive protectiveness of her, and of her broken children, Destin's own kin, even if they'd been hers as well. He didn't dwell on the surprise of information about Devon and Chiara with the threat of her in front of him. What he still knew was that Devon had died because of Chiara. She was the reason.

"We're going to kill your parents today." He said quietly, without retreating, even though he knew he should have started running out of Chainhome the moment he'd seen her. "And your brothers too, if they return in time. I would think out of any death you might care to witness in your life, it would be theirs you'd be most interested in. But here you are doing their bidding instead."

"They have too many things set in place to keep themselves safe for you and your family to ever reach my parents. Or my brothers." She heaved out a heavy sigh. "I will die before all of them, I'm certain of that." Chiara finally reached out to touch him, even though she knew he didn't want her to, and the moment her fingertips touched his skin he felt warm and comfortable. "Of course I want them dead, but that's not something I'm going to accomplish. And let's face it, even if I help you now, your people would kill me faster than mine would."

Destin couldn't deny that, and though a part of himself hated how easily she was able to manipulate him, he still relaxed against the bars, all will toward violence or running away gone in an instant. "The best thing you could do, if you want them dead, is stay out of our way. When all this is over, you and whoever else is left can do as you like with the ashes."

"I'll let that work itself out without my assistance either way." She ran her hand slowly up his arm. "What I really want, though," Chiara leaned in and he could feel her breath against his neck. "Is for my daughter to live." She kissed along his skin afterward. Her puppies with Devon had all been murdered, but Chiara had more at stake. "And I suppose having your puppies wouldn't be horrible."

The longer her touch remained on his skin, the fuzzier his thoughts became, but she could still feel his contempt for her burning beneath the warm haze she'd placed in his mind.

Would he remember anything she had said, if he survived the conversation? The question brought him to a momentary panic, but It did nothing to help his situation. The strength of his revulsion toward her only strengthened her further, but he tried, feebly, to move away from her.

"In the morning, all of this will be a ruin." He slumped against the bars, beginning to go weak under her disarming assault. "And you along with it."

"Me?" She chuckled and smiled as the bars of Adriana's cell moved slowly, since it had been left open after she had been moved to the birthing rooms. Slowly Chiara pulled Destin back up and dragged him into Adriana's cell. "Well, how about you stay here just to make sure of that?" She pulled her touch away from him and started to back away. "I'll just get rid of your lover's baby for you. No need to keep a squalling little rat around if no one is going to care for her, right?"

Anger returned to his eyes almost as soon as her touch left his skin, and one hand shot out to latch around her neck, slamming her back into the bars as he gritted his teeth in a growl. "No." He leaned in close, looking for any trace of fear in her violet eyes, but there was nothing in them at all, not fear, not cruelty, just an empty shell of a person without even enough of a soul left to be pitied. "You'll not harm her."

"Should I bring her to you, then? Do you think you can care for her in this tiny little cell that you left your true love in, day and night?"

"Better that than the cliff your parents threw your own children from." He said with ice in his voice, attempting to tighten his fingers around her throat even though the warm numbness was starting to spread through him again.

"As you wish, dear Destin." She said when he slumped back down again, his grip failing. Chiara didn't reach up and rub at her skin, even though she was sure she would have a bruise of Destin's hand imprinted into her skin the following day.

Without saying anything, a human slave appeared from the darkness carrying a wrapped bundle and Chiara stepped out of the cell in order to retrieve it. She sent the human on its way again and held out the sleeping child to Destin. "Here. Good luck leading a war from in here and with a tiny newborn babe in your arms."

Chiara stepped out again and tapped on the bars so loud that it would wake the child, and she looked toward the entrance before she walked out. There was a Stoneborn in Miris' place, and she barely glanced at him as she spoke. "Takas, seal Destin up in that cell."

The wolf moved in toward her and bowed as the stone around the cell folded itself around the bars to bind them in place. As soon as the babe woke, it was crying, and Destin moved back against Adriana's pallet, holding it close to try and soothe it back to sleep. Once it felt that it was warm again, the babe did seem to quiet down, but when Destin looked up, Chiara was gone and he was alone in the cell with nothing but the cold around him.

The darkness only seemed to deepen as the little girl settled back into sleep, and Destin was afraid to even set her down for fear of her getting too cold or waking her again. His mind was racing even if the rest of him was incapable of moving.

Adriana was dead. His mind was a jumble . . . there had been more, something about Devon . . . what else had she said? Everything was so heavy, the simplest thought was like trying to sprint through a snowbank. The one nugget of information she seemed to want him to retain was the knowledge of Adriana's death. That was the only fact in the world that mattered for all the meaning of his life to be drained out all at once.

The little girl didn't even have her coloring or her features to remind him of her. The girl's hair was a brilliant blonde that he vaguely remembered seeing on the man

Adriana had been paired with, and he could only assume the rest of her features had come from the man as well. He would know more certainly as she got older. If she survived childhood somehow, as the ward of a wolf. If any of them survived the day.

"Captain?" He heard a voice from the hallway and saw a tiny figure creep up to the edge of the cell. Destin knew he had once known the little boy's name during the time he'd overseen construction at the shipyard, but it escaped him, though the boy clearly still knew him. There were tears on the boy's face that Destin could feel, but his voice didn't shake, either with the sadness he was feeling or the cold, to which he was obviously accustomed. "I heard what the witch-wolf said about Ana. I'm sorry. I'll miss her too."

Destin just nodded, since he couldn't move otherwise, still lightly bouncing the little girl in arms that were growing more numb by the moment. "Your name is Malcom, right?"

The boy nodded, and scooted a little closer on his side of the bars, looking over the little girl in her wrappings. "Is that her daughter?"

Destin took in a slow breath before he nodded again, trying to steel himself to the void he faced. His mind still plummeted down hopeless corridors in which all he could do was tell the girl in his arms about how incredible her mother had been.

"She looks like Shian." Malcom said quietly, obviously mourning right along with Destin, but he had seen too much loss over the course of his short life to permit the loss of anyone, even Adriana, to break him completely. "What are you going to name her? We live longer if we get names, you know. We're just like you that way."

Destin hadn't been aware that their superstitions around naming a child had extended to the humans, but he was certainly familiar with them. "You said his name is Shian? The father?" Malcom confirmed it with a nod, and Destin went on, looking down into the little girl's face with a sigh.

"Sheena, then. So she'll remember both of them."

Malcom seemed appeased by that, and remained silent for a while before he stood up and flattened himself against the bars so as not to be seen. "Sheena's a good name. Ana would have liked it." He glanced furtively up and down the hall, and apparently saw something he didn't like, since he went tense all at once. "I'll find someone to wet nurse for her. Takas is grumpy most of the time, but he won't let the little girl starve. He hates it when they cry."

"Thank you, Malcom." Destin was touched by the boy's concern, but his help didn't stop the tears flowing down Destin's face. "Adriana always spoke well of you, and I'm glad you're still a good friend to her, even now."

"I'll make sure the baby is alright. We take care of each other here. We have to." He said sadly, before he reached in through the bars to pat the little girl on the head gently. "I'll be back, I promise."

When the boy was gone, Destin moved slowly up onto the pallet, still holding the newborn girl close against him and rocking her as his tears soaked the swaddling blankets wrapped around her.

"Sheena," he whispered to the baby, not wanting to wake her again, "I'm sorry."

He had to catch his breath before he went on, since for once the tears streaming down his face were accompanied by sobs that threatened to crack his own ribs with the force he had to use to suppress them.

"I'm sorry I didn't do more for your mother. That I didn't just run when she asked me to. I'm sorry that I wanted a better life for her, when the only life we could have had was taken away." He shook for a few moments in silence, but when the freshest batch of tears had cleared itself from his eyes, he looked down and the girl's own eyes had opened just slightly in sleep.

She blinked a few times, and Destin's heart finally drowned in grief inside him. Adriana's green eyes stared back up at him, as if accusing him from beyond life, and then closed again as the baby returned to sleep.

He couldn't breathe, couldn't speak, couldn't feel, and he knew that even when the dawn finally broke over the world, it would bring no warmth. Not for him. Not without her.

TWENTY FOUR

Miris wondered, for the thousandth time, about the change wrought in him during the last year of his life since his turning. He had been running for an hour through the forest on his way south, at a distance from the main road that led from Chainhome to the capital, and he couldn't even feel it in his limbs. The strength that surrounded him and pervaded his body was still a constant surprise for him, but he was grateful for it, especially at times like the present when he sorely needed it.

When the captain's estate finally came in sight, Miris slowed, since there were wolves milling around it and overflowing the outer walls surrounding it. He was obligated to approach slowly, though he understood there was no way for him not to appear threatening.

A few of the wolves present glared as he joined the group, but no one stopped him and no one condescended to speak to him as he made his way through the gathered crowd.

There was no way for him to even approach the house itself with the gathering of captains and other wolves who were packed into the great room. He could see Hassir and Daiva standing around a model of the capital that she'd formed from the stone of the floor, discussing strategy with the various leaders so that everyone would be prepared when morning came, but the guards outside the house weren't letting anyone else close for fear they'd be some kind of spy.

He paced outside for a while until he caught sight of Kaia and her brother going around giving out food. He stepped toward them, shouldering past a few Earthborn near him who seemed affronted at his presence, but he didn't pay them any mind.

"Kaia!" He called through the crowd, his fingers twitching at the clasp over the bag at his side.

Instead of ignoring Miris as most might have expected from Kaia, a wolf high above his class, she smiled when she finally saw who was yelling for her. Kaia made her way as the wolves parted for her, and she held out some roasted meat from the giant bowl in her arms. "You look exhausted and the battle hasn't even started. Do you want to eat something? I can get you some water . . ."

"I need to talk to your sister and your new brother." He refused the food, since he was still a little out of breath from his run and certainly not hungry given the news that he was bearing. "It's about the captain. He went up to Chainhome to see Adriana."

"We knew that he probably went to see her." She handed the bowl of food to an Earthborn also glaring at Miris, but she didn't look back. "I'll take you to them." She grabbed him by the arm so that no one would try to stop him following after her and she weaved her way back through the exceptionally large crowd.

"You shouldn't be here." He said in a low growl when they had to slow down to get in through the doors themselves. It was the closest he'd ever been to her besides his brief threat back at the shipyard, and when he came to a stop behind her, his voice came from well above her head. She came up to just beneath his shoulder, and he had to lean down just to make sure she heard him. "This place is going to be ripped apart by morning, and you along with it if you're still here when the fighting starts."

Kaia turned enough so that she could look up at him, which put their faces even closer. She was confused, though, since it sounded like he was actually maybe a little concerned for her life. Or maybe he just meant that she was weak and that she would get in the way, which was probably the real reason. "I'm just doing my part." She said softly, but she knew he could hear her. "Taimon and I are going to leave to help with the children before long. We were waiting for Destin to come back."

"Good. You'll be safer with them." He wasn't looking at her as he spoke, but his hand remained on her shoulder as they made their way through the crowd. "Don't wait for Destin to come back. You need to put as much distance between the children and the capital as you can before morning."

She was even more confused by his warning, and she felt uncomfortable with the fact that he was telling her not to wait for Destin. "We'll keep the children safe." Kaia spotted her sister, finally, and she led the rest of the way through the crowd. She stopped short to look up at him again before he went ahead to talk to Daiva. "Thank you for fighting on our side, and for the warning. I'll tell Leander what you said and we'll get the children to safety. Try not to die, all right? My agreement still stands, if you ever want to work it out."

"About that . . ." he took his bag off over his head and gathered up the strap to hand to her. "That's yours. It's not finished yet, but your family had to go and start a war before I got it done, so you'll have to cut me some slack on that. If we all survive, there'd better be a lot more of that bread in my future." He didn't stay to wait for her to even look at what was inside, though, and moved away to talk to her sister, as the Stoneborn and her Fireborn mate both gave him dirty looks at his approach.

Kaia was clearly surprised as she took the bag into her hand, and while Miris continued on his way, she stayed put to open it up. She looked inside the bag as if something was going to jump out and bite her, since she wouldn't put it past Miris, but instead she pulled out something dainty and beautiful.

She smiled as the bracelet laid out across her fingertips, and she didn't know what he was talking about when he said it was unfinished. Intricate loops of silver and gold had formed themselves into thousands of tiny flowers, on a dozen strands that would hang off the bracelet itself to catch the light. It was beautiful. Kaia put it on her wrist and slung the bag over her shoulder. "You have to survive to get the bread!" She yelled out, but then took off running so that she could show Taimon and help with the children.

Daiva watched her sister disappear, and though she wanted to ask Miris what in the world he was giving her sister, there were bigger things on her mind. "You better have something important to tell me, Miris."

"The Captain just got himself locked up in Chainhome by the princess." He said bluntly, since if there was one type of wolf he was familiar with, it was Stoneborn, and he knew she would prefer things direct and to the point. "Important enough for you?"

She was quiet for a moment before she glanced over at Hassir. "It sounds like our plan is going to change slightly." Daiva looked at Miris again and raised an eyebrow. "You decided to support us instead?"

"I'm here because I despise you people slightly less than I despise the royal family. I was turned by the crown prince and then dumped right back in the shitpile I grew up in. All Destin ever did to me was threaten to kill me once. I can deal with that." He didn't back down from Daiva or the glare from her mate, he just waited to see what she would do with him. "I passed a lot of Stoneborn on my way south, along with a few of Chiara's usual guards. Chainhome isn't going down easy, and unless you want to flatten your brother, you need to keep the fighting away from the prison itself."

Daiva growled softly and the model of the castle in the middle of the floor started to crack and crumble. "We'll . .

." She looked over at Hassir "We'll focus on the palace and deal with Chainhome later. They aren't going to kill their own slaves, even with Destin in there. And with his human there, well, that's where he would want to be."

"Let me deal with Chainhome, then." Miris volunteered. "Give me a dozen Stoneborn and I'll hand the place to you on a plate by noon, and your brother along with it."

The rest of the model of the castle crumbled before she looked at Miris. "And why should I trust you, Chiara's own toy, to free my brother and to open the doors of Chainhome?"

"Because toys eventually get tired of being played with, and slaves are born pissed off about being told what to do." A few of the wolves who first sneered glanced at Daiva instead, every eye in the room curious about what she would do. "I'm going back up there either way. I'm supposed to be on watch. So either I do this alone and most of the slaves die, your brother included, or I get some help, and only some of them die. Or you kill me just for being here. Your choice."

Daiva took only a moment to consider, and she thought about the information he gave. She also thought, briefly, about her sister. While she never would trust Kaia or Taimon in battle, and she didn't know if they had their wits about them for anything else, she did trust her sister as a judge of character. If Kaia led Miris to them because she knew he had something important to say, then Daiva could trust him just a little further.

"There's a group of Stoneborn gathered by the front entrance." She picked up a piece of the broken castle and shaped it so that her fighters would know she had given her command when Miris went to find them. Daiva tossed him the small piece of stone and nodded toward the door. "They'll follow you if you show them that. If they die because you have betrayed my trust, I will take great pleasure in making you pay for it afterward."

"One thing all you nobles have in common." He looked

over the piece of stone she'd given him as he turned away. "You all love the sound of your own threats." He shoved his way out of the room, and Daiva could hear him barking orders at the group she had put at his command. The shouting only lasted a few moments before Daiva could feel the group run out of the compound headed north, and the rest of the room settled back into their own conversations.

"No one trusts a Heartborn." Hassir said beside her, but he wasn't second-guessing her choice. "Depending on Chiara's interest in staying alive, we may have just sent her another dozen fighters to defend Destin's cell."

"Chiara supported this cause once. She's just as much a slave to her parents as any of those humans, or even Miris for that matter. I don't trust her, but I trust my sister. If she trusts Miris, then I will give him one opportunity to prove himself. Destin is trapped regardless, but at least this is a sliver of hope."

"It's a shame. Asira was very much looking forward to destroying something alongside him." Hassir sighed and turned his attention back to the gathered captains, Dola in particular. "You can assume Destin's command in the seaward side of the attack?"

Dola nodded, since before Destin's return, she believed she was going to lead the attack in the first place. "It will be greatly helpful to have your sister there in Destin's absence." She shook her head as she looked back at some of the members of her command, and sighed. "I'm beginning to wonder if that human woman is going to be the death of him after all."

Daiva nodded slowly. "I've assumed that all along. Enough about that, let's alter our plans so that we can compensate for this. Melyssa and Cadmos are waiting for our attack. We have no reason to delay."

Hassir obviously agreed, and turned to give orders to his own commanders, as they prepared to leave the estate and take their positions around the city. Daiva's force was larger and more threatening, but Hassir intended to burn the Isles to the ground. That called for some subtlety, at least at first.

"It looks like our contest for the right to kill Melyssa will come down more to a race than a fight to the death, my lady." The challenge was a low, self-satisfied growl as they walked out of the house, wolves scattering in every direction. "May the worthiest wolf prevail."

She looked back with a smirk before she grabbed his robes and pulled him in for a violent kiss. Normally they would be given time to spend alone, for days, weeks even, after a mating. Instead, only hours later they were already throwing their lives at a war instead of at each other. "I will." She teased as she let him go. "I will see you on the other side."

* * * * *

"What are we waiting for?" One of the Stoneborn beside Miris growled. None of them were happy about being led by an ex-slave.

"I know those wolves standing by the gate." Miris answered without looking away, inwardly cursing. Takas and his mate were on the ramp itself, and there were two dozen other wolves milling about keeping watch. All of them Stoneborn, by the way they stood completely still and almost faded into the foundations of Chainhome itself. "I'm curious. Do the lot of you prefer fighting your own kind, or would you rather mix it up a bit and keep things interesting?"

His companions weren't amused by his light-hearted tone, but they answered the question, even if they were scowling the entire time. "Fighting our own kind is easier. We know how they work, how they move. The same as I'm sure you would prefer to fight another rat instead of a true wolf."

"Actually, you're right about that. Rats are much easier to kill than we are." Miris had to concede that point, and he shrugged as he started walking forward. "Wait here. You'll know what to do when the time comes."

"What?!" The wolf moved forward and growled angrily. "What are you doing?"

"Your mistress put me in charge of the lot of you." Miris shot back as he turned around, glaring at each of them present. "Spread out in these woods and stay alert. The point is to kill our enemies, free your captain, and take Chainhome. That's what I'm doing. Now do as you're told."

None of the fighters were happy about being spoken to in such a way, but they were soldiers, and they had fought with Daiva for a long time. They were accustomed to taking orders. As soon as the first few wolves dispersed through the trees, the others followed, all of them laying low and watching the other wolves hundreds of yards away.

Miris shook his head at the stubbornness of Stoneborn and walked casually out of the trees toward the main road, where he turned and headed back to Chainhome's entry ramp.

Every wolf on the ramp turned and watched him approach as soon as he came in sight, but Miris didn't stop. He was a guard there, he had a right to come and go as he pleased. "Is the princess still inside?" He called out to Takas and his mate at the top of the ramp, walking without concern between the Stoneborn standing guard all around him.

Helana, Takas' mate, looked incredibly confused when Miris showed up, since they assumed he'd been sent off by Chiara. "No. We all assumed that you ran off because she wanted you ready and waiting for her somewhere."

He let out a frustrated sigh and shook his head. "No, she sent me south to make sure the Oceanborn wasn't followed on his way here. He has incredibly annoying friends." He got up to the top of the ramp, breathing heavily, and leaned on his spear as he gestured back at the tree line. "There's a dozen or so Stoneborn out there, they didn't think I saw them on my way by. There could be more. You lot are pretty much invisible at night. The ones I saw look like his sister's people."

She looked over at Miris and shook her head. "You better stay here, then. He's in there with a baby, and a wet nurse. We'll take care of the trouble out there." Helana looked out at the rest of the Stoneborn and motioned toward the trees without saying anything. The sooner they could clean up the mess, the sooner they could get back home and be done with it.

Miris shook his head as the Stoneborn wolves ran off, and he watched for a moment just to make sure Daiva's people did their jobs well. Helana and Takas' friends had expected scared rebels when they ran into the trees. From the screams that resulted in the clash, Miris could tell they had encountered much more than that, and it made him smile as he turned back into Chainhome.

Some of the humans woke at the commotion outside as the sound of stone and screaming filled the darkness, but Miris didn't pay it or them much attention. The bars on each cell he passed bent outward to leave enough room for their occupants to leave. As he went, he picked pieces of the bars and scraped them against the stone. The edges filed off like wet clay to form crude daggers and spears. He let each one clatter to the floor behind him as he went, and he didn't hurry along the way, making weapon after weapon for the occupants.

People began filing out of their cells behind him, picking up their weapons with confused looks on their faces, but he'd already rounded the first turn in the maze of hallways before someone finally grew bold enough to speak to him.

"Miris? What's happening?" Malcom's voice was almost shrill in the cold night air, and when Miris turned around, the boy was standing in the middle of the hallway with a small, crude knife in each hand, though the iron was almost too heavy for him to use effectively.

"You're leaving." Miris said with a laugh, the utter ridiculousness of the moment washing over him in waves. "All of you are leaving. Take your things, take yourselves, and those of you who are capable of picking up a weapon, take your pick and put it to good use." He ripped off a few more doors, the bars twisting and clanging on the ground like snakes until they formed wicked flat cleavers and spears for the humans to arm themselves. "Make for the docks. If any wolf tries to stop you, kill it."

There was a crowd of humans behind him already discussing what he'd said among themselves, and he could hear them asking themselves whether or not they could trust anything Miris said, given who he was. He didn't care. He was telling the truth and no one would believe him, but that was fine by him.

He moved to the cell that recently belonged to Adriana and removed the metal from the doors completely, shaping it into half a dozen small shields hastily behind him as he stepped inside. Destin sat with his back against the far wall, his eyes on the ground, and when Miris saw the baby nearby with a wet nurse, he put together quickly what happened.

"Come on, Captain." He said quietly. "There's still a war to fight."

Destin looked up slowly, his eyes glazed over with half-frozen tears after the past few hours of darkness he had lived through, and he couldn't bring himself to get to his feet at first. Miris got closer and helped him up, but still he stood in place catching his breath, trying to bring his focus back to the present moment.

What returned him to reality was the sight of Malcom outside the bars, standing with a few dozen other humans as they waited on him. They didn't trust Miris, but they would trust him. At least that was what Adriana had said once.

What had her trust in him gotten her? Only death.

"Malcom." Destin said quietly, his voice still shaky from hours of disuse and grief. He looked back at the wet nurse holding Sheena, and gestured the woman forward, though she looked fearful with Miris standing close by. Sheena was awake and crying, but Malcom stuck his knives into his frayed belt and took the baby from the woman's arms, rocking her gently as he looked up at Destin for his orders.

"Gather up the other children and the elderly, keep them close. Everyone else who can hold a weapon needs to gather around them to protect you as you move south. Don't let anyone stray, or run. Keep them all together, and get to the shipyard. The fighting in the capital shouldn't be anywhere near there. Some of my other people have taken all the wolf children who belong to us there already and hidden them near there. You find them and you stay with them until the ships arrive. You understand?"

Malcom shook with fear and not with cold, but he nodded and bounced a little with the baby, shushing her to tell her that everything was going to be alright. As soon as Destin said something, that meant it was really happening. Which meant they were really going to go free. "I understand. We'll get there."

Destin nodded. "Miris. Get the others. Make sure everyone is out, then stay with them."

Miris gave a salute and headed out of the cell, hastening his progress through Chainhome. He ripped the bars out of every cell in the prison, arming the slaves with their own cages as he went.

He finally got up to the highest level of the prison and sighed as he pulled the final door off its hinges. He wasn't looking forward to the birthing rooms. He didn't want to see Adriana's dead body if she had died giving birth to that weakling boy's child. She had died only hours before going free. But if she was dead, he intended to make sure her body made it out of Chainhome before the place was smashed to bits. Destin would want her buried at sea.

At first Miris was greeted with an eerie silence, but once he took a few steps inside of the birthing room, he could hear Adriana cry out while several nurses tended to her by wiping away the sweat from her forehead and supporting her while she suffered through a harsh contraction.

As soon as it passed, she was the first to notice Miris,

and she did not look happy about it. "What . . . are you . . . doing here?"

"Shit." Miris said breathlessly as he looked her over, Shian still seated beside her holding a waterskin and attempting to tend to her, but he looked just as exhausted as she did.

Miris actually stumbled over himself once on his way to run back out the door and down the stairs, but by the time he got outside, a large group of human men had gotten out of Chainhome and were standing guard while they waited for everyone else to arm themselves inside.

"Destin." He asked some of the men in front near the ramp. "Did Destin already . . ."

One of them pointed to the ocean, where Miris could see Destin walking over the rocks by the shore. Before Miris could even cry out, though, he had jumped into the surf, and Miris knew he was on his way south in the freezing water to help play his part in the plan, but that didn't stop him from swearing fluently as he turned back into Chainhome, returning to Adriana's room at the end of yet another contraction.

"Get her up." He said roughly as he started giving orders to some of the midwives in the room, grabbing some blankets and some of the remains of the iron door he'd torn off the hinges on the way in.

Shian got up from where he'd been sitting beside Adriana for most of the day and rounded on Miris. "You can't move her right now, are you an idiot? She's about to . . ." He was cut off by Miris' hand clamping around his throat and his back hitting the stone behind him, hard enough to hurt but not hard enough to do permanent damage.

"Listen to me. The Isles are about to get turned inside out, and this place along with them. Once the captain's people finish with the capital, they're taking the fleet and we're all going elsewhere. So if you want your woman left behind when all that happens, that's your problem. I'm not going to be the one who answers to Destin and tells him she was actually alive, but she missed the boat."

He threw Shian aside and turned some of the iron into poles so as to make an impromptu stretcher on which they could carry Adriana to where they were going. He had started his outburst trying to keep Adriana from hearing him, but her cries had ended just as he'd started losing his temper, so he was sure she'd heard just about everything he'd said. One more thing he didn't have time to worry about.

Adriana was about to respond when her face contorted with pain again, since her contractions were so close. She was about to give birth, and he wanted to haul her out into the cold. "Hurry up!!" She couldn't think straight, and she certainly couldn't think about how to help Destin when it felt like her insides were going to rip apart. "Just hurry up! I don't care . . ." She growled like a wolf as pain ripped through her again, and she wanted to hurt Miris most of all, especially since he'd thrown Shian up against a wall. "I don't care where you take me, just hurry!"

Miris hesitated for a moment at her growl, then shook his head and started ordering around the midwives, who were humans as well and were part of the night's excitement whether they liked it or not. "You heard the woman. Get her on the stretcher and get every blanket you can find. It's going to be a long walk to the shipyard."

TWENTY FIVE

Leander reached the top of the massive arch over the shipyard after climbing too long. It was hung below with pulleys and hundreds of pieces of rope that hung useless all through the winter, but the stone arch itself didn't seem to care what season it was.

The steps carved into the side did very little to ease his mind about how high above the ground they were. He knew Marella wasn't enjoying it either, but it was the best vantage point in the area to keep an eye on the ships, the harbor, the capital, and the palace. Even Chainhome was visible farther away to the north along the curve of the shore.

The cold air bit at his skin through his thick cloak, and the darkness all around them was both unsettling and complete. It wasn't yet time for Daiva and Hassir to strike, with the morning still so far away, but he still would have preferred some kind of movement, not the ghost of peace.

In case we ever needed more proof that Skyborn are insane. Leander looked over at Taimon and two of the other Skyborn who had accompanied them to the heights, so as to listen on the winds for signs of battle and give him updates on how things were progressing. The trio seemed absolutely relaxed, actually making jokes with each other about the climb the entire way. *Who would enjoy this? Under any circumstances?*

That's why they're crazy. They spend too much time up here where the air is thin. Marella shook her head and remained close to Leander, but she looked back down to where all the children were gathered. It was a crazy scene, puppies running all around, but they were contained in a shallow pit that she and the other Earthborn had created. *Do you think we're safe enough out here?*

I think it was a good idea on Daiva's part. Melyssa will be looking to her ships, certainly, but not to the shipyard. She'll be too busy with the capital to pay much attention to anywhere else. There's no military advantage to be gained here. By the time she notices where we are, it'll be finished.

He looked to the south along the coast, and shook his head as he picked out the lines of his friends' estate along the shore. *I really thought she would have assaulted their home by now. Either they have and decided to leave the place standing, or they really haven't even begun. I don't like it when Melyssa surprises me.*

There's no one there. Marella looked toward the house as well. *Why would she waste her time destroying an empty house?* She looked over at Taimon, who was focused on the winds. *It's cold out here for those pups. I should dig deeper. Make some kind of shelter for them.*

Your brother is working on it. He motioned down at the small shelter beside the shipyard, where the earth was still growing deeper and rising on all sides. There were several dozen small children inside, and just getting them to the shipyard safely had been a miracle. Leander hoped they managed to stay out of sight. It was difficult keeping all the pups in line without a fire to keep them warm, but there were some risks they couldn't take. There were a few Fireborn women among them, and the heat from their bodies had to be enough for the time being. Until the humans arrived, if they ever did.

With any luck, we won't have to be out here for too long, and the ships will . . . he stopped short, turning to look north in the direction of Chainhome. There was no sign of movement, but she could feel the spike that had gone through Leander nonetheless. *There. Wolves are dying. I can't tell who or how many, but I can feel it. Whoever it was, they just shed the first blood in this war.*

She wished that there was a way to make Leander more comfortable, to shield him from what she knew he was going to suffer, but there was nothing Marella could do other than distract him. *Let's go down with the children. They have it handled here. The humans will be here soon.*

Unless it was a large group of humans I just felt die, and not just a few wolves. He said with another look to the north, but no wolf could see that far with any kind of accuracy. He nodded and went back down the steps, putting a hand on Taimon's shoulder to encourage the man and reaffirm that Leander would be using his eyes whenever it was necessary. *Daiva can't lose a brother again. Or if she does, she needs not to find out about it until this is over with. That family has been through too much.*

It wasn't long before the humans started to trickle in.

Marella and the others dug pocket caves in the ground to give them places away from the wind, but there were so many of them, it was difficult to shelter them all. She left Leander on his own to help until she heard a scream, and she immediately popped her head up to get out of the pit. "Leander? What was that?"

"That was the captain's human." He answered more calmly than she could tell he actually felt, but he rushed to help Miris carry the stretcher that he'd been carrying Adriana on the entire way south.

Fires sprang up in various places as the humans came in, since there were hundreds of them and they all needed to survive until the morning for their efforts to mean anything. He guided Adriana closer to one of the fires along with several of the human children whose teeth were chattering uncontrollably.

"Kaia!" He shouted into the crowd, since he could feel the human woman thinking her name and looking around for her even through the pain she was in.

Kaia felt Leander calling for her more than she heard him call her name, and she put down the three puppies in her lap before she went looking for him. When she found him, though, she found Adriana, who was doing all she could not to scream out in pain. Kaia looked panicked, but she went to Adriana's other side. She could smell blood, as every wolf could, she was sure. "Adriana, it's alright, we'll . . ."

"No, no it is not!" She bit so hard on her lip that it was bleeding along with the other parts of her as she was put down on the ground. Adriana was vaguely aware that she was out near the shipyard, the last place in the world that she imagined giving birth. "Shian!" She gripped Shian's hand so hard that she was sure she injured him, but she looked up at him as tears streamed down her face. "Now, the baby is coming now, I can feel it!"

"Good." Shian managed to say as he bunched up a blanket behind Adriana so she could sit up and push the way he knew she needed to after an entire day around the midwives. He stayed out of the way of the fire so that it could warm her as much as possible after the exhausting journey they'd taken down from Chainhome, and tried to sound calmer than he was. "Go on, then. You can do this. You know you can."

Adriana didn't know how long she spent pushing her child out. All she knew was a painful eternity until she heard both the cries of her baby and Kaia's yelp of excitement. Adriana collapsed back against the blanket Shian provided for her, panting and crying. Kaia took up the responsibility of quickly wiping off the baby before she put the tiny squirming thing against Adriana's chest.

"A girl." Kaia put another blanket over Adriana and her tiny baby, trying to make her as comfortable as she could. "She looks a lot like you, doesn't she?" She smiled at Adriana before she looked over at Shian and smiled as well. "Pretty little thing, right?"

Shian nodded breathlessly, glad to hear the little girl

crying at last. He kept a close eye on Adriana, but all he could see in her face was relief that the night was over at last. She was still moving, still crying, still alive, even though the midwives had said they were concerned about how long the birth was taking to progress. "She is. And she's right, she does look like you, Ana."

Adriana couldn't find the strength to lift up her head to look at the little girl on her chest, but she kept the baby snuggled close to her skin to keep her new little girl warm and alive. She gave him a weak smile before she closed her eyes. The midwives were still buzzing around her to get her cleaned up and deal with the after-effects of the birth. "Shanna, right?" She mumbled in her exhaustion.

He chuckled once mid-sob and leaned down to smooth away her hair and leave a kiss on her forehead. "Yes. Shanna." He had one arm beneath Adriana's as she held the baby, just to support her as he'd been trying to do all day. "I can take her if you need to rest, Ana. She'll be here when you wake up."

"Mhm." She moved the blanket aside so that he could take their baby, and she opened her eyes just to watch Kaia wrap the girl snugly. Adriana watched Shian take their tiny Shanna from Kaia and she smiled. "When she gets hungry . . ." She said softly, her eyes drifting closed again.

"We'll wake you up, I promise." He patted her hand and tucked it under a blanket as he focused on holding the baby in his arms, moving closer to the fire so she would warm as they continued to tend to Adriana, even though she was already unconscious.

Kaia smiled as she watched Shian stand next to the fire and admire his child, and she walked up behind him and patted his back lightly in a friendly gesture. "You look pretty proud, as you should be. Baby humans aren't as cute as baby wolves, but they're still cute."

"Mine is!" A small voice from nearby said as Malcom came to join them. He stopped to look at Adriana's sleeping body for a moment just to make sure she was just sleeping, though he didn't want to disturb her, just like he hadn't wanted to disturb her on the way south when he'd found out she was actually alive. He was holding a small bundle of his own, but the little girl was awake and looking around at the world, having just eaten as soon as they stopped in the shipyard. "Look at her, isn't she cute too?" He sat beside Shian, bouncing the little girl as she fussed.

Shian just had to laugh, but he nodded anyway. "Yes, she's very pretty, Malcom, but why do you have a baby?"

Malcom hesitated at that explanation, and just looked at the little girl in his arms for a moment before he was cut off by a much older voice.

"Because Destin was told that it was Adriana's daughter." Leander chimed in from nearby, having been present for the birth. Second to a mating ceremony, a birth was one of a Heartborn's favorite things in the world, so long as it went well, and he could barely feel the cold all around them in the rush of power flowing through him from the proximity. "Chiara gave Destin a choice, either stay and be imprisoned or the child would die. He chose to save the little girl."

Malcom nodded, though he still didn't like Heartborn picking things out of his head, even if they seemed nice like Leander. He looked up at Shian with an apologetic smile. "He tried to name her the way he thought you two would want. Her name is Sheena."

That made Shian smile in spite of the circumstances, and he nodded. "He was close. And Sheena is still a very pretty name."

Kaia peered in at the little girl in the boy's arms, and she looked at Shian a few times, since it did look like he could have fathered the child himself. She looked back and forth between the babies, both so fresh and new to the world. "I suppose this means you get two baby girls at once, then."

Shian wasn't sure what he thought about that, but if Chiara had stolen the girl from someone else, he hoped the mother would come looking for the baby, or at least still want to raise it herself with their newfound freedom. There were too many uncertainties for him to think about it at the moment.

"You look like you're doing a pretty good job yourself right now, Malcom, so you go ahead and hang onto her for tonight." He looked up at the sky, just barely beginning to grow light along the eastern horizon. "We all have to make it through today before we can worry about who's taking care of who."

Before the eastern sky could turn lighter with the coming sunrise, though, they all felt the ground shake, and the sky to the south turned brighter instead. Pillars of fire rose around the capital as far as the eye could see, dozens of them fanning out to envelop the entire city.

Shian put a protective arm around Malcom's shoulders as the world trembled. He had no idea if the day was going to go their way or not, but he knew enough to be afraid of the conflict regardless.

* * * * *

Daiva smiled as she looked up at the palace, her people filling in behind her. Undoubtedly those within were primed and ready for battle, and so was she.

"Finally." She turned to give the order over one shoulder, her eyes still fixed on the structure. "Prison for those who surrender. No survivors among the rest. If they resist, they have made their choice."

Her wolves ran past her in every direction at first, all of them headed for the palace directly, closed off as it was after the threat of the night before. Rather than trying to break into the palace, her wolves stopped short of the walls and started pulling them down in sheets, tearing down some of the outer rooms entirely to crack the foundations from below. They weren't just there to defeat the queen and her armies, they were there to destroy the place completely.

There was an Earthborn leader with her who came with

Asira's reinforcements. Though he had been tasked by Hassir to stay close to Daiva, he and his mate didn't fit in very well with the rest of the wolves from the Reef, and it had taken her a moment to figure out why. Torren was an Earthborn, and his mate was Forestborn. Of all the wolves to be loyal to the Reef, they were easily the least likely.

That image of them changed, though, the moment the first wolves of the Isles came pouring out of the palace to confront them, and Torren put his fist directly through the chest of another Earthborn. The kill barely seemed to faze him, and he didn't look over at Daiva as they advanced.

"How long has it been since these wolves have actually seen an assault on their home?" Torren's concern was detached and almost amused. He stumbled on the stone for a moment as a pack of Stoneborn came upon them, but at the last moment, he dodged their attack and spun, cracking the knees of a wolf with the kick that resulted. "A century? Maybe more?"

"Several. Lifetimes, really." Daiva used a large piece of stone like a sword, crushing several more Earthborn easily and similarly. "That's why they hate the Reef. Because they're so human that real wolves look like barbarians."

"Well, that explains a lot." His mate caught one wolf trying to get behind Daiva, which made Torren smile as they continued toward the palace. "I know my lord is going to be disappointed. He expected much more of a fight than this. If he had known," he paused to get into a momentary one-on-one with another Earthborn who was almost his size but nowhere near his age, a fact the man realized quickly when Torren broke his arms and then crushed his skull between his hands, "he would never have waited for the advantage of you and your people before starting this insurrection."

"I am glad, for my own sake, that he did. I'd much rather be his mate than his prisoner." Daiva watched the dead wolf crumple to the ground before she plunged her stone sword into another wolf. She pulled it out easily and swung her weapon around to knock the wolf's head off. "I see a path to the entrance. Come with me, we'll go looking for the queen."

"As you say, my lady." He was her servant now as well, a fact that all of the wolves under Hassir's authority seemed immediately aware of.

As they made their way into the palace, two of his Stoneborn dove in front of a cadre of enemy Skyborn, deflecting the attack with their own bodies in order to protect her. A pair of Fireborn roasted the wolves of the Isles alive in the next moment, calming the winds again, but Hassir's people continued to move around her closely, constantly watching for nearby threats.

Daiva knew her way around the palace, and she took great pleasure in tearing down walls so her warriors could have access to whatever might be lurking on the other side. As they moved further in, there were suspiciously too few wolves to be seen. Daiva was angrier by the minute, and everyone could feel the stones shifting and groaning beneath their feet at her mounting rage. "Where are they?"

Torren took care to stay a little ahead of Daiva as they fought their way through the halls, but he had to agree, they were meeting very little resistance. By the time they reached the luxurious apartments of the royal family, there was almost no one in the halls, and what few they came across fled as soon as they caught sight of Daiva. The pillars and flowing arches of the royal suites had taken centuries to create and perfect, the long history of ancient rulers told in countless panels through the structure, but they were empty mosaics, with no one standing by to defend them.

"They've gone." A voice called out through the halls, barely audible against the noise of the war being fought outside in the streets of the capital.

It came from Melyssa and Cadmos' own private chamber, a cavernous vault of a room with open windows and a large bed on one side, a roaring hearth in the opposite corner. In the center of the room between the two, a Stoneborn had erected a thin pillar, to which was bound a young Skyborn with his hands wrapped painfully behind his back around the stone, like some kind of sacrifice waiting for Daiva's arrival.

"They fled the capital. They left me to tell you, if you made it this far."

"If I made it this far?" She growled loudly, and the pillar he was trapped against crumbled instantly, though the Skyborn wasn't hurt in the action. She wanted him alive, especially if he was able to give her more information. "Such noble monarchs, and they run away like rats?!?" Daiva was quiet for a moment, but her silence was worse than her growling, since they could hear the ceiling cracking above them from her fuming. "In their place they leave a boy to speak for them. They deserve to lose everything."

"I won't argue with you there, my lady." The Skyborn had prudently fallen to his knees as soon as the pillar was gone from behind him, and even though the ropes he'd been bound with were falling away, he didn't move any closer. "They told me to warn you that you would not be able to win against them in a single day. If the Reef desires a war, she intends to give you one properly, as she once did." He fell silent and dropped his face to the floor without pride or dignity, hoping she wouldn't kill him for bearing the message on the queen's behalf. "If I knew where they went, I swear to you, I would tell you. Please believe me."

Daiva looked down at him, disgusted at the groveling. She didn't barge into the castle to scare children, she came to rid the world of the wolves that thought they deserved to call themselves royal. "I don't believe you for a moment. But run fast enough, and maybe you'll survive the way out."

The boy didn't have to be told twice. He shifted and ran straight out the window into the night air, borne away on currents of air that would at least see him safely down into the ocean, which was more than he could say for his chances inside the palace with the wolves of the Reef.

Torren watched the boy go with a grunt, and looked around the rest of the chamber and the still-burning fire with a disappointed glare. "The queen values her life more highly than it's worth. By noon, this entire capital will lie in ruins. Even if she and her family survive, all of her fighters here will be dead, her fleet will be gone along with the slaves that built it, and her people massacred. What victory is there in survival if your own people despise you for abandoning them afterward?"

"She must have another plan, otherwise she wouldn't just back away like this. I know her well enough to know that she always has something brewing." Daiva went to the window where the wolf had jumped out, and she looked out at the fires scattered just beyond the castle. "Let us finish our work here, then. We'll find her. Today or tomorrow, she will not hide forever."

TWENTY SIX

Hassir walked along the shore casually as he watched the city burn around him. The sun had risen an hour before, and the fighting, such as it was, seemed almost finished. Screams still filled the air of wolves in single combat and a few pockets of resistance from the wolves of the Isles attempting to make a final stand.

The real battle, more than anything that was happening on the land, had moved to the ships of the fleet out at sea, and he watched closely for evidence of his sister's work among them.

Melyssa and Cadmos had not protected their own palace or their own people so much as their means of transportation, and Hassir almost applauded their priorities. It also moved the battle away from anything that he or Daiva could participate in directly, but his sister's people were no small force.

Dozens of ships throughout the harbor and beyond into the sea were either aflame or in various stages of sinking, but all Hassir could feel as he saw them was disappointment. He couldn't kill an enemy he couldn't find, and he had no doubt that was exactly the same sentiment that had been on Melyssa's mind as soon as the threat was issued.

He looked down the sand at two figures coming up out

of the water and moving to meet them. One was Asira, blood flowing from several deep gashes in her arms and legs, but obviously nothing that kept her from walking. The other was Destin, looking a great deal more exhausted than Asira, but bearing fewer injuries.

"Have you found Melyssa and Cadmos on the ships?" Irritation was rough in his voice, telling Asira everything she needed to know about the landward battle.

"No." The water rolled off of her easily and flawlessly, almost as though it couldn't touch her in the first place. "I do not think a Fireborn queen would make an escape to the sea, do you?"

"She made her escape somewhere. She and her mate tucked their tails between their legs and fled long before we even arrived." He looked at Destin without commenting on the fact that he'd obviously survived Chiara's imprisonment and been freed. Details of what had happened would be plentiful enough later on, Hassir was sure. "You lived under them closer than most. Where would they hide?"

"With their children." Destin's eyes were on the ground and he was breathing heavily after the fight. It was more than just physical exhaustion in his demeanor. Everything about the man had nearly surrendered to the conflict itself, and he was only still moving because he was supposed to be fighting. "But that could be anywhere. Cadmos' mind works around problems, not through them. He may have run to one of the other Isles, or he may have sequestered them away in some dark hole a few hours' walk from the shore to wait out the war. All I could do is guess, and that profits us nothing."

Asira looked around for Daiva, but she wasn't surprised that her brother had split from his mate during the fight. She looked over at Destin once before she looked back at the remaining ships. "We still have work to do. They may very well be waiting for us the moment we load up the ships and take the humans out of here. The problem with not being able to kill the enemy is that it means they might be lurking at every corner. It's exactly how the Isles like to fight, I suppose."

That clearly didn't mean Hassir liked it any better, but there wasn't anything he could do about it at the moment. "Finish with the fleet and we'll be gone, then. Daiva's fighters are about to bring down the rest of the palace and return it to the sea. My people are angry that Melyssa didn't see fit to send more of her army against us and are burning everything in sight. Let Cadmos breathe some of the smoke for a while." Hassir growled, but had to work to restrain his temper. "We'll meet you at the shipyard when we're finished with the capital. Tell the rest of the transport ships to start heading there whenever you feel the fleet is clear."

"I will, brother." Her brother started to walk away and she looked over at Destin again, who looked even more battered and worse for the wear, even though he hadn't really been touched. "Fighting the Genovin had to be worse than this. Come on, cheer up. We were cheated out of a war this time, but we'll get another one soon."

Destin shook his head as they returned to the surf, wading out into the water until it was waist-high before it began to carry them both out toward the ships at a faster pace. "That's the problem. I didn't want another one. I wanted this to be the last one. The last one before we could just live in peace."

"Peace never lasts. That's why wolves like us are necessary." She followed him out into the water and just before she dove back in, she looked at him once more. "Maybe you should head to the shipyard and let me handle this. Your sister and your brother are there, aren't they?"

"They'll still be there when this is over." He knew that her offer wasn't a compliment, especially coming from a wolf who had lived her whole life on the Reef and who, he'd seen personally, was every bit as vicious below the waves as her brother was above them. "In the meantime, it looks like the Isles have taken back the Guardian. That's my ship, and I intend to get it back." He said with a glare in the direction of the flagship, where he could still see Gale's massive form fighting on deck against half a dozen other Earthborn.

"If you think you can help them." She looked toward the Guardian as well, and she could see that they might be better off sinking the ship and creating Destin a new one. "I think the Isles have them cornered . . ." Before Asira could say anything else, Destin dove into the water and headed toward his ship at breakneck speed.

Dola and Gale were two of the few still alive on the ship, and Dola was doing worse than the rest of them. One of her arms was so broken that she couldn't move it, and her forehead was cut open so deep that she was bleeding down the side of her face and blind in one eye from her own blood. The gusts she was able to produce were getting weaker, and somewhere in the back of her mind, she knew she was going to die.

"Gale? Gale!" She wanted to be close to her mate, but she had a hard time seeing him, even if she could feel that he was still alive.

"I've got you." His growl came through to her the moment before he caught her, running along the deck away from the current pack of enemy Earthborn. They'd taken him and Dola and several others of their crewmates by surprise minutes before, swimming through the chaos of the shipwrecks all around them and climbing up the sides of the ship while he and Dola had been watching the rest of the battle.

He set her against the railing so she would have a point of reference to hold onto, then spun and engaged the other Earthborn, careful to avoid allowing any of them to get a solid grip on him. "Have you looked at the shore lately?" He screamed at the wolves attacking him, one of them even foolish enough to attack in wolf form, hoping for an advantage of teeth and claws. Gale shattered the wolf's face with his fist and kicked the crumpled corpse at another of the attackers. "Your people have already gone down in flames! What exactly do you think you're going to accomplish out here?"

"They just want the ship!" Dola snarled, holding on with her one good arm, picking up the wolf's body and throwing it into the water. She didn't know where Destin was, or why they had been so ill-prepared, but she could hardly think of anything through the pain. It felt like her arm was gone, it just didn't exist, even though she knew it was still attached and unmoving at her side. She was still bleeding profusely, but she couldn't get it to stop. "I can't . . . I'm so tired, Gale." She eventually said out loud, even though she knew it sounded ridiculous. Tired? Tired in battle?

He took down another wolf as he tried to get closer to her, throwing it off the side, but as he approached, one of the Isles fighters blindsided him and firmly planted a shoulder in his ribs, breaking a few of them on impact. He cried out in pain, but managed to hold onto the female who'd assaulted him and snap her neck. He had been thrown on the deck of the ship in the process, though, leaving another wolf to force his way closer to Dola through the winds she was using to defend herself. "On your left! Dola!"

There was a spray of water that rained down on them just as her attacker got close, and she was distracted enough that the attacker made his blow, a fist slamming into her ribs and breaking more than a few of them. The wind died down immediately, especially because she felt like she couldn't breathe, the worst feeling in the world for a Skyborn wolf like her. Dola gasped loudly as she crumpled to the deck, desperately trying to take a full breath even though she was sure that one of her lungs had collapsed under the impact.

The water that poured over the deck turned into a harsh weapon a moment later, but neither Dola nor Gale were capable of watching what unfolded after Dola went down. The wolves who had previously been attacking either ran for the other end of the ship where the new threat had emerged, or jumped overboard.

In the haze of pain that washed over her, though, Dola

felt Gale's hand laid over hers, soaked with seawater or blood, it was hard to tell. "Still here." He grunted across the soaked wood of the deck, but she could feel his hand shaking, and the strength she could normally rely on to flow from him dwindling by the moment.

"Don't go." She coughed out, but she could taste blood, and it felt like her whole chest was on fire from within. Dola tried to move closer to him, but slipped several times and cried out before she rolled into his chest from the movement of the ship. She whimpered as she looked up at him with one eye, now blurred with tears from both pain and sadness. "The . . . pups . . . you." It was nearly impossible to talk, but she had to try.

Gale's hand moved up to caress her face, but she could feel his chest heave as he attempted to breathe through his injuries, unsuccessfully. He managed to whisper out what sounded like an attempt at her name as his fingers wound with hers, but the strength left his muscles completely a moment later, as all the remaining strength that was a part of her nature borrowed from his own fled as well.

Dola whimpered loudly as she felt his life slip away, and just like that, there was no reason for her to continue to fight for breath. There was a shadow that fell over her as she heaved her last breaths, and she barely noticed her Captain looking down at her before she grabbed onto Gale's clothing once more and sighed out his name with her last breath. As devoted she was to fighting for her Captain, her love for Gale was stronger, but even that hadn't saved either of them from the Isles.

The silence that fell over the boat as Destin saw his oldest friend die in front of him was as cold and empty as the ship itself. It swayed in the morning breeze under nothing but the chaos of the ocean and the fight still going on in other ships in the distance, but Destin couldn't bring himself to care.

He looked from their bodies to those of the other wolves his friends had killed before their injuries claimed them, and he took the time to throw the bodies of their enemies overboard, regardless of the wolf's element. When the deck was empty, he walked slowly to the prow and looked out over the cold morning, his breath misting in the air in front of his face before it vanished as quickly as the dreams he'd held for the day itself.

Asira was right. Nothing they did mattered. No revolution would ensure peace, it would only prolong and provoke a war that had been raging between the great families of the isles for centuries, and he had been a fool to ever believe otherwise. Peace was every bit as much a fairy tale as the stories his parents had told him as a child, of an age when all the isles of the sea, from the Barren Isle in the north all the way to the southern wasteland of the Genovin kingdom, were all ruled under a single kingdom. A single council of rulers had unified the entire world in peace for generations before petty jealousies and feuds had torn it apart again.

There had never been such an age. Wolves were incapable of that kind of unity, that kind of peace. If wolves as honest and true as Gale and Dola, as true to their ideals as his own parents, could be killed for trying to build the kind of world they wanted, then the gods didn't care. The world would keep spinning, and the battles would keep raging between one isle and another. All that changed was the players and the arena.

Destin wanted no part of it. Not anymore.

The ship began to move north, away from the rest of the fighting. Asira could finish up with the rest of the fleet, he was sure. There were very few of the Isles' ships remaining, and those few were either already going down or thoroughly controlled by Asira's people.

Destin could see half a dozen more ships approaching from farther east out to sea, the transport vessels Hassir had mentioned, kept in reserve in case too many of the Reef's other ships were lost in the battle. He didn't pay them any attention as he headed north, straining at the force necessary to move the ship all on his own, but it was a worthy kind of exhaustion that would be waiting for him. He would get the humans to their new home. Perhaps that, he could call a victory for the day, if nothing else.

It was so busy around the shipyard that Kaia was surprised they hadn't been discovered somehow, but she did everything she could to help with the young. All kinds of children seemed to like her well enough, and Malcom kept by her side to help when he wasn't staying close to Adriana to guard her while she slept.

She heard Taimon's shout from above, which turned her attention to the water. She smiled when she saw the Guardian, hoping it meant her brother was alright, and she went running toward the water, leaving everything else behind.

Gathering all the humans at the shipyard had originally been Destin's idea, since it was one of the few places along the coastline where the water was deep enough for ships to come right up against the retaining wall set in place while ships were under construction. The Guardian did just that, the water pushing it right up against the stone wall where several of the humans rushed to tie it off so it would remain in place.

Destin appeared afterward, stumbling down a ramp one of the humans pulled down to the ground. He caught Kaia in a tight hug once she ran up to him, glad that she was obviously alright. Destin kissed her on the cheek once as he looked around at a few of the others who'd come to greet him, Leander and Marella included.

"Cadmos and Melyssa were nowhere to be found. Asira is securing the rest of the fleet. Daiva and Hassir are still busy laying waste to the city, but have assured me they will join us in time. There are more ships coming to carry everyone away."

It was impossible to miss the look of exhaustion and dejection on his features in spite of the victory he was reporting, and he brushed past Kaia and Leander with a final pat on his sister's shoulder. "I need to rest. Let me know when the ship is ready to depart. I need a crew of at least a few able-bodied sailors to replace those who've been lost."

She was surprised when he brushed past her, and she ran up to his side again, immediately supporting him when he continued on his way. "Here, follow me, I know where you can rest." She stood against Destin's side and put his arm around her shoulders to walk him away, and for once, he didn't protest the show of weakness.

She got him away from the ship, where others had taken over directing some of the humans onto the deck, still bearing most of his weight. "You've been lied to." She said abruptly by the time they got to one of the low fires built to keep the slaves warm and alive. She had to turn Destin and physically point him in the direction of an empty space beside the fire. Right next to Adriana.

He would have caught himself and kept from falling if not for the face that appeared above the blanket right in front of him, and all he could do was fall the rest of the way with one hand braced on the stretcher and the other on the ground. "You . . ." his heart was pounding in his chest and his mind was reeling, doubting what was in front of him after having been so thoroughly convinced that she was dead. "You're alive . . ."

His voice was dry and worn, and she could feel the hand closest to her shaking as the extremities of the night took their toll, but the look in his eyes desperately wanted to believe what he was seeing.

"I'm alive." Adriana smiled gently and nodded as she reached out and touched his cheek, since she was sitting up slightly as her baby was tucked in under a blanket and pressed against her breast. "This little girl sure made me fight for it, but I'm alive. I never thought I'd give birth in a shipyard, though." She laughed softly and searched his eyes afterward, since she didn't know what he'd been through since she had seen him last. No one had time to say much to her between birth and sleep. "Miris took us from the birthing room and brought us out here. I was worried that something had happened to you . . ."

He was silent for a long time as he just stared back at her, taking in the sound of her voice that he thought he would never hear again. "I came to see you . . . last night. Chiara . . . she told me you had died in childbirth, she brought . . ." he snapped out of his daze a little as he looked around blindly. "Where's Malcom?"

"He's asleep." Shian answered gently from nearby, since he hadn't wanted to speak up and disturb the reunion in front of him. "And Sheena with him."

Destin's eyes took in the human beside Adriana slowly, since it was the first time he'd seen the man awake and so close. He had been with Adriana when Destin hadn't been, but there was no anger in his Oceanborn eyes as he looked Shian over. "I'm glad they made it safely." His eyes returned to Adriana, and he pushed himself up a little more so that he could sit beside her. "I didn't think I would ever see you again."

Her green eyes held his deep blues, and she moved just enough so that she could lean her face in closer to his. "You freed us." She could feel her little baby squirming against her skin, so she moved the blanket just enough so that Destin could see the little baby against her chest. "I'm not going anywhere unless it's with you, Destin." She promised as he turned his gaze down to her tiny baby. "I love you."

He leaned his head down against hers, nuzzling the side of her face in a caress that was more wolf than human. The sigh of relief that escaped him at the scent of her seemed to drain all the tension and exhaustion out of him with the breath. "I love you too, Adriana. And this time, I'm not letting you out of my sight for a very long time."

"Good." She let out a sigh at the feel of his skin on hers again, and once she was able, she kissed him gently. Once Shanna seemed satisfied after feeding, Adriana wrapped her up snugly and gave her to Shian so that she could go back to sleep. As happy as she was to see Destin, she was still exhausted. Adriana did reach for Destin, though, since she wanted him to stay with her before she was willing to close her eyes. There were no bars separating them anymore, and no wolves that would stop Destin now. "Stay here with me, by the fire."

He nodded against her shoulder and kissed her once before he began to drift off along with her, giving no mind to anything else happening around them. Some of the humans volunteered as crew members on Destin's ship in the distance. Taimon and Miris took up impromptu positions supporting Destin in choosing who was capable and who wasn't, even though neither of them had served on a ship before.

Other ships came in as well, keeping their distance from the shipyard, but in that moment, none of it mattered. Victory didn't matter, Melyssa and Cadmos' survival didn't matter. The one and only important thing to Destin in the world was the beat of Adriana's heart beneath his arm as he held her.

Maybe, just maybe, everything they'd fought for hadn't been in vain. Maybe there was a chance for them to have the life they wanted. Maybe.

For the time being, maybe was enough.

TWENTY SEVEN

After hearing far too many reports, Melyssa was burning everything in sight from their hidden cliffside home on the opposite end of the island from her palace. She could still see everything burning, she knew her palace no longer existed, and she was furious.

Damos and his mate were with them, but Chiara had yet to return, if she was even still alive, and their other two sons had not arrived. "This was a mistake." She growled as another chair in the house was set aflame. "We should have stopped that Reefborn mutt the moment he . . ."

"Stopping Hassir here would have been meaningless." Cadmos responded quietly, not moving from the seat he'd taken by the window to watch the devastation the Reef had wrought on their home. "It would only have encouraged the entire force of the Reef to muster against us to finish what he attempted."

Melyssa really hated listening to her mate sometimes, especially when he was right. "I understand that. But we did nothing when they violated us, destroyed our homes, killed our people . . ." She shook her head as she glared at Cadmos. "Who is going to follow us into battle now?" They had preserved most of their armies by scattering them and sending them away, leaving only the weakest behind for

Hassir to contend with, but that did not mean that those lives lost counted for nothing.

"The lives lost, and the damage done, will permit us to push our kingdom to prepare for the real fight to come." He said without changing his tone, even if he knew Melyssa was close to killing him for his calm and infuriating nature.

He turned and caught her eyes without looking away, an intensity in his ice-blue eyes that matched her own, even if it was of a different kind. "When we called the captains together and sent them against the Genovin, we had to wheedle and coerce them into action. These Isles have been at peace for too long. They've become accustomed to the taste of it in their mouths, and the true dangers of the world have been kept at a distance."

"And that's a bad thing?" Damos interjected, obviously confused. "Hassir was always a threat, there's not much that could have been done to change that besides killing him, but even that would have provoked the Reef into a war. There were other things we could have done to try and keep the peace, though. Less restrictions on the commerce of the Reef, greater freedoms within their own borders . . ."

"Peace is useless, Damos." Cadmos shot at his thick-headed son, growing quickly impatient with his outlook on life. He might have been Melyssa's favorite child, but Damos was easily the least useful of their children, in Cadmos' eyes. Even Chiara understood more of the world they lived in than her brother did. "Until our family has control of all the isles, including the Genovin, we will not have the freedom to fulfill our designs. The plans your mother and I have made for you and your siblings are for nothing until that happens. And that will not be accomplished through peace."

"At least our best are unharmed and retained for battle, whenever that may actually come." Melyssa grumbled as she turned her attention to Damos again. "Soon your brothers will be here, and together we can plan for the war that Hassir seeks. I will not take this quietly."

"That possibility never crossed anyone's mind, Mother." Damos said before he thought better of it, but he didn't back down afterward, even if he did move in front of his mate protectively in case his mother decided to lash out at him for the comment.

Cadmos spoke quickly before Melyssa could lose her temper at their idiot son. "Your brothers will be here shortly, but your sister is another matter. Why hasn't she returned with Destin as she was instructed?"

"Maybe because you sent her to Chainhome with nothing more than a few dozen Stoneborn and those Ironborn she keeps as pets. In the middle of a war." Damos' anger turned to his father, since he was worried that Chiara had been killed or carried off during the conflict.

As soon as Damos moved in front of his mate, Melyssa narrowed her eyes at the female. She still did not understand why he had chosen the Forestborn. There was still a large part of her that was angry he had mated in secret without their consent. "If she is dead, then we will proceed without her." Melyssa was not the least bit disappointed to think that her daughter might be dead, but she did raise an eyebrow at her son. "That might cause a problem for you and your little flower."

Damos turned to look Bethalyn in the eye at that, and took her hand gently, even though he knew his mother hated it when he showed any affection for her in front of others. "Don't worry about us, Mother." The look in his mate's eyes was slightly hollow at the moment, as it had been for a long time, but he knew that, for the moment at least, it was probably for the best. He had seen Bethalyn when provoked, and she was capable of any manner of violence required of her, but she didn't have the heart for war, even at her best.

Cadmos ignored the conversation, since he had even less patience for Damos' choice of mate than Melyssa did. "Calis has arrived." Everyone immediately looked to the windows, where they could see a single ship coming up along the coast toward them, flying deep blue sails to proclaim his presence on board.

"Finally." Melyssa moved away from her mate and her son to go to the other. "Let's hope Malis is close behind." Melyssa left scorch marks on the door when she pushed it open. She shoved off her deep red robes and shifted so she could run faster to Calis' ship.

The ship drew into the deep waters of the cove nearby, and Melyssa could see several of Calis' Oceanborn servants around the vessel in the water to steady it. He and a few others were in a longboat already pulling up on the beach when she got close enough, and those who were with him undressed and shifted as well when they saw that she was in wolf form to greet them.

Calis was almost as beautiful a wolf as Chiara, his fur the pure white of his mother with only a few black streaks near his paws to distinguish him from Melyssa aside from his greater size. His mate, Ressa, ran behind him, deep brown and reddish fur in a dozen different shades catching the afternoon light as the sun began its descent toward the horizon over the ocean. Their eldest surviving son, Mavros, walked behind them, looking almost exactly like his father except for being slightly larger and leaner, his eyes only a ghostly Skyborn shade of the deep blue that belonged to both his parents.

We saw the smoke from the capital. Calis began without wasting any time. They'd had no word from his parents since they were informed of the threat as it had been issued the night before, and he was clearly itching to fight, as were the others disembarking from his ship behind him.

That is because Hassir and his dogs destroyed it. Melyssa said with a growl, but she was glad to see her son and his mate. Calis had chosen a mate that was clearly his equal, and she and Cadmos had approved of the match. *Your father . . . and I decided it was best to have more time to prepare for Hassir and his people. We pulled out most of our armies and scattered them to save them for the fight ahead. We decided to wait for you and your brother and your people. Hassir ran around and destroyed buildings, mostly. They took apart Chainhome.*

And our slaves along with it, I'm sure. Calis' mind was already churning through the implications. She could see that he mostly agreed with what they had done, given the time they'd had to prepare. *Hassir and his people will flee south and close their borders as well as they are able. He may come north again soon, though, if he feels he has an opportunity. It is you he wishes to kill. Nothing else will satisfy him.*

I know what he wants. Melyssa turned her attention to the water, and she looked in the direction of the Reef. *We are going to destroy him and his new mate and anyone else that stands in our way. That Reef is going to be ours again, and Damos will rule it himself in order to keep it from being defiled again.*

In time, perhaps. Calis agreed with his mother's ambitions, but he was perpetually grateful that his father was still alive to help keep her realistic. He started walking beside her back up toward the house on the side of the hill, his mind spinning through the details. *It's been a very long time since we've gone up against the Reef so openly, and Hassir is far more vicious than his grandmother ever was. We made him that way. If we're to have any hope of success, this will have to be accomplished slowly. A revolt like this has set us back years, not just days and buildings.*

I do not think we have years. Melyssa looked up at the house. *If Chiara is still alive, we might be able to swing the Genovin to back us. We can blame the attack on Destin and say that our fleet was led by a captain who sought to take us down. We might be able to convince the Genovin to help us.*

What do you mean, if Chiara is still alive? Calis sounded angry at the uncertainty. *Why isn't she with you? What about Damos and Bethalyn?*

Chiara was sent to take care of Destin, and clearly she did not do as she was told. She went to Chainhome last I knew, and Chainhome does not exist anymore. She probably did us a favor. Melyssa shook her head, and she did not look back at Calis. *Damos and his mate are fine. They are here with us.*

Mavros, go find your aunt. He glanced back at his son

walking behind him, and watched as he took off running up the hill on his way to where Chainhome had once stood miles away across the island. *If she is alive, we will need her assistance. And if you will forgive me for speaking so freely, you and Father need to give up on the possibility of her retaining Destin's loyalty or having his children. It's a wonder she hasn't tried to kill you herself after what you've put her through.*

Perhaps she already has tried. Melyssa wasn't the least bit apologetic, and she certainly would not be to Calis. *She tried to betray us with the family that just destroyed our home and declared war against us. If she's alive, then perhaps we can still use her. If not, we will not miss her intolerable character.*

That may be, but our chances of victory are that much slimmer without her. Calis reached the house and shifted, snatching a set of robes as they were handed to him by a servant near the door, then waited for his mother to do the same before he continued, shrugging the fabric over his shoulders and tying it at his waist. "Even your gods won't be able to help you if you anger Chiara's daughter."

Melyssa pulled her robes tightly around her waist. "We should start our discussions right away. We'll bring Malis up to speed when he arrives." She motioned to a much warmer room, with food waiting for all of them. Clearly whatever had been destroyed didn't stop them from being the royalty they were born to be. Now they just had to destroy everyone who was trying to get in their way.

* * * * *

The Guardian kept back to carry off the very last of the humans and the fighters from the shore. Destin wanted to allow Adriana as much time as possible to rest before embarking on a long sea voyage. He also wanted to be personally certain that all the humans who had escaped from Chainhome were carried off and all the wolves who wished to leave Melyssa's kingdom had a chance to depart.

Every ship remaining for the Reef departed carrying a

heavy load of wolves seeking asylum in the south, and several ships were underway with nothing but humans on board and a few wolves to help navigate the ocean. He wondered if any such voyage had ever been undertaken before, with such mixed cargo.

Destin approached Miris as some of the last of the humans helped the children board the second to last ship. Lines of worry creased his face, concerned that the voyage would be cramped and uncomfortable, but there was nothing else to be done. "Making new friends?"

Miris smiled back at Destin in the company of the Stoneborn around him, who were distinctly not smiling, but didn't seem to want to kill the Ironborn. At least not at the moment. "Resolving a misunderstanding, Captain, nothing more. They thought I betrayed them and tried to get them killed. I thought I was just setting them up to have some fun. Perfectly normal lack of communication."

"I see." Destin said without looking convinced, and nodded toward the north, his eyes scanning the dozen or so Stoneborn who remained of the group that Daiva had put under Miris' charge. "I want you to go back up to Chainhome and sweep the area while everyone is still too terrified to come out and face us directly. Make sure the place is leveled and swept into the ocean. Leave a monument, if you lot are feeling creative."

"Creative?" Miris looked behind him at his new 'friends' and shook his head. "Right. Creative. Let's go, then." He set off at a run before the other Stoneborn could raise any word of protest, and they ran after him, though none of them looked particularly happy about it.

The place had been mostly destroyed in the initial attack of the Stoneborn, but Miris stood back and watched as they gleefully finished their work. Or at least he thought they looked gleeful. It was hard to tell with Stoneborn most of the time whether they were actually enjoying their work or angry about it.

Miris remained by the tree line as huge hunks of stone

fell away into the ocean, and the Stoneborn paused for a moment to listen for screams before going further, judging by the silence that the structure had in fact been abandoned.

"You didn't leave much, did you?" Chiara said from behind him, and just after he heard her voice, he could feel her touch from behind. "I didn't expect there would be much left once Hassir and Daiva were finished. I'm sad you didn't come looking for me, though. Save the humans but not the lover?"

He flinched as soon as she touched him, but he didn't move away from her. He knew there was no point. She would do with him as she pleased, all because he'd been distracted enough not to be aware of his surroundings. "I've never been your lover, princess. I've been your plaything, and as much fun as you're aware it's been for me, that's all I ever would have been."

"I wouldn't say that, but you can label it however you please." Chiara pulled back her touch and moved to his side so he could see her. "I enjoyed you more than most." She looked at Chainhome once before she looked up at Miris again. "You made the right choice."

He looked over at her without moving away, since he was confused by her lack of an actual response. "You still could, if you wanted to. I'm not saying the captain would let you on board with his human after everything you've done to them both, but you're one of the most powerful wolves walking these isles right now. You really can do whatever you want. Go wherever you choose, do as you please when you get there. There's nothing keeping you here."

"There is always something keeping a Heartborn somewhere. But you're right about the nothing. I usually feel nothing. Especially not powerful." She sighed and looked down at herself, since she was actually bleeding from one arm. As soon as things had fallen apart at the castle and her family had left her without any information about where they had gone, some of the wolves turned against her. She was still alive, though, which was a testament to how powerful she really was. Even outnumbered. "There are a few lingering humans in the forest. Somehow they got lost, but I'm sure you can get them to the boats, right?"

"We'll make sure to round them up before we leave." He wasn't sure why she was actually helping him if she had no intention of leaving, but he wasn't going to question it. "I don't imagine I'll see you again. Honestly, I'm not even sure where we're going, so I can't even say that for sure, but I'm sure it's far away from here."

"Don't come back until you are ready. I'm sure Calis and Malis will be here soon." She stared up into his hazel eyes before she grabbed onto his robes and pulled him into a kiss. She made some kind of connection with many of the humans leaving and a deeper connection with Miris. More than he would ever remember. It was taking a painful toll on her Heartborn mind that they were leaving. "Goodbye, Miris."

She could feel the deep conflict of emotions in him at the kiss, and even as he looked at her afterward, he couldn't decide how to feel about the fact that she was letting them go. Rather than letting her move away, he stepped in closer to her and put one of his hands along the side of her neck, holding her close as he looked down into her eyes.

Someone told me recently that I deserved a better life than the one I already had. I didn't believe them at first when they told me either. I won't pretend to know you well enough to know what you deserve and what you don't, but you can have a better life than this, if you're willing to take it. The piercings in her ears hummed at his proximity, and she could feel some of his power moving through her, plentiful after an entire night and day in the fine armor she'd given him. *So take it, however you have to.*

Chiara enjoyed his touch on her skin, and it made her heart pound with renewed power, even if it was only just a little. *I'm dead no matter where I go, Miris. It's exactly what my parents wanted as soon as I was born, so I would have nowhere to turn but toward them.* She reached up and ran a hand along his arm. *I have someone I need to protect. That's my life.*

She liked the way the metal hummed against her skin and she sighed as she stepped away from his touch. *You should know something else.* She stepped up so that she could whisper into his ear. "Malis let your sister die. His mate was threatened by his attraction to her."

She could feel the armor covering him thrum and his anger darken the air around her as she said so. He growled low in his chest and sighed to calm himself, since it hadn't been Chiara's idea, clearly. "Then I look forward to seeing your brother and his mate again someday."

"I hope you do." She ran her fingers across his face to savor him a moment longer. "You better go before you get left behind." Chiara didn't understand it herself, the emotions she felt, except that maybe she had allowed herself to get closer to Miris than she had realized in the aftermath. She was sure that she was numb to caring anymore, but maybe not completely.

He gave her a final kiss before he pulled away, and waited for her to disappear into the trees before he approached the Stoneborn still destroying Chainhome. When they were finished, nothing remained of the place except a jagged coastline that looked like it might have been natural, and Miris approved. It was as though Chainhome had never even existed, and as far as he was concerned, it was good riddance.

TWENTY EIGHT

It was a rough trip for ships filled with humans that had never traveled so far by sea, but after days of travel, the island Destin had told Adriana about came into view. She was sitting out on the deck as the boat moved along at a steady pace, wrapped in several blankets, as was her little girl. Shian had fallen asleep beside her while Destin was guiding the Guardian, and she smiled as she looked over at him.

Shian was wrapped up tightly as well, but the constant spray of the sea was enough to ensure that he only ever slept lightly on the ship. The sleeping baby girl tucked against his chest looked more like him than he felt comfortable admitting, since he had never been intimate with anyone on the Isles other than Adriana. The mother of the baby that Malcom had cared for never came looking, even when the ships all gathered together on the ocean to distribute supplies. Instead of allowing the baby to be taken away, Adriana and Shian had decided that they would care for both of the girls as though Adriana had given birth to both.

She nursed both, snuggled both, and kissed them as though they both were her own. She'd lost three other children, two of which could have been among the other freed humans and she would never know, but these, these she could keep, and she wanted to.

"Shian." She said softly into his ear, and she nudged him carefully to wake him but not little Sheena in his arms. "Shian. I can see the island."

He woke up with a start, but looked down immediately to make sure Sheena hadn't woken up with him before he rubbed sleep from his eyes and looked around to see what Adriana was talking about. The island was barely visible against the horizon, a low, flat thing seeming to come just barely up out of the ocean. It was small wonder no other wolves had ever stumbled upon it.

He looked around the rest of the ship and saw a dozen other transport ships from the Reef nearby, all of them waiting on Destin's to approach first, since they had traveled to the island on his word alone, with no other guarantees that the humans would be safe or even welcome there.

"It's just an island." He said with skepticism heavy in his voice, since he had no idea of the actual reception that was waiting for them. He believed Adriana when she said she trusted Destin, and he had certainly made good on his word so far in freeing them from Chainhome and carrying them away from the Isles, but Shian's trust in a wolf would never go so far as to be absolute, on such short acquaintance. "It could have a thousand wolves on it, as far as I care right now, so long as it has some food and water."

"Don't be so grumpy." She kissed him on the cheek, and got up slowly to watch as the boat moved the rest of the way to shore.

It looked like they had stumbled upon just a scrap of land, but as soon as Destin swam away from the ship and onto the shore, the island seemed to come to life. Surely the people had seen the ships off the shore as they approached, and apparently they'd been waiting patiently to see who was coming to their island.

Destin came up out of the surf onto the sandy beach and walked up slowly once he allowed the water to recede back into the ocean. He was glad to see Elyra foremost among the people who had gathered, and he smiled as he saw her. "In all fairness, I did warn you that I would be back."

"You did. And we have been waiting." Elyra said with a smile as she looked back at his ship. "You had to travel a long way. There are houses that have prepared rooms and beds, and we've even erected some shelters for the people that won't fit into houses. We've put all of our efforts into getting ready while you have been gone."

Destin was glad to have been taken seriously, and he took Elyra's hand warmly to thank her. "There are only so many wolves with me as were needful to move our ships. If you're ready, I'll start bringing people ashore. Me and my crew would like permission to remain out here on the coast, at least until we can be certain our people have been settled."

She nodded and smiled even brighter as she looked at the wolf in front of her. "It was a hard sell, convincing the other Elders to let you and other wolves stay on the shore, but they'll let you. For now."

Destin pulled the massive ship closer through the water, until several wolves dropped from the prow and began to alter the shape of the beach in front of them. The sand moved away to accommodate the Guardian and flowed in again around it to hold it in place on the beach as several ladders dropped down from the railing.

There were some shouts of surprise behind him from the humans, obviously not accustomed to working with many wolves, but he ignored them as the other ships drew closer and Shian started down the ladder.

When Shian reached the beach, he breathed a sigh of relief and held Sheena tighter against his chest. He crossed the short distance to Destin and the woman beside him, who was older than any human he'd ever seen in his short life.

"You really are here." He said quietly, obviously still caught up in disbelief as he looked around at the group of humans moving toward the ships to help his own companions down, including Malcom and Adriana, who were among the next humans to descend to the sand.

"I can understand why you did not easily trust a wolf." Elyra looked down at the tiny baby in his arms. "You should not be out here with such a new little thing. Come with me to my house. There are beds prepared, and I have food."

Shian waited for Adriana to catch up before he followed, but soon they had both girls down to sleep in a pile of warm furs near Elyra's fire. Destin watched in silence as the tide of humans poured off the ships by the dozens, by hundreds, so many that he was amazed they had all been packed at one time into Chainhome. Many of them were still just as skeptical as Shian had been about their new home, but Elyra's people took all of them by the arm and led them to the shelters, each of which was already worlds better than Chainhome, rudimentary and crude as most of them were.

When the ships were empty, Destin smiled at the sight of Taimon and Kaia coming down the ladder last of all, with Daiva and Hassir coming from another ship in the distance to meet him. The lord of the Reef had wanted to see the island with his own eyes to be assured of its placement outside of his dominion, and Destin was glad of Hassir's silence as the man approached. It meant the humans would be left alone to live in peace, even by the Reef.

"I think we brought more than they were expecting." Taimon chuckled as he reached Destin, looking over the shelters already overflowing around the seaside village. He could hear some discussions among the townspeople of how they were going to accommodate the rest of the humans. Though there was a great deal of stress in the air, everyone was working on the problem rather than arguing, at least for the time being.

"I am sure they will figure it out." Daiva did not like the idea of being around so many humans and so few wolves any more than the humans liked the idea of the wolves being around. "They'll be safe here, and they won't get in the way when we have to fight the Isles again."

Destin sighed as he looked over at his sister. "Even here,

outside of anything the Isles have ever known, you still can't imagine peace? I realize that Melyssa and Cadmos are still alive somewhere, but even with their power and the entire population of the Isles, it's going to take them a long time to rebuild their fleet and regain the confidence of their people to come after us."

"I'm being realistic, Destin." She replied sharply, though she honestly could not imagine a life that was just . . . peace. It sounded boring, really. "You did a good thing for these humans, I think. That's what you should be happy about, but realize that peace comes and goes."

Kaia rolled her eyes as well. "You are truly terrible to be around sometimes. People died. Good wolves died. You don't have to be so severe."

Taimon cleared his throat and looked back and forth between Kaia and Destin sheepishly. "She's just being a ruler now. Better than Melyssa and Cadmos ever were, obviously. If they had still believed it was possible anyone could attack them and live to tell about it, none of us would be here right now. It's good to be worried about that kind of thing when you have to think about other people's safety all the time."

Daiva looked over at Taimon with obvious surprise in her eyes, but she appreciated he acknowledged what she was taking on, and that she wasn't trying to be cruel or violent. She was trying to be an efficient ruler. She gave Taimon a slight nod before she looked past her siblings and along the shore. "I am assuming we are meant to find or make our own shelter. I'll find something."

"I've gotten permission from the local Elders to make a home for my crew along the shore, so long as it's something low in profile that won't attract too much attention from the sea." Destin clarified before she moved away. "Miris and the Stoneborn you assigned to him will assist you, if that's alright. He's going to be one of my commanders aboard the Guardian now, so he'll be staying here with us."

"Really?" Kaia asked a little too loudly, but it was hard

for anyone to tell if she was surprised in a good way or in a bad way. She looked down at her bracelet again and stole a look over at Taimon who just shook his head. "What can I do, Destin?"

Destin smiled at the question, and gave her and Taimon a look that lasted long enough for both of them to start looking confused. "Sorry, I'm just remembering the little sister I had a year ago who would have run off to amuse herself as soon as she was finished with her chores rather than asking how she can help."

He chuckled at the memory and nodded toward the slight rise in the shoreline where Daiva started drawing stone out of the ground to assemble their home. "Make sure Daiva leaves space behind our new home for your garden. It's likely she'll forget. Until everyone's settled here and we can go south to the Reef, I want you to stay here with me."

"What about me?" Taimon could tell he was being excluded from that invitation, and the implications didn't settle well with him.

Destin's smile dimmed, but he had spoken about their brother with Daiva on the way to the Free Isle. "When Daiva leaves for the Reef, you'll go with her, if only for a while. You still have a lot to learn from Hadria and the other masters of your kind who are part of Hassir's councils. When Daiva decides you're ready to be on your own, you can live wherever you like, on the Reef or with the other exiles on Daiva's estates, but for now, you need to focus on your studies."

Taimon was clearly crestfallen at that, but he nodded without trying to argue. "Alright, if that's what you want me to do, I can do that."

Kaia clearly wasn't happy about that either, and she immediately went to Taimon's side, since they had never been separated before. She didn't want Taimon to be all the way at the Reef while she and Destin were not with him. "But Taimon and I . . ." She grabbed Taimon's arm and looked back at Destin, even though she knew he wasn't likely to change his mind.

"I know." Destin said with an apology in his eyes, but he shook his head afterward. "There's no place for you on the Reef, except at the Falls, and I don't trust strangers with your education. Maybe when we've come to know them better, you can go to study with Felja and Torren, but for now, I want you where I can take care of you, and Taimon needs to be on the Reef."

He and Daiva had been lucky enough to remain home for their entire childhood, but such a change for their siblings was one more casualty of the war they had started. "It won't be forever. For either of you."

Kaia was still frowning as she clung to her brother, but she looked up toward the house Daiva was building. "Can he come with me, then?"

Destin nodded and waved the two of them off. "Go on. Daiva won't leave for a few more days at least."

Kaia didn't start to cry until she was walking away with Taimon, and she buried her face into his arm as he led the way. She was already trying to think up an argument that would convince Destin to let Taimon stay. "I don't want you to go."

"I don't want to go either." He held his sister against him, but he was trying not to cry, trying to be more like Daiva and take on the responsibility that Destin handed him. "But Destin's right about a few things. I do have a lot I still have to learn. But I won't be staying on the Reef for very long once Daiva says I can live on my own, I can promise you that. I'll come back and get her to build me a house near yours with the rest of the exiles, or maybe we'll both go live on the Falls and let Destin and Daiva worry about fighting wars while we take care of feeding the kingdoms."

They stopped midway to the house so they could sit near some of the trees, though they were small and sickly-looking because they were so close to the sand and seawater. She leaned back on a thin tree trunk, and she sighed when she felt it against the back of her head. As soon as Taimon sat down, she grabbed his hand again, her new bracelet jingling softly as she reached out. "You can learn anywhere. The wind is everywhere. And Hadria is mean. I thought you would finally be rid of her. What if something happens to you at the Reef? I'm scared I'll never see you again."

"Something could happen to us anywhere." He said darkly as he squeezed her hand, shrugging afterward, since it wasn't in his nature to be so morose about anything. "I think if all this has taught me anything, that's it. I love Destin, but Daiva's right. Nowhere is going to be safe, not completely. And something could happen to me on the Reef, but I'm going to do my best to make sure it doesn't."

Taimon looked around at some of the hovels the humans were moving into, huddled together for warmth even though the days were finally getting warmer toward spring, and he thought about the Reef and the future ahead of him. The Reef was known for being severe and inhospitable. It was going to be his life until Daiva said otherwise.

"I think the two of them figured out a long time ago that nothing is alright and nothing is completely safe, and we have to learn to deal with that. Maybe this is our chance to figure that out." The wind whipped through Kaia's hair to push it back out of her face before she could reach up to do so, and he smiled over at her. "I'm going to miss you."

She curled in close and started crying again, even when he put his arms around her and held her. Kaia didn't say anything for a long time, mostly because she couldn't. "Mom, Dad, and Devon are already gone. Now you and Daiva are going to be far away. Who am I going to talk to about everything that goes on? Who am I going to run with during the Fulness? Destin has Adriana now."

Taimon rolled his eyes at that, since she was pulling out every line of reasoning possible, but that was Kaia's way. "You *could* just lock yourself in a tree for three days. That's always an option."

"Lock myself in a tree? Do you hear yourself?" She was laughing softly anyway, even with tears on her cheeks, but she sighed as she lifted her head up to look at her brother again. "I can't do that. That's boring."

He rolled his eyes at her and conjured a breeze to whip the tears right off her cheeks. He stood up again, pulling her up with him afterward. "Come on, let's go help Daiva, it's too cold out here for crying."

After getting settled into Elyra's house, eating a full meal, and helping as much as she could, Adriana could hardly believe she wasn't in the middle of a dream when she walked away from Elyra's house to the shore. Shian and Elyra were enjoying each other's company, captivated as he was by her stories, and both Shanna and Sheena were fed and sleeping snugly together near the warm fire. The wolves were busy making sure that their homes were satisfactory, the humans were settling in with their generous hosts, and for once, the world was quiet without feeling empty.

Destin was already sitting on the beach as the water came up and slipped over his legs and went back out again, and Adriana didn't say anything until she sat down next to him and leaned into him. "I feel like I'm dreaming."

He turned toward her and rested his cheek against her hair, taking in a deep breath of the scent of her as he closed his eyes. "A good dream, I hope."

"The only dream I ever wanted to come true." She wrapped her arms around his torso as soon as he turned toward her, and she held onto him as tightly as she could. "Well, there were others that I liked too, but this is definitely one of the best."

"We'll work on the others." He wrapped one arm around her shoulders, the other propped back to keep them up on the sand. "I have a few in mind, myself. Out here at least we have space to consider them. Work toward them for a change."

Adriana was quiet for a moment as she relished the fact that Destin was able to hold her out in the open and that no one was going to step in and stop them. No one was going to take her away and throw her back in a cell. They could be together. "And the time, I hope." She moved after that and slid into his lap to kiss him gently. Her body was far from healed after everything that she had endured, but she was glad to have some private time with the man that she loved. "When I'm better, I want to . . ."

"I know." The surf came up around them both again, but the water quickly left her dress so that she could stay as warm as possible in his arms. "I haven't forgotten, and I will keep my promise." He kissed her again and almost crushed her against him in his embrace, the coarse hairs of his beard harsh against her neck.

Following the bristles of his beard, she felt the teasing scrape of his teeth along her skin, sending ripples of power through her that her body had felt many times before, mostly during their lovemaking. The power of a wolf was not something a human body could endure for very long, but it would be a part of her turning, when that day finally came.

It also had a high chance of killing her.

She felt chills run down her spine as his power coursed through her, if only briefly. "I love you so much." She said without feeling like she needed to whisper it, and she trembled a little as he held her. "We can finally be together."

"For as long as you can put up with me." He leaned back to look up in her eyes, reaching up to run his fingers through her hair. "I love you, Adriana. I'll fight as many wars for you as I have to, but if it's up to me, I'd rather stay on a beach just like this one until I reach my decline and you're finally relieved to be rid of me."

"Never. I'll never want to be rid of you." She looked into his deep blue eyes a moment longer before she rested her head onto his shoulder. Their breaths rose and fell together, in time with the surf beside them, a slow rhythm that laid a spell of peace on both their hearts and minds that neither of them held any desire to ever see broken.

EPILOGUE

Seven Fulnesses later

Taimon was waiting for his family on the rocky promontory that qualified as a pier on the isles of the Reef, bouncing from one rock to another on his way down to greet them at the water's edge. Gone were the light blue robes of a noble wolf of the Isles, replaced with the more practical dark leather clothing worn by the wolves on the Reef. Still, a harsh change of wardrobe couldn't quite erase the playfulness in his step.

He smiled down at the longboat as soon as it was close enough for the occupants to hear him. "What took you so long? I sent word west to the exiles three weeks ago!"

"News takes time, brother." Destin smiled back at Taimon as he locked the boat in place and held it so the occupants could pile out of it. Kaia went first of course, but Leander and Marella weren't far behind, leaving Destin and Adriana to climb up onto the rock after them. "We came as quickly as we received word, but we didn't imagine Daiva or her pups would be going anywhere any time soon. Were we wrong?"

"No, I just like yelling at you for being late." He hugged Kaia tightly, not letting go as he continued the conversation.

"The pups were born almost a week ago. All but one of them have already opened their eyes. That's how late you are."

Kaia held onto Taimon as they made their way, though it certainly wasn't easy making it across the rock. She looked back only once to see Miris staying back with the boat, but then she let Taimon drag her along toward Daiva and Hassir's home. "We missed all of that already? Did they name them already too?"

"She says they have their names prepared, but they haven't officially named them in the presence of the other council elders yet. She's been waiting for you." He picked his way over the stones with the ease of experience, since he'd lived on the Reef for more than half a year already.

It had been a long and quiet spring and summer for everyone, and the weather was beginning to turn cooler again after the heat of the year. Time on the Reef had passed in a vigilant blur, as Hassir set all manner of security measures in place to warn them of any kind of attack forthcoming from the Isles or the Genovin. For all their watchful anxiety, the months had passed in uneasy peace.

The Reef itself looked anything but peaceful. The path they took, such as it was, led over a vast expanse of exposed stone with very few landmarks to show the passing distance. The plain seemed to stretch on forever even when they reached the top of a rise and could see the folds and dips of it extending its arms toward the horizon.

The only break in the perfect stillness was a cluster of buildings far in the distance, perched at the edge of a circular depression in the ground half a mile wide. It was also clearly their destination, as Taimon led them on, accompanied by several other Stoneborn of the Reef who were assigned to watch him at all times.

"This place is terrible." Kaia said softly as she looked around, since there was nothing that was even close to being alive, other than the wolves themselves. She already felt like she needed to run until she found a tree to wrap her arms around, but she kept herself tightly at Taimon's side. "Do you really like it here?" Kaia noticed a few wolves looking at her from afar as they wandered through, but she didn't think she could possibly be the center of attention just because she had green eyes. Adriana was human, for crying out loud.

"I admit, it's not as bad as I thought it would be." He shared some of his own abundant energy with her as they walked, since he knew Kaia would get none of her own in the barren landscape. "I'm the Lady's little brother, though, so I know I get a lot of preferential treatment. I don't think I would like it here quite as well if I had to fight for my own survival or my own food every day against wolves three times my size."

"They are scary." Kaia assessed as they got closer to Daiva's house. "It looks like they want to eat me."

Adriana couldn't help but laugh as she listened to Taimon and Kaia's conversation, and as much as she knew she should be nervous, she was so happy to be with Destin that it was hard to feel anything else. Her precious babies were back home with Shian and Elyra, and even though she missed them and their smiling faces, she was glad to have some time to simply be with Destin. "How did Daiva handle her pregnancy anyway? She does not seem like the motherly type."

"I'm sure she isn't." Destin laughed to himself, keeping a tight grip on Adriana's hand as they walked to make sure no one got any ideas about challenging him for possession of her. "The one time I saw her was right after the midpoint, so she was rather irritated about needing to be reliant on Hassir all the time. Otherwise, even if she was miserable, I doubt she complained much to anyone."

"It is so different from anything I'm familiar with." Adriana thought about what it might be like in the future, if she could actually convince Destin to turn her so that they could have a family together. It was further complicated by Shian and her daughters, since Shian wanted her to be able to stay and live with the girls, which would be difficult if she turned. "I'm beginning to worry that some of these Stoneborn are going to run across and snatch up your sister. Maybe we should have asked Miris to come up with us."

"They'll behave themselves." Taimon looked over his shoulder, nodding at Destin. "They know who Destin is. I know you don't do it on purpose, brother, but a lot of people around here are actually really scared of you. Apparently you won a reputation for yourself around here by, you know, coming back from the dead."

Destin seemed more amused by that than anything else, but he shrugged without letting go of Adriana's hand. "Good. If anyone does get any ideas, just warn me if you notice. I came here to see our sister, not kill other wolves, but it won't really be out of my way if the situation arises."

Daiva was sitting amongst her puppies when they walked into her home. She had just finished feeding them, and was barely tugging her robes back on after shifting back into her human form when her family entered. She stood up slowly and smiled when she saw Destin, since she truly was happier when her brother was around. "You decided you wanted to come by after all?"

"Autumn storms." He said by way of brief explanation, moving to a seat near her where he could get a good look at all of her puppies. "And we took a route somewhat out of our way to come along the Reef. Just in case." He hadn't wanted to sail in any way close to the Isles, since they were never sure how far out Melyssa's patrols would be sailing in any given season.

Rather than dwell on the reasons for his lateness, though, he looked down at the floor at the remarkably large number of puppies running rampant all over each other. It was incredibly rare for wolves to have a single child, though not uncommon to have a litter of two or three in which only one survived, depending on the wolf.

It was less common, but not unheard of, for wolves to bear a litter of four or five pups. Daiva had given birth to six, and all of them were still alive so far, though he noticed that two in the group were moving much more slowly and less certainly than the other four. "Does it feel good to be out of your wolf for a while again?"

"Yes, it feels excellent to have full control of myself again." She looked down at her pups as they remained more or less around her. Daiva picked one up and walked over to Kaia and held out a little male puppy. "I am glad you're here, Kaia. I think he could use your support." Daiva was just as surprised as anyone else that she had birthed six puppies, and, even moreso, that all of them had survived. It was unheard of, really, for all of the pups to survive, though she knew that she could still lose one or more in their early days.

Kaia looked down at the tiny squirming puppy in her hands, and she smiled when his little snout turned up and she could see into his green eyes. He had been trembling when Daiva handed him over to her, but as soon as she released just a little bit of her power into his tiny body, he relaxed as if she'd given him what he was looking for since the moment he was born.

"I told her the gods gave her a Forestborn as a means of revenge for giving you so much grief over the years." Taimon looked down at Kaia, glancing over at Daiva to acknowledge the glare he was getting for his comment. "She didn't think it was funny. I'm still laughing."

Destin grinned at the exchange, but he was looking over the others, picking them up one by one to examine the more rambunctious of them as they ran past him. There was a Stoneborn and an Earthborn, both male, who looked exactly the same. Destin nodded approvingly as he picked up another he managed to catch with Hassir's red fur, and red eyes to match her father. "It looks like you both received an heir on the first try. Congratulations."

Hassir was grinning from nearby with another of the pups sitting contentedly in his lap. "Her name is Sephessa." He announced quietly as the little Fireborn pup ran after her brothers on the stone, all of them falling over themselves as they learned how to stay upright on their own. "She'll rule the Reef one day if she doesn't die of her own stupidity first. No Oceanborn, though. My sister will have to produce her own heir, it seems."

Daiva nodded, though she thought it was only appropriate that Asira create her own heir, certainly. She watched as three of her pups chased each other, and she pointed at the one in Kaia's hands. "That is Caipher, the smallest, of course, but he seems to keep up." She moved her finger to point at the three growling and falling over each other. "The males with Sephessa are Raphis and Zephys. Raphis is the Earthborn, and Zephys is the Stoneborn." Daiva couldn't help but smile a little bit brighter as she looked at Zephys, strong and wild, even when he was so young.

"That one . . ." She turned to point at the female in Hassir's lap. "Is Aphira." She knew once she said the pup's name that the little girl would turn her head, and the group went quiet as they looked at her eyes. Violet eyes. She looked at her mother first at the sound of her name, but then took in the rest of the group, and focused on Leander, who had been quiet the entire time.

Leander's lips turned up in a smile, and he turned to bow slightly to Daiva. "My congratulations, Lady Daiva. It's not often the gods bless the world with one of my kind."

She nodded and smirked as she looked at her collection of pups, not a single one the same kind as any other. A Fireborn and a Heartborn in the same litter, though, was quite a lot. "She will be raised quite differently than Chiara, so it is my hope that she turns out more like you than she does the princess. An advisor to her sister."

Lastly Daiva went to pick up the pup that was sitting close to Hassir but away from his other siblings, mostly because he had not yet opened his eyes and he was content to just wait for them to come back to him so that they could all snuggle and sleep together. She picked up the little male and then stroked his fur lightly before she ran her finger along his little snout. "This one seems to be quite stubborn.

We have a name chosen for him, if he ever decides to open his eyes and introduce himself to the rest of us."

The male nuzzled his mother's finger as soon as he was in her lap, but when she settled into her seat, he moved a little to claw his way up on her robes, climbing shakily until he rested on her chest as she leaned back. There was a streak of afternoon sunlight coming down through a window nearby, and he pawed along the edge of her robes until he settled his body completely in the light, obviously relaxing at the feel of it on his fur.

"It looks like he prefers the warmth." Destin volunteered, grinning at the small pup, whose coloring was nothing like the rest of his siblings. The others had either brown or red fur, but the stubborn male had a mixture of both in patterns that seemed almost to glimmer in the sunlight.

"I told her." Hassir said with a confident chuckle across the room, still absently holding Aphira while everyone focused on the last pup with its eyes closed. "Another Fireborn, is my guess."

"And what happens then? If there are two eldest Fireborn?" Leander asked with his eyes on the last pup, chuckling at its scattered thoughts.

"Well, historically, if there are two in a litter, one will typically kill the other to gain dominance and secure their birthright." He shrugged. "We'll see what they become when they get older. It's conceivable they'll be friends, and if that's the case . . ."

"We don't have to worry about that for a long while." Daiva looked down at her pup again, though she was constantly glancing across the room to make sure the others hadn't gotten themselves into trouble. Raphis was famously getting himself stuck in places where he shouldn't be, and Sephessa often went running into the fire, tricking Raphis and Zephys into thinking that they could follow her. Zephys still had a patch of singed fur from the last time.

Adriana watched the little puppy in Daiva's arms, finding

herself fascinated as she watched him cuddle against his mother as though Daiva was the most important thing in the world. She did not think that any creature could find Daiva comfortable to be around, but he did.

The others were distracted by the other puppies running around, and so when the little unnamed pup sniffed at the air where the sunlight was hitting his fur, Adriana blinked a few times just to make sure she saw what she saw.

"Destin, he's opening his eyes." She said softly from beside him as Destin had reached down to give Raphis a scratch. "I can't see what color, though, with the sun in his eyes."

Destin moved to lean across Adriana so he could get a better look as everyone else in the room waited for him to declare what the last child was, what new element he might bring to the family or which of his siblings he might end up being in competition with.

When he met the pup's eyes, though, he was just as confused as Adriana for a moment. The sun was, indeed, in the little boy's eyes, but he wasn't squinting or wincing at the brightness of it staring down at him. His eyes were fully open, drinking in the sunlight, and the shade of his irises was nothing that Destin had ever seen before. It was like the sun his eyes had seen in their first moments opened to the world had been drawn in and mirrored right back out. They were a brilliant gold that seemed to radiate their own light, shining out at Destin as the pup looked directly up into the face of the sun and seemed content.

The smile on Destin's face faded as the reality of what he was seeing hit him in waves, stories and legends crashing through his mind. There were myths his parents had told them as children, of the single rarest kind of wolf, so rare and precious that they were universally believed to be something out of history's imagination. Too powerful to truly exist, too rare for anyone to be certain they were even possible, and too precious to be anything but a closely guarded secret.

"Lightborn." Destin finally breathed into the silence, but he couldn't take his eyes off the golden irises of the puppy in front of him. "Daiva, your son is a Lightborn."

"He . . . what?" She looked down at her last unnamed puppy and lifted him up to her face so that she could see for herself. Certainly Destin was wrong, there was no way she had a Lightborn among her children. She had never heard of one attested, much less met one. There was no way she could have given birth to one. When she looked into the pup's eyes and he licked her face, she was speechless.

Hassir moved over beside his mate quickly at that announcement, looking to confirm the evidence with his own eyes, but he was similarly speechless. One by one, everyone in the room looked into the little boy's eyes, and even when he was removed from the sunlight, the glow of his eyes and the brilliance of the gold within them was incontrovertible.

Leander was the one to finally break the breathless silence that fell over the room, but his face was somber as he looked back and forth between Hassir and Daiva. "No one can know of him." He said quietly, the import of what had happened distilling on everyone present as their thoughts jumbled together. "Whatever else Melyssa and Cadmos want with the Reef, however much they wish to kill us all, the moment they learn that this boy exists, they will stop at nothing to claim him for themselves. Nothing."

"He will be protected." Daiva said softly but fiercely, since she was not going to let any harm come to her pups as long as she had control over it. When they were adults, their lives would be their own. Until then, their lives were hers to guide and protect.

She ran a gentle hand along his fur, and she knew all those present would keep the secret of the pup in her arms. They were family that she trusted, even Leander and Marella.

"Dephir. His name is Dephir."

ABOUT THE AUTHOR

D. Brumbley is a husband/wife duo from Kansas City who spend most of their time in each other's heads. In suburbia the duo lives in a simple house with a dog and two feisty kiddos. One half of the duo loves football, baseball, libraries, and romance. The other half of the duo likes D&D, Fantasy novels, Marvel Comics, and cheesecake. A country girl and an east coast boy met online, became best friends, fell in love, and somewhere along the way decided that telling stories together would be fun.

Best. Decision. Ever.